Under a Vampire Moon

Carolyn stared, watching the muscles in his arms and chest ripple under his black t-shirt as his bow scraped so quickly over the strings of his violin that she expected to see sparks flying and smoke rising. His eyes were closed, his face transported as the music moved through him. She couldn't seem to tear her gaze from him as he played song after song . . . and then his eyes suddenly opened and met hers.

Carolyn felt like someone had jammed an adrenaline shot into her heart. She was sure it skipped a beat, but when he caught her gaze and didn't release it, her heart started thumping again, charging ahead at a frightening rate that left her breathless and almost dizzy.

LYNSAY SANDS

Under a Vampire Moon

Moon

AN ARGENEAU NOVEL

AVON

An Imprint of HarperCollinsPublishers

AVON BOOKS
An Imprint of HarperCollins*Publishers*
10 East 53rd Street
New York, New York 10022-5299

Copyright © 2012 by Lynsay Sands
Excerpt from *The Lady Is a Vamp* copyright 2012 © by Lynsay Sands
ISBN 978-0-06-210020-7
www.avonbooks.com

First Avon Books mass market printing: May 2012

Avon Trademark Reg. U.S. Pat. Off. and in Other Countries, Marca Registrada, Hecho en U.S.A.
HarperCollins® is a registered trademark of HarperCollins Publishers.

Printed in the U.S.A.

10 9 8 7 6 5 4 3 2 1

Under a
Vampire
Moon

Prologue

'I don't see any tables,' Carolyn said, glancing over the busy open-air restaurant.

"We can sit at the bar," her friend, Bethany, said with a shrug. When Carolyn frowned, she rolled her eyes, and caught her arm to drag her toward the bar, adding, "We'll move to a table as soon as one opens up. Besides, we're only going to be here until Genie arrives and our table is ready next door anyway."

"Right," Carolyn breathed and slid onto the stool Bethany directed her to. She then glanced over her shoulder self-consciously, her gaze skittering over the young, laughing crowd surrounding them. Despite the setting sun, it was still hot and most of the patrons were dressed casually in shorts and summer dresses. This was the more casual restaurant at the resort, with bare wooden tables crowded onto the railed deck, and Caribbean music barely covering the sound of talk and laughter. In comparison, the indoor restaurant next door, where she, Bethany, and

Genie were to eat was a four-star affair with proper tables, table cloths, silverware, candlelight, and four-star prices. They'd dressed accordingly, which left Carolyn feeling a little like they stuck out like sore thumbs amongst this more relaxed crowd.

That wasn't the only thing making her uncomfortable, however. It was the clientele here, as well. Most of the people seemed to be half their age, though there were some older people. But no matter their age, they all seemed to be paired off. She and Bethany were the only single females, or single anything as far as she could tell. Everyone else was part of a couple.

Probably on their honeymoons, Carolyn thought unhappily as she noted all the intimate smiles and gentle kisses being exchanged around them. The sight made her sigh and turn her eyes forward to stare at the bottles of liquor lining the back of the bar as she wondered if this hadn't been a huge mistake.

"What can I get for you two pretty ladies tonight?"

Carolyn blinked as her view was suddenly blocked by a smiling bartender. The man wore a white shirt and dark slacks. His eyes were dancing and his teeth looked incredibly white against his dark skin as he beamed happily at them. Everyone here seemed to be happy and beaming, she noted.

Must be something in the water, Carolyn thought and forced a smile. "A glass of white wine, please."

"The same for me," Bethany announced. "And two shots of tequila as well."

"Tequila?" Carolyn asked as the bartender moved away.

"Yes, tequila. And we are downing them the minute they arrive and then ordering more," Bethany said firmly.

Carolyn hesitated. She wasn't really interested in tequila shots, but simply asked, "Are you sure your stomach can handle it?"

Bethany had been complaining about her stomach since they'd eaten their dinner on the plane here. Carolyn had taken the rubber chicken, but Bethany had opted for the salmon and had been swearing ever since that it had been bad.

"I'm hoping the tequila kills whatever nasty little parasites the salmon had growing in it," Bethany said. "Failing that it will make me puke it back up and get it out of my system. Either way, I'll recover quicker than without it."

Carolyn gave a disbelieving laugh. "Yeah, well, I don't think I—"

"Good, you shouldn't be thinking," Bethany interrupted firmly. "I brought you here so you *wouldn't* think, remember? And to make you relax and enjoy yourself for the first time in God knows how long. And you *are* going to relax, Carolyn Connor, if I have to personally pour every last drop of alcohol there is in St. Lucia down your throat."

"I *am* relaxed," she protested at once.

Bethany snorted. "Sweetie, you're as wound up as a clock and have been for years. And, as your friend, I *am* going to see you unwind if it kills us both."

Carolyn stared at her blankly, and then felt the tension in her shoulders ease. A small, real smile claiming her lips she said, "What would I do without you?"

"Lock yourself in your house, leave it only to go to work, and die lonely, old, and bitter," Bethany said promptly.

Carolyn laughed, but it was a hollow sound, because the sad fact was that Bethany was probably right. If it weren't for Bethany she'd be locked down already, either in her house or at her office, her head buried in business as she struggled to forget the last ten years and pretend she wasn't heartbroken and, yes, bitter.

"So . . ." Bethany arched an eyebrow. "Let Aunt Beth nurse you back to health and happiness. I promise you are going to have a very good time on this trip. You will laugh and have fun and even get laid. It will be the time of your life."

"Right," Carolyn said dryly, some of her tension returning. The last thing she wanted at this point was to get involved with another man. Been there, done that, got the divorce lawyer to prove it, she thought grimly, and then glanced to the bartender as he returned with two wineglasses and two shot glasses, both with golden liquid in them.

"Thank you," Bethany said cheerfully, pushing one of the shot glasses toward Carolyn and then lifting the other as she turned on her bar stool to face her. "So . . . " She paused and waited pointedly.

Carolyn picked up her shot glass with resignation.

"To a good time in St. Lucia," Bethany said firmly and tossed back her shot.

Carolyn raised the small glass to her own lips and took a sip, grimacing as the liquid burned its way across her tongue.

Bethany set her glass down with a gasp, glanced to Carolyn and frowned when she saw her still full shot glass. "Down it," she said firmly. "Dr. Beth's orders."

"But—"

"Down it," Bethany repeated pushing the glass to her lips.

Carolyn did as ordered, gasping and coughing as the liquid burned down her throat and slammed into her stomach.

"That a girl," Bethany said with approval. Slapping her

back with one hand, she took the empty glass from her with the other and set it in front of the bartender, saying, "Two more."

"Beth," Carolyn got out, her voice raspy, "I haven't drunk in ages. I—"

"You haven't done a lot of things in ages," Beth interrupted as the bartender refilled their shot glasses. "And you're going to do them all here. So don't even try to fight it. Trust me, I know what's best for you."

Carolyn shook her head, but accepted the shot when the bartender pushed it toward her.

Beth clinked her glass and said, "To freedom."

Carolyn downed the shot without prompting this time and waited for the coughing fit to follow, but suspected her throat was still numb from the first shot. This one went down more smoothly, and she only had to clear her throat a little afterward. She set the glass down and pointed out, "I'm not free yet."

"Semantics." Bethany gestured for the bartender to pour them both another. "The worst is over. Now it's just a matter of waiting for the courts to do their thing."

"Yeah," Carolyn murmured as another shot appeared before her.

Raising her glass, Bethany said, "Here's hoping they're quicker about it than they have been with everything else."

Carolyn drank, but as she set the empty glass back, she said, "I don't really care. I'm in no rush."

Bethany scowled as she gestured to the bartender again. "I swear, every time you say that it sends a shudder down my back. It makes me think you don't want the divorce at all. That you're still hung up on him and want to get back together."

"No," Carolyn assured her solemnly. "That isn't the case at all. But I'm also not eager to rush into a new relationship. In fact, I've decided marriage just isn't for me. So what do I care if it takes a while to resolve the old one?"

"Right." She smiled. "It doesn't matter. You got everything you wanted."

Carolyn snorted. "What I wanted was a happy marriage. Failing that, I wanted a fair divorce settlement."

"Then that's our next toast," Bethany said cheerfully. "To the incredible Larry Templeton, lawyer extraordinaire who is going to get you everything you deserve and more."

Carolyn raised her shot glass, but found it hard to smile. Bethany was trying to cheer her up and ensure she enjoyed this vacation, but she simply wasn't in the mood. Carolyn was heartsore, bruised, disillusioned, and, frankly, depressed. And she suspected being at this resort in the Caribbean wasn't going to help. It was obviously a popular place for honeymooners. Everyone was smiling and happy and full of love and hope. It was a depressing counterpoint to her own state, mid-divorce and traveling with a friend. At forty-two she was also old. Or at least she felt old. Christ, she'd never felt so old in her life, Carolyn acknowledged unhappily; old, jaundiced, beaten down. How had she gotten this way?

"Oh."

Carolyn pushed her less than pleasant thoughts away and lowered her shot glass to glance at Bethany. Her eyebrows pulled together when she saw the uncertain look on her face and the way she was suddenly clutching her stomach.

"Are you all right?" she asked, leaning toward her with concern.

"I don't think the tequila killed the bugs like I was hoping," Beth muttered.

Carolyn bit her lip. "Do you want to go back to our villa? We can give dinner a miss tonight and just—"

"No, no, Genie is supposed to meet us here," Bethany

interrupted, and then her gaze slid past Carolyn and she brightened. "Oh look, a table has opened up. Why don't you take our drinks over while I go vomit."

Carolyn glanced instinctively over her shoulder to see a couple leaving a table on the lower deck overlooking the beach. She then glanced sharply back as Bethany's last word sank in, but Beth was off her stool and already weaving through the crowd toward the washrooms between the open-air bar/restaurant and the fancier dining establishment beside it.

"I'll bring your drinks," the bartender announced, scooping up the two full wineglasses and her shot. When he started around the bar, she stood, thinking she'd claim the table, but if Beth took more than a couple moments, she'd check on her.

Carolyn started to walk, but bit her lip when the room shifted a bit around her. It seemed the tequila was hitting her already. Great, she thought, following carefully as the bartender led the way through the crowd.

When he paused suddenly, she glanced around his shoulder to see that a couple had approached the table from the opposite direction.

"It's okay," Carolyn said to the bartender at once. "We can wait at the bar."

"No, no, no," he said beaming from her to the couple. "The table sits four. You can share and make friends."

"Oh, no, that's okay," Carolyn said, cringing at the very idea as her gaze slid over the young couple. They looked to be about twenty-five or so. The man was dark-haired and dark-eyed with the swarthy good looks of an Italian. He was also smiling faintly, one possessive arm around the woman; a curvaceous, auburn-haired beauty who was peering at Carolyn with a discomfiting interest. Definitely honeymooners, she thought unhappily.

"Don't be silly." The woman suddenly beamed. "We'd be happy to share. We're only waiting for our table to open up in the restaurant next door."

"So are this pretty lady and her friend," the bartender announced happily, setting the glasses down and moving to pull out a chair for Carolyn even as the other man pulled out one for his wife.

Carolyn gave in and said, "Thank you," as she slid into the chair.

After asking the couple what they'd like, the bartender slipped away to get their order.

"Well, this is lovely," the woman said with a pleased little sigh and then held out her hand. "I'm Marguerite Argeneau."

"Argeneau-Notte," the man corrected gently, pronouncing it Ar-zsa-no-No-tay, and the woman blinked, then laughed with embarrassment.

"Marguerite Argeneau-Notte," she admitted wryly, and explained, "It's new. I'm not used to it yet."

Carolyn managed a smile and accepted the offered hand as the woman continued, "And this is my wonderful husband, Julius Notte."

"Carolyn Connor." She held on to her smile as the man now took her hand in a firm, warm grip, then sat back and cleared her throat. "Honeymooners?"

"Yes," Marguerite chuckled. "But we've been married for weeks. I should be adjusting to the name change by now."

"You've been here for weeks?" Carolyn asked with interest.

"Oh, no. We only arrived a couple days ago," Marguerite said. "We had some family matters to tend to back in Canada before we started our honeymoon."

"Oh." Carolyn blinked. "You're Canadian?"

"I am." Marguerite smiled. "You?"

"Yes, Toronto." Carolyn lifted her wineglass to her lips, but paused and set it back down thinking perhaps it would be better to switch to water or Diet Coke. She really wasn't much of a drinker and didn't want to end up in the bathroom stall next to Bethany. That thought made her glance in the direction her friend had disappeared to as she wondered if she should go check on her now.

"What a small world. I'm from Toronto too," Marguerite said happily, reclaiming her attention.

"Are you?" Carolyn asked turning back.

Marguerite nodded, and then smiled at her husband and leaned into the arm he'd placed along the back of her chair, adding, "But Julius is from Italy, so we are going to split our time between Canada and Italy for now despite the fact that his business and family are in Italy."

"You'd miss your family if we stayed only in Italy, *cara*. I want you happy."

Carolyn managed another smile as Julius bent his head to press a gentle kiss to Marguerite's lips, but just barely. Their love and happiness was actually painful for her to witness. Turning her head away, she glanced again in the direction Bethany had taken, thinking she should definitely check on her. And where was Genie? Their reservation was for seven thirty and it was nearly that time now.

"Are you on vacation?"

Carolyn glanced back, relieved to see that Marguerite had straightened, putting some distance between herself and her husband.

"I—yes." She raised her glass to her mouth to hide her expression as a grimace claimed her lips. A moment of silence passed as she sipped her wine, but it was just a sip. The tequila appeared to be ruffling its way through her brain as it was, leaving her confused and depressed. Alcohol was not a cure for depression, Carolyn thought, and promised herself she wouldn't let Beth urge any more on her.

She set down her glass and glanced up to find Marguerite eyeing her solemnly, her expression concentrated. It felt like the younger woman was looking right through her and seeing the failed wasteland of her life.

"Perhaps I should check on Beth." Carolyn pushed back her chair and stood, but paused as Genie suddenly appeared and caught her up in a hug.

"Oh, my God, I'm so sorry. I meant to be here half an hour ago, but just as I was leaving the office I got a call that the band I hired for the next week had to cancel. They were supposed to start tomorrow night, but there's been a death in the drummer's family." She released Carolyn and turned to drop into the empty chair beside hers. "I've been making frantic calls ever since, trying to replace them, and then saw the time and thought I'd better get down here and explain."

Carolyn sank back into her chair as Genie grabbed Bethany's glass of wine and took a deep swallow. Carolyn glanced to their table companions. "This is Genie Walker, a friend of ours from university, and the reason we decided to vacation here. Genie, this is Marguerite and Julius Notte."

"Hello, I hope you're having a nice stay," Genie said, her professional face sliding back into place as she set down Bethany's glass.

"Yes, lovely," Marguerite assured her. "You work here, then?"

"She's the entertainment coordinator for the resort," Carolyn said.

"Soon to be ex-entertainment coordinator if I don't find a replacement band that can be out here by tomorrow night," Genie moaned and stood up. "I'm sorry, Caro,

I have to go. I ran into Beth on the way here. She was headed back to the villa. She says she's fine, but wants to lie down. I promised I'd keep you company for dinner, and I will, but I really need to find a replacement band first. I'll come back and join you the minute I find one. But it might be a while. I—"

"That's okay." Carolyn stood up as well. "I'll just go back to the villa and order room service. We can have dinner tomorrow night instead."

"Sit," Marguerite ordered.

Carolyn stiffened at the sharp order, but found herself immediately sinking back into her seat though she didn't recall deciding to. Genie, too, sat down again, she noted with confusion and felt concern begin to stir within her, but as soon as it began to rise, it immediately receded, leaving her calm and relaxed.

"You will both be joining us for dinner," Marguerite announced with a smile. "I have just the band for you."

At least, that's what Carolyn thought she'd meant, though band had sounded like man. But then the tequila was really kicking in now so she'd probably misheard.

"Carolyn?" Julius asked and Carolyn glanced to him, but he was looking at Marguerite.

Nodding, the woman beamed at him. "Christian must come."

Julius's eyebrows rose and he turned to peer at Carolyn with new interest, and then pulled a cell phone from his pocket and began to punch in numbers.

One

'So... what do you think your mother's up to?'

Christian Notte tore his attention from the cliffs sloping down to the sea and glanced over his shoulder to his cousin. Despite the question, Zanipolo was peering out the window of the resort van, his eyes glued to a scenery none of them normally saw . . . at least not in daylight.

He eyed the man briefly, noting that he'd slid sunglasses on and let his black hair out of its usual ponytail so that it partially curtained his face, offering more protection from the sun glaring through the windows. His gaze then slid to the other passengers in the van. Giacinta shared the seat with Zanipolo, sitting directly behind Christian. Her eyes were positively eating up the passing scenery through the huge sunglasses she'd donned, her long blond hair offering her some protection as well.

Behind them sat Santo. The drummer had been the first to get in and had immediately laid claim to the back bench seat, sprawling out and rubbing his ringed fingers wearily over his shaved head as the others had settled in. He was getting sun from all three sides, and with no hair to protect his head from it, but then that was probably why he'd claimed the backseat, Christian thought grimly. Santo would always take the worst, most uncomfortable position, and leave the better spots for the others. It was his way . . . and never failed to annoy Christian.

"Well?" Raffaele asked, drawing Christian's gaze to the man who sat on the first bench seat, beside him. The last member of the band, Raffaele was dark-haired like the other two men, or like both of the other two men would be if Santo didn't shave his head, but his hair was cut short. He also had the Notte black eyes with flecks of silver that all of them had.

"Don't ask me," he said, settling back in his seat and returning his gaze to the passing seascape. "She said the scheduled band had to cancel and we would be perfect to replace them."

"Uh-huh," Zanipolo said with a laugh. "Because every couple wants their son and niece and nephews hanging around on their honeymoon."

"It's possible," Raffaele said thoughtfully. "Marguerite hasn't let Christian far from her side since finding him and Julius again."

Before Christian could comment, Giacinta said, "She's found him a life mate."

The words were spoken with a certainty that brooked no argument and Christian had to resist the urge to glance back and ask if she really thought so. He'd suspected it himself when he'd gotten off the phone with his parents. His father had been the one who had called. Julius Notte had simply said, "Your mother wants you here. Gather the band together and fly to St. Lucia at once."

Christian had just stiffened up over the autocratic

order when Marguerite took the phone and began to babble excitedly about the resort's scheduled band canceling, and the resort needing a replacement band, and she was so proud of him she'd played the video she had of them on her iPhone for the entertainment coordinator, and the woman had thought they were brilliant too. Everyone would love them she'd assured him. Besides, she was missing her handsome son, and . . .

Well, really, by the time she'd finished gushing in his ear, Christian had found it hard to refuse his mother.

Mother. He smiled at the word. Christian had lived more than five hundred years without one, dreaming of having both a mother and a father like his cousins had, imagining what she would be like. What his life would be like. And now he was finding out. It was even better than he'd imagined.

Marguerite Argeneau-Notte was the most nonjudgmental, loving woman he'd ever met. She showered those she cared for with a love and warmth that slid around them like a soft, warm blanket, a cushion from the rest of the world.

"Well?" Raffaele said, nudging him when Christian remained silent.

"Well what?" he asked, pulling himself from his thoughts.

"Do you think she's found you a life mate?"

"I don't know," he said and pondered the possibility. Since his parents had found each other again, Christian had spent a good deal of his time in Canada, getting to know his mother and other siblings. Each of those siblings was newly mated. While he'd enjoyed getting to know them, he'd also found it almost painful to be around such happiness and joy while he was still single. The thought of joining their ranks was . . . well— He shook his head.

A life mate. He had been alone so long now it was hard even to grasp the idea of having a mate of his own.

"It's a life mate," Giacinta announced firmly. "There is no doubt."

This time Christian did glance back and ask, "Why are you so sure?"

"Because that is the only reason in the world that your father would allow her to send for you on their honeymoon," she said with a shrug.

"Yeah," Zanipolo agreed. "She's right . . . you lucky bastard."

"Don't get his hopes up," Santo growled from the back. "What if you're wrong, Gia?"

"Well, I guess we'll find out soon enough. We're here," Raffaele announced, drawing their attention to their surroundings as the van slowed at a large sign with the resort name and logo on it. They turned down a curving lane and Christian glanced around. There wasn't much to see at first and then the way ahead opened up and he noted the buildings and villas climbing the mountainside on their left. On the right it was flat and littered with what appeared to be stores and shops. A large main building lay ahead, and there was a walkway between it and the shops on the right. Through the opening they could glimpse beach and blue sea and then they were turning into a circle in front of the main building and coming to a halt.

Christian followed Raffaele out of the van when the driver opened the door. He tried to tip the man, but the driver grinned and waved his money away, assuring him it was all taken care of as he moved over to speak to someone in a white shirt and dark pants with a clipboard and a name tag.

"Where's our luggage?" Giacinta peered up the road the way they'd come.

"I'm sure it's coming," Christian said mildly, but couldn't resist looking for the second van himself. It didn't hold just their luggage, but the coolers of blood they would need while here.

"Oh yes, it is coming." Their driver was suddenly beside them again, and began to usher them toward another van, explaining, "I cannot drive you to your villa, but they will take you."

Christian glanced toward the new van with the resort logo on it, and supposed outside vehicles weren't allowed on the private roads.

"They will bring your luggage when it arrives," the man added as he urged them into the new van. "Have a nice stay."

Before anyone could respond, he'd closed the door and stood smiling and waving as the van moved slowly away from the entry.

"You are the new band."

Christian tore his gaze from their old driver to turn forward and peer at their new one, noting the white shirt and dark pants. "Yes."

"I'm Adam. Genie will be relieved that you are here," the man said, flashing a wide smile at them in the rearview mirror.

"Genie's the entertainment coordinator?" Christian asked, recalling his mother mentioning the name.

"Yes. You must be famous to be in the estate villas. Usually bands stay in lower rooms or find their own accommodations, but you are in one of the big villas."

"One of the big villas?" Christian asked with a frown.

"Oh, yes. They are beautiful with their own pool and chef. Yours has four bedrooms."

"All right! Our own pool," Zanipolo said. "Midnight dips after the gig. Awesome."

The others smiled, but Christian scowled, knowing his father had arranged it. Not that he wasn't glad to be in a villa rather than one of the "lower rooms," but he'd rather have arranged it himself and wasn't pleased with his father paying his way. The man tended to forget he was grown up and his own man now.

Well, he'd just have to pay him back for it, he decided as the van crawled along the curving, narrow private road that wound its way up the side of the mountain. The lower roads held long two-story buildings with balconies running their lengths. He supposed those were the single suites or lower rooms. At the end of the first road, they turned in a small turnaround and headed back, taking the upper road to another turnaround allowing them to head up yet another road where another set of long buildings stood. Two more turnarounds brought them to a road where villas were set out side by side and clinging to the mountain like ivy. After two more turnarounds they were cruising past more villas.

There wasn't enough room for two vehicles on the narrow lanes and Christian was just wondering what happened if a vehicle was coming down when another was going up when a vehicle appeared on the road before them. Their driver slowed, but the other driver spotted him and immediately stopped and backed up, pulling tight to the side of the road at the turnaround. He waited there until they had pulled into the turnaround and then scooted past and down the lane, waving cheerfully as he went.

"Man, I see why they don't let just anyone drive their vehicles up here," Zanipolo muttered as the two vans passed within a whisper of each other.

Christian grunted, but didn't comment and they were silent as they went through two more turnarounds, all of them peering curiously at the tropical vegetation on either side. Green plants and flowering bushes spilled out between buildings and along the road. It was quite lush and beautiful and they soaked it in, knowing it would be the only time they'd see it in sunlight. None of them would waste the blood necessary to come out during the day to see it again. Instead, they would have to make do with enjoying their surroundings at night. They wouldn't be seeing it now but it had been a scramble to get everyone together, pack, and get here. Arriving in daylight had been unavoidable.

"Here you are."

Christian glanced toward the two-story white villa the man was stopping the van in front of. The moment he'd followed Raffaele out of the vehicle, Christian walked along the road until he was past the villa and could peer beyond it and down the mountain. It was beautiful, the green mountainside dotted with white buildings with salmon-colored roofs, running all the way down to the sea. The sun sparkled off the blue Caribbean as if it was full of diamonds. Christian simply stood there soaking it in.

"Man, daywalkers have the best of both worlds," Giacinta said with a sigh, drawing his attention to the fact that she had followed and stood at his side.

"But only for a short time," Santo pointed out, rubbing his bare scalp with a pained expression.

"We should go in," Christian said reluctantly.

They all turned as one, then paused as the van went zipping past, the driver smiling and waving.

"Where's he going?" Zanipolo asked with alarm. "What about keys? He didn't give us keys."

Before anyone could comment a second van rolled past and slid to a halt in front of the villa. The door immediately opened, and a smiling woman in a royal blue skirt suit leaped out.

"Christian Notte?" she asked, eyeing them questioningly.

Christian moved forward, aware that the others were following.

"I am Bellina," she announced, beaming as she took his hand in a firm shake. "I will be your social coordinator during your stay. Here, let me show you your villa."

Turning away she led them down the walk to the front door, unlocked it, and quickly led them inside.

Christian followed and felt a tension he hadn't realized had been there slipping from his shoulders as they stepped into a cool, shady entry. The mortal woman Bellina was chattering away as she led them through the building, taking them through a large open living room, a big beautiful kitchen/dining room with a waiting fruit tray and bottle of wine, and then on to show them the terrace and pool. But he wasn't paying much attention. Christian was following silently, his tension returning as his gaze slid over the white walls, the generous windows, and the multitudinous skylights. His mind was screaming that this definitely wasn't a place made for immortals.

It wasn't until they reached the upper floor and the bedrooms that he began to relax again.

"Mr. Notte said you find it difficult to sleep after ending a set and wanted to be sure we had blackout curtains while you slept, and we do," Bellina said chirpily, crossing the darkened master bedroom to reach the drapes. "We left them closed so you could see how well they work, but once you wake up—" She yanked the curtains open and turned to beam at them.

Christian instinctively flinched, one hand rising to protect his face as he turned his head away from the bright sunlight that immediately poured in. He nearly laughed when he saw that his cousins were all reacting in much the same way. You'd think it actually burned them or something from the way they were responding, he thought with wry amusement. Shaking his head at their instinctual reaction, he lowered his hand and forced himself to turn back. Spotting the startled expression on Bellina's face, he smiled and strode forward.

"Sorry, it's been a long day for us what with the scramble to arrange everything and then the flight here," he said, excusing their behavior as he took her arm to urge her from the room.

"Oh, yes, of course. You must be exhausted," she said, smiling sympathetically.

"Yes. And we have to play tonight so a nap would probably be in order."

"Of course. We do not want you falling asleep onstage."

"No," he agreed wryly as they started downstairs to the main floor again.

She nodded. "There is still much to explain about your personal chef and so on, but I can do that later. Perhaps if you call me when you wake up, I could come back," she suggested.

"Thank you," Christian said. They were halfway down the stairs when he noted two men waiting patiently next to their neatly stacked luggage in the entry.

"If you tell them where to put the luggage, they will distribute it for you," Bellina said.

"That isn't necessary," he assured her as they stepped off the stairs. "We'll get our own luggage."

"Very well." She gestured to the men, who immediately opened the door and filed out. "Call the main building when you wish to come down and a van will be sent for you. And call me if you have any questions at all. There is much to do while you are here, and you'll only be playing three hours a night so will have time to enjoy the activities."

"Yes, thank you," Christian said, ushering her out the door, but she stopped on the front step and turned back.

"I almost forgot your keys," she said with a laugh, pulling five envelopes from her pocket and holding them out.

Christian accepted the envelopes, nodded, smiled one last time and then closed the door with relief as she hurried away toward the waiting van.

"Blood," Santo grunted.

Christian turned from the door to see that the others had followed and were now pulling the coolers away from the luggage.

"We should stack it in the fridge now," Christian said. "It's hot enough here the blood will go bad in no time if we leave it out too long."

The coolers were immediately carried to the kitchen, and all but one emptied. They left several bags in the last one and took it with them as they headed back to the master bedroom.

At the front of the group, Giacinta rushed to close the curtains Bellina had opened. Santo carried the cooler to the dresser and set it down. As he opened it, Christian glanced around the room, his gaze sliding over the tasteful furniture, and pausing on the king-sized bed as he took note of the flowers and robes arranged on the comforter. The robes had been tied at the waists and spread out to look something like snow angels, while flowers and leaves had been arranged to spell WELCOME on the comforter.

"Fancy," Raffaele commented, appearing at his side to hand him a bag of blood.

"Hmm." Christian popped the bag to his already descending fangs, only to frown as a ringing sounded from his pocket.

"Phone," Raffaele pointed out with amusement. He'd just been about to pop his own bag to his teeth, but arched an eyebrow and asked, "Want me to answer it?"

Christian pulled the phone from his pocket, read the caller ID, and shook his head. He then hit the button and raised it to his ear, grunting a version of hello.

"Christian Notte, are you talking with your mouth full?" Marguerite's voice admonished gently.

Christian found his lips curving in a smile around the bag in his mouth as he mumbled yes around the obstruction, the word coming out "es."

"Oh, I'm sorry to interrupt your feeding, then, dear. I just wanted to be sure you and your cousins got in. Is everything all right there?"

Christian said "es" again and then tore the bag away with relief when he realized it was empty. "It's beautiful. A bit sunny though, don't you think?"

"Well, this is the Caribbean, darling," she pointed out with a laugh. "It's all right though. The curtains do a good job of keeping the sun out while you're sleeping and it's lovely at night."

"Hmm." Christian glanced around when Santo whistled. When his cousin immediately tossed him a second bag, Christian caught it, but merely held the bag as he spoke. "Did Father arrange for the villa?"

"Yes, dear. He felt that since you're doing us a favor by coming here, you should all be comfortable. Besides, if he hadn't, Gia would have been the only one with her own room and you boys would have had to share and that's no good."

"And why, pray tell, would that be no good?" Christian asked with interest.

"Oh, well, I remember how much you disliked it when

we were in England and you and the boys were sharing there," she said lightly.

"Uh-huh," he said with disbelief.

"Anyway, I should let you go. You're probably exhausted after your flight and would like to sleep, and we want you well rested and perky for tonight."

"Why? What's happening tonight?" he asked at once.

"Well, you'll be performing, of course," she said on a laugh. "Genie is so grateful you were willing to fill in for the band that canceled, she's coming to the show tonight and offered to buy us all drinks during your break. So make sure you join us then."

"Right," Christian said. "Tell Father I'm paying for the villa."

"Now, Christian—," Marguerite began.

"I'm hanging up, Mom. Good sleep," Christian interrupted and started to hang up, but paused when he heard his father say, "Marguerite? What's wrong, *cara*?"

"He called me Mom," Christian heard her say in a sniffly voice.

"Ah, *bella*," Julius Notte crooned. There was a rustling and the line died.

Christian smiled faintly and pressed the button to end the call, then set his phone on the bedside table and glanced around.

"I'm guessing you're taking this room?" Zanipolo asked, pulling a bag of blood from his fangs.

"You guessed right," Christian said dryly.

The other man nodded and glanced around at the others. "That leaves three rooms and four of us."

Gia chuckled at their expressions and headed for the door. "Well, there's one other room with a double bed. The other two have twins, so I'll take the double bed and leave the other two to you guys to fight over."

"I'll share with someone," Santo offered.

Zanipolo grimaced. "No offense, cousin, but you snore like a foghorn. There's no way I'm sharing with you."

"I guess that means Zani and I are sharing and you get your own room, Santo," Raffaele announced, heading out with Zanipolo on his heels.

Santo stared after them with surprise. "I don't snore, do I?" He frowned. "Can immortals snore?"

"You don't snore," Christian assured him.

"Right." Santo frowned. "So why—"

"You shout and thrash and scream," he said quietly.

Santo stiffened, his expression freezing. Then he nodded, ran one hand across his bald head and left the room.

Christian watched Santo leave, then slapped the bag of blood to his teeth and pushed his door closed. He was exhausted and couldn't even be bothered to go get his suitcase.

Moving to the bed, Christian quickly brushed aside the robe and flowers and lay down. He stared at the ceiling as he waited for the bag to empty, and pondered whether his life was about to change or not. He suspected Gia was right and Marguerite had found a possible life mate for him. He suspected it was the entertainment coordinator she kept mentioning.

"Genie," he murmured, pulling the empty bag from his teeth, and then his eyes closed and he fell asleep.

TWO

'Caro?'

"Here!" Carolyn set her brush down on the bathroom counter and walked to the door to her bedroom, pausing when she saw Bethany standing in the hall door in her pink silk robe, her dark hair up in a ponytail. "You aren't ready."

"No." Bethany grimaced. "Would you mind if I didn't go?"

Carolyn frowned and started across the bedroom. "I thought you were feeling better."

"I was when I woke up from my nap this afternoon, but now not so much," she said with a grimace. "I'm thinking it might be better to stay here and just rest tonight. Hopefully, if I do, I'll be good for tomorrow so we can enjoy the rest of the trip . . . and since Genie will be there tonight to keep you company, I thought it would just be best to rest tonight." She hesitated and then added, "Well, unless you mind. I mean I know I dragged you here, so if you want me to—"

"No, no," Carolyn said quickly, though she really would rather Bethany came, but if she wasn't feeling well . . . she managed a smile and shrugged. "Like you say, Genie will be there. Besides, I want you feeling better for the rest of the trip too."

Bethany smiled. "I promise I'll make it up to you. Tomorrow we'll do something fun, maybe a tour or something, then come back here, party our faces off, pick up a couple of men and rock their world."

"Considering that every single male here appears to be on his honeymoon, I don't think that's likely," Carolyn said with amusement, moving to the closet to scoop up her shoes. Carrying them to the bed, she sat to put them on, thinking she was actually glad that this was the case. She sincerely doubted she could "rock" anyone's world, and she also didn't really want to "party" her "face off." Last night had been more than enough partying for her.

Carolyn grimaced at the memory. Thanks to those tequila shots Bethany had talked her into, she'd spent the evening trying desperately not to slur her words, first in the lounge and then in the restaurant where Marguerite and Julius had insisted she and Genie join them. Truthfully, they seemed like a nice young couple, but just the fact that they were on their honeymoon had left Carolyn somewhat at a loss and avoiding personal questions. The last thing newlyweds needed to hear was about her divorce.

Mostly, Carolyn sat and listened as Genie and Marguerite chattered away about the band that was coming and various events on the island, while trying to ignore the strangely intense way Julius kept looking at her. There had been nothing sexual in the way the man had eyed her, more like he'd been sizing her up for something. It had been a bit weird and made her uncomfortable. Carolyn had been glad when the meal ended and she'd been able to use the excuse of checking on Bethany to escape.

Of course, after returning to the villa and finding the other woman sound asleep, Carolyn had crawled into her own bed and soon drifted off as well. It had been an early evening, but then she'd had a long day what with the flight and what not. Traveling always wiped Carolyn out.

"Perhaps the guests here are all on their honeymoons, but there are other resorts with restaurants and lounges, you know . . . not to mention some clubs in town as well. Besides, the people who work here aren't all on honeymoons or even married. That driver who brought us to our villa was a cutie," Bethany said with a grin as Carolyn finished with her shoes and stood up. "And I think he liked you. He kept calling you pretty lady."

"Who? Adam?" Carolyn asked, and couldn't keep the shock out of her voice.

Bethany arched an eyebrow. "You have a problem because he's not white?"

Carolyn snorted. "No, I have a problem because he's a baby. Adam has to be at least twenty years younger than me," she pointed out with a laugh.

Carolyn was sure Bethany was just teasing her, so was a bit shocked when Bethany arched an eyebrow and said, "So? Men do it all the time. Rich, successful men are always dumping their wives for sweet young things." She shrugged. "You're a rich divorcée. Why shouldn't you have a boy toy?"

"Oh, I don't know," she said dryly. "Maybe because the entire time I was with him I'd be resisting the urge to change his diapers and burp him."

Bethany laughed. "Honey, if Adam dropped his drawers in front of you I'm sure the last thing you'd be thinking about is diapers."

"Beth, he called us both pretty ladies, and so did the bartender. I suspect the male workers here do it with everyone. It probably gets them bigger tips. And I hate to tell you this, but if your plans to cheer me up include my having a sordid little tryst with a cabana boy, you're going to be terribly disappointed on this trip."

"It doesn't have to be one of the guys who works here, necessarily. What about those band guys who are coming tonight?" Beth asked, moving out of the way as Carolyn grabbed her purse and approached the door. "They're Italian, right? Well, Italian men are supposed to be stallions."

"And bands have pretty young groupies chasing them around," Carolyn pointed out as she crossed the foyer. "They'd hardly be interested in an old broad like me."

"All right, we'll find you an adult playmate then." Beth trailed her to the front door. "But I think you're making a mistake. Younger men have a lot more stamina than men our age. They hit their sexual peak from eighteen to twenty-five or something like that, while women don't become sex machines until their forties. In truth, it's almost like mother nature wants us to play with the young ones."

Carolyn just shook her head and opened the front door as she sang out, "Good night, Beth."

"Have fun," Bethany instructed as Carolyn pulled the door closed.

"Have fun," Carolyn muttered, starting up the walk to the wending mountain road. "Yeah, right."

Honestly, the longer she was here the more Carolyn regretted coming . . . and it had only been a little more than twenty-four hours. But so far she'd had an uncomfortable meal with Genie and strangers, gone to bed early, gotten up early, and sat on the beach alone with a book . . . mostly in the shade because everyone knew the sun wasn't good for you. She hadn't been reading the book, but had basically pretended to, keeping it propped on her chest while she watched the people around her under the cover of her sunglasses.

It had been a depressing exercise, Carolyn thought as she started along the dark lane. Watching all that billing and cooing around her as she sat alone without even Bethany for company. She'd found herself lying there wondering what was wrong with her. She was okay when it came to looks with a nice face, shoulder-length blond hair, and . . . well, all right, she could stand to lose a few pounds, but she was average. Why didn't she have someone to love her too? Of course, then the heckler, the voice in her head that sounded like her ex-husband, had helpfully listed all her faults. It was a never-ending list and had taken up most of the day.

"Depressing," Carolyn muttered, moving automatically to the edge of the road as she heard a vehicle approaching from behind. Unfortunately, she moved too far to the side, her heels promptly sank into the grassy verge and nearly sent her splat onto her face. Managing to stay upright by doing a little dance that took her right out of one shoe, Carolyn sighed and bent to pull it out of the dirt. She then cursed under her breath when her purse promptly slid off her shoulder and dropped to the ground.

"Pretty lady, what are you doing walking? You should have called down for a ride. Come, get in, we have room."

Carolyn froze at that voice and didn't need to look to see that a vanload of resort guests were getting a lovely view of her behind. It just had to be the case. It was her kind of luck. Sighing, she pulled her shoe free, grabbed up her purse, and slung it back over her shoulder as she straightened and turned to the van to find Adam beaming at her from the driver's seat. That just figured. With Beth's words ringing in her ear the last person she wanted to see was the first one she did.

"Don't they ever let you go home, Adam?" Carolyn asked, managing a smile.

"Two drivers are sick. I am working overtime. Overtime pays well," he said with a grin. "Come, get in. We will take you down. You can sit in the front with me."

Carolyn hesitated, but then limped around the van to the passenger-side door with one shoe on and one off. She was running a little late and would get there faster with a ride. Mind you, it was going to be uncomfortable making small talk with Adam while Bethany's words rang in her head. Good lord, he really didn't look more than twenty-one or twenty-two.

Shaking that thought away, she opened the door and climbed in, smiling at Adam as she did.

"There, see? It's all good," Adam said cheerfully, sending the van moving forward again as soon as she'd settled in the seat and tugged the door closed.

"Yes, thank you." Carolyn quickly undid her shoe, slipped it back on and did it up only to frown as her heel immediately slipped out again. She stared at it blankly, slow to realize that her foot hadn't worked itself out of the shoe, but that the sandal strap had actually broken.

"Damn," she muttered.

"This pretty lady is Caro," Adam announced to the van at large, and then added, "Caro, this is the band, the NCs. It stands for the Notte *cuginos*. Notte is their last name and they say *cugino* means cousin. I am taking them down to the main building so they can perform."

Carolyn briefly forgot about her shoe and glanced around with surprise, her eyes skating over the shadowed faces of the five other people behind her. It was hard to see much. The roads weren't exactly well lit; all she could really make out was that she thought one of them might be a woman. Maybe two, she thought as she noted the long hair on the one in the seat directly behind hers. Although, if that was a woman, she was one hell of a big female.

A snicker came from the smaller one she'd thought was a female and Caro glanced to her curiously.

"Say hello," Adam ordered cheerfully.

"Hello," Carolyn murmured even as the riders in the back did as well. At least, most of them did, the one in the back who had moonlight glinting off his bald head remained silent and she eyed him curiously, wondering if he shaved his head as some sort of fashion statement, or was balding and trying to hide it by shaving his head. Really, that sort of thing fooled no one, she thought. Although he seemed to have a nicely shaped head, the sort that took well to the style.

"Caro is a friend of Genie's," Adam announced and then glanced to her and asked, "You are sitting with Genie tonight to watch them play?"

"Yes," she said, smiling as she settled back in her seat. "Genie and a young couple on their honeymoon, Marguerite and Julius."

Adam nodded, but the sudden tension in the back of the van was actually palpable, and Carolyn recalled that Marguerite and Julius had arranged for the band to come here. She bit her lip, wondering if she should say something to acknowledge that, but didn't have a clue as to what she should say.

"We are all related to Marguerite and Julius."

Carolyn turned in her seat again to see that the smaller female had sat forward . . . and she was definitely female.

Not that Carolyn could see her any better, but the woman's voice was a beautiful, husky singsong that could only be female.

"Really?" she asked with a smile. "How are you related?"

"Raffaele, Zanipolo, Santo, and I are all nieces and nephews," she said, pointing to each dark figure in turn. She then gestured to the second figure with long hair, the possibly very large female, and added, "And Christian here is their so—"

"Their brother," the one called Raffaele interrupted.

"Julius's brother," the woman agreed, and then jabbed Christian in the shoulder and taunted, "Put your hair back in its ponytail, *cugino*. Surely you realize you could be mistaken for a woman like that?"

"What?" the man asked, glancing over his shoulder with what appeared to be confusion, though it was hard to tell in this light.

The woman leaned to whisper something in his ear and then sat back with a laugh as Christian muttered under his breath. He turned to peer toward Carolyn then and she stared back curiously, wishing she could see his face. Like the girl, he had a nice voice, though his was definitely all male.

Growing uncomfortable under the man's stare, she slid her gaze to the others, noting that every one of them appeared to be peering from him to her and back almost expectantly, their heads in silhouette as they turned forward then back, then forward again.

Finding it all a little too strange, Carolyn started to turn back in her seat again, but paused as the big man in the back rumbled, "Since she named everyone but herself, I'll do it. The girl is Giacinta."

"Giacinta," Carolyn murmured the alien name with interest. She'd never heard it before.

"Everyone calls me Gia," the woman said absently, her gaze on Christian, and then sounding somewhat awed, she said, "You can't read her, can you?"

Carolyn was raising her eyebrows at the strange question when Santo growled, "Gia," in warning.

"Here we are," Adam announced cheerfully and Carolyn glanced around to see that they were approaching the front of the main building.

"Thank you, Adam," she said as he brought the van to a halt.

"No problem," Adam said as the band began to pile out. "You call for a ride next time. It's a long way to walk and uneven. We are happy to collect you."

"Thank you," Carolyn repeated with a smile and opened her door. She turned on the seat to get out, only recalling that her shoe was broken when it slipped off her heel and to the side before she could plant it on the ground. Carolyn immediately grabbed for the door to keep from twisting her ankle or stumbling and then gasped in surprise as she was suddenly caught around the waist and lifted away from the van.

Clutching the arms holding her, she stared blankly down at the young man carrying her, noting the long, deep auburn hair; the chiseled features; and then the wide, deep black eyes with flecks of some lighter color in them. Eyes very like Julius Notte's, she thought absently, though this man's were larger, with an almond shape.

"Grab her shoe," he growled, never taking his eyes from hers, and it was only when she heard his voice that she realized it was the one called Christian.

Flushing under his intense stare, Carolyn glanced over his shoulder in time to see a man with short, black hair bend to collect her shoe and follow them, and then Christian was setting her down.

He didn't just set her down though, but eased her to the ground, holding her close as he did so that their bodies rubbed against each other in a long, slow, full-body caress that left her flushed and breathless and completely flummoxed. Her feet finally landing on the cool tile gave her something of a jolt and had her tugging free and then dropping to sit with a little bump on the bench he'd set her in front of.

"Thank you," Carolyn breathed, looking everywhere but at him. Her gaze slid over the other band members, noting their resemblance to each other and their differences. Zanipolo had long hair like Christian, but his was tied back in a ponytail; it was also black like Raffaele's, whose hair was shorter. She suspected Santo's hair would be black as well if he let it grow; at least his eyebrows were black, she noted, taking in the thick metal rings on each of his fingers as he ran one hand over his bald head. The rings looked more like some modern kind of brass knuckles in silver than actual jewelry. Her gaze slid to Giacinta then, a pretty, petite blonde and the only one of the group not wearing all black. Her outfit was a short red skirt and white tank with an open white blouse over it.

Spotting her shoe in Raffaele's hand as he approached, Carolyn held out her hand, but Christian took it to examine.

"It's broken," he said with a frown.

"Yes." Carolyn risked glancing his way, and felt another flush rise up through her. Biting her lip, she looked away and briefly considered taking the next shuttle back up to the villa for new shoes. But she was already late, and really, she was so flustered and embarrassed all she wanted at.that moment was to get away from the man presently holding her sandal.

That left one option, Carolyn decided, and quickly

removed the still good sandal. She then stood, snatched
the broken sandal from Christian's fingers, murmured,
"Thank you," and hurried away through the main building on bare feet, aware that every member of the band
watched her go. She could feel their eyes burning into her
back. They probably thought her a crazy lady for rushing
off barefoot like that, but she didn't care. She—

"Carolyn?"

Sliding to a halt, Carolyn glanced around to see Marguerite and Julius crossing the lobby toward her.

"I'm so glad you made it. I was starting to worry,"
Marguerite said, giving her a hug in greeting. She then
turned her toward the front of the building saying, "We
were just going to check and see that Gia and the boys
made it down all right."

"They have. I rode down with them," Carolyn said, resisting her pull.

"Oh." She smiled. "Well then, come, and I'll introduce
you to them."

"Oh, no, I—" Carolyn grimaced and held up her shoes.
"My strap broke and I can't wear them and I'd really
rather just go sit down. Besides, they introduced themselves to me," she added in a babble, beginning to back
away. "I'll just go sit down. You two—" She paused and
gave her head a shake as the strangest ruffling sensation
went through her head. Then forced a smile. "I'll go save
us a table."

"Don't be silly," Marguerite said, suddenly beaming.
"We'll all go down together. We can talk to Christian and
the others on their break. Or perhaps even before they
start."

"Right," Carolyn muttered, suddenly aware that she'd
probably have to meet them all again if she stuck with
Marguerite and Julius. The idea made her ridiculously

uncomfortable and she found herself frowning and trying to come up with a reason to leave. They were almost to the open-air bar when she suddenly realized she was carrying the perfect excuse.

"You know," she said, coming to a halt, "I think I should probably go back up to the villa and switch my broken shoes for—"

"Don't be silly, Caro. You're here already," Marguerite said with a gentle smile. "Everything will be fine."

Carolyn stared at her silently as her eagerness to escape the possibility of having to again face Christian eased and a soothing calm slid over her. Then she smiled and nodded and allowed Marguerite to lead her into the open-air bar, wondering what on earth all the fuss had been about. Christian had helped her after her shoe broke. She was making a mountain out of a molehill. Everything would be fine.

"She is your life mate," Raffaele said quietly.

Christian tore his eyes away from the lobby as his parents and Carolyn were swallowed up by the crowds. Turning, he considered the group eyeing him silently, his cousins and band mates. They'd known each other all their lives, but had only played together the last ten years or so.

"Well?" he asked. "What was she thinking?"

"She thought you were a big female at first," Zanipolo said with amusement.

"Yes, I know," Christian said dryly. "Gia giggled that into my ear. It's why I tried to read her."

"It was dark in the van and she hasn't our eyesight," Raffaele said soothingly. "All she could make out was long hair and a large frame."

"She thought you were very handsome once she saw

your face," Giacinta said, patting his arm as if he might need the reassurance. She then bit her lip and added, "Which kind of horrified her."

Christian frowned. "Why?"

Gia arched her eyebrows as if that should be obvious. "She's forty-two."

Christian's eyes widened. He would have placed Carolyn in her mid- to late thirties. She carried her age well. Still, he didn't get Giacinta's point. "So? She's forty-two?"

"Well, you look about twenty-five or twenty-six," she pointed out gently.

"I haven't been that young for a very long time," Christian said grimly.

"But you *look* that young," Gia pointed out and when he stared at her blankly, she added, "She is mortal. She thinks you are young enough to be her child and is upset to have sexual feelings for someone she thinks is so young."

"She had sexual feelings for me already?" he asked with a grin.

Gia threw up her hands in exasperation. "*Uomini! Idiota, non essere cosi stupido!*"

Christian blinked at the explosive rant of "Men! You idiot, don't be so stupid!" and then cleared his throat. "I gather this is a problem?"

"*Si, cugino, è una problema,*" Gia said dryly. "I read her. She is not the type of woman who would be comfortable having an affair with a younger man. She will now avoid you to avoid those uncomfortable feelings."

Christian frowned. It wasn't a problem he'd considered when he'd contemplated the possibility that his mother had found him a life mate.

"Don't worry, we'll help you with her. And I am sure Aunt Marguerite will help too," Raffaele rumbled and then slapped a hand on his shoulder and urged him into the building. "Now let's go find our equipment and get set up. When you called Bellina, she said Genie had our instruments kept in her office until we arrived, *si*?"

"*Si,* all but the drums and keyboard. She had those set up on the stage." The words were said absently, Christian's mind was on the problem of Carolyn, and the disturbing assurance that his mother and cousins would help him woo her. Cripes, he thought with dismay as he imagined that scenario.

"I hope your friend Bethany feels better soon," Marguerite said with a sympathetic smile.

"So do I," Carolyn assured her. They were seated at one of the tables on the edge of the lower deck, the sandy beach close enough to touch if she just slid her foot over the slightest bit, which she'd done several times already, digging her bare toes into the cool sand and allowing it to slide around and between them. "And I'm sure she will."

Marguerite nodded. "Well, we're here to keep you company tonight, so she couldn't have picked a better time to recuperate."

Carolyn smiled, but shook her head. "Don't be silly. You two are on your honeymoon. You don't need me hanging around. Besides, I have Genie. As soon as she gets here we'll move to another table so you two can be alone."

"Cara," Marguerite said with amusement. "We like having you here, dear."

Carolyn smiled wryly, finding it odd that Marguerite always managed to make her feel like a child when she was probably twenty years older than the woman. Her gaze slid to Julius then to note the solemn expression on his face as he eyed her, and Carolyn found herself wondering if he or Christian was the older. The brothers looked like they could be about the same age, but her instincts told her Julius was probably the older one, though she couldn't say why for sure except that it was something about the eyes.

"Oh, here they are," Marguerite said happily, and Carolyn followed her gaze to the stage where drums and a keyboard had been set up. Genie was now leading the band members onto the low stage and taking up the microphone to introduce them as they moved to their spots. Santo settled behind the drums, Raffaele stepped behind the keyboards and began to check things, Zanipolo and Giacinta both carried guitars, and Christian was holding a . . .

"Violin?" Carolyn said with surprise.

"Yes!" Marguerite beamed. "Isn't he clever?"

"Er . . ." Carolyn stared blankly. The men all wore black T-shirts and either black jeans or leather pants, making Gia stand out in her red and white. And their hairstyles were all kind of punk rock. Gia's hair was now gelled and wild around her head while Raffaele's hair stood up in shiny spikes all over, like a porcupine. Then there was Santo's bald head, and Zanipolo's and Christian's long hair, although Zanipolo had let his out of its ponytail, while Christian had pulled his back into one. All in all they looked like a rock band . . . except for the violin.

"Christian was trained in classical violin, but he prefers hard rock," Marguerite said, sounding more like a proud momma than a new sister-in-law.

"Hard-rock violin," Carolyn murmured, a bit befuddled. She'd never heard of such a thing. She liked modern music, pop, hip-hop, alternative, and some hard rock, but she'd never heard of hard rock done with a violin. This should be interesting, she thought dubiously.

"Just wait till you hear them." Marguerite grinned.

Carolyn smiled doubtfully as Genie finished introducing them and stepped off the stage to hurry to their table.

"Oh, my God, they are so hot, Marguerite," Genie gushed as she fell into the chair next to Carolyn's. "You didn't mention that they were all gorgeous."

"I showed you the video," Marguerite pointed out with a laugh.

"It didn't do them justice at all," Genie assured her and then glanced back to the stage. Heaving a sigh, she muttered, "If only I were twenty years younger. I don't suppose any of them would be interested in a fling with an older woman?"

Marguerite chuckled, "Oh, Christian happens to like older women. But he generally prefers blondes."

"That leaves me out then," Genie said with a sigh and then elbowed Carolyn. "But it means you might have a chance."

Carolyn nearly spat out the wine she'd just sipped. Swallowing it quickly and managing not to choke, she glanced to Marguerite to find the woman smiling at her encouragingly. Carolyn could feel the blood rushing to her face with embarrassment. She shook her head and turned quickly to the stage as Gia stepped up to the center mic.

The young woman stood there for a full minute, garnering the attention of everyone in the room, and then she opened her mouth and released a high pure note that pierced the silence. Her hand crashed down across the strings of the electric guitar she held and the band suddenly kicked to life, all movement and sound. Santo's body vibrated as he beat his drums to death. Zanipolo was working his electric guitar like a cross between a lover and a submachine gun. Raffaele was pounding on his keyboards, his head bobbing to the music. Gia was alternately making love to her own electric guitar with long riffs, and singing into the microphone with a clarity that Carolyn had never encountered before. And Christian . . .

Carolyn stared, watching the muscles in his arms and chest ripple under his black T-shirt as his bow scraped so quickly over the strings of his violin that she expected to see sparks flying and smoke rising. His eyes were closed, his face transported as the music moved through him. She couldn't seem to tear her gaze from him as he played song after song . . . and then his eyes suddenly opened and met hers. Carolyn felt like someone had jammed an adrenaline shot into her heart. She was sure it skipped a beat when his eyes opened, but when he caught her gaze and didn't release it, her heart started thumping again, charging ahead at a frightening rate that left her breathless and almost dizzy.

The music ended as abruptly as it had started. At least it seemed that way to her. Surely it hadn't been an hour and a half already, she thought faintly as the band suddenly began to set their instruments aside and move off the stage.

"Break time," Genie announced over the microphone and Carolyn blinked. She hadn't even been aware of the woman leaving the table.

"Weren't they great?" Genie asked the audience. "They'll be back in fifteen minutes. I can't wait. How about you?"

The bar erupted in claps and cheers, but Carolyn's eyes were still locked with Christian's as he led the band toward their table. He hadn't even looked away while setting down his violin, and the intensity of his stare made her feel like a gazelle being stalked by a tiger. What remained of her intelligence pointed out that she was being ridiculous, but her instincts were screeching at her to run. Before she quite knew what she was doing, Carolyn stood, tore her gaze free of Christian's, mumbled something about the ladies' room, and fled in that general direction at little short of a dead run.

"I told you she'd avoid you," Gia said as Christian watched Carolyn flee. His instincts were telling him to give chase, to run her to ground like a panther with prey. The problem was what to do with her once he caught her. He knew what he wanted to do, but it was entirely inappropriate behavior in a public place.

Christian shook his head as that last thought registered. He already wanted her, he acknowledged on a sigh. The moment in the van when he'd realized he couldn't read her, he'd immediately been curious. And he'd felt a strange flutter and tingle as he'd touched her to lift her out of the van, which had grown as he'd carried her to the bench. It was what had urged him to deliberately let her body slide along his as he'd set her down, which had only increased those sensations. But when he'd felt her watching him while he was onstage and opened his eyes . . . He'd been captivated by the emotions flitting across her face. He'd recognized awe, appreciation, loneliness, and raw need and it had called up similar responses in himself. By the time the set had ended all he'd been thinking about was getting to the table to claim her.

Christian hadn't been clear on how he'd intended to do that. Actually, he hadn't been thinking clearly at all, his blood was up after performing, and he suspected it might be a good thing she'd fled.

"I'll go get her and bring her back," Gia offered as they reached the table.

"No, it's better she doesn't return until he's back onstage," Marguerite said at once, and when Christian glanced at her with surprise, she smiled apologetically. "Your passions are too hot right now. If you carry her off, as you were thinking about while playing, you'll scare her. It's why I didn't stop her from going."

"I wasn't thinking that," Christian said quickly.

"Darling, that was the most G-rated thing you were thinking," Marguerite said gently.

Christian flushed as his cousins chuckled, but couldn't deny it. He hadn't really been thinking of carrying her off, but images of that and much more had been running through his mind. Grimacing, he dropped into a chair at the table.

Marguerite patted his hand, then glanced to Gia and said, "You could go talk to her. Calm her and make sure she returns to the table once you're all back onstage. I think you'll like her, Gia."

"Okay." Gia started to turn, but paused when Santo caught her arm.

"You need water," he said, spotting a waiter nearby and concentrating on him briefly.

"I don't drink water," Gia said with a scowl.

"But we don't have what you do drink here and there is no time for any of us to make a run back up to the villa to get it. Water will deal with the dehydration from the performance for now."

Gia clucked impatiently, but when the waiter suddenly appeared with several bottles of cold water dripping with condensation, she accepted one and moved off in the direction of the ladies' room.

"So . . ." Christian accepted the bottle Santo passed to him. "How am I supposed to woo her if I can't go near her?"

"I don't think you should . . . for tonight at least. I think you should let us work on her first," Marguerite said thoughtfully.

Christian stiffened at the suggestion. "Mother, don't confuse me with Father. Unlike him I know how to woo a woman."

"Excuse me, I know how to woo a woman." Julius slid his arm around Marguerite, pulling her close as he added, "And here's the proof."

Christian nodded. "Which wooing technique do you think did it? When you attacked her and Tiny in that hotel? Or when you threw her over your shoulder and carted her back to that townhouse in York?"

"What? He did that?" Raffaele asked with surprise as Julius's eyes narrowed.

"I'm just asking so I don't use the wrong technique on Caro," Christian said, holding his father's gaze and ignoring Raffaele for now. Lips twitching, he added, "Maybe you could school me in how to talk to her. Should I practice in my head?"

"Oh man, I'm so missing something here," Zanipolo muttered.

Julius suddenly relaxed. "Go ahead and laugh, son. But it's you in the hot seat now." Expression solemn, he added, "And Carolyn isn't immortal, with an immortal's understanding of life mates. She's also been hurt and has a natural resistance to getting involved with men at the moment, not to mention utter horror at the idea of even being attracted to someone she thinks is as young as you are. She will be difficult. Accept your mother's help."

Christian frowned at the thought that anyone had hurt his Carolyn, but let it go for now and glanced to his mother. "What do you suggest?"

Marguerite relaxed, though he suspected it was the brief verbal exchange between her son and husband that had made her tense to begin with. Now she said, "Well, I think we should see how Gia's talk with her goes. Then Genie can help."

"Genie? The entertainment coordinator?" he asked with bewilderment.

Marguerite nodded. "They are friends and she seems open to the idea of a vacation romance for Carolyn. As is her other friend Bethany."

"I'm not interested in a vacation romance," Christian growled.

"Yes, dear, I know," Marguerite said patiently. "But it's a start. You have to work your way up to this."

He shifted impatiently, but knew she was right. "Okay, so how can Genie help?"

"With the right prodding, I'm quite sure she'll help convince her," Marguerite assured him. "But, in the meantime, I don't think you should even talk to Caro again until tomorrow."

"Tomorrow?" Christian sat up abruptly. Cripes, he wanted her now. Waiting till tomorrow was—

"You have waited five hundred years. One day won't kill you," Marguerite said, patting his hand soothingly. "Besides, it won't really be tomorrow."

When he allowed his confusion to show, she smiled. "Shared dreams."

"Oh, man." Zanipolo punched Christian in the arm. "Shared dreams are supposed to be hot."

"Hopefully, with talking to Gia, encouragement from Genie, and the shared dreams she may be more willing to overlook the age difference."

Christian suspected it wouldn't be that easy, but merely asked, "Is she close enough to have shared dreams?"

"She's in the villa below yours," Marguerite said, grinning. "We arranged it."

"Thank you," he murmured.

"Don't thank us. We haven't won her for you yet," Marguerite said, and then warned, "And I suspect no matter what we do, she'll still run eventually."

When Christian stilled, she shrugged. "All of your brothers' life mates ran at some point or another," she said quietly. "It's a frightening prospect for a mortal. They have not only to accept our existence, but to trust in nanos, something they didn't even know about before meeting an immortal."

Christian glanced up as Genie suddenly appeared at the table, smiling widely.

"Oh, you guys are great. Everyone I've talked to loves you," she announced happily, and then asked, "Where's Gia? And Carolyn?" she added as she noted her friend was missing as well.

"They are in the ladies' room. I'm sure both will be back soon," Marguerite answered. "Speaking of Carolyn, Christian was just asking about her, but I don't know her as well as you. Perhaps you can answer his questions?"

Genie's eyebrows rose as her gaze shifted to him. "Sure. What did you want to know?"

Taking his mother's cue, Christian smiled and said, "Everything."

Three

Carolyn stepped out of the stall and headed for the sinks, her footsteps slowing as she recognized the blonde fluffing her hair in front of the mirror.

"Oh, hi," she greeted self-consciously when Gia met her gaze in the mirror. Suddenly uncomfortable, she gestured to the stall and mumbled, "I was just . . . er . . ."

"Using the facilities?" Gia suggested with amusement.

Carolyn nodded and continued to the sink to wash her hands, silently berating herself for an idiot. It was guilt over her attraction to Christian and the way she'd fled that had made her say that, as if she needed a cover for leaving the table.

Gia chuckled, and Carolyn glanced at her uncertainly.

"Sorry, but you should see your expression," Gia said with amusement. "You look as guilty as a kid caught with his hand in the cookie jar."

Carolyn looked back to the sink as she washed her hands.

When Carolyn moved to dry her hands, Gia asked, "So the entertainment director, Genie, is a friend of yours?"

Carolyn smiled. "Since university. And so is Beth. She came here with me, but has been under the weather since arriving," she explained. "Which is a shame since this is the first time the three of us have been together since we roomed together at uni."

"The three of you were roommates?" Gia asked curiously. "On campus?"

"No, we rented a house with another friend. Brent."

"Brent." Gia grinned. "One man and three women. That must have been interesting."

Carolyn chuckled. "Brent was more like one of the girls than a guy."

Gia's eyes narrowed and then she murmured, "Gay."

"Yes," Carolyn answered, though it hadn't really been a question. "Few in school knew it though. He was still in the closet back then. His parents were older and he didn't think they'd accept him if they knew." She smiled faintly. "The funny thing is, he dragged me home as his 'girlfriend' for years to keep his parents from finding out, and when he finally came out of the closet, his mother wasn't surprised at all. She'd known all along I was just his beard."

Gia turned her back to the counter, hefted herself up to sit on it, and picked up a bottle of water that had been resting beside her. She eyed Carolyn as she opened it and took a sip, then lowered it and asked, "Beard?"

"It's a fake girlfriend basically, so people don't know the person's gay," she explained, wondering what the Italian equivalent would be. Marguerite had said the band members were all Italian relatives of Julius's.

She glanced toward the door, but hesitated, not anxious to go back out while Christian might still be there. Carolyn was afraid of making a fool of herself over the man by drooling or otherwise revealing her attraction to

him. It just seemed better to avoid him. She'd go back
after he'd returned to the stage and then slip away before
the second set ended and avoid the lounge until the band
left, she decided.

"Sit with me," Gia suggested, patting the counter beside
her. When Carolyn glanced at her uncertainly, she smiled
wryly and said, "I'm supposed to get to relax during the
breaks, but if we go back out, guests will want to talk to
me and then it's not relaxing. Talking to you is relaxing."

Carolyn didn't particularly want to go back out anyway,
so moved over to settle on the counter next to her.

"So, you didn't mind being this beard for your friend?"
Gia asked at once.

"No, not at all. Brent was a sweetheart and a great
friend. He still is. Besides, I felt for him. He really struggled with his sexuality back then. He wanted to be straight
to please his family and basically fit in, but he just wasn't
attracted to women. He had it tough there for a while. I
was happy to help out," she said with a shrug.

"My *cugino* has the same problem," Gia announced
when Carolyn glanced to the door again.

Carolyn looked back uncertainly. "*Cugino*?"

"Cousin," Gia translated. "He's gay, but . . . well, Italy
is terribly into the whole machismo thing, and especially
in our family, so he keeps it to himself. I'm the only one
who knows."

"Oh, that's a shame. It must be hard for him," she said
with sympathy, recalling many late-night talks with Brent
on the subject. He really had struggled with it and it didn't
seem fair to her. She didn't understand the anger and rage
homosexuality caused in some people. Some acted like
they thought the individual woke up one day and said,
*Well, I think I'll piss off the universe today by switching
my sexual preference.* She was no expert on the matter,

but it seemed to her that thinking a person could choose
what gender they were attracted to was like thinking you
could choose what you preferred to eat. Some preferred
chocolate over vanilla, and others preferred vanilla to
chocolate; it wasn't a choice, but a matter of taste and
what appealed to their palette. Why did they think sexual
preference would be any different?

"*Si.*" Gia nodded sadly. "It wasn't so bad for a while,
he had a—what did you call it? A beard?" When Carolyn
nodded, she continued, "He had a beard for years. They
were good friends and she would go to family functions
and such with him. But she married last year and he has
not had a beard since. Everyone in the family is bothering him about bringing home another girlfriend and he's
afraid some of them are beginning to suspect. Especially
Julius and the other boys in the band."

"This cousin is one of the guys in the band?" Carolyn asked with surprise, wondering which one it could
be. She was pretty sure it wasn't Christian or Santo, and
Raffaele didn't seem likely. That left Zanipolo. Of course,
she could be completely wrong. It wasn't as if you could
tell just by looking. Well, sometimes you could, she supposed, but not always, and definitely not if they were still
in the closet.

"You could help him," Gia said now, and Carolyn
peered at her blankly.

"Me? Help him? How?" she asked with bewilderment.

"You could be his beard," Gia said with a smile. "If
they thought he was having an affair with you, it would
lay their suspicions to rest for now and take the pressure
off of him for a little while, even after this trip."

"Oh, Gia, I don't know," she began with dismay.

"Oh, but it's perfect," Gia said at once, moving to clasp
her hands. "You have done this before so know how to be

a beard. He will be able to relax with you and not worry that you will try to drag him to bed, or be hurt or complain if he doesn't try to drag you there because you know he can't possibly be interested."

"But I'm so much older than all you guys," she pointed out, her voice rising along with her alarm.

"No you're not. We aren't as young as we look," Gia assured her. "We just have to keep the youthful image to be in a band. And we age well in our clan," she added when Carolyn narrowed her eyes on her, looking for crow's-feet or any other telltale sign that the woman might be older than the twenty-five or so that she looked. "Besides, his last . . . er . . . beard was about your age, and everyone thinks he prefers older women because of it. They won't doubt it for a moment."

"Gia, I'd like to help, but I don't think—"

"It would be mutually beneficial," Gia interrupted persuasively. "He's smart and funny and good company . . . well, perhaps not funny," she muttered with a frown. "Actually, he's a little serious, but I'm sure that's just because he's always worrying about others finding out and the family turning from him. He is good company though, and could be your escort and companion while your friend, Beth, is ill."

"I don't know . . . ," Carolyn murmured, but was growing tempted to say yes. She really hated the idea of anyone suffering like Brent had. And it would be nice to have company while Beth was ill.

"And you would be doing me a great favor," Gia said solemnly. "I worry about him. He has been so morose over it all, I fear he will do something to hurt himself. But if you were to act as his beard and get the pressure off of him, I wouldn't have to worry so much."

Carolyn's eyes widened. "It's that bad?"

"Our family is very much into machismo," she said solemnly.

Carolyn bit her lip. It really was very tempting. In fact, the only thing now holding her back was the realization that if she agreed, she would probably have to be around the band at least occasionally, which meant being around Christian, and with her ridiculous attraction to him, that didn't seem like a good—

"And I know Christian would be grateful," Gia said suddenly and Carolyn stilled, and then raised wide eyes to the blonde.

"Christian?" The name came out a squeak. Dear God, she thought when the girl nodded. She'd been lusting after the poor guy and he was gay. How sad was that? And where the hell was her gaydar? She'd always thought her twenty-plus-year friendship with Brent had sharpened it to a fine point. Apparently not.

"God," she muttered.

"So? Will you do it?" Gia asked, and then eyes twinkling, added, "You can take lots of pictures of you and Christian together and e-mail them to your ex-husband so that he thinks you are having a grand time with a buff young stallion."

Carolyn burst out laughing at the thought, and then glanced to her with surprise. "How did you know I have an ex-husband?"

"Your finger." She nodded toward her hand and Carolyn glanced down, sighing when she saw the mark her wedding ring had left. It was like a brand of sorts, she thought with disgust. It might actually be gone now had she taken her wedding ring off back when she'd left Robert, but she'd worn it so long she hadn't even thought about it until Bethany had insisted she remove it when they left on this trip. "You're single. Advertise it," she'd said.

"He's not actually my ex-husband yet," Carolyn admitted unhappily. "The divorce isn't final. The lawyer says another three months and it should be done, but right now it's still in the process."

"Hmm. Well, then you should definitely take pictures of you and Christian and send them to him."

Carolyn chuckled at the thought, but knew she wouldn't do it. She had no interest in any kind of contact with Robert, except to sign the final divorce decree.

"So? Can I tell Christian you'll do it?" Gia asked.

Carolyn hesitated. She'd like to help him out, and the idea of company while Beth was ill was definitely a tempting one, and she was pretty sure now that she knew he was gay her attraction for Christian would die a natural death. The only real issue was what others would think. They'd all think she was some kind of cougar, playing with someone twenty years her junior. That thought bothered her and she said, "I'd like to help, Gia. But I'm kind of uncomfortable with the idea of everyone thinking I'm having a fling with someone so much younger than me."

"Well, neither Marguerite nor Julius, nor certainly anyone in the band will think anything of it," she reasoned patiently. "As I said, they all think Christian prefers older women. But aside from that, women in Europe take younger lovers all the time, at least among our people. No one thinks anything of it," she said with a shrug. "And you can always tell Genie and Bethany the truth so long as they don't tell anyone. As for everyone else, who cares about them? You're not likely to meet anyone from here again, that's the beauty of a vacation . . . Come on," she cajoled. "It would be fun having you hang with the band."

Carolyn hesitated, but then blew her breath out. "What the hell. Yes, I'll do it."

"That a girl!" Gia said with a grin. "I promise you won't regret it."

"Let's hope you're right," Carolyn muttered, already having second thoughts.

"That's my cue." Gia slid off the counter as the sound of a guitar tuning up reached them. "Back to work for me. You should return to the table and enjoy the rest of the show."

"Yes, I suppose so." Carolyn slid off the counter as well. There seemed little reason to avoid Christian anymore. She'd obviously been imagining the sparks that had seemed to fly between them as he'd stared at her. He'd probably been wondering if he could persuade her to be his beard. Now that she knew the lay of the land, Carolyn was almost embarrassed by the wild thoughts that had run through her head. Shaking her head, she followed Gia to the door.

"Caro, dear, will you order Julius and me another drink if the waitress comes around again, please?" Marguerite asked as she stood up. "We're just going to go see if Gia and the boys are up to joining us or not."

"Sure," Carolyn said as the couple stood and moved toward the stage where the band was now winding up cords and putting away instruments.

"God, every single one of them is hot," Genie said, her eyes eating the band alive as they moved around the stage. "Even that Gia. I'd switch teams if I had a chance with her."

Carolyn laughed. "Sure you would."

"Okay, maybe I wouldn't, but I'd seriously consider it."

Carolyn shook her head and glanced toward the band again.

"So what about that Christian?" Genie asked.

"What about him?" Carolyn's eyes found the man on his haunches, setting his violin in its case.

"He was asking me loads of questions about you. You might get lucky there," she said, elbowing her.

"Brent would have more luck than me," Carolyn assured her.

Genie blinked. "What?"

Carolyn nodded. "I was talking to Gia in the washroom during the break. The family's very into the macho thing and he's gay but firmly in the closet, and she asked me to be his beard."

"No. God, why are the good ones always gay?" Genie moaned, her eyes moving back to the stage. "Are you going to do it?"

"Yes," she admitted. "I don't mind helping him out, and it will give me company while Beth's sick."

"True." Genie glanced back to the stage. "You could do worse than eye candy like that to keep you company. Of course, every single woman here is going to envy the hell out of you and hate your guts."

Carolyn laughed at the suggestion, her gaze shifting to Marguerite and Julius as they reached the band.

"Well?" Christian asked, bending down for Marguerite to kiss his cheek.

"You were brilliant," she assured him, beaming. "I was very proud."

Christian flushed, but smiled and admitted, "I meant Carolyn. Do I go back and try to sleep now?"

Marguerite bit her lip and glanced to Gia. "You didn't tell him yet?"

Gia shook her head. "I take it you read her?"

"Yes, dear, and that was brilliant thinking on your part. Absolutely brilliant."

"Thank you, Aunt Marguerite," Gia said, beaming under the praise.

"What was brilliant?" Christian asked at once.

Marguerite bit her lip, which didn't seem good, but it definitely worried him when she suggested, "Why don't we go somewhere more private to discuss it."

"We have to take the instruments back to Genie's office," Raffaele rumbled. "You can talk there."

"Won't Genie—"

"She gave us the key," Christian interrupted.

"Right, then we'll do that," she decided.

Christian glanced toward the table as he followed the others offstage, his gaze finding Carolyn. Much to his shock she gave him a tentative smile when their eyes met and Christian felt something unclench a little in his chest. He'd been worried sick about how to woo her ever since she'd fled the table earlier at his approach. It would be impossible to woo her if she wasn't around to woo. However, it appeared that Gia's brilliant idea was actually working. He couldn't wait to hear it.

Unfortunately, he appeared to be the only one eager to get to the office. Everyone else was moving at a snail's pace as Marguerite gushed with praise over the performance. Christian forced himself to be patient. He'd waited for Carolyn for five hundred years, another five minutes wasn't going to kill him . . . hopefully.

"All right." Christian closed Genie's office door and turned to glance from his mother to Gia. "What's this brilliant idea?"

When Marguerite and Gia exchanged a glance, he felt trepidation crawl up his spine again and narrowed his eyes.

"Well?" he growled.

"Now, dear, I just want you to take everything into consideration here before you react," Marguerite cautioned, just increasing his trepidation. "You have to think where Carolyn's head is at."

"She was superfreaked at being attracted to you," Gia put in solemnly. "I mean, seriously, ready-to-run-and-never-come-near-the-lounge-again freaked."

Christian frowned, but wasn't terribly surprised. This not-aging business could be a real pain in some ways, but he supposed it wouldn't have been any easier had he looked five hundred. Then she wouldn't have given him a second glance.

"And?" he prompted, when neither woman continued.

Gia glanced to Marguerite. When she nodded encouragement, Gia cleared her throat. "So I got her talking to try to figure an angle. It was obvious that just trying to convince her to overlook your age and give you a chance wasn't going to work. She's not the kind of woman who would be comfortable with a boy toy."

"A boy toy?" he choked out, and then scowled when his father snickered.

"Yes, well that's how she was thinking of you, Christian," she said, and then pointed out, "We do look a lot younger than we are."

"Right," he growled. "So?"

"Well." Gia paused to lick her lips. "I got her talking about her friends . . . Genie and Bethany and . . . er . . . Brent."

Christian stiffened, eyes narrowing. "Brent?"

"Yes, he's . . . er . . . well, he was her roommate in university. Actually they were all roommates. They shared a house," she added quickly when he began to scowl. "Brent was a good friend. Kind of like a girlfriend."

Christian blinked. "Kind of like a girlfriend?"

"Yes, well, you see . . . er . . . Brent is gay," she explained.

Christian relaxed. That was all right. He'd started worrying there that Gia was going to tell him Carolyn had some long-lived, unrequited love for the guy.

"Okay, so she has a gay friend," he said, not getting where this was going.

Gia glanced to Marguerite again and shifted her feet. "Well, see, he wasn't openly gay, he was in the closet, and she used to pretend to be his girlfriend on occasion to help him stay there. It's called being a beard, apparently."

Christian waited.

Gia shifted nervously again, and this time he noticed that she was shuffling a little away from him. When his eyes narrowed, she continued, "And then it struck me. She was very sympathetic to this Brent. They were good friends and she felt bad for the struggle he had and so on . . ." She paused and shuffled another step away before blurting out, "And so I told her you were gay."

Christian blinked once, twice, and then a third time and squawked, "*What*?"

"Now, Christian, just listen for a moment," Marguerite said, patting his arm.

Christian glanced toward his mother, but paused as his eyes got caught on his father chuckling silently behind her. He glared at the man, but glanced at Zanipolo when he said, "Wait, whoa. Are you *serious*? You told her he was *gay*?"

"It seemed like the perfect solution," Gia said on a sigh.

"What the hell do you mean it seemed like the perfect solution?" Christian asked with disbelief. "You told her I was *gay*."

"Yes, but see—"

"And she *believed* you?" he asked with horror.

"Yes, of course. Why would she think I'd lie about something like that?" she asked with exasperation.

"Julius," Marguerite chastised gently when his father gave a muffled guffaw.

"Sorry, darling, but he gave me such grief over my wooing of you that I can't help but think this is funny," Julius said, slipping his arm around Marguerite.

"It isn't funny," Christian growled. "She told my life mate that I'm *gay*."

Zanipolo gave a bark of laughter. "And she believed it."

Christian scowled at the man, considering violence until Gia said, "Actually, at first I just said my *cugino* was gay and didn't tell her which one. She thought it must be you before I said it was Christian."

"What?" Zanipolo cried. "Why would she think that? Do I look gay?"

Christian growled impatiently, and turned on Gia. "I don't see how her thinking I am gay is supposed to help."

"Is it my hair that made her pick me for the gay one, do you think?" Zanipolo asked suddenly. "Maybe I should cut it."

"It could be," Santo said, eyeing him consideringly.

"Nah. Christian has long hair too," Raffaele pointed out.

Christian scowled at them, but then glanced back to Gia as she announced, "I said you were in the closet and afraid to come out for fear the family would turn on you."

"What?" he asked blankly.

"We would never turn on you, Christian," Marguerite murmured, patting his arm. "Gay or not, we love you."

"*I'm not gay*," he pointed out, his voice rising an octave, and heard another snort of laughter from his father.

"Well, no dear, of course not," Marguerite said quickly. "But if you were, we'd still love you. You wouldn't have to hide in the closet with the smelly old shoes."

"It's not literal, Mother. I wouldn't actually be hiding in a closet. It's a—never mind," he muttered and turned back to Gia. "How the hell is my being a closet gay supposed to—"

"She's agreed to be your beard," she interrupted quickly.

"I don't want a damned beard," Christian snapped. "I want my life mate."

"Maybe I should grow a beard. Maybe that would make me look less gay," Zanipolo muttered, rubbing his cheek.

Gia ignored him. "I know you want her for a life mate, not a beard, Christian, and this way she won't be uncomfortable spending time with you. You can get to know each other without the risk of her fleeing because of her attraction to you."

"Because she thinks I'm gay so won't be attracted," he pointed out grimly.

"Now, Christian, your being gay won't affect her attraction to you," Marguerite said soothingly.

"*I'm not gay*," he bellowed, scowling at his father when he released another guffaw.

"No, of course not, dear. She'll just think you are," his mother agreed.

"But I'm not!" he roared. "And how the hell am I supposed to get close to her when she thinks I am?"

"Christian," Marguerite began with concern.

"Allow me, *cara*." Julius took Christian's arm and urged him away from the rest of the group. It did little good since they all immediately crowded forward behind them, but Julius ignored that and put his arm around Christian as he said, "Stop thinking about the gay bit, and think about her being your beard. That's a pretend girlfriend, right?"

He frowned but nodded.

"So, you'll get to spend time with her, take her out for dinner, talk, get to know each other, and"—Julius added firmly—"you'll get to hold her hand, put your arm around her, dance with her, and so on, like a boyfriend does. It will be expected. At least in public, right?"

Christian nodded slowly, considering this.

"We can even make sure she lets you kiss her," Julius added.

"How are we going to do that?" Marguerite asked with interest.

Christian scowled. "I don't want you taking control of her and—"

"That's the beauty of it," Julius interrupted. "We won't have to control her to get her to do anything. All I have to do is say something like, you two never kiss or anything, I don't believe you're dating, and you'll be obliged to kiss her and she'll let you to uphold her position as beard."

"Oh, Julius, you *are* clever," Marguerite praised.

"But if she thinks I'm gay, she'll hardly be attracted to me and want me kissing her," Christian said unhappily.

"Her thinking you're gay isn't going to affect her attraction to you," his father said firmly. "Nothing can affect that. The nanos somehow control that. She'll want you no matter what she thinks you are. All this gay and beard business does is make it so she just won't be afraid that you're attracted back. So she won't fear having to deal with, or face up to, an attraction she feels is inappropriate. She'll have no reason to run. You'll be free to woo her."

Christian could see how that could be helpful. It was certainly better than having her avoid him and not getting to spend time with her at all. Still . . . "All right, but what happens then?"

"What happens when?" Julius asked uncertainly.

"Well, once I have her liking me and get her to know me, how do I then roll it over from I'm gay to I'm not?" he asked dryly.

"Oh." Julius removed his arm with a shrug. "I have no idea."

"I'm sure nature will take its course, dear," Marguerite said at once. "The important thing is that this allows you to at least begin the wooing process."

Christian sighed and nodded wearily.

"It's not my clothes," Zanipolo said with certainty. "My clothes are no different from what you guys wear."

"Now," Marguerite murmured, ignoring Zanipolo's mutterings. "I told the girls we were going to see if you guys were up for joining us. Are you?"

When Christian hesitated, unsure if he was ready—or even knew how—to play a gay man, Marguerite added, "If so, you can ask her to go for a walk, tell her Gia told you she agreed to be your beard and you appreciate it and then kick it off. Ask her to dinner tomorrow night, maybe."

Christian hesitated. "I don't have to talk in a higher octave or start walking or behaving effeminately, do I?"

"Is my walk effeminate?" Zanipolo asked suddenly.

"Not that I noticed," Santo assured him. Zanipolo was just relaxing when he added, "But then I don't really watch you walk, *cugino*."

"You don't have to walk or act effeminately," Gia said with exasperation. "There are all sorts of gay men, some more effeminate, some more butch, and then some perfectly average. They are just like everyone else, for heaven's sake."

"Right," Christian muttered.

"Just be yourself," Marguerite advised.

"Right," Christian repeated.

"Let's go get her, son," Julius said cheerfully, slapping him on the shoulder. "I want to be bouncing your babies on my knee in nine months or so."

"Oh," Marguerite said on a little sigh and rubbed Christian's arm. "My baby having babies."

"I'm over five hundred years old, Mom. Hardly a baby."

"You'll always be a baby to me," she assured him, leaning up to kiss his cheek.

Christian shook his head and turned toward the door, but heard her murmur in a weepy voice, "Did you hear, Julius? He called me Mom again."

"*Si, cara,* and so you are," his father said gently.

"Yes, but I missed so much of his growing up," she said on a sigh as Christian opened the door.

"You did," Christian heard his father agree solemnly. "Maybe we should have another one to make up for it."

"It won't make up for all I missed," she whispered. "But it would be nice."

"Then we'll start working on it tonight," Julius murmured.

"You two have been 'working on it' since finding each other," Christian pointed out dryly.

"Yes, we have," Julius agreed as they started through the lobby. "Jealous?"

"Damned right," Christian muttered. He wouldn't mind doing a little "working on it" with Carolyn. But that wasn't likely to happen for a while with her thinking he was gay. God!

Four

'Oh, here they come.'

Carolyn glanced around at Genie's warning.

"They're all coming, not just Julius and Marguerite," Genie pointed out.

As if she could have missed that fact, Carolyn thought dryly. Cripes, the men were a wall of male flesh that pretty much engulfed the two smaller females. They were all so tall it was like watching a walking forest.

"Do you think Gia got the chance to tell him you agreed to be his beard?"

"I don't know," Carolyn muttered, suddenly nervous.

"I guess we'll find out soon enough. Gad, you're so lucky. I wouldn't mind being his beard. Getting to hang on his arm, and cuddle up to him and stuff."

"What?" Carolyn blinked at the words.

"Well, you'll have to make it convincing," Genie pointed out. "You can't just sit there like a bump on a log. Brent used to put his arm around you all the time. He held your hand and kissed your forehead too when you were doing it for him."

Yes, he had, Carolyn realized with dismay. Good lord, she'd forgotten about that part of it. It had just seemed natural with Brent, brotherly affection rather than anything untoward, but then she hadn't been lusting after Brent, and despite the fact that she knew Christian was gay, she still found him damned attractive.

"I'm sure Christian will expect the same," Genie pointed out. "I mean you're supposed to convince them all that you're having an affair."

Carolyn was just beginning to hyperventilate at that thought, when Genie added, "Of course, you're not supposed to be having the affair yet, so tonight will probably just be exchanging glances and smiles and stuff. But don't forget to do it."

"Right," Carolyn muttered, calming a little. She could do glances and smiles. Tomorrow she'd worry about hand-holding and that other business. Maybe once she got to know him, her feelings would shift to the more sisterly affection she had for Brent . . . Right, she thought as her eyes slid over Christian in his tight black T-shirt and even tighter black jeans. He was a beautiful man.

Gay, gay, gay, she reminded herself grimly. It wasn't nice to lust after young gay men, no matter how studly they were. Hell, she shouldn't be lusting after anyone his age to begin with.

"You're on," Genie whispered just before the group reached the table, and then noting the look on Carolyn's face, muttered, "I'll wave down the waitress and order you a drink. A nice stiff one."

"Thanks." Carolyn suspected she'd need it as she pasted a smile on her lips.

Christian was at the head of the group, his eyes locked

on hers again, and the moment she smiled, his lips quirked into a responding one. He also moved around the table, his fingers brushing along her back above the chair as he passed behind her to claim the chair on her left.

Carolyn's smile became strained as she fought off the shiver that tried to ride up her back at the light—no doubt unintentional—touch.

"Two slushy lime margaritas," Genie said as a waitress appeared at their table. Glancing around, she asked, "What else?"

"I'll have the same." Christian's deep voice sounded by Carolyn's ear, and she turned with a start to see that he'd turned sideways and pulled his seat closer. He'd also placed one hand on the back of her chair and the other on the table in front of her. It made her feel surrounded. She started to glance nervously away, but paused when he leaned forward to whisper in her ear.

"Gia told me. Thank you."

Carolyn couldn't stop the shiver that claimed her this time when his breath brushed her ear. She tried to cover her reaction with a nod, but thought, *Cripes, what have I gotten myself into here?*

"I know I told you before, but you guys were great," Genie announced suddenly and Carolyn turned to her gratefully.

"Yes, you were all very good," she agreed, frowning when her voice came out huskier than usual. Maybe she was getting Bethany's bug, Carolyn lied to herself desperately.

"What's your favorite song?" Christian asked, drawing her gaze again. His eyes were sleepy as he added, "I'll play it just for you tomorrow night."

Carolyn's eyes widened, but all she managed to get out was a weak, "Er."

"Christian can play anything from the sixteenth century on," Gia announced, drawing her attention next. "He's very talented."

"The rest of us are no slouches either, but Christian is the family prodigy," Zanipolo said in an extremely deep voice she didn't recall from the bus. Perhaps he was getting a cold too, she thought.

"Do you play an instrument?" Christian asked, drawing her reluctant gaze back to find he'd leaned in closer, his face just inches away.

Carolyn couldn't even manage an "Er" this time and simply shook her head.

"But she loves music. She loves to dance," Genie announced cheerfully.

"Christian loves to dance too," Gia said at once. "We should find a nightclub in town after the show tomorrow night and go dancing."

"Oh, that's a brilliant idea, Gia," Marguerite said at once. "I'd love to go dancing. You two will come, won't you, Carolyn? Genie?"

"Sure we will," Genie said for both of them.

"I'll look forward to it," Christian murmured in her ear.

Carolyn swiveled her head to glance at him and nearly kissed the man he was leaning so close. She felt his breath on her lips and swallowed.

"Oh, good. Here are our drinks," Genie announced brightly.

Carolyn turned with relief.

The waitress had returned with a tray of drinks. As the woman distributed the other drinks, Genie took a margarita off the tray and handed it to Carolyn saying, "Pass it along."

Carolyn automatically took it and turned toward Christian, but froze when his hand closed over hers, his fingers caressing hers briefly before they shifted to take the glass.

"Thank you."

"Er," Carolyn muttered and quickly turned back to take the second margarita Genie was now holding out. Lifting it to her mouth, she took a big gulp. Sharp pain immediately shot through her head.

"What's the matter?" Christian asked with concern when she set the glass down and raised her fingers to the bridge of her nose.

"Brain freeze?" Genie asked. When Carolyn nodded, she said, "Rub your tongue across the top of your mouth and cup your hand over your mouth and nose then blow hot air into it. That always helps me."

"Here." Christian caught her chin and turned her face to his, then cupped his own hands around either side of her mouth and nose and blew his warm breath into the cave he'd made. He had nice breath, she thought vaguely, wide eyes staring into his as he blew again.

"Don't forget to rub the top of her mouth with your tongue too, cousin," Zanipolo laughed.

Flushing, Carolyn pulled back to turn abruptly to her drink. She nearly took another swig, but caught herself. Slow sips, she told herself firmly. Brain freezes were painful, and her brain was useless enough already. Damn he was good at this. She herself almost believed he was interested. Gay men shouldn't be this sexy.

Genie suddenly muttered by her ear, "Damn he's good at this. I'm almost believing he's hot for you myself and I *know* he's gay."

Since she'd just had the very same thought herself, Genie's words shouldn't have affected her, but for some reason they depressed the hell out of Carolyn and her shoulders slumped a little as she lifted her drink to her lips for another swallow.

A sudden reduction in the heat along her side made Carolyn glance around, and she watched Christian lean toward Marguerite as she whispered something in his ear. When he started to straighten, she turned her gaze quickly back to her drink and took another sip. But now she was aware of the heat he was radiating. It seemed to prickle along her side like an electrical current.

"The moonlight on the water is beautiful at night," Christian said huskily. "Would you take a walk with me?"

Carolyn blinked at the request, her eyes shooting to his face. When she didn't respond other than to stare at him wide-eyed, he took her free hand and started to stand. "Come. We won't go far and I'll bring you right back."

Carolyn reluctantly released her glass as he tugged her to her feet, then moved in front of him at his urging to weave her way through the tables to the opening in the railing where they could step down onto the sand. She was very aware of his hand at her back as they walked, aware too that the table had gone silent behind them. Carolyn was pretty sure everyone was watching them, even people at tables they were passing were looking, and she suddenly felt self-conscious as their eyes slid from her to the man behind her . . . an obviously younger man.

Christian moved up beside her and took her hand once they hit the sand.

"What's wrong?" he asked quietly when she stopped.

"Nothing, I'm just getting sand in my sandals. I thought I'd take them off," she said, which wasn't a complete lie, but also allowed her to pull her hand free. Relief immediately rushed through her, but it turned to dismay when he knelt at her feet and began to undo her sandals before she could bend to the task herself. Good lord, he was playing Prince Charming to her Cinderella!

"You fixed your shoe," he said with surprise.

"Not really. Genie took it to her office and stapled the strap back into place. It's a temporary fix, but it's working for now." She bit her lip as his fingers brushed against the bare flesh of her feet as he worked. Cripes! Since when had her feet been an erogenous zone? Carolyn wondered with dismay as his touch sent little tingles skating up her leg. She had definitely been too long without the touch of a man if his undoing her shoe could affect her like this, she thought, gritting her teeth and just refraining from grabbing his shoulders to steady herself as her knees went weak.

Carolyn managed to hold herself upright until he finished, but it was a close call, and she couldn't help releasing a relieved little sigh when he straightened.

When she held out her hand for the shoes, he took it in his instead and drew her forward, her shoes caught in his other hand. Carolyn fell into step, but she was thinking that this had been a really bad idea and that maybe she couldn't do this after all. She was trying to think of a way to say so when he suddenly said, "Thank you."

Carolyn glanced at him uncertainly. "For what?"

"For agreeing to help me," he said as if that should be obvious, and she supposed it would have been had she not just been trying to figure out a way to wiggle free of the promise. When she remained silent, he added, "I really appreciate it. My family wouldn't understand."

"They all seem like lovely people," she murmured, and then added almost hopefully, "I'm sure they would be more accepting than you think."

Christian shook his head firmly. "No. They're very old-fashioned. I wouldn't just be disinherited, I'd basically be cut from the family if they found out."

Carolyn frowned. It was hard to believe that Marguerite and Gia would turn their backs on him. She was less sure about Julius and the others though.

"So I really appreciate your willingness to help me with this," Christian continued. "I'll try to make it as easy as I can for you."

Well, that put paid to her backing out now, Carolyn supposed. She'd feel a complete heel if she did. It wouldn't be so bad, she assured herself. They'd hold hands once in a while, maybe he'd put his arm around her a time or two and look at her all sexy and sloe-eyed while he talked to her. She could handle it, she assured herself. It wasn't like they were going to be around his family all the time, and when they weren't they could both relax and just be natural . . . whatever that was.

"It's beautiful here," Christian said suddenly, pausing at the edge of the surf and peering out over the moonlight-dappled water.

"Yes," she agreed, taking it all in herself. It really was the perfect place for a honeymoon. Which just made her wish she was here with someone who was actually interested in her and not—

"May I kiss you?"

Carolyn turned to peer up at him sharply. "What?"

"The whole table's watching us. They'll expect it," he explained wryly, his gaze sliding to the side as if looking toward the table.

Carolyn started to turn her head, but he caught her chin and slid his hand into her hair to stop her.

"You'll give away that we know they're watching," he warned quietly. "And Julius is very sharp. He's also suspicious at the moment. I think someone's been carrying tales to him."

Carolyn frowned.

"It's okay if you don't want me to kiss you," he said with understanding. "It would be helpful, but I know it's a lot to ask." He hesitated and then added, "I could just kiss your ear. That would be enough to satisfy Julius. I—"

"The ear," she said quickly, thinking that would surely have less effect than his kissing her lips. It certainly carried less chance of her doing something stupid like kissing him back and giving away her attraction to him.

Carolyn thought he smiled, though she wasn't sure in this light, and then his head lowered. He slid his hand into her hair, drawing it back from her face and ear, using the hold to tilt her head up and slightly to the side. Then his mouth was there and her eyes widened as a whole new world of erogenous zones opened up and swallowed her whole.

Dear God, her stomach actually jumped. Or something moved inside her, and then she was nothing but a mass of sensation as his lips, teeth, and tongue explored her ear. Carolyn was hardly aware of reaching for his arms to steady herself, or that her body moved instinctively closer to his, and when he whispered, "Thank you," by her ear and slowly straightened, she was more disappointed than she'd ever been over anything in her life.

"Christ, I need to get laid." The words slid out before she'd realized she was going to say them, and Carolyn slapped a hand to her mouth and stared at him with horror. She couldn't believe she'd said that. She couldn't even believe she'd thought it. She just wasn't all that sexual. Robert had always said she was frigid. She'd never— Seeing how wide Christian's eyes had gone, she pulled her hand away from her mouth and said quickly, "Not by you, of course. I just mean, I—it's been a long time since—I can't believe I even said that," she muttered on a groan. "It's been seven years since I had sex and I haven't even wanted to or anything. I—" She stopped trying to stammer her way out of that one when he pulled her into his arm and patted her back soothingly.

"It's all right. I understand. It's been a long time for me too," Christian growled, but was thinking, *It had been seven years since she'd had sex?* He was sure Marguerite had said Carolyn and her husband had split only two years ago. But she hadn't had sex in seven years?

"Really? It's been a long time for you too?" she asked, pulling back with surprise. "Is that because you have to be so careful? I mean, Brent seemed to be forever flitting off with a new lover before he met Stanley."

Christian released her and stepped back, both regretting that he had to do so and relieved to be able to at the same time. That brief nuzzling had affected him much more than he'd expected. It was the shared pleasure. There was definitely no question that Carolyn was his life mate. Only life mates shared pleasure as he'd just experienced. Every scrape of his teeth, and every lave of his tongue along her ear had sent pleasure cascading through his own body as if she were actually doing it to him. It was something Christian had never experienced before, so he hadn't realized how powerful a punch it would carry.

Christian had only stopped when he had because he'd been a heartbeat away from bearing her down onto the sand and completely blowing his cover story of being gay. He'd actually had to argue himself out of doing it. But when she'd blurted out those words about needing to get laid . . . well, that was when the real struggle had taken place. He'd pulled her into his arms to keep from following through on the first urge. He was definitely going to have to be more careful in the future. He would have to keep some distance between them, or at least not breach that distance unless they were around the others, whose presence would help to rein him in.

"Brent," Christian murmured the man's name as he

stepped back to give them both a little space. He couldn't resist catching her hand in his as he urged her to walk again, but it was better to keep moving. There was less temptation to kiss her if he wasn't looking at her. "Brent is the friend Gia was telling me about?"

"Yes." He felt some of her tension slip away. Whether it was because they were walking again, or just because she was thinking of her friend he wasn't sure.

"Tell me about him," he urged.

"Well, he's my age," she said slowly.

"What's he like?"

A fond smile came to her lips and—despite himself—Christian felt jealousy slither through him. He didn't like the fact that someone else was the recipient of an affection he couldn't yet lay claim to.

"Well, you'd probably like him actually," Carolyn said, her smile widening. "He's smart, funny, and certainly not lacking in looks. He's about as tall as you, with dark hair and a nice smile too." Carolyn grinned and then teased, "If he were still single I'd call and suggest he fly out so I could introduce the two of you. He likes redheads."

"I'm not a redhead," Christian muttered, trying not to show his horror at the thought that his life mate, a woman he'd waited more than five hundred years for, wanted to set him up with her gay school chum. Dear God! He hadn't expected this when he'd gotten the call that Marguerite wanted him in St. Lucia.

"You do have red in your hair," Carolyn said, drawing his attention again. "It's a lovely dark chestnut with red highlights. Dark auburn I guess."

Christian grunted. It was hair. He'd never thought much about it other than the fact that he'd obviously inherited it from his mother. Most Nottes had black hair, unless they dyed it like Gia.

"Anyway, Brent and I were both majoring in business when we met, but both wanted business law. We had a couple of classes together, found we had a lot in common, and started hanging out." She shrugged. "We became best friends."

"Gia said you were his beard?" Christian asked curiously, wondering how that had come about.

"Yes. That just kind of happened. As I said, he was good-looking and not effeminate at all, so naturally drew a lot of attention from girls at uni. But when we started studying and hanging around together, they backed off." Carolyn smiled wryly. "It took us a while, but then we realized that because we were always together, people assumed we were a couple. Then when we moved into an apartment together in our second year, they *really* thought we were a couple," she said with amusement. "Which worked out nicely. It kept the she-wolves away."

"It would have kept the men away from you too, though."

Carolyn shrugged. "I didn't have time for them anyway. I was on a scholarship. I had to keep my grades up."

"Your parents couldn't afford to put you through school?"

"Parent," Carolyn corrected quietly. "My mother was the only family I ever had, and as a single parent she worked two jobs to make ends meet. There was always lots of love, but not much money. I knew quite young that I'd have to earn a scholarship to go to university, so worked hard through high school. I was a complete geek," she admitted wryly. "Always studying, always working for extra credit. But Mom was proud of me for that."

"And where is your mother now?" Christian asked, worry sliding through him. If there had just been the two of them, they were probably very close. He could easily see that she loved her mother dearly. Carolyn might resist turning to avoid leaving her mother behind.

Carolyn blew her breath out, sadness sliding across her face. "She worked herself sick to raise me, and then died just before I graduated."

Christian was silent for a moment, considering everything he'd learned. It sounded like—thanks to all her studying and hard work in high school and university—she'd missed out on a lot of the sexual experimentation mortals now indulged in during their late teens and early twenties.

"So you spent your university years working hard and hanging out with Brent?" he asked finally, trying to figure out just how much she'd missed out on and what made her tick.

Carolyn smiled faintly. "And Genie and Bethany. We were all housemates."

"And you're still friends with all of them," Christian murmured, somewhat surprised. From what he understood, university friends tended to drift apart as life took them down different paths, but Carolyn nodded.

"Genie's major was travel and tourism, and after graduation she got a job at a resort in Puerto Vallarta. But she and I were pretty close and kept in touch through letters and e-mails. We've kept writing all this time as she's moved from job to job."

"And Bethany?" he asked.

"Bethany and I kind of drifted apart after graduation. We only reconnected three years ago when my husband and I sold one house for another. She's a realtor now," Carolyn explained. "And when I started to search for one and saw her name, I called her on impulse. We had coffee a time or two then, but Robert—well, he discouraged my having outside friends," she admitted with discomfort and rushed on, "but when we split and put the house up for sale for the divorce, she handled that one as well and she was a rock, very supportive. We've grown close again since then."

Christian was silent as he absorbed her words. That little bit told him a lot about her marriage. The only kind of man who discouraged outside friends was an abusive one. They liked to isolate their victims so they had no support and were less likely to leave. Letting it go for now, he asked, "And Brent?"

"Oh, so you *are* interested in him," she teased.

Christian forced a smile, but didn't comment. He was interested, but not in the way she meant. If Genie and Bethany and her mother were all gone by the end of university, then Carolyn had been on her own except for Brent.

"Brent and I both got jobs in the city. Junior positions, of course, both underpaid and overworked to start. But we pooled our money and took an apartment together." Carolyn chuckled. "It's amazing how much fun you can have on little money. It helped that both our companies were big on family gatherings and had numerous dinners and parties where a date or a spouse was encouraged to attend. I'd go as his date and we'd stuff ourselves and—"

"Still his beard?" Christian asked with a frown.

"The law firm he got a position with was kind of conservative," she explained. "He was worried about getting a partnership if they knew he was gay. It was just easier to take me." She shrugged. "I didn't mind though, because it meant he had to be my date for my firm's functions. It worked out well."

"And neither your boyfriends nor his minded?"

Carolyn shifted uncomfortably. "His didn't mind."

"And yours?" Christian asked, eyes narrowing as her discomfort grew.

Finally, she admitted, "I didn't date much. We both worked long hours and when we did have spare time there wasn't much money. We might go to a bar for a drink once in a while, sometimes a gay bar, sometimes straight, but . . ." She looked uncomfortable. "There aren't a lot of straight men in gay bars, and in straight bars people thought we were together. Not that I'd have picked up a guy from a bar anyway," Carolyn added wryly. "I guess I'm old-fashioned."

They were both silent, and then she admitted quietly, "Or maybe it's more that I'm socially backward or something. I'm not all that comfortable around new people most of the time, at least not in social situations. I'm a whiz at dealing with people at work, but put me in a social situation and I turn into this brainless twit. I lose the ability to speak with any kind of intelligence and— Frankly, I often start to feel like I'm drowning."

"You didn't get much chance to practice," he said gently when she fell silent. "You were busy earning your scholarship when most kids learn to socialize."

Carolyn bobbed her head, but didn't comment and Christian watched her silently. She'd eschewed any kind of social life in high school and worked her butt off to get her scholarship, then had continued to avoid social entanglements in university to keep it. No doubt with her mother, Genie, and Bethany gone after graduation, she'd clung to Brent as her only friend, and probably the closest thing to family she had. But it had hampered any chance of a social life for her.

"How long did the two of you share an apartment?" he asked abruptly.

She raised her head and peered along the beach, her eyes narrowing. "Let's see, it was four years to get my undergrad degree, then three for the law degree, so we moved into the apartment when I was twenty-five and he moved out west when I was thirty-one, so six years I guess."

"He moved out west?" Christian asked, thinking that would have left her completely alone.

Carolyn nodded. "He got offered a position with the promise of a junior partnership in two years if it worked out so he moved out to British Columbia. It all turned out for the best though. The head of the firm there was openly gay, which made things easier for him, and he eventually met Stanley there. They got married and have been together for . . . wow, it's ten years now," she said with surprise and then muttered, "Time flies when you're busy."

"And what did you do when he left?" Christian asked quietly, imagining her alone in the big city.

"Well, fortunately, by that time I was making more money and could afford the rent on our apartment on my own, so I just stayed there."

"I meant socially," Christian said patiently. "It sounds like Brent was both family and friend to you until then. How did you cope with losing him?"

"Oh." Carolyn shifted uncomfortably. "Well, I missed him, of course."

That was undoubtedly the understatement of the century, Christian thought grimly.

"My phone bills were crazy huge the first year and so were his . . . But then he met Stanley and I met Robert and . . ." She shook her head and said wryly, "Marriage is not an antidote for loneliness."

Christian turned to look up the beach. He suspected her husband had been her only lover, or at least one of a very few . . . and apparently he hadn't been her lover long. If she was thirty-two when they met, was forty-two now and hadn't had sex for seven years—and the sex wouldn't have stopped abruptly, but would have slowed to a trickle and then dribbles—good lord, he thought, it was no wonder she was horrified by the prospect of an affair with what she thought was a younger man. The idea of an affair at all probably gave her palpitations with the little bit of experience she'd had.

Gia's plan probably *had* been the only way for him to get to know her, he realized. Now he just had to try to keep his hands to himself, he thought grimly. Which definitely wasn't going to be easy. Life mates weren't known to have a lot of control around each other, but he suspected it was vital to keep them out of the bedroom for a while if he wanted to earn her trust and win her.

Sighing, he said, "Tell me about your husband."

"No." The word was sharp and Christian glanced over to see that her expression was closed. He felt as if a door had just shut in his face, and was more disappointed than surprised when she stopped walking and said, "We should go back. We've walked quite a distance and they'll be wondering where we are."

Carolyn turned back without waiting to see if he would follow, and wasn't very responsive to his comments and questions after that even though he avoided the subject of her marriage. Obviously, it was a subject to stay away from in future if he wished to spend time with her.

Five

Genie was missing from the table when Carolyn led Christian back. She peered to Marguerite questioningly as she took her shoes from Christian and settled in her seat. "Where's Genie?"

Marguerite smiled. "She said she had to get up early for work, but that she'd talk to you at breakfast."

"Oh." Carolyn concentrated on putting her sandals back on, and then glanced at her margarita. It had melted while she was gone, she noted, and then stiffened when Christian rested his arm along her chair back, his hand cupping her shoulder. His skin was warm on hers, sending out little currents of electricity that made her skin tingle.

It had been hard to handle his closeness before their walk on the beach, but she simply couldn't bear it now. Carolyn wasn't sure if it had been his nuzzling her on the beach, or all she'd revealed while talking to him . . . or perhaps she was just too tired to deal with her attraction to him, but she couldn't handle it now.

"I guess I'd better go to bed too if I want to get up to have breakfast with her," Carolyn said, standing abruptly.

She caught the surprise on Christian's face out of the corner of her eye, but he immediately stood too. "I'll see you back to your villa."

"Don't be silly." She scooted out from in front of her chair. "Stay with your family. I'll be fine."

"I'm a bit tired myself," Marguerite said.

"Then I guess we'll join you for the ride back," Julius announced, ushering Marguerite to her feet.

"And us," Gia announced.

Carolyn frowned as the whole table rose. She glanced to the drinks on the table. Marguerite's and Julius's glasses were the only ones that were empty. Everyone else's still looked full, and she said desperately, "But you haven't finished your drinks."

"Neither have you," Gia said with a laugh, and moved around the table to slip her arm through hers. "Come on. You do look tired. We'll all ride up together."

Carolyn sighed, but didn't argue further. She was just grateful it was Gia ushering her out and not Christian, though she could feel him at her back. He must be nearly on her heels for her to be able to feel his heat, she thought as Gia led her out of the bar and around the pool toward the main building, chattering away.

"I don't think we'll all fit in one van," Carolyn said as they reached the waiting vans. "Why don't you all go ahead in the first one and I'll just grab this other—" She'd started to move toward a second van, but Gia pulled her back.

"Don't be silly. It might be a little tight, but we'll all fit," she said, urging her toward the first van.

"Santo, you're the biggest. Take the front seat," Julius ordered as he slid the side door open. "It will leave more room for the rest of us in the back."

The moment Santo moved toward the front-passenger door, Julius added, "Zanipolo and Raffaele, you're in the back. We don't want any of the ladies to have to crawl all the way back there in their high heels and dresses."

Neither man even hesitated, but immediately climbed inside to maneuver their way around the two front bench seats to the back one. The moment they were out of the way, Julius ushered Marguerite forward, saying, "We'll take the second seat and you three can take the first one since Carolyn has to get out first. Christian, you're on the outside so you can handle the door."

The words made Carolyn sigh, but she obeyed like the rest. Julius was like a drill sergeant, she thought as she followed Gia inside the van. She settled on the bench next to the other woman and squeezed up against her to make room for Christian. The seats were really made for only two, she decided as Christian closed the door and wedged himself in next to her. It was a very tight fit, and he lifted his arm to rest it along the back of the seat behind her to make more room.

"Out of the pan and into the fire," she muttered. This was worse than just his hand cupping her shoulder. Not only was his arm still around her, but she was now plastered against his side as well, their bodies touching from shoulder to knee.

"What was that?" Gia asked.

"Nothing," Carolyn sighed.

"The seat is really too small for the three of you," Marguerite said as the van pulled away. "Christian, why don't you sit Carolyn on your knee? It will make more room."

"Oh, no, that's—" Carolyn bit off her protest and clutched at his arms as he suddenly scooped her onto his lap.

"Relax," he said quietly, settling his arms around her waist. "We'll have you back at your villa in a minute."

"But—seat belts," she choked out, grasping hopefully at the excuse.

"Are there seat belts on these vans?" Zanipolo asked from the back. "I haven't noticed any."

Carolyn hadn't either, and if there were, no one bothered with them. The vans didn't exactly go quickly on the hill roads.

"What are your plans for tomorrow, Carolyn?" Marguerite asked.

"I'm not sure," she admitted, trying to sound calm. "It depends on Bethany and whether she's feeling better. She—" Carolyn paused on a gasp as they bumped over a pothole, the action bouncing her on Christian's lap so that his arm accidentally bumped into the underside of her breasts.

"You were saying?" Julius asked.

"Er . . . ," Carolyn muttered weakly.

"She doesn't know. It depends on Bethany and whether she feels better," Christian said for her, his fingers shifting back down to her waist.

"Do you and Bethany have any tours booked while here?" Marguerite asked.

"Er . . . I . . . er . . ." Carolyn paused and closed her eyes, trying to calm herself, and then suddenly she was calm. It slid through her like cool water, freeing her tongue. Taking a breath, she said, "We're supposed to take a boat tour to Soufriere to see a drive-in volcano and a cocoa plantation one day, and there's a shuttle to the markets another. There are a couple of other things, but I don't recall them at the moment. Bethany made most of the bookings," she finished, just grateful to get the words out.

"But nothing tomorrow?" Marguerite asked.

"Not that I know of. We were just going to relax on the beach the first few days." Her eyes dropped to Christian's face. He was peering up at her, his head tipped up and his eyes—She stared at them, her own widening as she took in the way they glowed like a cat's eyes in the dark.

"The beach sounds nice and relaxing," Marguerite said, and Carolyn tore her gaze from Christian to glance at the woman, noting that her eyes too seemed to be catching and reflecting what little light there was in the dark van. Carolyn glanced to the others then and saw the same thing. She shook her head. It must be a trick of the light. She hadn't noticed this in the van earlier. Her own probably looked the same way, she decided.

"Here we are," the driver announced, stopping in front of her villa.

Carolyn immediately tried to get up, but Christian held her in place with one arm around her waist as he opened the door. Only then did he release her.

"I'll walk you to the door," she heard him say as she scrambled out of the van.

"Oh, no that's—"

"A man always sees his mate to her door," Julius interrupted from inside the van and Carolyn snapped her mouth closed, only to have it drop open when he added, "Besides, you wouldn't deprive him of a good-night kiss, would you?"

Christian was out of the van by then and gently pressed her mouth closed with one finger under her chin, then caught her hand and tugged her to the stone walk to her villa.

"I don't think I like your brother," she muttered. "I think you're right, he probably wouldn't take the news about *you know what* well. He seems an autocratic dictator type, who likes to boss people around and—"

Her words ended on a gasp when Christian suddenly turned, tugged her forward by her hand so that she fell against his chest, then lowered his head and laid one on her. As kisses went it was sparklers and rockets. Carolyn completely forgot she was playing a role here and melted against him with a little moan, her arms sliding around his neck. She moaned again when Christian's hands molded her body to his, then felt him lift her, thought they were turning and then her feet settled on the ground again and he broke their kiss.

Carolyn blinked up at him with confusion and then glanced down when she felt his hand at her breast, but he was just pulling her key card from her breast pocket. She supposed he'd either felt it while they were kissing, or had seen the outline earlier that evening and recognized it for what it was.

With one arm still around her waist, he reached around with the other to unlock and open the door. He'd carried her the last few feet to it, she realized, as he straightened and slid the key card back into her breast pocket. When he then released her, Carolyn slowly withdrew her arms from around his neck.

Christian smiled faintly and brushed one finger affectionately down her nose. "Fa— Julius *is* an autocratic dictator. He's the head of a large corporation and used to bossing people around. He also likes you."

"He does?" she asked uncertainly as he clasped her shoulders and turned her toward the door.

"Mmm-hmm." His breath stirred her hair as he urged her forward into the villa. "Otherwise he wouldn't have made sure I kissed you good night."

The sound of the door closing punctuated the sentence and Carolyn spun back to stare at the wooden panel. She then shifted sideways to peer out the window as Christian jogged lightly back to the van. She watched him get in and the van head off, then turned slowly away only to pause when she saw Bethany standing at the top of the stairs in her robe.

"Who was that?" Bethany asked, eyes wide.

"I . . . er . . . Oh, it's a long story." She ran one hand wearily through her hair.

"Well, then you'd better start talking, girl. Cause you do not get yourself kissed silly by a handsome young hunk like that and think you can get away without telling me every little detail."

"There's nothing to tell," Carolyn said quietly. "He's gay."

Bethany stilled and then shook her head. "Carolyn, gay boys do not kiss girls like that."

"They do if they're in the closet and their family is watching and they want to convince them they're straight," she assured her. "And how did you see the kiss anyway? We were outside."

"I was at the window, watching like an anxious mother," she said wryly. "I heard the van and came to greet you, but when I saw that guy practically ravishing you on the doorstep, I was afraid you were going to bring him in, so I started to hurry out of sight, but stopped when he just pushed you through the door and left."

"Oh," Carolyn muttered.

"So, start talking. I want to know everything," Bethany said firmly.

Carolyn headed for the kitchen saying, "Fine, but I need a drink."

Bethany followed, and waited patiently as Carolyn opened a bottle of wine and poured herself a glass. The fact that the other woman passed up a glass herself told Carolyn that she still wasn't feeling well. Bethany never passed up a glass of wine. Carolyn took a long swallow of the crimson liquid and then set down her glass and explained everything.

"So you're playing beard again, this time to this kid in the band?" Bethany asked quietly.

Carolyn nodded.

"It's Brent all over again." Bethany was starting to sound angry.

"Not exactly like Brent," Carolyn muttered uncomfortably.

"Yeah, no shit, Sherlock. Brent never did more than kiss you on the forehead. He never pushed you through the door looking the way you did just now," she said grimly, and then accused her, saying, "You're falling for him, aren't you? You know he's gay, and you're just stupidly falling for him anyway."

When Carolyn winced and bowed her head without answering, mostly because she was definitely in lust with the guy, Bethany snapped, "What are you thinking?"

"Apparently I'm not," she admitted with frustration. "I didn't mean to get into this in the first place, and I don't know what the hell I'm doing. I just . . ."

"Tell him you can't do it," Beth said firmly.

For some reason the very idea caused panic in Carolyn, and she blurted out, "I can't. He's counting on me."

"Who cares?" Beth said with exasperation, and then stared at her hard. "You're falling for a boy who likes boys . . . And you're letting him stick his tongue down your throat so his family doesn't know?" She clucked with disgust. "If that kiss didn't convince them he's not gay, nothing short of his screwing you in front of them will. Cut him loose. Tell him to go stick his tongue down some younger girl's throat."

Carolyn flinched, tears glazing her eyes, and Beth sighed. "I'm sorry, sweetie. I don't mean to be so harsh, but

I don't feel well and . . . I worry about you. At this rate you're either going to end up some crazy old woman with a hundred cats, or a dirty old lady with Gigolos-Are-Us on speed dial."

Carolyn gave a half-sob, half-laugh and wiped the tears from her eyes. "That's not going to happen. Well, the cats maybe, but not the gigolos on speed dial."

Beth pushed herself off the stool she'd settled on. "I'm going to puke again and then go to bed. We can talk more in the morning."

Carolyn frowned. "You still aren't keeping anything down?"

"I think it's the flu rather than food poisoning," Bethany muttered unhappily. "Figures I'd come down with it on my first day of vacation. Go to bed, Caro. I'm fine."

"Right," Carolyn murmured and glanced along the counter, then walked out into the entry to peer around there as well.

"What are you looking for?" Beth asked following her.

"My purse. I need to set my phone alarm to meet Genie for breakfast."

"You didn't have your purse when you came in."

"I must have. I took it with me," Carolyn said even as she realized she hadn't been holding anything but Christian when he'd kissed her. She hadn't had it in the van either, she realized, recalling clasping his arms when he'd lifted her onto his lap. She couldn't have done that and held a purse too. Carolyn clucked impatiently. "I must have left it in the bar."

Beth raised her eyebrows. "Do you want me to call the bar and see if someone found it?"

"No, thanks." Carolyn moved wearily to the door. "I'll walk down and get it. I can use the exercise and the walk will tire me out and help me sleep."

"Well, don't forget your key card. I'm going to bed and might not hear you knock if you forget it."

"Got it," Carolyn assured her, patting the breast pocket of her silk blouse just to be sure as she opened the door.

"Good night then," Beth said, heading for her bedroom.

"Night." Carolyn slid out of the villa. She paused on the doorstep briefly to wipe her eyes again, but then let her hands drop and started up the walk.

"Well, what do you think, Mom?" she whispered, lifting her eyes to the stars overhead. "How much more of a mess can I make of my life?"

Probably not much, Carolyn decided for herself when there was no answer. She had it pretty well screwed up right now as far as she could tell. Mid-divorce and lusting after a guy who wasn't only too young, but had no interest in members of her sex. Shaking her head, she stepped onto the road.

The night air was cooler than it had been all day, but still felt warm after the air-conditioning in the villa. It was also dark. The only light from the stars overhead and the villas she was passing, it left the narrow road shadowed and made Carolyn wish she'd switched to flat sandals for the walk. Aside from the fact that she couldn't see that well and was likely to stumble over something and break her neck, one sandal was broken, the fix only a temporary one. With her luck it would give halfway down the mountain and she'd break her neck that way. Either way, she'd have a broken neck, which wasn't looking all that unattractive at the moment all things considered, she thought glumly, and then glanced around when she heard a rustling in the vegetation behind her on the right.

Not seeing anything, Carolyn turned and continued walking. She wasn't too concerned about whatever she'd heard. This was a private resort, after all, with only honeymooners and staff running around. She figured she was safe enough, but glanced around again when the rustling came once more, this time behind her on the left. As far as she could tell there was no one on the road, or in the bushes alongside it, but it was dark.

Carolyn's imagination kicked into action. Were there wild animals on St. Lucia? If so, how big were they and were they carnivores? Death suddenly didn't seem that attractive after all.

Biting her lip, Carolyn briefly considered heading back to the villa and calling for a van, but it would mean walking back toward whatever was making the sounds she'd heard. Breathing out slowly, she listened for another moment, her ears straining for sound behind her.

"Cara?"

Carolyn whirled around, pausing when she saw the dark figure in the shadows ahead. Whoever it was, was tall and big and had apparently just come around the corner at the turnaround. She stared uncertainly until the man moved closer. He was a foot away before she recognized Christian.

"Oh." She sagged with relief, and then immediately tensed up again. Really, he was the last person she wanted to see at the moment. She was confused and had made enough of a fool of herself tonight what with falling all over him when he'd kissed her, and God he smelled good. What was that cologne he was wearing?

When he paused in front of her, she cleared her throat and asked, "What are you doing here?"

"I couldn't sleep." He took her arm, urging her to walk again.

"Probably jet lag," Carolyn muttered, wishing he'd let go of her arm. He smelled too damned good and she didn't like the tingles his touch sent through her. Or to be more honest, she liked them too much.

"I'm sure it is jet lag," Christian agreed as they turned the corner and started down the next road. "I thought a nice walk would make me relax and hopefully help me sleep. What about you?"

"I left my purse at the bar earlier," she admitted. "I'm going down to get it."

"You should have called for the van." He sounded like he was frowning.

"Yes, well, I thought I'd be safe enough on resort property," Carolyn muttered.

"Few places are safe for a woman alone anymore, especially at this hour," he said solemnly.

Carolyn grimaced. In the city, she never would have risked a long walk at this hour, but it was easy to forget such built-in cautions in this paradise.

They walked in silence for a bit, Carolyn worrying her lip as she tried to think of something to say. Unfortunately, the only thing she seemed able to think of just then was the kiss. And her reaction to it. And how much of a fool she was.

"I'm glad I ran into you," Christian said suddenly, and then proved he'd been thinking about that kiss too when he added, "I wanted to apologize for the way I kissed you earlier."

"Apologize?" she echoed uncertainly. She hadn't been expecting this.

"Yes. I appreciate your help in this difficult situation, and that you were kind enough to go along with it, but I realize that kiss was expecting a bit much. I caught you by surprise and apologize if my kissing you like that made you uncomfortable."

Uncomfortable? Was that what he thought her reaction

had been? Good lord, he didn't know women at all if he mistook her response for discomfort.

But then, Carolyn supposed, she hadn't really responded at all other than to cling like he was a life raft on rough seas. It wasn't like she'd kissed him back or started groping him, Carolyn realized. He *had* taken her by surprise. That kiss had curled her toes. It had been better than any kiss she'd experienced in her life, actually. Affected her more than anything her husband had ever done too. And Christian was gay.

She wondered what that said about her. Or perhaps it said more about her soon-to-be ex-husband's skills in that area. Robert hadn't been much of a kisser. If she hadn't seen his tongue flapping about inside his mouth over the years as he'd lectured or insulted her . . . well, she would have been hard-pressed to say for sure that he had one. Certainly, it had never left his mouth for hers.

What other areas had he not been up to scratch in? Carolyn wondered. What had she been missing out on? If other men out there kissed like Christian . . . well, it seemed to her she'd been missing out on a lot.

Perhaps it wasn't really him she'd responded to, Carolyn thought, feeling a little better about the whole thing. Perhaps had any man she found attractive kissed her with the same skill . . . well, maybe they would have stirred the same reaction. The thought was intriguing, because she definitely wouldn't mind experiencing that heady passion again . . . with someone who was feeling it too, though.

"I think we can avoid situations like that in the future," Christian continued. "I don't want to take advantage of your generosity in helping me."

Translation: He didn't want to swap spit anymore, she thought and couldn't help but think it was probably a good thing. While she did want to experience more of that passion he'd shown her, she'd rather do it with someone straight. Too much of the kissy-face business with him would just confuse her, she was sure. She was probably too new to this business to be able to separate her body's natural response from her emotions.

"My family won't think anything of it if we slip away to be alone, maybe on tours, or out for dinner and such. They'll just assume we want to be alone. That way we could avoid the necessity for such actions and get to know each other better."

"Good idea," she said brightly, feeling much better about all of this. She was now positive it hadn't been him she'd been reacting to at all, just his skill. And being that skilled, he obviously had a lot of experience. Of course, that experience was with other men, but it was still experience. He might be able to help her with this business of sex. Give her some tips and pointers. She obviously had a lot to learn, and Carolyn had been able to talk to Brent about almost anything. They'd never really discussed sex much, except for him to lecture her about her needing to get out, have fun, and get laid, which she'd always laughed off. But she would have felt comfortable talking about sex with him. He'd been more like a girlfriend than a male friend. Probably because he was gay and therefore not interested. It lowered a lot of the male/female barriers when it came to talk. It should be the same with Christian once they got to know each other a little better, she thought now. Then she could grill him about kissing and other stuff she might have missed out on, about how it was supposed to be. She suspected what she'd experienced in her brief marriage wasn't the way it had to be.

"I'm glad. I'd like us to be friends," Christian said, drawing her gaze. Not that she could see much in that light or lack thereof.

"I'd like that too," she assured him, patting his arm. "I could use a friend."

"Aren't Bethany and Genie your friends? I thought they'd been friends since university?"

"Yes, but—" Carolyn paused and frowned, unsure how to explain the situation to him. The fact was while Beth was a friend, she'd never discuss sex with her. It would mean revealing parts of her marriage it was just too humiliating to admit. And while she'd revealed all to Genie in e-mails the last two years, she already knew any mention of Robert or what had gone on in her marriage was likely to make the other woman angry. She didn't want to have to wade through Genie's upset for her, to be able to discuss what she wanted to. Christian seemed the perfect solution. He was experienced, knew nothing of her marriage, wouldn't get angry, and wasn't interested so could be like a girlfriend. It was almost too perfect.

"There are some things I just wouldn't be comfortable discussing with them," she said finally.

"Like?" he prompted.

"Just stuff," she said vaguely, not ready to start talking to him about things like that yet.

Six

Christian glanced at Carolyn curiously. Just moments ago he'd been standing on his terrace, staring down at her villa below. He was supposed to be trying to sleep so that the shared dreams would come, but sleep had evaded him and he'd pulled his clothes back on and walked outside to simply stare down on her lighted villa as his mind filled with imaginings of what he would do to, and with her, once they'd gotten past all this and were life mates. His fantasies had definitely been in the not-gay category, but had been interrupted when he'd seen her leave the villa to start walking down the road.

Christian couldn't have stayed on that terrace had his feet been Krazy Glued to the tiles. He'd leaped over the railing and run down through the sloping hill of vines and foliage to the road, then continued past her villa and down to the next road so that he could come up the lane in front of her as if their meeting was accidental.

"Stuff I'll need to get to know you better before I'll be

comfortable discussing it," Carolyn added, drawing his mind back to their conversation.

Christian murmured in understanding, but wondered what the "stuff" was. He didn't ask though. He suspected he was on shaky ground at the moment. The minute he'd left her at her villa Christian had begun to worry that the kiss may have scared her off. He was walking a fine line here, using the cover of homosexuality to keep her from avoiding him so that he could build a relationship and earn her trust, while also fighting an attraction that was only going to grow between them.

The irony that he was lying to gain her trust didn't escape him. Although he wasn't the one who had actually spoken the lie, Gia had. But he'd let it stand and furthered it. As for the growing attraction, that was going to be the hardest part. Even now it was a struggle not to simply pull her into his arms and kiss her again.

That kiss at her door had hit him even harder than the ear nuzzling earlier. It had been too long since he'd experienced desire for him to be able to handle it with any kind of equanimity. It had been centuries since he'd even been interested in sex. That wasn't uncommon for his people. They often became weary of food and sex after a century or two. Both became more a bother than a pleasure, so immortals generally stopped troubling with them.

His interest in food had ended by the time he was about a century and a half old, sex at about the same time. Both had just slowly seemed to lose their flavor and excitement. But since encountering Carolyn his long dead desire was like a lion in his gut, yawning itself awake and hungry after a long sleep. If he hadn't been aware of everyone waiting and watching in the van, Christian wasn't sure he could have ended that good-night kiss as he had. He certainly hadn't wanted to. He'd wanted to peel away her clothes and— Hell, had he followed his instincts, Christian wasn't sure he could have managed the willpower to take her inside, he might have ravished her right there against the door, or on the cold stone walk. He definitely needed to keep his hands and mouth off her when they were alone, Christian acknowledged grimly. He just hoped he could do it.

Grimacing at the thought, he tuned back in to Carolyn's voice as she chattered away about St. Lucia. She was much more relaxed than when he'd first encountered her. It reassured him that he'd chosen the right tactic by voicing an apology and mentioning the bit about avoiding the others to avoid the need to kiss her again. If the passion of their kiss had scared her, his words had obviously reassured her.

"I was really bummed when we got here and I saw all the honeymooners around," she was admitting now. "And then with Bethany out of commission . . . well, it was really getting depressing. It'll be nice to have a buddy to hang around with."

Buddy? Christian grimaced, but kept his mouth shut. Friend first, lover second, and then spill the beans and convince her to turn and be your life mate, he reminded himself grimly of the plan.

"But it is a lovely spot," Carolyn continued. "Even at night."

"Yes." He glanced around. It was lovely, but he doubted she could see just how lovely with her mortal eyesight. He could give her the gift of seeing at night. He'd like to see her reaction once she had immortal eyes.

"Oh, good, the bar's still open," Carolyn said as they walked through the main building several moments later. Christian glanced ahead and could see the bar lights twinkling over the happy guests.

"I hope my purse is still there," Carolyn said fretfully. "I can't believe I left it behind. I guess I was a little distracted."

Christian supposed the distraction had been her eagerness to escape him. He was sure that was the reason she'd decided to leave once they'd gotten back from the beach. He'd known he'd upset her by asking about her husband, but hadn't realized how much until they got back to the table. He would definitely steer clear of the subject for a while. At least until he was sure it wouldn't send her running again.

"Darn, it's not there."

Christian followed Carolyn's gaze to the table where they'd sat earlier. It was now occupied by a couple in their thirties who were smiling and kissing each other, but he could see that there was no purse on the table.

"Oh, pretty lady!"

Christian turned a scowl on the bartender at the call and followed when Carolyn headed that way.

"You forgot this." Smiling widely, the man reached under the bar to retrieve a small black purse.

"Oh, thank you!" Carolyn rushed the last few feet to claim it, laughing and relaxed again. "I was afraid it was gone for good when I didn't see it there."

"No. I saw it when I was clearing the table and brought it here. I knew you would come back for it," the bartender assured her.

"Thank you," Carolyn opened her purse. "Let me tip you."

"No, no, you buy a drink, I take a tip, but otherwise, it's not necessary."

"Oh." Carolyn frowned.

"Let's have a drink then," Christian said, his scowl fading as the man inadvertently offered him an opportunity to get to spend more time with Carolyn.

"Oh, but I have to get up early to meet Genie for breakfast before she starts work," she said reluctantly.

"One drink," Christian coaxed.

Carolyn hesitated, then nodded, "All right then. But I can't stay long."

"Right. We'll be fast," Christian assured her.

Carolyn turned to the bartender, taking out her money. "I'll have a white wine, please, and whatever he's having."

Christian caught her hand and urged her away. "I'll get it."

"But—"

"I'll tip him. Besides, I want something to eat. I haven't eaten in a while." For about three and a half centuries, he added silently as his eye was caught by a passing waitress with a tray of something giving off the most delectable smells.

"Oh." She hesitated.

"Go find us a table. I'll follow with the drinks." Christian watched as Carolyn turned to survey the available tables. When she started to move off, he pulled out his wallet and asked the bartender, "What's good?"

"Our wraps are very popular," he said at once.

"Two of those then, please, and—" He paused, at a loss as to what to order to drink. It had been a while since he'd indulged. Smiling wryly, he said, "Whatever your most popular drink is."

Nodding, the bartender accepted his money and said, "Go sit down. I will bring your drinks and change."

"No change. Just the drinks," Christian said and turned to follow the path Carolyn had taken. She'd found a table in the corner along the rail overlooking the beach and was peering out over the sand and sea when he joined her.

"It's beautiful, isn't it?" she said on a little sigh.

"Yes," he agreed without bothering to look. She was the most beautiful thing there was here for him to see. His life mate. It made her more precious than diamonds and more beautiful than the loveliest flower to him.

Carolyn turned and smiled at him. "So tell me how you got into music."

Christian hesitated and frowned. She needed to get to know him to trust him. The problem was in this area, as with most others, he had to be careful. He couldn't tell her he'd been born in the late 15th century, etc. etc.

"The usual," he said finally, deciding just to avoid too much detail. "I liked music, so my father suggested I try various instruments. I showed an aptitude for the violin, so he sent for a teacher to give me classical training."

"Classical training?" Carolyn said with amusement.

Christian smiled faintly. That was pretty much the only kind of training there had been back then, but he supposed it surprised her because he played in a rock band. "Yes, classical. He hired the best in the country to teach me. I think he was hoping I would become an Italian Johannes de Sarto . . . Sarto was a Franco/Flemish composer who was popular a long time ago," he explained when she looked blank at the name.

"Ah." She nodded and then smiled wryly. "I take it your interests didn't lie in that area though?"

"They did for a while, but it got boring playing the same songs over and over again. So I put down the violin and went to work for the family instead, and then picked it up and put it down over and over. I guess this is one of my picking-it-up-again phases."

"Hard-rock violin?" Carolyn asked with a grin.

Christian chuckled. "Gia dragged me into it. Come play with us, she said. I did, and—" He shrugged. "I like it. It's more interesting. The music gets into your blood. I've been playing with the band for ten years and am not yet bored."

Carolyn's eyes widened. "You must have been a child prodigy."

He shrugged. "I was five when I started to play."

"Ah." She nodded. "And then Gia dragged you into the band. What was it? A high school band in someone's garage?"

"Oh, God no. We were well out of school when we started. No doubt old enough to know better," he added with a laugh that faded when he saw the way she was looking at him. "What?"

"Ten years ago you couldn't have been more than fifteen or sixteen," she said slowly. "And you said you put down the violin and worked for the company several times before that, but—"

"I'm older than I look," he interrupted quietly.

"Gia said that too," Carolyn murmured, peering at him more closely.

He'd thought he was being careful, but he'd obviously have to watch every word he said. Carolyn wasn't a stupid woman. Much to his relief the bartender arrived then with their drinks to distract her.

Christian picked up his drink to try it, searching his mind for a way to *keep* her distracted from his slip. But he grimaced and set the drink down after tasting it. It was far too sweet. He'd much preferred the drink he'd tried earlier, the slushy green one Genie had ordered and he'd copied. That had been sweet/tart, much more to his taste. He would have ordered it again if he'd thought of it.

"No good?" Carolyn asked sympathetically.

"I preferred the earlier drink," he muttered. "But the bartender said these were popular."

"I like the sweet/tart of lime margaritas too," she said wryly. "Not too keen on sweet, sweet drinks."

"No." Christian repeated lime margarita in his head several times to be sure he recalled it for the next time. Not having consumed anything but blood for centuries, it was hard to know what he would and wouldn't like whether it was food or drink. Everything was new to him now.

"How old were you when—"

"Oh look, the food's here," Christian interrupted with relief as a waitress approached with two plates.

Carolyn glanced around and they both sat back as the waitress set the plates on the table.

"Thank you," Christian said, and then lifted his drink. "Could you take this away and bring me one of those slushy lime margaritas?"

She took the glass with a smile. "Of course. I'll have this taken off your bill."

"Oh, no, that's not necessary. I . . ." Christian let his words trail off. The woman had just walked away with the drink.

Carolyn chuckled at his vexed expression. "It won't go on the bill."

"But I ordered it," he pointed out.

"On the bartender's recommendation and you didn't like it," she argued.

"She didn't know that."

"Yeah, but they're all about service here, and considering the prices, they can afford to be," she said with a shrug.

Christian peered at her silently. It *was* pricey here, and it made him wonder how she afforded it. She'd started life poor and worked hard to get a degree and a good job, but had the money situation changed that much through her hard work? Or had she married money? Unfortunately, he couldn't ask without touching on her marriage, which was a subject he had to avoid to prevent her from withdrawing again. Or, at least, he'd have to approach it like disarming a bomb, delicately and with a prayer on his lips.

"What's this?" Carolyn asked curiously, examining the rolled sandwich and chips on her plate.

"The bartender called it a wrap."

"I can see it's a wrap," she said with amusement. "What kind is it?"

"Oh." He hesitated but then grimaced. "I'm not sure. He said it was the house specialty and popular, so I ordered us both one," Christian answered and then smiled wryly and pointed out, "Mind you, considering the lack of success of his recommended drink, however, this could be a mistake."

Carolyn chuckled, but shook her head. "I don't know. It smells delicious."

Christian had to agree. The wrap was looking more promising than the drink had turned out to be. His stomach apparently agreed. Deprived of anything but blood for centuries and not complaining about it before this, it now gave a rumble loud enough that Carolyn actually heard it.

She laughed at his embarrassed expression. "You'd better feed that beast or it might crawl up your throat and do it for you."

Christian smiled faintly, and picked up one half of the sliced wrap. He peered curiously at the pinwheel opening, trying to sort out what was in it. It looked like chicken, rice, peas, and other vegetables.

"Mmmm." That moan from Carolyn drew his gaze to see that she'd taken a bite and was now rolling her eyes with apparent pleasure. "Try it. It's good."

Christian needed no further prompting. He took a bite, and immediately closed his eyes as flavor drenched his tongue. Food. Dear God, it had been centuries since food had appealed to him, but even when he'd been eating, he didn't recall anything having tasted this good.

"Good, huh?" Carolyn asked with amusement.

Christian opened his eyes and stared at her, knowing she was the only reason the wrap tasted as good as it did. She'd not only reawakened all his appetites, but added an extra sparkle and excitement to them . . . and all with the simple fact of her existence.

It was rather bewildering really, Christian thought. He had no idea how the nanos chose mates, or how his mother seemed to sense when someone was a possible life mate for an immortal . . . and really, Carolyn was the most unlikely life mate he could have imagined. A wounded bird. But then, so had he been until little more than a year ago. Not as wounded as Carolyn perhaps, but wounded just the same. A son without a mother until Marguerite reentered his life. And Carolyn was a woman without a family. He could give her that. Parents-in-law, grandparents, and even brothers and sisters and a niece, as well as all the cousins and aunts and uncles anyone could want. Probably more family than any sane person would want to interfere in their life, he thought wryly.

"What are you smiling about?" Carolyn asked curiously.

"My family," he admitted honestly, and when her eyebrows rose, he shrugged. "You make me think of them."

She blinked and then chuckled. "If you were straight, I think I'd be insulted. Fortunately, you aren't, so . . ." She shrugged. "I think I understand. You make me think of Brent too, and he's the closest thing I have to family."

Great, Christian thought on a sigh. He reminded her of her gay buddy. Wow, was that sexy or what?

"I didn't realize how much I've missed him until now," Carolyn said suddenly.

"Do you see him at all?" Christian asked.

"Oh sure, I go to BC at least once a year and he and Stanley come to Ontario two or three times a year to see his family. We get together then."

Christian wanted to ask what Brent had thought of her husband, but knew better than to broach that subject.

The waitress arrived then with his margarita and he thanked her and took a drink, relieved to find it as good as he'd recalled. They ate in silence for a bit, and then Carolyn asked, "Do you travel a lot with the band?"

Christian took a drink to clear his throat and shook his head. "We mostly play locally. This is the first time we've played away from home."

"Really?" She didn't hide her surprise. "You're very good. I would have thought you'd be in demand all over."

Christian shrugged. "We've had requests to do gigs farther away, but always turned them down."

"Why?"

"Because we all have day jobs we can't be away from."

"Really?" That had her curious. "What do you do during the day?"

"I work for the family construction firm. Most of us do," Christian added. It was how they'd gotten time off so easily. Marguerite wanted them here, so Julius, his father, and their boss, had said to come. Christian also did occasional work for the council as an enforcer, but he couldn't tell her about that.

"I can see you in construction," Carolyn decided, her gaze sliding over his shoulders and chest.

Christian's body reacted as if she'd physically touched him. His nipples even hardened, something he didn't think anything but cold could cause. Well, at least not in a man. It had certainly never happened to him before that he'd noticed.

"I can see you working a jackhammer or slinging a sledgehammer," she said with a nod and took a drink of her wine.

Christian chuckled. "Nothing so physical. I'm basically an overseer. I check on the sites, make sure they're keeping on schedule, handle any problems that arise to hold up jobs."

"Oh," she sighed with feigned disappointment. "Well, scratch the sexy image of you shirtless and sweaty with a hard hat on."

Christian's eyes widened incredulously. Was she flirting? That had sounded flirty. On the other hand she thought he was gay, so probably felt safe flirting with him now. This was definitely going to be a challenge, he decided.

"So which do you prefer?" Carolyn asked as she picked up her wine for another sip.

"Construction or music you mean?" he asked and when she nodded, he considered the question briefly. "Music."

"Then why not give up your day job and pursue music full time?"

"Because none of us is interested in fame and fortune, and the way things are, we can play our music without worrying about either."

"I thought every musician wanted to be famous," Carolyn said with surprise.

Christian shrugged. "Perhaps they do. I don't know. I'm sure there are some who aren't interested in it, and just want to do what they love. Perhaps they want their music to gain acclaim, but I doubt anyone wants the kind of fame that plagues performers now. We certainly don't." It would make life very difficult to have their faces splashed everywhere. Perhaps not right away, but that kind of fame would make it hard to be anonymous and hide what they were since they didn't age.

"Okay, but what about fortune?" she asked.

"All of us already have fortunes, or are well on the way to it," he said with disinterest. For some reason that made Carolyn still.

"You do?" she asked with obvious surprise.

Christian nodded and took another bite of his wrap, wondering what had caused the odd expression now on her face. He wasn't even sure what the look was, a sort of stunned one, but with something else, something akin to, but not quite, longing. Finally, he asked, "What?"

Carolyn shook her head and smiled crookedly. "Nothing. You're just enough to make a gal wish you were fifteen years older and straight."

"After my money, huh?" he teased, not believing it for a moment. He didn't yet know how she'd gotten it, but she had money. Her clothes and the few pieces of jewelry she wore said as much, not to mention the fact that she was staying in a villa. Genie might be a friend, but he didn't think she could get Carolyn and her friend a reduction on the price of the villa they were in, and he knew they didn't come cheap. He'd made arrangements to switch the billing for their villa to him before they'd gone down to the bar to perform and the price had raised his eyebrows.

"Yeah, that's me. The gold-digging divorcée, looking for her next victim."

Christian eyed her silently. There was something in her tone of voice that sounded almost like bitterness. It raised questions in him, but questions he couldn't ask without touching too close to her marriage.

"Julius is your older brother, right?" Carolyn asked suddenly.

Christian hesitated. He didn't want to lie to her, but

she wouldn't believe him if he claimed Julius Notte as his father. Finally he said, "Julius is older than me."

"And the construction company, it's the family business?" she asked.

He nodded.

"So, what about your parents? Are they retired?" Carolyn sipped her wine.

"My parents are presently on an extended vacation," he said carefully. It wasn't a lie, a honeymoon could be considered a vacation . . . couldn't it?

"Any other siblings besides Julius?" she asked.

"Three half brothers and a half sister, through my mother." A smile curved his lips as he thought about the relatives he'd just recently become acquainted with.

"Wow, a big family then," she said enviously. "What are their ages? I'm guessing Julius is the oldest if he runs the company. How many years are there between you?"

Christian silently cursed. There was no way to answer without lying through his teeth, so he did the only thing he could think to do and stuffed his mouth with food while he scrambled to come up with a way to deflect the question.

"Hey, you two," Gia said brightly, suddenly appearing at the table.

"Gia, hi." Carolyn smiled at his cousin as she joined them.

Christian merely grunted and continued to chew, but knew Gia had just saved his bacon. He also had no doubt his mother had sent the woman down to keep an eye on things in case he needed help. Christian just wondered how long and where exactly she'd been skulking around. He hadn't seen her approach.

"You couldn't sleep either?" Carolyn pushed away her half-eaten sandwich.

"Jet lag is a bitch," Gia said wryly. "Makes me glad I don't have to travel much."

"Yeah, Christian was telling me you guys only play locally," Carolyn said. "Do you work for the family company too?"

"No, I'm a hunter," Gia answered and Christian froze.

When Gia's expression froze as well, he realized she'd recognized the slip, but before either of them could react, Carolyn said, "A corporate headhunter?"

Christian relaxed as Gia quickly nodded. "Yes, a corporate head hunter."

"Really?" Carolyn smiled. "I use those all the time. Do you work only in Europe or do you do work in Canada and the U.S. too?"

"Mostly Europe," Gia murmured.

"That's a shame. I haven't been too happy with the company we usually hire. If you worked in the U.S. and Canada I'd have hired your firm next time." She laughed and added, "I already know you can be persuasive at getting someone to take on a job they may not be eager to do."

Gia and Carolyn chuckled and Christian forced a smile, knowing Carolyn was talking about Gia's persuading her to be his supposed beard.

"Well," Carolyn said, glancing at her wristwatch. "It's good you showed up. You can keep Christian company. I need to get back to the villa and get some sleep."

Christian quickly swallowed his food and stood. "We'll walk back with you."

"Don't be silly. Stay, finish your— Oh." She peered blankly as he grabbed up the last of his sandwich and stuffed it in his mouth.

"I guess he's done," Gia said with amusement.

"I guess," Carolyn said dryly, watching him chew and swallow the mammoth mouthful he'd taken.

"Don't forget your purse," Christian said quietly as Carolyn started to turn away from the table.

She came to an abrupt halt and turned back to snatch it up. "That would have been good. Especially since that's what I came down for in the first place."

Christian followed the women out of the restaurant. He listened idly to their happy chatter all the way to the vans, and then opened the door and saw them in. He then closed the door and climbed into the front passenger seat, leaving them alone together on the first bench seat. It was better that way. Less tempting. He was determined to see her back to her villa without kissing or touching her.

The moment the van stopped, he was out and opening the door for her.

"Thank you." Carolyn took his offered hand to disembark. When he released her, she turned toward the stone path to her villa, saying, "Good night."

"Good night," Christian said quietly as he closed the door. He watched her walk away as he got back into the van. The moment she slipped inside, the driver pulled away and Christian forced himself to relax back in his seat.

"Are you going to try to sleep again?" Gia asked as they walked from the van to their own villa moments later.

Christian grimaced. "I slept all afternoon. I'm not likely to sleep now. It's why I was awake to see her leave for the lounge earlier."

Gia nodded. "Your parents saw you leave. Marguerite called and asked me to keep an eye on the two of you and make sure you didn't need help."

"She has such faith in my abilities," he said wryly, opening the door for Gia.

Gia chuckled as she entered the villa. "She was only

worried because you can't control or wipe Carolyn's mind and she feared she might ask something that you would have difficulty answering honestly . . . as she did," she pointed out dryly.

"Yeah." Christian followed her inside. "Thanks for intervening."

"Hey, you're my favorite cousin," she said lightly, bumping his arm with her shoulder, and then added with a grin, "Well, one of them."

"Right," he said with a laugh.

"So what are you going to do?" she asked, as she closed the door.

"Wait for dawn and then find her tomorrow morning, spend the day with her, and earn her trust."

"Out in sunlight?" she asked with concern. "And when will you sleep?"

"I'll sleep tomorrow night. By then I ought to conk right out. And I don't see any alternative to going out in daylight. Between the shows at night and her mortal hours, it's the only way to spend more than a couple of hours a day with her. I need to gain her trust."

Gia nodded solemnly. "Well, you may as well come hang with us then. Maybe you can get Zanipolo to shut up about Carolyn's thinking he must be the gay one. He's questioned why she would think that ever since returning. He's now determined to cut his hair and grow a beard to look more manly."

Christian chuckled and followed her from the foyer.

Seven

A squeal and a laugh made Carolyn glance to the right, the sunglasses she wore hiding the fact that she was watching a young couple romp on the shoreline. A young redhead was apparently reluctant to enter the water and a dark-haired young man had grabbed her around the waist from behind, lifting her off her feet. Definitely honeymooners, Carolyn decided as she watched the young man carry the laughing woman into the sea.

So young, so happy, so in love, she thought sadly, just watching them made her want to weep. She didn't think she'd ever been all of those things. Oh, she'd been young once, and happy on occasion, but not happy like they were, and while she'd thought she was in love with Robert, it turned out the man she'd loved hadn't even existed. Her in-love stage had been very short and mostly self-conscious as she struggled to please a man who could never be pleased.

Grimacing at the unhappy memories, she raised her

book again and pretended to read, but instead continued to glance around under the cover her sunglasses offered.

Carolyn had awakened that morning to the sounds of retching coming from Beth's room. Bethany was still sick, definitely some sort of bug and not food poisoning, which was a worry with her diabetes. When Beth joined her in the kitchen some moments later, Carolyn had suggested seeing if there was a doctor on the island, but Beth had refused. She just needed more sleep, she'd insisted. Carolyn should go have breakfast with Genie and then hit the beach. She'd join her later.

As if that was likely, Carolyn thought on a sigh. It seemed she was destined to spend the next two weeks alone, surrounded by happy honeymooners, whose very joy was a counterpoint to her own situation. That or hang out with her gay buddy Christian. The thought was unkind, she told herself as soon as it slipped into her mind. Christian seemed like a nice guy. Besides, without him to keep her company at least part of the time, she might very well be moved to do herself harm.

Seriously, all these loving couples made her feel . . . Well, frankly, she felt damaged. A freak. She kept looking around wondering why she didn't have someone to love her. Why Robert hadn't loved her. What was wrong with her? It was disheartening, being surrounded by all the couples who were young. There were some older couples, and even one or two women she thought she might be better looking than. Yet they all had these happy, smiling, loving partners while she was alone . . . as usual. But then Carolyn had felt alone most of her life. She'd been a latch-key kid with a mother who she knew loved her dearly, but who, because of circumstances, had spent most of her time working, and then . . . Well, she'd just never felt like she belonged anywhere or had a real family.

Carolyn grimaced at her own selfish thoughts. She'd been very lucky to have her mother. She'd at least known she was loved. Some kids didn't even have that. She forced her gaze back to her book again, trying to find where she'd left off, then stiffened with surprise as someone dropped onto the sand beside her lounger.

"Morning."

Carolyn recognized Christian's voice before she actually turned her head to look at him. He had a deep, sexy voice, very distinctive and hard to forget. She smiled at him, her relief at no longer being alone adding warmth to it.

"Morning," she said and frowned as she noted the rings under his eyes. "Did you get any sleep at all?"

"Not much. I drifted off at dawn." When concern pulled at her face, he shrugged. "It just means I'll sleep great tonight."

Carolyn smiled wryly. "As it happens, so should I. I woke up at dawn."

"Ah, that explains it," he murmured and she quirked an eyebrow.

"Explains what?"

"Why you look tired too," he said quickly. "What woke you?"

"Beth. She got up to get a drink and dropped a glass in the kitchen. By the time I sent her to bed and cleaned it up, I was wide awake. I tried to go back to sleep, but gave up after lying there for an hour."

Christian nodded. "How's she doing?"

"I think it's the flu and she should see a doctor, but she insists that so long as she takes in lots of fluids and sleeps, she'll be fine," Carolyn said, her eyebrows rising as she glanced over his black jeans and T-shirt. "That's not exactly beachwear."

"I have something of an allergy to the sun," he excused himself.

"Should you be out here then?" she asked with concern.

"So long as we're in the shade, I'm good."

"Hmm. You aren't going to be comfortable out here in jeans and a T-shirt, though. It's too hot. Maybe we should—" Her voice died abruptly as he stood and quickly removed his T-shirt. Her eyes widened. She'd thought his tight T-shirts pretty much gave away what his chest would look like naked, but she'd been wrong. He looked good in the T-shirt, but he was a bloody Adonis without it.

When Christian undid his jeans and began to push them off his hips, she tried to tear her eyes away, but it was just impossible. She watched avidly as he stepped out of them to reveal a pair of loose, black swim trunks. His legs were as impressive as his torso. The man was built like an athlete, all rippling muscles and taut olive skin. He must be popular at gay bars, Carolyn thought, but frowned as she noted that his impromptu striptease had drawn every female eye for a hundred yards.

"Damn, Christian, you're likely to cause a riot on the beach doing that," she said with disgust.

"What?" he asked, glancing around with surprise.

"Never mind." Carolyn glanced around again to notice that some of the women were now enviously looking her way. If they only knew. "You should have grabbed a lounge chair before stripping. Do you want me to get you one?"

Christian shook his head, and unfurled a large beach towel next to her chair. "I'm good."

"Hmm." She watched him stretch out. When he turned his head and smiled, she automatically smiled back and then returned her gaze to her book, thinking it was a shame she'd never dated anyone as attractive as him when she was younger. Every woman should get to enjoy such male beauty at least once in their life.

Her mouth quirked. She'd actually been asked out by such a man once during university. Well . . . the term "asked out" was a bit misleading, she supposed. He'd walked up and started talking to her on one of the rare occasions when it had just been the three girls out. Amazed that such a good-looking—translated: hot—guy was paying her such attention, she'd hung on his every word for the full three minutes it had taken before he'd said, "I'd love to have breakfast with you. Your place or mine?" Carolyn had shrunk from the offer like the virgin she'd been at the time, but now wondered how her life might have turned out had she accepted it.

It might have ended up different, or it might have wound up the same, Carolyn supposed. Really, regrets were a waste of time. You simply couldn't change the past. The present and the future were all you had to work with.

"What are you reading?"

Carolyn glanced to Christian. He was lounging on his back, his hands under his head and smiling at her easily. She turned the cover for him to read. "It's very popular at the moment, but I'm finding it a bit slow myself; too much about German politics, at least at the beginning. Hopefully the story picks up soon."

"Let me know if it does. I've got that at home on my TBR pile," he admitted.

"Really?" she asked, eyes wide.

He arched an eyebrow and asked, "Why so surprised? Did you think the only thing I could read was music?"

Carolyn chuckled. "Well, you *are* a rocker. I thought all you guys did was party and have sex."

Christian snorted. "You'd be surprised. It's been a long time for me, and I don't even remember when Santo and Raffaele last had a lover."

"And Zanipolo and Gia?" she asked.

"Gia hasn't for a long time either. Zanipolo, on the other hand, is something of a slut," he informed her.

Carolyn grinned. "He is, is he?"

"Yes," Christian assured her, and chuckled. "And he was very upset to learn that he was the one you first thought must be the homosexual in the band when Gia was talking to you."

Carolyn stilled. "I didn't tell Gia that's who I suspected was gay."

Christian's grin froze, and then he relaxed and shrugged. "Perhaps she was teasing him then."

Carolyn frowned. It must be the case, of course, because she hadn't spoken her thoughts aloud . . . still . . . Still what? It wasn't like Gia could read her mind. She must have just been teasing Zanipolo. It was a coincidence, she thought, and then, realizing what Christian had said, asked, "So Zanipolo knows you're gay?"

His gaze flickered. "Zanipolo knows my sexual preference."

"Oh. Does anyone else?"

Rather than answer, he sat up abruptly and glanced around until his eyes found the small drinks shack in the middle of the crowded beach. "Do you want a drink? I'm thirsty."

"I am kind of thirsty," she admitted.

Christian immediately dug his wallet out of his jeans pocket and loped away across the sand. Out into the sun, she noted, worrying about his allergy. Fortunately, it was a slow moment at the booth and he was back quickly with two margaritas.

"It's kind of early for alcohol, isn't it?" Carolyn asked as he bent to give her one of the drinks. By her guess it wasn't yet noon. Maybe 11 a.m.

"I didn't know what else was good," Christian said with a shrug as he settled on the sand next to her. "One shouldn't hurt us."

"Hurt us, no," she agreed. "But I'll probably fall asleep."

"Considering neither of us got a full night's sleep, that doesn't seem a bad thing. A little nap in the shade sounds good to me."

Shrugging, she sipped her drink. It really was good, cold, tangy, refreshing, the perfect drink for a hot, sunny day with a book.

"Do you think Beth will feel better by tonight?" Christian asked, sipping his own drink.

"Probably not. Why?"

"Julius wanted to know for the reservations," he explained.

"The reservations?" Carolyn asked uncertainly.

"For dinner." Seeing her blank expression, he reminded her, "Dinner and dancing tonight. Dinner before we play our set, dancing in town after?"

"Oh, right." She'd forgotten that business from last night. But now supposed that meant she could expect kissing or nuzzling to take place tonight to convince his family they were witnessing a blossoming love affair. The thought made her raise her glass, but she remembered about brain freezes at the last moment and only sipped the drink.

"It's just one night," Christian said quietly. "I'll book tours and dinners for the rest of the week to ensure it doesn't happen again."

Carolyn nodded at the reassurance and took another swallow of her drink.

"Do you have any tours you're particularly interested in?" he asked.

Carolyn shook her head. "I don't even know what's available. I know we're booked for a market shuttle and Bethany booked us for the day sail up the coast to see a drive-in volcano and a cocoa plantation. But other than that, I'm clueless when it comes to what's available."

Christian tossed back the last of his quickly melting margarita and stretched out next to her again. "I'll grab a pamphlet when we go to lunch and we can check out what's available while we eat."

Carolyn nodded and drank the last of her own drink, then set the empty glass in the sand beside her seat and lay back to open her book again. But she was smiling now, she noted. It was a comfortable, relaxed smile. She wasn't alone.

"Cara?"

"Hmmm?" she murmured sleepily, blinking her eyes open to find she'd turned onto her stomach on the lounger. The sun had moved in the sky and their shade had slipped away. She was now lying out in the open, the sun beating down on her. She was hot and sweaty, the skin of her back sizzling under the midday sun.

"You'll burn. You need lotion."

Christian's voice from her other side made her lift her head and turn to peer at him. He sat, one hip perched on the edge of her lounge chair, and was still in only his swimming trunks, but now held a bottle of lotion in his hand. Opening the bottle, he squirted some into his palms and then let the bottle drop to the sand.

"Should I put some on for you?" he asked, rubbing his hands together to spread it over his fingers.

Carolyn opened her mouth to say no, she'd do it, but

bit off the sound before it was even quite formed when he bent to run his hands over her back. The way he massaged the cream into her back and shoulders should have been soothing. She was pretty sure it would have been with anyone else, but it just wasn't with him. Her skin tingled everywhere his hands moved and rather than relaxing, she found herself growing tenser under his touch. Biting her lip, she closed her eyes and tried to force herself to relax, but it was impossible. Gay or not, he was a handsome, sexy guy and he smelled damned good.

"You're getting a tan line." He'd leaned forward to speak, his naked chest pressing warm and hard against her equally naked back and his breath soft against her ear. "Shall I undo your bathing suit top?"

Carolyn blinked her eyes open with alarm at the suggestion, and then wondered with confusion when she'd removed her T-shirt and shorts to reveal the bathing suit she'd worn beneath. She'd been too self-conscious to do so when she'd first arrived, but now her clothes were gone, her bathing suit her only covering. A tug on the string at her back dragged her attention from this concern to another as her bathing suit top fell away to pool on the lounger on either side of her, leaving her back completely bare, and her sides exposed. It wasn't indecent or anything, her breasts were still squished beneath her on the lounger and hidden, but it made her feel oddly vulnerable, and then Christian bent forward to whisper in her ear again.

"*Hai la pelle bella, cosi dolce.*" His voice was husky and soft, his hands running down her back, sliding toward her bathing suit bottom. "*Ritiene buon sotto le mie barrette.*"

"Hmm?" Carolyn mumbled with confusion, not understanding what she presumed was Italian.

"You have beautiful skin, so sweet," he translated, his

hands massaging and kneading her lower waist. "It feels good under my fingers."

Carolyn stilled with surprise, but bit her lip as his hands slid from her back to her sides. His palms were against her sides, but the tips of his fingers curved under her waist just above her bathing suit bottom and glided upward. She gasped when they brushed the bottom of her breasts, then the sides of them as his hands continued upward dragging his fingers along. Carolyn didn't breathe again until his hands slid back down.

She let out a small breath of relief as they moved to her waist again, but then Christian shifted and his hands skipped over her bathing suit bottom to find the flesh of her upper legs.

Surely he had to stop and get more lotion now, Carolyn thought, almost desperate for a moment without his hands on her. Her body was tingling everywhere he touched, but also in places he wasn't touching as his fingers cruised down to her calves and ankles. He then shifted both hands to her left leg for the upward journey, one hand strong and firm on the inside of her ankle, the other outside, his thumbs sliding up the back as his hands made their way up her calf.

Carolyn felt herself tensing. She didn't care if he was gay, there was just no way to lie still and unfeeling with his hands traveling over her body. She wanted to ask him to stop, but didn't think she could speak to save her soul as his hands moved toward the apex of her thighs. She was tightening like a wind-up clock, and Carolyn bit her lip almost hard enough to draw blood as she fought not to squirm.

Much to her relief, Christian paused just short of the top of her leg, and then his hands shifted to her other leg to travel slowly down that one. This time, however, on their upward journey he allowed them to ride all the way up, and her breath left her on a gasp as the hand on her inner leg brushed lightly against her bathing suit bottom between her legs.

"Christian," she choked out in protest as her body responded to the grazing touch, and then his hands were on her back again, sliding out from her spine to her sides. Carolyn let her breath out slowly, her head turning to search the beach, widening when she saw they were now alone, the beach littered with nothing but empty lounge chairs. The sight confused her. Where had everyone gone? It was close to lunchtime, but surely they hadn't gotten up en masse to hit the restaurants?

"Such pale skin," Christian murmured as his fingers slid along her sides, moving upward. "So beautiful."

The words sounded by her ear, his breath hot on her already heated flesh, and she started to turn her head toward him and then froze as his tongue suddenly slid along the outer edge of her ear before he claimed the lobe with his lips.

"But you're gay," she choked out with confusion as he began to suck on the lobe, sending a new wave of tingles through her.

Hands pausing halfway up her sides, he released her lobe and growled, "No. I'm not," and then while she struggled to accept that, his lips drifted to her neck, nibbling and kissing, sending shudders rushing through her body as his hands continued up her sides again.

"Give me your lips," Christian whispered as his hands paused, the sides of them just grazing the undersides of her breasts.

"Christian, I don't think this is a good—" Her words died on a gasp as his hands suddenly curved under her breasts. He squeezed gently, and then raised her away from the lounger so that he could reach and cover her mouth with his.

Carolyn moaned as his tongue slid past her lips, kissing her with the same passion she recalled from the night before when he'd seen her to the door. It drew the same shattering response from her body now, causing a small explosion of passion and need that poured over her like the sparks from fireworks. Moaning again deep in her throat, she twisted in his arms, her breasts slipping from his hands as she turned over.

Christian's mouth clung to hers and the second she was on her back, sliding her arms around his neck, his hands found her breasts again. His fingers closed over the tender flesh, squeezing and kneading, drawing gasps and moans from her in turn as his tongue thrust repeatedly into her mouth.

Carolyn had never experienced such passion. It seemed to be riding through her in waves that matched the rhythm of the ocean waves pounding on the shore, rushing over her one after the other, as tireless as the sea itself.

She moaned his name when his mouth left hers, then gasped when it dropped to her breast. He drew on the nipple, grazing it with his teeth and she groaned and writhed on the lounger. When his hand slid down and slipped between her legs, Carolyn cried out, her fingers clenching in his hair.

"*Bella cara,* moan for me," he whispered against her breast as his fingers began to caress her through the thin cloth . . . and Carolyn did moan, her entire body shuddering at the touch.

Lifting his head, Christian claimed her mouth once more, his lips moving over hers as his fingers stirred her passions. This time when his tongue thrust into her mouth, she let her own tongue move tentatively to join in the dance. When his mouth broke from hers again, she cried out in protest, but his fingers continued to stir her passions and he chuckled then nipped her ear, whispering, "Touch me."

Carolyn immediately pulled one hand from his head to obey, her fingers gliding down his chest, and then dropping to seek him out through his swimming trunks. She found him hard and—

Carolyn stilled, her eyes popping open with surprise.

Christian paused and raised his head with concern. "What is it, *cara*?"

"I . . . er . . . you're so big," she said with embarrassment.

He looked confused and shook his head. "No I'm not."

Carolyn stared at him with disbelief. "But Robert—"

"I am not Robert," he said solemnly, "and I assure you I am only on the high end of average, so if I seem so much bigger than he is, he must have had *un pene molto molto piccolo*."

Carolyn didn't ask him to translate. She suspected he'd just said something along the lines of Robert having had a piccolo for a penis or something, but frankly she didn't much care. Christian had suddenly removed his hand from between her legs. She was struggling to hide her disappointment, and regretting she'd said anything when she felt a sudden tug on the bathing suit tie at her hip.

Even as Carolyn glanced down, Christian was reaching to tug on the other tie. Her eyes shot back to his face and his mouth covered hers again, and then she felt his hand brushing aside the scrap of cloth that her bottoms had become and replacing it with his hand.

Carolyn cried out into his mouth as his fingers dipped between her legs, finding and gliding over her warm, slick flesh. For a moment she was all sensation, and little in the way of thought, and one hand clenched desperately in his hair while the other tightened around his erection.

When she was rewarded with a groan from Christian and his caresses and kisses became more demanding, she immediately released him to find the bottom of his roomy trunks. She slid her hand up one leg to find him again without the cloth in the way and his flesh was hot, and even harder than it had been a moment ago. Carolyn began to move her fingers over him, eager to increase his pleasure.

Christian's response was most gratifying; he stilled for the count of a heartbeat, and then growled into her mouth, his tongue lashing her almost in punishment. But he also changed his caress, leaving his thumb to circle the nub of her excitement as he slid a finger inside her.

Carolyn's hips bucked and she arched on the lounger, crying his name as their kiss was broken. Christian continued what he was doing, but shifted his mouth to her nipple then, drawing it into his mouth and suckling hard until she released his erection and removed her hand to tug fretfully at his swim trunks. Much to her relief, he responded at once, his hands leaving her so that he could stand and quickly shed himself of his swimsuit. In the next moment, he was climbing on top of her, his knees urging hers apart.

Carolyn reached eagerly for him, her hands pulling his head down to hers once more as he settled between her thighs. He didn't enter her right away. While he claimed her lips and thrust his tongue into her mouth, he merely ground himself against her, his hardness rubbing firmly across the center of her excitement.

Carolyn moaned and wrapped her legs around him in response, her kiss becoming more desperate. Her hands dropped to clutch his behind, digging in with a demand that wouldn't be satisfied by such half-measures. Still, Christian held back, his mouth devouring hers briefly before he suddenly thrust himself into her.

Carolyn tore her mouth away on a cry as he filled her, and then arched, little gasps coming from her lips as her body fought to accept an invasion it wasn't used to.

"*Cara?*" he asked uncertainly, not moving, and she blinked her eyes open. Seeing the concern on his face, she pulled his head back down. As she reclaimed his lips, her hips instinctively moved to urge him on and then he was moving again, his body withdrawing and then thrusting back into hers. His mouth caught her moans and cries as he drove them both to the edge of a precipice and then the ringing of a phone intruded, making her frown against his mouth.

"Ignore it," Christian gasped, thrusting into her again, but a second ring made Carolyn blink her eyes open and peer uncertainly around at what at first seemed an alien scene.

She was on her lounger on the beach as expected, but still in the shade. The beach was alive with laughing and chatting couples. Her T-shirt and shorts were back in place over her swimsuit, her book lay flat on her stomach where it had apparently fallen when she'd dozed off, and Christian was reclining on the sand beside her chair. Even as she noted that, his eyes popped open and he lunged to his feet. In the next moment, he was running for the surf, apparently eager for a dip.

Carolyn stared after him, her brain slowly calming from its agitated state and accepting that it had all been a dream. Of course, it had been a dream. Only in her dreams would Christian be straight and interested in her.

The ring of the phone sounded again, and Carolyn

glanced to her purse lying in the sand. Giving her head a shake to try to clear it, she leaned to the side, snagged the strap and dragged the purse closer. She then pulled it onto her lap and quickly dug inside to find her phone. It rang for the last time just before Carolyn hit the talk button, and then she pressed it to her ear to say, "Hello?"

"Caro?" Bethany said.

"Yes." She sat up, sending her book toppling to the sand. "Are you feeling better? Are you coming down to the beach?"

"No. I just wanted to check on you. I feel so bad about leaving you on your own."

"Don't worry about me," Carolyn said on a sigh. "I'll be fine. You're the sick one."

"Yes, well I do worry about you. I insisted on dragging you to St. Lucia and then, basically, abandoned you. I feel awful."

"Don't. You're sick. There's nothing you can do about that. But you'll be better in a couple of days and we'll still have loads of time to have fun."

"Right," Bethany murmured. "That band kid's not hanging around bothering you, is he?"

"I—no. He's nowhere near me," Carolyn said, her eyes finding Christian as he swam steadily out to sea. It wasn't a lie, she told herself. Christian was nowhere near her at the moment.

"Good," Beth said firmly. "If he shows up, tell him to take a hike. You don't need to waste your vacation playing beard for another Brent."

No, because sitting around on her own in honeymoon hell was so much better, Carolyn thought, but merely murmured noncommittally. "Is there anything you want me to bring you when I come back?"

"Umm . . . well . . . if you wouldn't mind, could you

stop at that little store across from the main building and see if they have any ginger ale?" Bethany asked. "And maybe some crackers? It will help settle my stomach."

"Of course," Carolyn said. "I'll bring them right up."

"No. Go ahead and have your lunch first. I can wait until you've eaten."

"All right," Carolyn murmured, recalling that Christian had said something about looking over pamphlets during lunch.

"And Carolyn?"

"Yeah?" She watched Christian turn and head inland again.

"Everything's going to be all right. If worse comes to worst we could always become lesbian lovers and grow old together. Who needs men anyway, right?"

"Right," Carolyn muttered, not finding their old joke remotely funny.

"Have fun. And don't rush back. Just enjoy the sand and surf. There's no hurry for the ginger ale and crackers. I'm going to lie down and sleep awhile anyway."

"All right." Carolyn hung up, her gaze on Christian as he swam the last ten feet to shore. He was a very good swimmer, she noted absently, but if he was allergic to the sun, she didn't think he should probably be out there in the water.

She sank back on the lounge chair, thinking that Bethany's efforts to encourage her had had the opposite effect and she was now depressed. Or perhaps it was the fact that she had apparently taken to having wet dreams about her poor gay companion that was depressing her, Carolyn thought grimly. She almost felt like she should apologize to the poor man for dream-raping him.

Grimacing, she pushed her sunglasses more firmly up her nose, and watched Christian walk, dripping, out of the surf. He was a beautiful young man . . . and she couldn't help her dreams, she told herself. Besides, that dream sex had been hotter than anything she'd experienced in real life. It was also the most fun she'd had so far on this damned trip. And she was the only one who knew about it, so no one had been hurt by it. She just had to remind herself, firmly, that all it had been was a dream and that it would never happen in real life. Christian was gay, and that was that. He would never want her. Ever.

Eight

"So Bethany booked you for the shopping tour and the day sail to Soufriere," Christian murmured, looking over the pamphlets.

"I'm pretty sure she mentioned those two. She might have booked others, but if so, I don't recall her telling me."

Christian nodded. "Well, it looks like we're out of luck this afternoon. Most of the tours start in the morning."

"Probably because it's cooler then." She leaned closer to read the description of the Jeep jungle tour. That sounded interesting, they stopped at a banana plantation and there were some falls and stuff on that tour too. The zip-line adventure looked interesting as well, zipping along through the trees 150 feet above the ground to see the forest from such an unusual angle. They would have a bird's-eye view, even of the birds. At least that's what the pamphlet claimed.

"Hmm." Christian frowned, and pointed out, "That leaves only the shopping shuttles this afternoon though."

Carolyn chuckled at his expression. "You look so thrilled."

"Yeah." He smiled crookedly. "Not keen on the shopping thing."

"Well, we don't have to do anything this afternoon," she pointed out with amusement. "I have to take some ginger ale and crackers up to Beth and check on her. Then we could lounge around on the beach for a bit. I mean, it's already after one and our food hasn't even come yet. By the time I get back from checking on Beth it will probably be two or three, we could lie around and read or talk, then get ready for dinner and . . ." She shrugged. "The rest of the night is pretty much spoken for."

"Yeah." He raised his eyebrows. "Would you mind?"

"No. Bethany and I planned to just chill for the first day or two anyway," she assured him and it was true, they'd planned to just relax and recuperate from the cares of the world. She supposed if Beth had to get sick, she'd picked the best time to do it. Surely she would be recovered by the time their tours came up.

"Okay, but I really think we should do the zip-line adventure or the Jeep tour tomorrow," he suggested.

"Sounds like a plan," she agreed, pleased that his interests seemed to coincide with her own. She then sat back as the waitress arrived with their food. Carolyn sighed with pleasure as the burger was set before her. She knew she shouldn't have it, she'd been trying to watch her weight since leaving Robert, but she was on vacation, what better time to have one? And Christian had ordered the same thing.

"Mmm, this is good," he announced around a mouthful of burger.

Carolyn shook her head with amusement. "Don't tell me they don't have burgers in Italy?"

"I'm sure they do, but I've never had one," he said, picking up a fry and popping it in his mouth.

"Never?" she asked with surprise and then smiled. "I suppose you eat a lot of pasta over there. It seems to be what Italy is known for."

Christian grunted, but his mouth was full of burger and she turned her attention to her own food. It was several moments before either of them spoke again and then it was Christian who said, "So what does a business lawyer do exactly?"

Carolyn smiled wryly and picked up a fry, as she admitted, "I don't really use my degree at all anymore."

When his eyebrows rose, she shrugged.

"Life kind of took a turn in an unexpected direction several years ago."

"Oh?" Christian asked curiously.

She nodded, and contemplated her plate, but then decided there was no reason not to tell him. It wasn't likely to affect their budding friendship and that was all it was ever likely to be. "You remember I said my mom was my only family?"

He nodded.

"Well, it turned out that wasn't exactly true. It seems we had loads of family. She just didn't dare go near any of them for fear my father would find her."

Christian paused in his chewing, his eyes narrowing. "Spousal abuse?"

She wasn't terribly surprised he'd guessed. What other reason would make a woman flee her husband and family and raise a child on her own in abject poverty?

"Yeah. I guess he was free with his fists. She told me she nearly lost me when he threw her down a flight of stairs while she was pregnant." She grimaced. "She put up with it so long as he only hit her, but when I was four he started in on me."

"Is that from him?" Christian asked.

Carolyn paused in confusion, but then realized she was rubbing the small tear-shaped scar by her right eye. Retrieving her hand, she reached for her burger, but then paused. "Yes. I guess I had my elbows on the table."

Christian's expression darkened. "And for that he scarred you for life?"

Carolyn shrugged. "I gather he had a temper. Besides, it was kind of an accident I guess. I mean, he apparently hit me and sent me flying into a glass or pitcher or something on the table. It was the glass that cut me, not him, but the fact that he'd hit me that hard was enough for her. She was afraid it wouldn't be the last time, so she took me and ran. She changed our name to her maiden name of Johnson, and worked a series of horrible low-paying jobs under the table to avoid leaving a paper trail he could follow to find us."

"And did he look?" Christian asked.

Carolyn nodded. "He apparently hired several private detective agencies and kept them working for ten years before giving up."

"He never thought to look under her maiden name?" Christian asked.

Carolyn grinned. "Johnson is almost as common as Smith. He could have looked till the cows came home and he wouldn't have found us. Besides, she was working under the table," she reminded him.

"Right." Christian nodded. "And you found this out, how?"

"Some of it I found out when Mom was sick, just before she died. The rest I found out from him when they found me," she admitted quietly. "Before Mom got sick, I thought my father had died just before I was born."

"When he found you?" he asked. "You didn't go looking for him?"

"Heck no," Carolyn said with amusement. "I mean, he was just a name, and from what my mother described, hardly someone I wanted to know."

"So what made him start looking for you again?"

"Cancer," she answered at once. "He'd never remarried, didn't have any other kids, got cancer, and decided it was time to try to find us again. Only this time he figured I'd be working so he had them search for me." She popped a fry into her mouth, chewed and swallowed and then continued, "It took a while, but he was lucky to find me at all. I almost changed my name legally to Carolyn at one point."

"Carolyn's not your real name?" he asked with surprise.

"Yes, well, it's my middle name."

"And your first name?" he asked.

Carolyn grinned. "Guess."

He blinked at the suggestion. "How could I even begin to—"

"It's Christiana," she interrupted with amusement.

Christian blinked and then raised his eyebrows. "You're kidding?"

Carolyn laughed at his expression. "My birth name was Christiana Carolyn Carver. My parents were into alliteration, I guess."

Christian flopped back in his seat and she chuckled softly, but continued, "Anyway, I went through life as Carolyn Johnson, my middle name and my mother's maiden name. I don't know how she managed that. I thought they needed birth certificates or some form of ID to register a kid in school, but if so, she must have bought some fake IDs." Carolyn pondered that briefly, trying to imagine her hardworking and upright mother dealing with black market types to buy fake IDs. It was very hard to imagine. Still, she must have, she supposed.

"While she apparently didn't mind fake stuff for my schooling, she used my real name and birth certificate to get me a social insurance number when I was a teenager. But she insisted I expend my energy on schoolwork and would never let me get a part-time job to help out, so I never actually used it until I graduated from university and started to work." Carolyn laughed. "It was really rather weird to have to learn to sign everything Carver. And anytime someone called me Chris or Christiana, I had no idea who they were talking to. I still went by Carolyn."

"And that's how he found you? Through your social insurance number?" Christian asked.

"Eventually," she agreed. "But Rob—" She paused, her mouth tightening, and then simply said, "It took a while. By the time his private detective tracked me down my father was in the final stages of cancer and on his last legs."

Christian was silent for a moment, his eyes solemn and she knew he wanted to ask her what she'd started to say about Robert. She wasn't ready to answer that and was tensing up at the thought of his even bringing it up, but he merely asked, "What was your father like?"

Carolyn's tension eased and her lips twisted. "Repentant. But then isn't everyone when they know they're about to meet their maker?"

Christian's eyebrows flew up at the words and she smiled wryly.

"Why so surprised that I would say that?"

"I guess you just don't seem the type to be so cynical," he admitted quietly.

Carolyn glanced down. He was right. She'd always been a little Pollyanna according to Beth and Brent, but she'd learned a lot the last couple of years. Still, Christian hadn't known her long, so it was surprising he had figured that out about her already.

"Anyway," she said. "He was full of apology and regret both for what he'd done to drive Mother away, and for the hard life she'd had because of it. He wanted to make up for it by leaving me his business and fortune."

When Christian's eyebrows rose, she smiled bitterly.

"It seems my mother gave up a lot to keep me safe. Daddy was wealthy as hell, with a couple of companies and loads of land. It's why she'd feared he would hunt for us; he had the funds to do it," she said dryly.

"And he left everything to you?"

Carolyn nodded. "The companies were based in Quebec. I sold a couple and moved the head office for the one I kept to Toronto and took over running it on his death."

"What business did you keep?" he asked curiously.

"An advertising agency," she admitted with a self-deprecating laugh. "I don't know why I chose to keep that one. I don't know a damned thing about advertising, or I didn't. But I just left the creative stuff to the staff at first and concentrated on the business end of things and now I know a heck of a lot more than I did."

"So you don't even use your law degree?"

"Well, I do, I suppose. When it comes to contracts I'm a whiz. It's handy there," Carolyn admitted, and then glanced down to her plate to see that she'd finished her meal. When she saw that Christian had finished his as well, she sighed and peered at her watch. "I suppose I should get the ginger ale and crackers and head back to the villa."

Christian nodded and ushered her out of the restaurant. The one they'd chosen was on the little strip across from the main building and Carolyn glanced curiously in the windows of the few small shops along the boardwalk as they went. When she saw the selection of T-shirts in one window, she paused.

"Did you want to go in?" Christian asked.

She glanced at his dark T-shirt and jeans and nodded. It was a tiny shop, full of baubles and clothes, and Carolyn wove her way through the place until she reached the clothing section where a selection of shorts and shirts waited. Her gaze slid over a group of Hawaiian-type prints, but didn't pause. She just didn't see Christian wearing them. Smiling at the thought, she continued on to the T-shirts and picked up a white one with the resort logo on the bottom-right hem.

"What do you think?" Carolyn asked, turning to hold it up to Christian.

He shook his head. "I don't need anything."

"Uh-huh," she said with disbelief. "So you have something in your suitcase that isn't black?"

"What's wrong with black?" he asked with a frown.

"Nothing. And you look good in it," she assured him. "But it's too hot here for it. You need shorts too."

"I don't do shorts," Christian assured her grimly, his nose rising and Carolyn laughed.

Leaning up to whisper in his ear, she teased, "You're pretty lame about fashion for a gay guy."

"I'm glad to hear it," he said dryly, his hand rising to graze her back before she lowered to her feet.

Shaking her head, she turned to pick up a pair of

canvas shorts to look them over and Christian immediately winced. "Caro, I won't wear them."

"Why not? You have good legs. You should show them off."

"Jesus, Carolyn. I'm not Beth. Men don't have good legs," he said with disgust.

"I meant nice guy legs," she said quickly. "All muscular and sexy."

Christian blinked, his annoyance giving way to a grin, and he asked with interest, "So you think my legs are sexy?"

Carolyn flushed. "I'm sure you know they are. Just see if they have a changing room and try these on. It makes me hot just to look at you all in black."

His eyebrows rose, his grin widening. "So, you're saying I make you hot?"

"I didn't mean—" she began with alarm, aware that she was flushing. But catching the twinkle in his eyes, she shook her head and said with exasperation, "Who knew you could be such a smart-ass?"

"I'll get the shirt," he conceded, chuckling, and took it from her, then led the way to the till. She supposed that was better than nothing.

They stopped in at the little grocer's for the ginger ale and crackers and then headed up the hill on foot, chatting as they went.

"How long do you need before heading back to the beach?" Christian asked as they neared the villa she shared with Beth.

Carolyn hesitated. If she just dumped the stuff and left, she'd only need a minute. However, she kind of felt she should stay and visit with Bethany, at least for a little bit. "Give me an hour?"

He nodded easily. "It will give me time to shower, change, and feed."

"Your Italian is showing, it's eat, not feed," she said with amusement. When Christian stiffened with what she thought must be embarrassment, she regretted teasing him. He was really very good with English. "Besides, you just ate. How can you be hungry again already?"

Christian relaxed and shrugged. "I just am."

"Hmm, you must still be growing then," she decided.

"*Cara,* I am well past the growing stage," he said firmly.

Carolyn ignored the Italian endearment. They seemed to use it freely enough. She also ignored his words and simply turned up the walk to her villa saying, "I'll meet you down there in an hour then."

The villa was cool and silent when she entered. Carolyn carried the bag into the kitchen and stored the ginger ale in the refrigerator, then set the crackers on the counter and went in search of Bethany. She found her sound asleep in her room, and gently eased the door closed. After a hesitation, she then headed back to the kitchen to write a note stating that she'd been back and gone and to call if she needed anything else or just wanted company. Carolyn then slipped out of the villa again and headed down the road. She'd almost reached the turnaround when the sound of pounding feet made her glance over her shoulder. Spotting Christian jogging toward her, she paused and smiled.

"You're early," he said as he stopped beside her.

"She was asleep," Carolyn said with a shrug. "Besides, so are you."

"I saw you head out and thought I'd catch up," he admitted.

"What about showering and eating?" she asked with surprise, wondering that he'd caught up so quickly . . . and wasn't the least bit out of breath.

"I grabbed a bite," Christian said easily. "And I decided why shower when I can just take a dip in the sea again."

Carolyn stared at him and then glanced back up the road to the villas, hers and then his on the next level up. It was hard for her to believe he'd even gotten back to his villa that quickly, let alone eaten something and come down again.

"We need to stop in the grocer's on the way back to the beach," Christian announced suddenly.

"I knew it," Carolyn said, starting to walk again. "You didn't even make it back to the villa and want to get munchies."

"Yes, I did, I—," he began, and then shifted gears and said, "Maybe, but they had a rack of novels in there. I thought I'd see if there was anything to read."

Chuckling at catching him out, she nodded. "Sounds good. I wouldn't mind something to replace the book I'm reading anyway. It's just too slow for my mood. I'll read it another time."

They chatted about books they'd enjoyed as they walked, and Carolyn found herself really wishing Christian was older and straight. He was interested in the same outings she was, the same food, and now she learned he had the same damned taste as she did when it came to reading. It made her think maybe mother nature had messed up and she was supposed to be a gay male. She considered that briefly, but shook her head. She just couldn't imagine finding it amusing to sign her name in the snow with urine. What was with that anyway?

"That was band boy, wasn't it?"

Carolyn froze and turned guiltily from the door to find Beth standing in the kitchen doorway, expression grim and arms crossed like a disapproving mother. Forcing a smile, she asked, "Did you find the crackers and ginger ale?"

"Yes, thank you," Bethany said. "And don't change the subject. I saw him. That was band boy who walked you to the door."

Carolyn rolled her eyes, wondering why she felt like a teenage girl caught messing around with the local bad boy. "His name is Christian. And he's very nice."

"He's using you, Caro," Bethany said with exasperation.

"Actually, today I was using him," Carolyn said dryly, moving past her to get to the fridge and grab a bottle of water. "He kept me company."

"While you played his beard," Beth said grimly.

"I wasn't playing beard. No one was around. We just hung out and had lunch together," she said firmly, opening the bottle and quickly downing half of it. While they'd avoided the sun all afternoon, the heat was enough to dehydrate anyone. She needed water.

Beth moved to retrieve the ginger ale from the fridge, and then collected a glass before asking, "Are you seeing him again?"

"We're meeting in an hour to have dinner before his show," she admitted and then added reluctantly, "And then we're all going dancing after."

"All being his family too?" Beth asked grimly, pushing her glass against the ice dispenser bar. When Carolyn nodded, she asked, "So tonight you'll be his beard again?"

Carolyn sighed. "What is your problem here? I don't mind, why should you?"

"Because I watched this for years with Brent. You avoided entanglements with straight men by hanging with him all the time. Now you're doing it all over again," she said impatiently, opening the ginger ale and pouring some into her glass. "How the hell am I supposed to get you laid if you have band b—Christian," she corrected herself dryly when Carolyn scowled. "How am I going to get you laid if you have Christian hanging around, scaring off all the prospects?"

Carolyn sighed and walked over to give her a hug. "I know you're worried, but I'm really not ready for a relationship anyway."

"Well, when are you going to be ready, Caro?" Bethany asked quietly. "You're forty-two years old and have been separated for two years. You're not getting any younger and it just gets harder the older you get." Beth shook her head and picked up her glass to take a sip, then set it back with a sigh. "Well, go get ready. You don't want to be late for your date."

Carolyn winced, but simply turned and headed to her room.

"So? How did it go?"

Christian turned from closing the door, a smile pulling at his lips. "Good. We talked a lot and joked and"—he shrugged—"she's starting to relax around me."

Gia had been peering hard at his forehead as he spoke and continued to for a moment afterward. He knew she was searching his memories as he talked . . . which was damned annoying really. But he knew new life mates were easily read and simply waited for her assessment. He felt oddly relieved when she nodded.

"It's the lack of sexual pressure," Gia said with a slow smile. "It's working. So long as you aren't putting on the Latin lover moves with her she relaxes. She's still attracted, I can see that from your memories, but she can put it aside and just enjoy your company." She grinned, and hopped across the foyer to give him a quick, hard hug. "This is going to work, Christian!"

"Yeah, I think it might," he agreed with a grin. Throwing his arm affectionately around her shoulders, he urged her toward the kitchen. He needed blood. They'd sat in the shade most of the afternoon, but between runs to the drinks shack and walks up and down the hill, he was low and needed a refill.

"But we should probably lay off the Latin lover business for a while to allow her to stay relaxed," Gia murmured as she watched him retrieve a bag of blood.

Christian frowned. He didn't really want to lay off the "Latin lover business," as Gia had called it. The afternoon had been both enjoyable and hell for him. He'd enjoyed talking to Carolyn and how she was opening up to him, but he'd also had to constantly fight the urge to touch her hand or arm, and kiss her as they'd chatted. He wanted her, and remaining so well behaved and cool around her was hard as hell. The only way he'd managed it all afternoon was by promising himself that tonight he could at least hold her hand, put his arm around her, and hold her close on the dance floor, their bodies sliding together to Caribbean music.

"Gia's right."

Christian lowered the bag he'd just raised and glanced to the door to see Marguerite entering with Julius on her heels. "How long have you been here?"

"About fifteen minutes. We were in the living room when you entered," she answered, pausing at his side to kiss his cheek.

Christian frowned as he hugged her, wondering how he'd missed noting them in the living room. The foyer opened up on it.

"And I think Gia's right about keeping the pressure off for a bit," Marguerite said as Christian popped the bag of blood to his mouth. "It shouldn't be hard though. We're dining in the fancy restaurant tonight. No one would expect you to drape yourself over her chair there. And then you'll be onstage during your show." She paused and frowned. "I'll make sure Genie is there, then I'll have her sit on one side of Caro during the show and I'll take the chair on her other so you can't sit beside her during your break."

Christian scowled as he saw his opportunities for touching and kissing narrowing.

"What about the dancing?" Gia asked. "We're supposed to go to the club for dancing afterward."

Christian began to smile around the bag in his mouth. He could put up with behaving himself for the first part of the night if he could look forward to holding her in his arms on the dance floor. He'd run his hands down her back, molding her body to his, and bend his head to inhale her sweet scent as he nuzzled her ear and—

"Down, boy," Julius said, snapping Christian out of his imaginings. "If Gia and your mother think you shouldn't dance with her, you shouldn't. We'll go to a nightclub that plays mostly fast music."

"Even those play the occasional slow song," Gia pointed out with a frown, inadvertently raising Christian's hopes again.

"Then the boys will dance with Carolyn so Christian can't," Julius said firmly.

Christian dragged the now empty bag of blood irritably from his teeth. "Don't you think she'll be suspicious if that happens? Besides, we aren't at work now. You can't force the boys to dance with her."

"I'll do it," Zanipolo announced, making his presence known, and Christian turned to scowl at the man. Men, he corrected himself as his gaze slid over his three cousins. They had apparently entered the kitchen while he was distracted and were now lounging around the dining room table, all three of them nodding, apparently happy to dance with his woman.

"And she won't be suspicious if you complain and your cousins make it appear that they are deliberately torturing you," Julius said with a shrug.

Christian cursed and turned back to the fridge for a second bag of blood.

"It's for the best, dear." Marguerite stepped to his side to rub one hand up and down his back as he slapped the second bag to his teeth. "And you can still have a good-night kiss. That will be expected. Your father will make sure of that again, won't you dear?" she asked, glancing toward her husband.

"Of course. I'm happy to help him get his woman," Julius said generously, and Christian's eyes narrowed. The man was just enjoying this way too much. He supposed he deserved it though. He'd given him rather a hard time about his romancing skills when it came to Marguerite.

Sighing, he shook his head, his mind turning to the promised good-night kiss to come. At least they were allowing him that. It wasn't much compared to what he wanted, but it was something, he supposed.

"It won't be long, Christian. A little patience now will make all the difference," Marguerite assured him solemnly.

Tearing the empty bag from his mouth, he muttered, "Right," and turned to retrieve another.

"If you keep looking at her like that, she's not going to continue to believe you're gay."

Christian scowled at Santo's words, but didn't tear his eyes from Carolyn. He just couldn't seem to. The way she moved to the music was beautiful to behold, there was no inhibition in her now. The usually tightly constrained, boxed-up woman was all fire and passion when she danced . . . just as she'd been in his arms in their dream. She'd come alive then, as if waking from a dream rather than drifting into one, and that afternoon when they'd been alone and he'd been struggling so hard to behave, she'd revealed a wicked sense of humor that had drawn several startled laughs from him.

Christian was coming to see that the true Carolyn hid from the world behind the calm conservative exterior she presented. Whether held there by fears or simple self-consciousness he didn't know, but she was a sleeping beauty waiting to be awakened and he was dying to wake her.

His eyes narrowed as a mortal male insinuated his way into the foursome of women, sliding in to dance between Genie and Carolyn. He saw her step falter, and uncertainty flash across her face as she was forced from whatever world she'd slipped away to as she'd danced. The mortal saw it too, and like a predator smelling a weak member of the herd, began to try to isolate her, turning his back to Genie, Gia, and Marguerite, focusing on Carolyn as he began to move forward, forcing her back and farther from them.

Christian could have controlled the mortal and sent him on his way, but in truth, he was so sexually frustrated at the moment that a more physical response appealed to him, and between one breath and the next he was on the dance floor. He'd used a speed his kind usually avoided to prevent drawing attention, so was surprised when he arrived only to find his father and cousins all there as well, moving to surround him, a wall of hard flesh.

"Back to your seat," his father said firmly.

Christian scowled, his gaze sliding past him to see that either his mother or Gia had taken control of the mortal and was already sending him away. Carolyn was moving back to return to the square they'd made on the dance floor since arriving at the club half an hour ago. She had also lost that uncertainty again, her body moving to the beat without the self-consciousness the mortal's interest had caused.

"Now," Julius said grimly.

Knowing his cousins would just drag him there if he didn't go willingly, Christian turned and moved back to the table. Dropping back into his seat, he ignored the other men then, his gaze locking on Carolyn again and staying there as he imagined she was dancing for him. He would ask her to dance for him once they were mates, he decided . . . naked. He wanted to see her naked, her hips grinding, and her breasts—

"You're wound pretty tight," Julius said grimly as he settled back into his own seat and let his eyes slide back to the women.

Christian grunted. "Are you surprised?"

"No, I would be too," he admitted. "But you have to tone down the intensity before she comes back to the table. You'll terrify her like this. She's not ready for it."

When Christian merely scowled harder, he sighed and added, "Son, Caro has never experienced any kind of passion before you. The level the nanos induce will—"

"None at all?" Christian interrupted with amazement, finally managing to tear his gaze from Carolyn. He knew she hadn't had sex for seven years, but had thought surely there must have been some passion at the beginning of the marriage.

Julius hesitated, and then said, "Her mind is an open book, and her relationship with her husband—"

"Ex-husband," Christian snapped. "She's mine."

"Soon to be ex-husband," Julius said quietly. "And she isn't going to be yours if you don't listen to me on this."

He ground his teeth together, but nodded grimly. "Go ahead."

"Her marriage is on her mind a lot because of you," he said solemnly. "She is comparing him to you in every way, and he's coming up very short," he added when Christian started to get riled again.

He relaxed a bit at that news, and held his tongue for his father to continue.

"Her husband was after her money. He served her up sweet words and milquetoast kisses and romanced her into a quick marriage. He even kept it up for a while afterward, but eventually it was too much effort and he began to neglect her, and then to insult and abuse her."

"But you said she hadn't experienced any passion," Christian reminded him.

"She didn't," he said dryly. "In her mind, his kisses were pleasant when he was first making the effort, and sex wasn't horrible."

Christian winced. Sex wasn't horrible? It wasn't much of an endorsement of Robert's bedroom skills, he thought and then began to grin. Carolyn was in for a gigantic surprise. There was *so* much he could give to her: family, passion . . . lots of passion. Hell, they'd be lucky if they didn't go into comas after their first time rather than just pass out if she had that little experience with passion.

"Yes, well, you're not going to get to show her anything if you don't dial it down now," his father said dryly, obviously reading his thoughts. "And you'd best try to control yourself when you kiss her at the door too."

Christian cursed, and shifted impatiently in his seat. "I suppose you want me not to sleep when she might be sleeping and avoid shared dreams in future too?"

"No," Julius said at once and when Christian glanced at him in surprise, he shrugged. "That is tempting her without the added fear and worry about what she thinks is your age difference. She's not totally comfortable with the dream the two of you shared this afternoon. She suffered some guilt over it, but she doesn't know you shared it. She also enjoyed it enough to overlook her guilt and tell herself it wasn't her fault for having it. Besides, the passion in the dreams is muted. Perhaps half the passion we can experience for real. It's like an appetizer, while the real deal is the appetizer, a four-course meal, and dessert all in one."

Christian's eyebrows rose. If that was muted and just the appetizer—

"Hell," he muttered under his breath, and almost didn't believe his father. But then he recalled the kiss they'd shared on her doorstep and changed his mind. That simple kiss had carried as much punch as the entire dream and had left him just as hard and aching. And that had only been a kiss without the caressing and . . .

"Hell," he muttered again, his eyes widening.

Julius nodded solemnly. "If you ever want to enjoy the full meal deal I suggest you get yourself under control . . . and now," he added with a grim expression. "A slow song is on. The women are returning to the table."

Christian turned sharply to see that this was the case and was immediately seized by panic. His intensity wasn't dialed down at all. If anything, everything he'd learned had just ratcheted it up several notches.

"Hell," he muttered for a third time, and this time there was an edge of panic to the word.

"Men's room," Julius ordered, catching his arm and pulling him to his feet. "Zanipolo, dance with Carolyn," he ordered loud enough for the women to hear as he dragged Christian off to find the bathrooms.

Nine

Carolyn stopped walking to stare as Julius dragged Christian away, and then glanced around at a touch on her arm. She blinked at Zanipolo's solemn face and then, recalling Julius's last order, she assured him, "Oh, we don't have to dance."

"Don't be silly, it's always a pleasure to dance with a beautiful *woman*," Zanipolo said, tugging her toward the dance floor.

"Oh," she mumbled on a sigh.

A slow song was playing, and Carolyn wasn't used to dancing to slow music anymore. Robert had always refused to dance and it had been years since she'd accompanied Brent to business functions with dancing, so she felt awkward and stiff when Zanipolo took her into his arms.

"Relax," he chastised. "I'm a good dancer, I dance a lot . . . with *women*. Because I like women. A lot."

Carolyn stared at him blankly. "Ah. Well, that's nice, I guess."

"It is," he assured her, and asked, "Do you like my new haircut?"

Carolyn glanced at his hair. She'd noticed that he now sported a brush cut. It actually looked good on him, though, and she nodded. "It's very nice."

"Very manly," he pointed out. "Not gay at all."

"Ah." Carolyn bit her lip to keep from laughing as she realized he was still bothered by the fact that she'd thought him the homosexual in the band. Relaxing completely now, she patted his arm. "Don't worry, Zanipolo. Gia was just teasing you. I never said I thought you were gay," she assured him, and then added, "I'm not even sure how she knew I thought that. I didn't say it out loud."

Zanipolo had started to relax after her first words, but looked stricken by her last ones, and Carolyn could have kicked herself as she realized what she'd said.

"I mean— Ignore that last part. I was just . . ." Unsure what to say to repair the matter, she cleared her throat, and asked, "Why was Julius rushing Christian away?"

Zanipolo hesitated, and then suddenly brightened and announced, "Julius caught him winking at one of the waiters. No doubt he is demanding an explanation."

"Oh dear," Carolyn breathed, glancing anxiously toward the bathrooms.

"No, this might be good," Zanipolo assured her. "Christian will tell the truth and then he won't have to hang all over you and make you uncomfortable anymore."

Carolyn frowned, part of her relieved at the idea and the other part just worried about Christian and how Julius would react if he did come out of the closet. Cripes, if he was really as homophobic as all that . . . at the very least it would be unpleasant, but it was possible the two men could come to blows. Halting, she said, "You have to go check on Christian."

"Julius said to dance with you."

Carolyn clucked with exasperation. What control did Julius have over these people that they obeyed his every order without question? she wondered with irritation. Tugging herself free of his arms, she said, "Well, you can tell Julius I refused. And I do," she assured him firmly. "Now go check on Christian or I'll march into the the men's room and check on him myself."

"Fine, I'll go, but only because I have good news to impart," Zanipolo announced as he began to lead her back to the table. She didn't bother to ask what the good news was, merely smiled, grateful Christian would have support in dealing with his brother.

"If the passion is that strong, surely she won't be able to resist," Christian muttered, pacing the bathroom, his mind working on overdrive as he sought excuses to go out there and drag Carolyn straight back to the resort.

But the resort was so far away, he thought with dismay. There must be hotels nearby they could go to. Yes, a hotel would do. Even a cheap, dingy one if necessary so long as it was close. He just needed to get her alone, get her naked, and show her what they could have together.

"Once she sees what I can offer her, she can't possibly run from it. She'll want it. She'll want me. She—" He stopped abruptly as cold water suddenly splashed across his groin. He stood gasping for a second, but raised his head, gaping when he saw that his father had turned on the taps in the sink, and cupped his hand under the faucet to send a stream of the liquid at him.

"What are you doing?" he cried, stepping quickly to the side.

"Putting out the fire." Julius simply turned his hand to

make the water jet follow. "Your pants were about to start smoking."

"Christ!" Christian snapped, moving again. "Stop that."

"In a minute," he said calmly. "You're halfway back to human again."

"Halfway back to human? What the hell?" Christian shifted again, only to be followed once more, but he began to understand what the man was saying when he saw the bulge in his jeans. He'd been half-erect since he'd started to watch Carolyn dance on arriving here. But his talk with his father and the resulting thoughts it had stirred in him had probably raised it to a full erection before the first gush of water. It was definitely receding now, however.

"That's better," Julius announced cheerfully, turning off the taps. "Good talk, son. Let's go back and join the women."

When Christian just stood there dripping and glowering at him, he sighed.

"Your pene was doing your thinking for you. But I'm sure you're a little more clearheaded now and can see that you need to continue on the path that was set."

"No, I don't see that," Christian growled. "She's had enough time to get to know me. We're friends now. She won't—" He paused with surprise when his father cuffed him in the back of the head.

"Snap out of it!" Julius roared. "It's only been twenty-four hours for Christ's sake!"

"What?" Christian asked with amazement, and then protested hotly, "It has not."

"It has," Julius said at once, and then sighed and pointed out, "You only met her yesterday evening before the show, son."

Christian blinked several times, his mind going back over the events in his head. It felt like months, but he knew that wasn't the case. Still, surely it had been longer than twenty-four hours?

"It feels like months have passed because your adrenaline has been on high and your emotions and hormones have been going crazy," Julius said quietly, apparently reading his mind. "But it's only been a day."

"Jesus," Christian muttered, sagging with defeat.

"So," Julius said after a moment. "Do you think you can control yourself for the rest of the night?"

Christian nodded wearily. He'd have to.

"Good." Julius patted his back, and then glanced down at his jeans and muttered, "Maybe you should stand under the hand-dryer for a bit or something. You look like you wet yourself . . . a lot."

Christian glared. "And whose fault is that?"

Julius grinned, but before he could respond the bathroom door opened. His smile was immediately replaced with a scowl when Zanipolo entered. "What are you doing here? I told you to dance with Carolyn."

"I did, but then she wanted to stop and she insisted I come check on Christian," he explained as the door closed behind him.

"Why would you need to check on me?" Christian asked with surprise.

"What happened?" Zanipolo asked rather than answer the question. "You look like you wet yourself."

"Zanipolo," Julius gasped. "What have you done?"

Christian glanced to his father with surprise. Judging by his expression, he was reading Zanipolo's mind and was horrified by what he'd found there.

"Uh." Zanipolo eyed Julius warily and then glanced to Christian and said, "I was helping."

"Helping?" Julius asked with disbelief. "That wasn't helping, you idiot."

"What did you do?" Christian asked, alarm beginning to crawl up his spine.

"Uh, well." Zanipolo was beginning to look worried. "Carolyn asked me if you were all right because of how Julius dragged you off."

"And he told Carolyn that I had caught you winking at a waiter and I'd dragged you in here for an explanation," Julius said heavily.

Christian grimaced, but relaxed a little. She already thought him gay, telling her he'd winked at a waiter wasn't great, but he couldn't see it really being a problem. He could explain everything when he revealed all later.

"And then he told Carolyn that this might be for the best and if you came out of the closet you wouldn't have to hang all over her anymore."

"What?" Christian squawked.

"But this way you don't have to kiss her and stuff. You can keep your distance and just gain her friendship and trust," Zanipolo said quickly. "I mean, I thought the kissing and having to control yourself was proving to be a problem." He glanced to Julius with alarm. "Isn't that why you dragged him in here?"

Christian growled deep in his throat and headed for Zanipolo, physical violence on his mind, but Julius caught his arm.

"We can fix this," he assured him quickly when Christian turned on him.

"Fix what?" Zanipolo asked with confusion. "She already thought he was gay. Now she just thinks you might know."

"Which means he doesn't need a beard," Julius snapped.

Zanipolo frowned. "Well, yeah, but they're becoming friends and—"

"We can't trust in that," Julius growled. "It's only been twenty-four hours. It's a very tentative friendship at best right now. Should that roommate of hers wake up in the morning feeling better and ready to have fun, Carolyn could drop spending any time at all with Christian."

"Oh," Zanipolo said, with dismay. "I didn't—I mean, I thought—" He paused when Christian began growling again and sighed. "How do I fix this?"

Julius thought briefly and then said, "An orchid. You'll find one and—"

"Where am I going to find an orchid?" Zanipolo interrupted with a frown.

"I don't care. Rob a florist's if you have to, but if you do, leave the money in the till for it," Julius added with a frown. "But find an orchid, or something equally exotic and have the waiter bring it to her along with a card saying that she is as beautiful and rare as the flower."

Christian cleared his throat, and asked, "How is that going to fix—"

"Because you are going to tell her that was the explanation you gave me when we got in here, that you'd paid the waiter to go get the flower for her. That he'd winked to let you know that he had found a flower and that you winked back to indicate you understood. And, of course, you'll tell her that Zanipolo is out getting a flower now to uphold the lie."

"Right," Christian muttered on a sigh. Honestly, he'd never thought he'd find himself telling lies to make his life mate think he was gay of all things. It was just . . . well, he didn't know what the hell it was. He was so confused he didn't know what to think.

"Okay," Julius said. "Zanipolo, go find that flower. Christian, let's you and I get back to the table."

"Does this mean I can dance with her and—"

"No!" His eyes narrowed. "Do I need to take you back to the sink?"

Christian scowled and pushed past him to get out of the room in case the man decided to splash him again. Once in the hall, however, he asked, "So how am I supposed to tell her all this at the table with everyone there?"

Julius paused abruptly and cursed. He thought briefly, and Christian was just getting his hopes up when he suddenly relaxed. "You don't have to explain anything. She won't ask in front of everyone and once the flower arrives, I will explain that I nearly ruined the surprise when I caught you and the waiter communicating across the room with your eyes and misunderstood." He nodded. "That should do it."

"That should do it all right," Christian said glumly.

"Can you manage the good-night kiss?" Julius asked suddenly. "Or should I arrange it that—"

"I can manage it," Christian snapped. Cripes, there was no way they were taking that away too.

Julius nodded, but patted his shoulder and said, "Well, if you find yourself losing control, just remember you have sweet dreams to look forward to."

Christian just nodded and led the way up the hall. Zanipolo broke away, heading for the exit as they stepped out into the main room, but Christian hardly noticed. Carolyn was at the table, looking worried. He offered a reassuring smile and found himself picking up speed to reach her side.

The moment he settled in the chair next to hers, she

turned to him, her hand resting on his knee as she leaned up to ask in his ear, "Is everything all right?"

"Fine," he assured her, but Carolyn wasn't paying attention. Her gaze had dropped and she was now feeling her way up his leg. He sucked in a breath as her fingers crept up, but didn't move to stop her until he noted the way his father was eyeing him.

"Christian, you're all wet. What—?" she began, but paused and glanced up with surprise when he caught her hand.

"It goes all the way up," he growled, his voice not the only thing affected by her touch. Christ, at this rate his father would be pouring his drink in his lap, he thought with disgust.

"Oh." Flushing, Carolyn glanced away, looking embarrassed. "Sorry. I—"

"It's water," he added gently, releasing her hand. "There is a problem with the taps in the washroom."

"Oh." She grimaced. "I hate when that happens."

"So do I," Christian said dryly, casting his father a scowl.

"What?" Julius asked innocently. "I didn't have any problems. It was you who couldn't handle his taps."

"I can handle my taps just fine," Christian growled.

"It didn't look that way to me, son," Julius said and when Marguerite elbowed him, added, "Shine. Sunshine."

Christian rolled his eyes at the effort to cover the slip, and glanced at Carolyn to see her peering from him to his supposed brother with confusion.

"Come on, Caro," Gia said suddenly, standing up. "They're playing fast music again. Let's go dance."

Carolyn peered uncertainly at Christian. "Will you be all right? Is everything okay?"

Obviously the sniping between him and Julius had her

worried that things weren't as fine as he'd claimed. He forced a smile. "Yes. Go ahead. Have fun."

"Aren't you going to dance?" she asked, still hesitating.

"I don't do fast dancing," he said at once.

A surprised laugh slipped from Carolyn's lips and she shook her head. "You are so lame for a gayyyy"— she drew the word out, her eyes widening with horror as she realized what she was saying and then quickly tacked on —"mer."

"Gamer?" Julius chuckled as if not noticing the slip. "Has Christian been telling you about his love for that vampire game of his brother, Etienne's? What is it? Blood something?" he asked Christian.

"Wouldn't he be your brother too, Julius?" Carolyn asked.

Christian sighed as everyone went still, and said calmly, "Julius and I have different mothers." At least that was true. "And Etienne and the others and I share the same mother and different fathers."

Carolyn frowned. "So you and Julius have the same father and different mothers, and you and this Etienne and the others have the same mother and different fathers."

"It's very complicated," his mother intervened. "Why don't we dance now?"

"Wait a minute. Etienne? With a game called Blood something?" Carolyn asked with amazement. "Not Etienne Argeneau of Blood Lust?"

"Oh, you've heard of him?" Marguerite asked and Christian had to hide his grin as his mother preened with pride. She was proud of all her children.

"Of course," Carolyn said at once. "My advertising agency is pitching ideas for the ad campaign for his latest version of the game."

"My, what a delightfully small world," Marguerite said,

beaming, and Christian narrowed his eyes on his mother, but she ignored him. "I'm sure you'll win him over and get the contract, Caro dear. We'll put in a good word for you."

"Oh, no, don't be silly," Carolyn said at once. "If he likes the ideas that's one thing, but—"

"Nonsense, men do it all the time with their old boy's club business. We can start a girl's club," Marguerite said, slipping her arm through Carolyn's to draw her away toward the dance floor with Gia and Genie following.

Christian watched until they were swallowed up by the crowd, then settled back in his seat, waiting for them to reappear on the slightly upraised dance floor so he could watch Carolyn dance again.

"Take Gia's seat, Christian," Julius said suddenly.

He glanced around with surprise. "Why?"

"Because I don't want to have to take you back to the bathroom for a second round with the taps before we head to the resort," Julius said dryly.

Christian scowled, but switched seats so that his back was to the dance floor. He wasn't happy though, and was suddenly positive it was going to be a very long night for him.

"We'll leave as soon as Zanipolo returns with the flower," Julius said quietly.

Christian nodded silently.

"Thank you for my flower. I mean, I know it was just to cover for—"

Christian caught her arm and drew her to a halt as they reached the door to her villa. She'd been chattering nervously since he'd helped her out of the van. It was a notable difference from the relaxed woman he'd spent the day and dinner with. She'd grown a bit tense when the others had joined them for dinner, but as the evening had progressed without his kissing or putting his arm around her, she'd relaxed again. Now, however, just the thought of his kissing her had her all atwitter and it made him sad to see her like this. He couldn't wait for the day when she was relaxed with him all the time, well, except for when she was excited, he thought wryly and then sighed as he noted the way she was peering up at him.

"I'm going to kiss you," he said solemnly.

She nodded, but grimaced which really wasn't very flattering, or wouldn't be if he didn't know that the passion he stirred in her upset and embarrassed her mostly because she was afraid he would realize she was attracted to him and be offended.

"I know you're not attracted to me," he lied, "but I'd appreciate it if you could maybe close your eyes and pretend I'm someone you'd really like to kiss." He smiled and suggested, "Consider it practice for when you find someone you want to kiss."

"Practice?" Carolyn echoed blankly.

"Well, you said it had been seven years since you'd been intimate with anyone. I suspect that alone will make you a nervous wreck about it. But a little practice ahead of time with someone you aren't interested in and who you know won't take it the wrong way and expect you to go further might reassure you."

She blinked at the suggestion and suddenly smiled. "You know, it just might."

For some reason, that reaction sent a shot of alarm through Christian, but he nodded, drew her into his arms, and lowered his mouth to hers . . . and immediately understood the reason for the alarm. He'd meant to relax her and lay a quick gentle kiss on her lips, then leave . . . which proved what a fool he was. He doubted he'd have managed that even if he hadn't calmed Carolyn's nerves first, but his saying he knew she wasn't attracted to him and to think of it as practice without the worry of it going further . . . well, it seemed to have freed Carolyn somehow. The moment his lips touched hers, she opened her mouth for him and moved closer. That startled him enough that he paused briefly, but then she slid her tongue out and past his lips and slid her hands up to curl around his neck. The move raised her breasts and pressed them against his chest. It also snugged her hips to his, her softness rubbing against his sudden hardness. When she then tentatively lashed his tongue with her own, he just lost it. In the next heartbeat, Christian had one hand on her bottom, pressing her forward as he ground against her and the other hand sliding up under her top in search of her breast.

When Carolyn gasped and moaned, her body shuddering at his touch, he backed her up to the door, used his hand on her ass to lift her, and then pinned her there with his hips so that both his hands were free. His second hand immediately joined the first under her top, and then he was tugging at her bra cups, trying to pull them aside to free the bounty he'd found. He'd nearly accomplished it too when a sudden sharp pain in his ear made him break their kiss. Turning his head, Christian hissed, so far gone he bared his fangs before he recognized that it was his mother who had grabbed him by the ear.

"Uh, sorry," he muttered, retracting his fangs.

Marguerite nodded, but held on to his ear and said, "Release her."

Sighing, Christian closed his eyes briefly, and then slowly turned to peer at Carolyn. She was still and silent, her eyes vacant. His mother had taken control of her. Christian slowly retrieved his hands from under her shirt and clasped her arms to lower her to the ground as he eased away. He then stepped back and stood silently as his mother concentrated on Carolyn's forehead. After a moment, Carolyn turned, opened the villa door and moved silently inside before closing it behind her.

"I veiled her memories of what happened so she thinks it was just a very pleasant kiss and she's comfortable with it." His mother shifted to peer through the window beside the door, dragging him with her.

"Thank you," Christian said uncomfortably. "Do you think you could let go of my ear now, Mom?"

"Calling me Mom is not going to lessen my annoyance with you, Christian Notte," she announced grimly, still watching through the window. "I cannot believe you would jeopardize your entire future for one minute of pleasure."

"I'm sure it would have been more than a minute," Christian muttered, but felt himself flushing. He felt about twelve years old. How did parents do that to you? How could they make a five-hundred-year-old feel like a teenager caught parking with their girlfriend?

"Don't flatter yourself," Marguerite snapped, finally releasing his ear. "I read your thoughts as I approached. You were about to pull her legs around your hips, reach under her skirt, tug her panties aside, and slide home. A heartbeat after that the two of you would have been an unconscious heap on the stone."

Christian didn't try to deny it. But really, it was incredibly embarrassing to have his mother talking to him about this stuff.

"I don't care if it's embarrassing," she said with exasperation. "It has to be said. And just be glad it's me. Your father was going to intervene, but I managed to convince him to let me do it."

Christian glanced to the van where five pairs of eyes

were watching. The only one not gaping out the van windows at them was the driver of the resort van.

"Your father's controlling him," Marguerite announced. "I sent Carolyn in to go to bed. We had best get you back to the villa so you can do the same. And the first dream you enter with her, I suggest you move it out in front of the villa here for at least a quickie so that if my veiling of her memories doesn't hold, she'll just think those memories are from dreams."

"Right," Christian agreed, suddenly eager to get to bed.

"But Christian," she said solemnly, "you need to take this as a warning. You have to control yourself. If something like this happens when one of us isn't around to intervene you could send her running for the hills."

"Right." He nodded again. "Control myself."

Marguerite shook her head and led the way back to the van.

Ten

Christian followed Carolyn off the ladder onto the platform. When she moved to peer over the rail, he followed, noting that the ground looked a long way down. The pamphlet had said they'd be as high as 150 feet. His gaze slid over the wild beauty surrounding them and then to Carolyn's pale face and he asked with concern, "Are you sure you want to do this?"

She glanced to him and managed a laugh. "Why? Do I look terrified?"

"A bit," he admitted gently.

Smiling, she shrugged. "I'm just nervous because I've never done this before. I'll be fine once I get going," she assured him and stepped up to the guide to allow him to clip her harness to the cable.

Christian listened absently as the guide told her to sit and stick her legs straight out in front of her. He then gave her instructions on keeping her right arm behind the pulley, and lightly grasping the cable with her gloved hand to help keep herself steady. Carolyn was nodding, but she still looked pale and Christian was about to ask again if she was sure she wanted to do this when the guide suddenly released her and Carolyn went zipping away.

He expected her to shriek her head off all the way across, so was amazed when a happy "weeee" sounded that lasted the entire ten seconds before she reached the next platform, and Christian relaxed and found himself grinning as he stepped forward for his turn. His woman had surprised him again. There was more to Christiana Carolyn Johnson Carver Connor than first met the eye, but then perhaps he should have expected as much from a woman who carried so many names, he thought as he was suddenly sailing through the sky toward the platform where she waited.

"Isn't it a blast?" Carolyn cried, hopping up and down beside him as the guide worked to free him from the cable. "Oh my God, we have to do this again."

Christian chuckled at her enthusiasm, as he was freed. "We will. There are something like eight or nine more platforms."

"Yeah. But I mean another day even," she said quickly. "Every day. We should do this every day we're here."

Christian laughed and urged her out of the way as they waited for the rest of their party, but paused when she said, "This is better than sex."

That was damned insulting, considering they'd had sex three times in their sleep last night, and he'd thought it had been damned hot. As instructed he'd ensured that the first dream moved to her stoop and he'd happily repeated what had happened in real life, but even more happily had completed it pretty much the way his mother had suggested he would, but taking a little more time and care about it.

"Well, except for dream sex."

Christian barely caught the mutter and asked quickly, "What?"

"Nothing," she said flushing, but he'd heard her and it soothed his hurt ego and returned his good mood for the rest of the zip-line adventure.

"I think I'm going to try the pistachio-crusted chicken breast."

Christian glanced up from his menu at Carolyn's words and smiled. It had been after noon when they'd returned from zip-lining and they'd decided to hire a car and head into town to have lunch and tour the market. Genie had sent for a car for them and they'd asked the driver about restaurants during the ride. He'd delivered them here, to this lovely, open-air pavilion on the seaside with artwork littered about and benches heaped with pillows.

"Sounds good," Christian decided, setting his menu aside.

"You always order what I order," Carolyn said on a laugh.

Christian shrugged. "And I always like it."

"Hmm," she said with amusement. "Well, if we have room for dessert, do me a favor and order the chocolate banana cake."

He quirked an eyebrow. "Why?"

"Because I'm going to order the apple strudel, but I want to try the chocolate banana too. We can share."

"Sounds good," Christian repeated which made her laugh and shake her head as the waiter arrived. He poured them each an icy glass of water, took their order and slipped away, and Carolyn sat back against the pillow on her bench seat with a pleased little sigh. She glanced around at their picturesque surroundings, and then turned back and blurted out, "Beth wants me to have an affair while I'm here."

Christian raised an eyebrow and teased, "Here? The benches look comfortable, but I think the other restaurant guests might not appreciate it."

Carolyn blinked, flushed, and then tossed her napkin at him. "Not here, here. In St. Lucia, smarty-pants."

"Oh," he drawled with a grin and then asked, "How's she feeling, by the way?"

"Well, she wasn't retching this morning for a change, so I think she may be turning a corner," Carolyn said, and then grimaced and added, "I sincerely hope so since the cruise to Soufriere is tomorrow."

Christian nodded mildly, hoping she wasn't. If Bethany was better and they went on the cruise it meant he wouldn't get to see Carolyn all day. He'd already checked into getting a ticket on the day sail, but had been told it was fully booked. It was apparently a popular cruise.

"Anyway, she's been bugging me about this vacation fling thing," Carolyn said, returning to the subject she'd brought up.

"And how do you feel about it?" he asked. She seemed to want to talk about it.

"I'm not sure," she admitted, biting her lip. "At first I was totally against it."

His eyes narrowed. "But now?"

"Well, I've been thinking about what you said last night . . ."

"What I said?" he asked uncertainly.

"You know, when we had to kiss? And you said to think of it like practice for when I met someone I wanted for a mate or whatever."

Christian just blinked at her. She was completely re-laxed about their kiss the night before which was rather

unexpected considering her reactions to everything the
first night. His mother had said she'd veiled things and
made Carolyn think it was a pleasant kiss so that she
would be comfortable with it, but he hadn't expected this
much comfort. What the hell had Marguerite done? He
wondered and then recalled that Julius had said Carolyn
hadn't experienced real passion and that in her mind her
husband's kisses had been pleasant. Cripes, he thought
picking up his glass of water, his mother had made the
memory of their kiss a milk toast event.

"How am I at kissing?"

Caught by surprise, Christian choked on the water he
was drinking and spat it everywhere during the coughing
fit that followed.

"Oh, dear. That bad?" Carolyn asked dryly, helping him to mop up the mess he'd made when he finally
stopped coughing.

"No, of course not," he snapped and then sat back in
his seat to stare at her. "What the hell does that have to do
with Bethany wanting you to have an affair?"

"Well, like you said, kissing you is practice. But so
would an affair be." When his eyes widened incredulously,
she rushed on, "I mean, I haven't got a lot of experience
and five years of sexual rejection from my husband—"

"I thought it was seven years," he interrupted with a
frown.

"It's seven years since I've had sex. We've been separated for two though," she pointed out.

"Oh, right," Christian muttered.

"Anyway, that hasn't exactly left me feeling confident in my attractiveness or skill in that area," she said
with a grimace. "I mean, frankly, up until now I haven't
even considered ever getting involved with a man again.
I figured I'd just work and get a cat for company—or a

hundred," she muttered with a self-derision he didn't understand. "And just grow old and wait to die, I guess."

Christian frowned at the depression that settled over her, wanting to reassure her that she definitely wasn't going to grow old alone with nothing but cats. Hell, if he had it his way, she wouldn't grow old at all. But he couldn't say any of that, of course, so bit his tongue and waited.

Still he was surprised when she suddenly brightened and said, "But now I'm thinking maybe it doesn't have to be that way."

"Oh?" he asked warily.

She nodded and leaned forward eagerly. "I think I've hit early menopause."

Christian blinked several times. "Huh?"

"I'm having these dreams at night," Carolyn admitted, flushing.

"Oh?" he repeated, one eyebrow sliding up his forehead. He knew exactly what dreams she was talking about, but he wasn't supposed to. Besides, she looked half-embarrassed and half-eager and wholly adorable and he just wanted to hear her admit to having sex dreams. "What kind of dreams?"

"Er . . ." Her flush deepened, but she straightened her shoulders and admitted in a whisper, "Wet dreams, and they're really . . . um . . . steamy," she admitted turning an even brighter red and then rushed on, "And I've never had them before so it must be menopause. Right?"

"Steamy, huh?" Christian asked. They hadn't just been steamy for him. They'd been hot as hell. Widening his eyes innocently, he asked, "Who was in them?"

"Er," she said again, and then dropped her gaze and waved her hand vaguely, "Oh, just some celebrity sort."

"Like Brad Pitt?" he asked, feeling bad for making her

uncomfortable and thinking to offer her an easy lie, but she recoiled in horror at the suggestion.

"Oh, good lord, no! He isn't hot. I mean I suppose he is, but he isn't as hot as— And he's a blond," she said, her voice rising as she cut herself off.

"Ah." Christian bit his lip. She thought he was hotter than Brad Pitt. Gia said every woman on the planet wanted Brad Pitt. But he was hotter to Carolyn. God, he loved her.

The thought resounded like a gong through the sudden dead silence in his head. Christ, had he really just thought that? Yes he had, Christian acknowledged, but supposed he shouldn't be surprised. She was his life mate. It was inevitable that he'd come to love her. But up until now he'd just been thinking lustful, claim-her-and-make-her-his thoughts. He hadn't expected these other softer feelings to creep up on him so quickly.

"Anyway, aside from the dreams I think I'm having hot flashes." Carolyn's words caught his attention.

"Hot flashes?" he echoed uncertainly. She was far too young to have hot flashes, wasn't she? He didn't know. It wasn't something often discussed among his people, but it was on the news on occasion and he'd always thought it hit later.

"Yeah," Carolyn said with a sigh. "At least I think so. I woke up last night in a terrible sweat and . . . er . . . all worked up."

Well, that explained the abrupt end to the third and final sexual dream they'd shared last night, he thought. It had stopped abruptly, stirring him from sleep and leaving him too frustrated and wound up to sleep again.

"I was shaking too and kind of panicky," Carolyn said with a frown. "It was a bit scary, actually, but it got better after I got up and had something to eat." She grimaced at the memory. "Anyway, I think it must have been a hot flash, although I don't recall reading anything about anxiety and shaking with hot flashes."

"So," Christian said and paused when his voice came out a husky growl, cleared his throat, and tried again. "So, having these dreams and . . . er . . . hot flashes has made you decide maybe you want to have an affair?"

"Well, there're your kisses too," she said with an embarrassed laugh.

"My kisses?" he asked with interest.

Expression turning solemn, she nodded. "I know you're gay, and you would be far too young for me even if you weren't, Christian. I know better than to be attracted to you or anything."

"Er," he muttered, not sure how he was supposed to respond to that one.

"But you are a very good kisser," Carolyn assured him.

"Er," he said again, but he was grinning this time.

"And I've decided I like kissing, and want more of it," she announced.

Christian continued to grin until she rushed on, "But with a straight man my own age, of course. I mean I know you and I will probably have to kiss again while you're here, for your brother's sake, and I honestly don't mind. It's good practice, like you said, but it makes me think I might want to find someone else to kiss me too."

"What?" Christian scowled.

"Well, not while I'm helping you, of course," she reassured him. "I mean, it's not like I'd find anyone at honeymoon hell anyway. But I'm thinking that after you guys leave, Bethany and I should move to another resort, one where there are more single men, and then I can practice kissing and other stuff."

"What other stuff?" he asked, outraged.

"Well . . . you know," she said, with a grimace. "Other stuff."

Christian scowled at her for the very suggestion, but she wasn't paying attention. She was peering thoughtfully upward, several expressions flitting across her face. "Although, you know, now that I think about it, maybe we don't have to wait until the end of the week."

"*What*?" he asked with dismay.

"Well, think about it," she said cheerfully, her gaze returning to his. "If Bethany and I were to move to another resort, you could tell them you were coming to see me and we could hit the nightclubs and pick up guys together."

"*Pick up guys together!*" he cried, and then glanced around when she shushed him. Several people were looking their way. He scowled at them briefly, but turned back and lowered his voice. "Let me get this straight . . . a day or two ago you were totally not interested in a fling, but a couple of dreams and hot flashes later and you're ready to go out and—"

"Well, they're *very* hot dreams," Carolyn said almost apologetically. "I mean, if the real thing is even half as nice, it's miles ahead of anything I've experienced." She paused and then admitted, "I don't think Robert was very good at it. Which means I probably haven't got a clue. I mean some of the things in those dreams . . . " She flushed and waved her hand in front of her face. "I don't even know where they came from. I mean, you—" She paused abruptly, looking alarmed, and then cleared her throat. "I mean, the guy in the dreams seemed to really know his business. But of course, that was in my mind." She sighed. "It must come from books I've read or something. I usually skip the sex scenes, but I must have picked up a thing or two in the few I've read." Carolyn glanced at him. "But, still, a dream is one thing and real life is another."

"Exactly," Christian said firmly.

Relief coursed through him, until she added, "So, it seems to me it might be best to get the nerve-wracking and awkward first time or twelve out of the way with someone I'm never likely to run into again."

Christian gaped. He'd created a monster. Not that her wanting to explore her sexuality made her a monster, but she was supposed to want to explore it with him, dammit. Of course, that was impossible since she thought he was gay, he supposed.

Jesus, what had his family done to him? And what the hell was she doing discussing this with him anyway? She wasn't comfortable wanting him, but was burbling on cheerfully about menopause and wet dreams and having a fling or *twelve* with some guy she hadn't even yet met?

Obviously, she'd totally accepted him as gay. He'd completely replaced her buddy, Brent, who she'd once said she could discuss anything with. Again, what had his family done to him?

"Don't you think?" Carolyn asked, drawing him from his increasingly agitated thoughts.

"No, I don't," he snapped.

"You don't?" she asked, her shoulders drooping with disappointment, but then said, "Wait, what don't you think? That I should move to another resort? Or that I should have a fling?"

"Either," he growled. At least not with anyone but him, and then it wouldn't be a fling. He wanted her for life.

"Well . . ." Carolyn sat back blinking, and then almost whined, "Why not?"

Christian frowned. He couldn't tell her the truth, and without that he didn't have a single good goddamned reason to give her. And then it came to him, and calm flooded him, his agitation leaving him as he said, "Carolyn, you obviously aren't the type of woman to run around having flings."

"But I can change. I want to be that kind of woman," she said at once.

"What kind of woman exactly do you think that is?" he asked staying calm.

"Confident and sexy and comfortable in herself," Carolyn said at once. "The kind of woman who has sex on a beach, or up against a door, or in the wading pool, or on the terrace rail under the moonlight."

Yeah, that had been pretty hot, Christian thought with a little sigh of remembrance. The moonlight had shone down on her passion-filled face as he'd— Christian shook his head, and cleared his throat to say, "That's passion, not confidence or being comfortable with oneself. And do you really think you'll find that with some stranger you meet at a nightclub?"

"Well, why not? Even you manage to stir some passion in me and you're gay," she said grimly. "There must be loads of it in me somewhere. Surely a straight man could stir up even more?"

Christian ground his teeth, sure if she mentioned his supposedly being gay one more time, he'd—

"Pistachio-encrusted chicken breast for two."

Christian glanced up at that announcement, and immediately sat back for the waiter to set down their dishes. Once the man had gone, he suggested, "Why don't we shelve this conversation for right now and enjoy lunch?"

Carolyn didn't protest, but her jaw was set as she picked up her fork and began to pick at her food. She was angry and disappointed by his lack of support, Christian realized, and was suddenly worried. So long as she was willing to talk to him about it, he would have some warning if the passion building between them, not to mention the sexual frustration, moved her to do something stupid . . . and he could prevent her doing something she'd regret. However, if she got so annoyed she wouldn't share her thoughts and plans, he wouldn't have that opportunity.

Christian considered the matter as they ate their main dish, and when the plates were taken away, said, "I'm sorry. You're an adult, and know what you want. However, I just worry that you might rush headlong into something when going slow might be easier for you. I mean, you said yourself that you think the first time will be awkward and nerve wracking and I don't think you're considering that. It's not likely you're going to experience much passion in that state."

She frowned, but was listening, and Christian continued, "I mean, you're obviously comfortable with me . . . and knowing I'm not likely to try to push you into bed, you relax, which is probably why it allows your body to react as it does. And then in the dreams you're in control," sort of, he added to himself. "Your dream lover doesn't do anything to make you uncomfortable or rush ahead to . . . er . . . completion without exciting you first." At least he knew that was true. Carolyn was definitely with him every step of the way in the dreams, including orgasm . . . well, when they weren't interrupted, he thought, and wondered if she was buying any of this tripe he was feeding her. It was hard to tell from her expression. "So, wouldn't it be better for you to wait until you're comfortable with someone and not rush out and pick up the first guy who looks your way in a bar?"

Carolyn sat back with a sigh. "I suppose."

Christian almost melted into his seat his relief was so strong. But then he glanced to the side as their waiter appeared with their desserts. When the man left again,

Carolyn and Christian arranged the plates in the middle of the table between them to share.

"So," Carolyn said on a sigh as she scooped up a bite of apple strudel. "What are you going to do tomorrow while Bethany and I are on the cruise? If she's feeling up to it," she added, rolling her eyes.

Christian relaxed and smiled. She wasn't angry anymore. That knowledge stirred a relief in him like none he'd ever experienced.

Carolyn closed the villa door and turned to carry her bags to her room, but paused abruptly when she spotted Bethany at the top of the stairs in a bathing suit.

"You're up," she said with surprise. "And obviously feeling better."

"Yes." Bethany grinned, moving forward to help her with her bags. "I think it's finally done."

"Well, great," Carolyn said with a smile. "Why don't you go get dressed? It's almost dinnertime. We could—"

"Oh no, I don't want to push it and risk not being ready for tomorrow's cruise," Bethany said at once, leading the way to Carolyn's room with half the bags. "Instead, I was thinking we could order room service and eat here, have a glass of wine by the pool, and maybe a swim under the stars. Relax for a bit. Then we could have an early night so we're both well-rested for tomorrow's cruise."

"Oh," Carolyn said with surprise, and bit her lip as she followed Bethany to set down the bags she carried.

"I'm so glad to be feeling better," Bethany said as she sank onto the side of the bed. "I've been alone so long I think I'm ready to start climbing the walls."

"Oh, of course you are," Carolyn said, guilt immediately claiming her. Turning, she bent to hug her, saying,

"Honey, I'm sorry, I should have stayed and kept you company. I—"

"Don't be silly," Bethany laughed. "You offered, but I just didn't feel well enough for company. I mean, it's not like we could have talked anyway while I was hanging over the toilet," she pointed out with a grimace. "Still, I'm ready for company now . . . if you don't mind a quiet night in?"

"No, of course I don't mind," Carolyn assured her. "That sounds lovely."

"Good." Bethany stood. "Then let's go look at the room service menu and you can show me what you bought while we wait for dinner to show up."

"You go ahead," Carolyn said, moving toward the bathroom. "I'll be right out."

"Okay, but hurry," Bethany said cheerfully. "I suspect it will take a while for dinner to get here."

"I will." Carolyn closed the bathroom door behind her. Pausing then, she heaved a sigh and withdrew her phone. She'd made plans to have dinner alone with Christian and then sit with Marguerite and Julius while the band played. She'd have to call and cancel. Carolyn felt bad about it, but what could she do? She'd come here with Bethany. Christian and the others were new friends. She owed her loyalty to Beth . . . whether she'd rather go out or not, she thought unhappily, as she called the main building and asked to be put through to Christian's villa.

Carolyn paced the large bathroom as she waited for someone to pick up the phone, and felt an odd sense of relief when she recognized Gia's voice saying hello.

"Hi, Gia. How are you?"

"Caro!" Gia greeted. "I'm good, but Christian's in the shower. Do you want me to see if he'll—"

"No, no, that's okay," Carolyn said quickly. "I'm afraid

I was just calling to explain that Beth is feeling better."

"Oh, that's great," Gia said cheerfully. "I'll tell Christian when he gets out of the shower. He can call down and add another person to your reservation then."

"Uh, well," Carolyn dithered, but finally said, "Actually, no he doesn't have to do that. Bethany wants a nice quiet evening in and an early night so we can rest up for the cruise tomorrow."

There was a pause, and then Gia said, "I don't understand, if she isn't going to join you why—?"

"Well, that's the thing. She's feeling well enough that she wants company, so she suggested ordering in room service and relaxing here," Carolyn said quietly.

"Ah," Gia murmured. "So you're canceling on Christian."

Carolyn sighed as a wave of guilt assailed her, but said, "I'm afraid so."

"So he won't see you again until tomorrow night?" Gia asked.

"Uh, well . . ." Carolyn grimaced. "I'll have to call you back on that. It kind of depends on Bethany. I mean I came with her and can't just dump her to hang around with new friends. Especially when she's been so ill."

"Right," Gia breathed. "Well, have a nice night. You'll be missed."

"Thank you," Carolyn whispered and hung up. Letting her breath out slowly, she stared at herself silently in the bathroom mirror, wondering why she was suddenly so depressed.

Christian was whistling softly to himself as he walked into the kitchen to get a bag of blood. He'd grabbed two to take with him to the shower, but it had been another long day out in the heat with bits of sun here and there and he figured he needed a couple more before he left to collect Carolyn for dinner.

His whistling died slowly and his footsteps faltered halfway to the refrigerator when he spotted everyone standing around looking grim. Christian raised his eyebrows as his gaze slid over his parents and cousins. "What's up?"

"Carolyn called," Marguerite said quietly and something about her solemn tone made worry slip through him.

"What's happened?" he asked sharply. "Is she all right?"

"Yes, she's fine," Marguerite said quickly, and then added reluctantly, "In fact, she called with good news . . . It seems Bethany's feeling better."

Christian's eyes narrowed as the implications hit him one after another. His few days of having her to himself would be at an end. Either it would be he, Carolyn, and Bethany, or it would be Carolyn and Bethany and he would be out.

"I'm afraid it's the latter," Julius said, obviously reading his mind. "At least for tonight and tomorrow. She called to cancel dinner. Bethany feels better but wants them both to stay in, and have an early night in preparation for tomorrow's sail . . . and Carolyn feels she has to do so."

Christian cursed and turned to jerk the fridge door open.

"It's all right, Christian, we can deal with this," Marguerite assured him.

"How are you going to deal with it, Mother?" he asked sharply, retrieving a bag of blood. "Carolyn isn't the sort to abandon a friend she's on vacation with. She's going to stay in tonight, then sail off tomorrow and— Christ," he muttered, suddenly slamming the door closed and turning to them with alarm. "Bethany will encourage her to continue with that cockamamie plan of hers and sleep with the first guy who looks at her cross-eyed."

"What?" Gia asked with surprise. "What plan?"

"Oh dear," Marguerite murmured, her gaze focused on his head and pulling out the information without his needing to say it. "I hadn't considered something like this coming up."

Nobody asked what she was talking about. Everyone was now focused on his head, no doubt retrieving his memories of the entire lunch conversation. It was certainly there on the surface for them to find, he thought grimly.

"Oh, man," Gia muttered.

Marguerite said, "It's all right. We can handle both problems very easily."

"How?" Christian asked grimly.

"Well, Bethany is a simple matter of distraction. We have one of the boys romance her a bit and keep her busy, freeing Carolyn to be with you," Marguerite pointed out, smiling.

"I'll do it," Zanipolo offered at once. No one was terribly surprised. He was still into sex with mortals and something of a slut as Christian had said. But Marguerite shook her head.

"Thank you, Zanipolo, but I think Santo would be the better choice."

"Me?" Santo asked with shock. "Why me?"

"You have that mysterious silent man thing going for you and all that masculine virility. It will definitely distract any woman."

"I'm virile," Zanipolo protested at once.

"Yes, dear," Marguerite patted him soothingly. "I have another task for you."

"What's that?" he asked suddenly wary.

"You need to find an opportunity to kiss Carolyn."

"*What*?" Christian squawked.

"Well, it will kill any ridiculous notions she has that just any man can stir the passion in her that you do," she pointed out, moving to pat Christian's arm now.

"*What*?" Zanipolo cried. "I'm a good kisser."

"I'm sure you are," Marguerite said, turning to pat him again. "But the fact that Carolyn believed you might be the one in the band who was homosexual, suggests you are the one she finds least attractive, so—"

"What?" Zanipolo interrupted mournfully. "But why? Women like me."

"Yes, dear, of course they do. You're very funny."

"Funny?" Zanipolo asked with horror.

"In a charming way," she assured him quickly. "Women like amusing men."

"He's not kissing her," Christian said grimly.

"Now, Christian," Marguerite said, turning to pat him again. "Zanipolo—"

"Isn't laying a finger on my woman, let alone his filthy mouth," he snapped.

"Filthy?" Zanipolo turned on him with outrage.

Marguerite began to pat him again. "I'm sure Christian didn't mean—"

"The hell I didn't, his lips have been on more women than have died of cancer in all of history. And not just their damned lips. He's not kissing her."

"Now, Christian," Marguerite started to turn to him again, but Julius stepped forward and caught her arm.

"You're making me dizzy," he muttered, pulling her away. He then scowled at both young men. "Zanipolo, you'll kiss Carolyn. But no tongue, and no passion. And, Christian, you'll let him. Once she sees how lame his kisses are compared to yours, she'll give up this nonsense of taking a lover."

"*Lame*?" Zanipolo gaped. "I am *not* a lame kisser."

"Julius just means that the nanos aren't there with shared passion so they will seem lame," Marguerite said quickly.

"He's not going to kiss her," Christian repeated.

"Would you rather she kissed some random mortal?" Marguerite asked.

"She's not kissing anyone but me," he said grimly.

"We're trying to help you here, Christian," Julius said impatiently.

"It's your bloody help that caused this in the first place," he snapped. "Telling her I'm gay of all things. I should just march down there right now and tell her the truth about everything."

"Do you think she's ready for that?" Julius asked quietly.

"She may be," Marguerite murmured, surprising everyone. When Christian peered at her hopefully, she said, "She did feel comfortable enough to talk to him about sex." She frowned. "Of course, that may be just because she thinks he's gay and therefore safe, but I think if she isn't ready she's very close . . . Unfortunately, close isn't good enough. I'd rather you wait just a bit longer to be sure, son."

Christian shook his head. "I want to tell her everything and take my chances."

"In front of Bethany?" Julius asked.

"No, of course not, I'll ask Carolyn to come outside."

"And tell her on the stoop about immortals and life mates and that she's yours?" he asked dryly.

Christian frowned with frustration.

"And what will you do if she runs?" Julius asked.

"Chase her," Christian said without hesitation.

"You can chase her, but you can't keep her if she's unwilling. We'd have to wipe her memories of you, and you could never go near her again."

"What?" Christian gasped with horror.

"It's what is done," Marguerite said quietly. "We can't take the risk that she'd repeat what you've told her. It would endanger not just you, but our entire people."

"But you said Lucern, Bastien, and Etienne's women ran," he said desperately.

"Yes, but Kate, Terri, and Jackie already loved them and wouldn't have turned them in. It would have ripped out their own hearts to harm them." She tilted her head and asked, "Does Carolyn love you already?"

Christian frowned. He'd realized today that he loved her, but . . .

"Do you want to take that chance?" she asked.

Christian sighed in defeat and shook his head. Not yet. He wouldn't take the chance and lose her.

"Why not sleep on it tonight and wait and see what happens tomorrow?" Julius suggested sympathetically. "If Bethany comes down to dinner, Santo can put the moves on her and act as a distraction."

"Put the moves on," Santo echoed dubiously.

"And you can get more time alone with Carolyn. If your mother's right, she's gaining trust, and she likes you. Perhaps love isn't far behind."

"Right," Christian muttered, and finally slapped the bag of blood to his teeth.

Eleven

'The captain wants you to sit by him.'

Lowering the water bottle she'd been drinking from, Carolyn blinked at the big man in front of her. She then glanced to the helm to see the captain smile and nod, his shoulder-length brown hair blowing in the breeze.

Putting the cap back on her water, Carolyn slipped it in her bag and stood to move shakily toward the bow, wishing even as she did that she could just get off the boat and go back to the resort. She'd felt fine when she'd first woken up, but wasn't feeling so hot now. She was shaky, going hot and cold, and oddly off balance. But she'd been like that all night and suspected she was coming down with whatever Bethany had. If so, this trip was going to be one long torturous affair.

Thoughts of Bethany made Carolyn grimace. After their dinner, Beth had left her alone and gone to bed early. Carolyn had paced the villa for a bit, but then had gone to bed as well. However, she hadn't slept well. Her night had been one erotic dream after another, all featuring Christian Notte. And every dream had seemed to be interrupted before completion by a serious case of the sweats that had sent her to the kitchen in search of juice or food. She must have been up and down five times, she thought with a sigh. And every time she'd dropped off to sleep, she'd found herself starring in another porno with Christian.

Still, other than being a little tired, she'd been fine on first waking that morning and so had Bethany. Although, Carolyn had been in such a tizzy about waking up late that she hadn't really noticed other than to ask how Bethany was as she'd scrambled to get ready and rushed down to the boat with her. However, by the time they'd reached the main building and run into Genie, Carolyn had begun to feel bad again: a little queasy with hot flashes and an odd disorientation. She hadn't wanted to ruin Bethany's first outing, however, so had kept her increasingly alarming state to herself as Genie had rushed them to the dock and the waiting boat.

Genie had followed them onboard to have a word with the captain. The way she'd gestured repeatedly to them hadn't made it hard to figure out that she was giving him special instructions to make sure they had fun. Genie had left as the last of the guests got onboard and the captain started the engine. The crew had been untying the boat when Bethany had suddenly stood, muttering, "Oh God, I'm going to puke," and rushed off the boat.

Carolyn had stared blankly after her, her thoughts too muddled to grasp what was happening at first. By the time she'd figured it out and moved to follow Bethany, the boat was slipping away from the dock.

"No! Go! Have fun! I left the cooler with the water and suntan lotion there. Make sure you use both," Bethany had called, waving her back as Carolyn had stared at the growing distance between the boat and the dock, trying to sort out if she could manage the jump. She might even have tried it despite the swiftly yawning distance had not one of the crew caught her arm and pulled her away with a shake of the head. Frowning, and a little befuddled as to how she'd suddenly ended up all alone on a cruise full of honeymooners, Carolyn had returned to her seat.

It seemed, however, that the captain was taking a special interest thanks to Genie, Carolyn thought as she made her way to the helm where the captain stood watching her unsteady approach with narrowed eyes. She was going to get to sit at his side like the teacher's pet in class, she thought as she reached him. Great.

"Caro or Beth?" the captain asked, urging her to the seat next to the helm.

"Caro." Carolyn climbed onto the stool with resignation.

"I'm Jack," he announced.

"Captain Jack." She nodded, and smiled wryly. "Like the pirate."

He grinned, but simply dropped a necklace of flowers over her head, announcing, "This makes you the ship mascot. We have one every trip."

Translation: charity case, Carolyn thought as he signaled to the big, brawny guy who had fetched her. He was obviously a crew member, though he could have passed for a guest. There were no uniforms, everyone onboard wore shorts and T-shirts, including her. The signal was apparently to bring a drink, she realized, when the man appeared before her with a plastic cup of what looked like orange juice.

"Your morning vitamin C to ensure you have a good day," Captain Jack said as she accepted the drink. "Best toss it back quickly, we're about to hit choppy water."

Carolyn glanced out at the water, noting that it was indeed choppy ahead. She supposed they were about to pass the coral reefs. She wasn't sure, but thought those kept the waves down some. Whatever the case, drinking the juice quickly seemed smart if she didn't want to wear it, and she drank half of it in one gulp, only to come up gasping.

"Sorry, should have warned you that we put a little firewater in to keep your blood up," Captain Jack said on a laugh, slapping her back as she began to cough.

"It's seven thirty in the morning," she got out, her voice raspy and shocked.

"Yeah, but you looked like you could use it to help you get in the mood," he said with a shrug.

Carolyn grimaced. "The mood for what?"

"Fun. Genie said to show you a good time and that's what we're going to do. Right, boys?"

Carolyn glanced toward the men who were all grinning and nodding. They were an eclectic crew. While Captain Jack was a tan and buff white man who looked to be in his late thirties, his crew ranged in age from young to late twenties with one large, brawny fellow who could be mid-thirties. They also ranged in color from a freckled redhead to a couple of men who were obviously native islanders.

"Drink up," Captain Jack said, gesturing to her still half-full glass. "It will loosen you up. You can't have fun when you're as tense as a virgin on her way to be sacrificed. Besides, I don't want everyone else to get wind of the fact that there's alcohol onboard. They'll want some and it's not supposed to come out until the trip home."

Carolyn grimaced, but the orange juice had actually eased some of her queasiness. And she was pretty sure one drink wouldn't hurt, so she shrugged and tossed back the rest of the drink.

"Good girl." Captain Jack took her empty glass to discard, and turned back to the helm, but then glanced over. "So your friend left. Sick?"

Carolyn nodded. "Since the night we arrived. We thought it was food poisoning, but I don't think it should last this long."

"Probably flu," he said. "It's been going around the island."

"Hmm." Carolyn grimaced. If it was the flu, she'd probably get it next.

"Any other friends here?" Captain Jack asked, adjusting course a bit.

"Genie," Carolyn answered.

He nodded, his gaze drifting to her hand. "And you're not married but were?"

Carolyn rubbed the telltale indent on her ring finger. "On the tail end of a very long, two-year divorce."

"Two years . . . so not still at the screwed-up stage. Ready to date?"

Carolyn chuckled at the exaggerated leer he produced. "I don't think Genie meant you had to go that far to make sure I have a good time."

"I'm sure she didn't," he agreed with a grin. "But you're a pretty single lady and I'm a handsome single guy and everyone knows captains make the best lovers. We know how to harden up."

"Oh," she groaned. "That's a horrible play on words."

He raised an eyebrow. "You know what 'harden up' means?"

"Sailing close to the wind." She'd read it in a book just a couple of weeks ago.

"Damn," he breathed. "I'm impressed. I usually have to explain that joke. Sometimes after I'm slapped."

His words made her laugh as she suspected he'd intended.

"You have a nice laugh. You should do it more often. It makes your eyes twinkle," he said with a smile. "So how long are you here?"

"Another week and a half."

"Nice. Gives us lots of time to get to know each other," he announced. "I came here for a week ten years ago. It's been a long week."

"I'd say so," Carolyn agreed with a laugh, wondering why she wasn't uncomfortable with his compliments and flirting. She suspected it was because she knew he was only doing it under Genie's orders. The man wasn't really interested in her. He'd do his job, show her a good time, then set her ashore at the end of the cruise and not give her another thought.

Captain Jack glanced aft again and straightened. "Looks like we're about to hit those waves I mentioned. Don't mind me if I'm a bit distracted until we get around the point. You just sit there and look pretty while I impress you with my naval mastery."

Carolyn smiled. "If you say so."

"That's 'Aye-aye, Captain' to you, wench," he said lightly, turning to place both hands on the wheel.

Carolyn shook her head with amusement and wondered what the hell was in the punch as Captain Jack concentrated on riding the waves toward the point. She wasn't generally this comfortable with someone this quickly, and she normally didn't know how to handle attention from men. Not that she received it often, but on the rare occasion when she did, she tended to get flustered and uncomfortable and do her best to escape the situation.

"Right-o," Jack said moments later as the boat began to pitch a bit. "This shouldn't last long. It'll calm once we get around the point."

Carolyn nodded and retrieved her water from her bag

to take a drink. She then put it away and turned in her seat to peer toward the bow as they moved through the choppier water.

"Like I say, it'll be less rough once we get around the point," Captain Jack repeated, glancing her way as he pushed up on the throttle to send them moving faster. She didn't understand the reason for his repeatedly saying that until he asked, "You don't get seasick, do you?"

"Not that I know of. This is my first time on a boat," she said.

His eyes widened at the admission. "You're kidding?"

"No."

"Well, hell, woman, where do you live? The desert?"

Carolyn chuckled and shook her head at the suggestion. "Toronto, Canada."

"Yeah?" He grinned. "I have family there."

"You're Canadian?" she asked with surprise, and when he nodded, she muttered, "I keep running into them here."

"I'm not surprised. St. Lucia was a British colony like Canada and our two countries have a good relationship. A good number of the tourists who come here are Canadian and British."

She nodded and held on to her seat as the ride got a little bumpier. When she noticed Captain Jack eyeing her with concern, she raised her eyebrows in question.

"You look pale. How's your stomach?"

Carolyn hesitated. She was queasy again, but she was also feeling flushed and shaky as well, just as she had before she'd had the drink earlier. Her heart was also racing in her chest as if she'd run a marathon. She'd been experiencing those symptoms since yesterday, though, they just seemed a little worse now. She didn't think it could be seasickness, and was wondering if it was even flu now. It didn't feel like any flu she'd ever had. Recalling that the drink had helped if only temporarily and suspecting it was the orange juice, she shook her head. "I'm okay. I think I just need some juice or something."

"Diabetic?" he asked with a frown.

"No, I skipped breakfast and—" She paused as he turned to gesture to one of the crew again. A heartbeat later the big, bulky guy was in front of her with another full glass and a big grin. She eyed it suspiciously. "It's just juice this time, right?"

"Sorry, all the juice is already mixed into the punch," Jack said apologetically. "Just sip it and see if it helps again."

Carolyn grimaced, but took the drink. Noting that Jack's concern appeared to have deepened suddenly, she raised her eyebrows. "What?"

"Your hand's shaking," he said grimly and then turned and began searching through a small open shelf by his hip. Straightening a moment later, he turned and handed her a chocolate bar. "Try this."

Carolyn set her glass between her knees to free both hands to open the chocolate bar, frowning when she found the task taxing. Aside from disoriented, she was suddenly extremely clumsy. It was a bit scary actually, and she was relieved when she got the bar wrapper open. Sighing, she took a bite.

"If it's low blood sugar it will take a couple of minutes for you to start feeling better," Jack said as she finished the bar moments later.

Carolyn nodded and balled up the wrapper, placing it in Jack's hand when it appeared before her.

"Thank you," she said as he discarded it in a small bag on the open shelf.

"My pleasure."

They were silent for several minutes, and Carolyn retrieved her drink and continued to sip it, thinking the added sugar should help. But she was aware as she did that Jack's gaze kept shifting repeatedly from the water ahead to her and could feel his concern. However, after a bit she started to feel better.

"Your color's better," he said suddenly, holding his hand out for her now empty glass.

"I'm feeling better," she admitted, handing it over for him to discard as she stood up. She then leaned against the stool and peered out over the water as she said, "Thank you."

"Like I said, my pleasure," he assured her, and then his gaze on the water ahead, he added, "You know what this means, right?"

"What?" she asked uncertainly.

"Well, I've showered you with flowers, bought you drinks, and given you chocolate . . . we're practically going steady now."

Carolyn blinked and then burst out laughing. "You're a terrible flirt, Captain."

"Actually, I'm a wonderful flirt," he assured her. "I'm charming as hell."

"Yes, you are," she agreed with amusement.

"But you seem to be immune," he said conversationally. "Is it the boy?"

"The boy?" Carolyn asked uncertainly.

"I came into the bar a couple nights ago after the midnight cruise and you were with some young buck. Ambrose behind the bar said he was from the band."

"Oh, you mean Christian." Carolyn laughed suddenly and shook her head. Funny she hadn't thought of him right away. While she'd seen him as a boy herself when they'd first met, the longer she spent with him, the less young Christian seemed to her. "We're just friends."

"Good friends?" he asked meaningfully.

"No, he's ga—" Carolyn cut herself off abruptly and slammed her hand over her mouth as she realized what she was saying.

"Gay?" Captain Jack asked with surprise.

"No," she said at once, but then scowled and added, "Don't tell anyone. I promised not to tell." Shaking her head, Carolyn muttered, "And I said Bethany was the blabbermouth. What the hell was in those drinks?"

Jack grinned. "Sugar and spice and everything likely to loosen a girl's lips."

"Hmm," Carolyn said, glowering out at the water.

"So the young buck's a buckette," Jack marveled. "Who woulda thunk it?"

Carolyn groaned and he patted her shoulder soothingly.

"His secret's safe with me . . . Certainly safer than it is with you," he teased.

"Did I say you were charming?" she asked with a grimace.

"No, I said it, you just agreed," he assured her.

"I must have been drunk."

Captain Jack chuckled, but then his laughter faded and he asked seriously, "So what's with all the hand-holding and his having his arm around you business?"

"He wasn't holding my hand or anything when we were in the bar alone," she said with a frown.

"So maybe I've noticed you more than once the last couple of days," he said with a shrug.

Carolyn's eyebrows rose.

"So?" he prompted, when she remained silent.

"His family doesn't know, so his cousin asked me to play his date while he's here," she admitted quietly.

"Ah." He nodded. "Good to know."

"Why?" she asked at once.

"It means you're still on the market," he said lightly and grinned at her.

Carolyn shook her head and settled back in her seat, her gaze sliding over the two dozen passengers. Every single person was part of a couple, of course, except for herself and the crew. How depressing was that?

"So is it always honeymoon central here?" she asked abruptly.

Captain Jack shrugged. "It's that time of year. From Valentine's till June we usually have a lot of honeymooners." He took in her expression, and then stepped back from the helm and held out his hand. "Come here. The mascot gets to steer the boat for a while on these cruises. It's in the rules."

Carolyn hesitated, but then decided, why not? It was better than sitting there staring at the couples billing and cooing around her.

"Here come the shuttles for the tour."

Christian followed the driver's gaze to three minibuses trundling toward them. After a night filled with incredibly erotic, but frustratingly interrupted dreams, Christian had gotten up and stood watching at the windows until he'd seen Carolyn and Bethany leave their villa to board one of the resort vans. He'd turned away then and gone into the bathroom to splash water on his face and brush his teeth, and had been coming back out ten minutes later when he saw the van pull up in front of the villa down the hill again. Frowning, he'd paused, watching with surprise as Bethany had gotten out and rushed inside.

Christian had wondered briefly why the woman wasn't on the cruise, and where Carolyn was, and then had found himself throwing on clothes and hurrying down to the main building.

He'd found Genie almost at once and learned that Bethany had returned on her own, leaving Carolyn alone on the boat. When she'd then offered to transfer Bethany's ticket to him, and arrange for a car to take him to Soufriere to meet up with the tour, he'd immediately agreed.

"And there is the boat," the driver said now, drawing Christian's attention to a large boat with a crowd of people on it. It was still a distance away, but he thanked his driver, tipped him, and slid out to walk to where the boat would dock. It took him a moment to spot Carolyn, mostly because he'd started out looking for her among the passengers. Not finding her there, he turned his attention to the helm. His eyes widened and then narrowed as he spotted her at the wheel, laughing at something a shaggy-haired mortal was saying.

Christian scowled when the shaggy-haired guy stepped up behind Carolyn, his arms enclosing her as he clasped the wheel around her body. Christian's mood and expression didn't improve much when Carolyn laughed and ducked out from under the man's arm to escape the intimate hold. She didn't move far away, just to a seat next to him and she seemed to be having far too good a time. Christian didn't like the appreciative way shaggy was eyeing her either.

A growl caught his ear, and Christian actually glanced around before he realized there was no one nearby and that the sound had come from his own throat. Forcing himself to relax, he tried for a casual smile as he waited for the boat to dock.

* * *

"Isn't that band boy?"

Carolyn lowered her water bottle to glance around to where Captain Jack was peering, her eyes widening when she spotted Christian onshore.

"He doesn't look happy."

"He plays in a band, I doubt he's a morning person," Carolyn murmured as she noted that while Christian was smiling, it was more a baring of teeth, and tension was in every line of his body. "I wonder what he's doing here."

"Joining the tour would be my guess," Jack said. "He must have missed the boat. That's one of the resort cars leaving."

Carolyn glanced toward the car now trundling away from the dock, noting the resort logo.

"Well, at least I know you'll have a girlfriend to keep you company on the land side of the tour," Jack commented.

Carolyn turned to scowl at him. "That's just mean."

"No." He grinned. "That's relief because I don't have to worry about competition from a younger man who's built like a fricking male model."

Carolyn just shook her head, not taking him seriously. The man really was a flirt, and he was just doing as Genie had asked and making sure she enjoyed herself, she thought as her gaze slid back to Christian. He really was well built, tall, with wide shoulders that narrowed down to slim hips. His T-shirt was tight enough that you could see the curve of his pecs and his six-pack stomach.

"You should have fun on the tour," Jack commented. "But we'll be waiting when you come back and the return ride is tons of fun. By then it's sunny and hot, and we break out the punch to loosen everyone up for the contests."

"Contests?" she asked, forcing her gaze away from Christian and to him again.

"Wait and see. I don't want to spoil the surprise." The wicked tilt to his grin was a bit worrying, especially when he added, "As ship's mascot you are expected to join in by the way so save some energy."

"Uh huh," Carolyn said, her eyes narrowing on the twinkle in his eyes. She suspected she wasn't going to like these contests. "Speaking of ship's mascot, you'd better have this back. I don't want to ruin it while land side." Carolyn removed the necklace of flowers and raised her eyebrows in question. "Where do I put it?"

Captain Jack grinned and removed one hand from the wheel to turn toward her. When he bent his head, she slipped off her seat and leaned up to lift it over him, her eyes widening when she felt his hand at her waist.

"You're pale again," he said quietly, his hand sliding around her back and steadying her when she stumbled against him. "Do you need another chocolate bar?"

Carolyn dropped the necklace around his neck and moved back with a sigh, but he didn't release her and she was partially flustered by that fact and partially grateful. She was shaky and off-kilter again and his hold kept her from stumbling around like a drunken idiot. The queasiness had returned as well, but despite that she shook her head, not wanting to be a bother. "I'll be fine. We eat at the cocoa plantation."

"Hmm." He eyed her silently, and then said, "Hang on to the wheel for a minute." When she reached out to place a hand on it, he immediately turned to dig through his shelf again, coming up with another chocolate bar. "Take this anyway, just in case. It's a long way to Fond Doux."

"Thank you," Carolyn murmured. She slipped the chocolate bar into her bag and settled on her seat once more as he took the wheel. "Fond Doux is the cocoa plantation, right?"

Jack nodded, but he was looking ahead again and his eyes narrowed. "Yeah, band boy definitely isn't a morning person."

Carolyn glanced back to the dock. Christian was now pacing, arms crossed and a scowl on his face as he watched them approach. She didn't comment, but simply watched Christian curiously as Jack eased back on the throttle. The moment he steered the boat up to the landing, the crew burst into action, grabbing lines of rope and leaping off to fasten the boat in place.

"Stay put," Jack ordered when Carolyn started to slip off her seat to join the other passengers lining up to disembark. "Shaky as you are you're likely to take a dip in the drink if someone bumps you as you're getting off."

Carolyn grimaced, but settled back in her seat. Mostly because she knew he was right. She wasn't happy doing it though. Now that they'd docked, she wanted off . . . and it had absolutely nothing to do with a sudden eagerness to talk to Christian, she assured herself. After all, he was gay. Right?

"Okay," Jack said finally, and then immediately caught her arm when she leaped off her stool and nearly overbalanced and fell on her face. Frowning, he said firmly, "You should have eaten that chocolate bar. And I think you should be tested for hypoglycemia when you get back to Canada."

"Hypoglycemia?" she asked with surprise.

He nodded. "I have an aunt with it and you're acting like she does when her blood sugar's low." He led her across the boat. "It's not something to be messed with."

They'd reached the side of the boat, and Carolyn gasped in surprise when Jack suddenly caught her by the waist to lift her over the foot-wide gap between boat and landing. Christian was immediately there, clasping her waist above Jack's hands, his thumbs just below her breasts as he tried to take her, but Jack didn't let go and she dangled briefly over the water between the two men as he said, "She keeps going pale, gets the shakes, and gets a bit disoriented. I think her blood sugar's low. Keep an eye on her and make sure she eats the chocolate bar in her bag."

The scowl on Christian's face eased somewhat, replaced by concern as he peered sharply at Carolyn.

"I skipped breakfast," she muttered with embarrassment, wishing they'd put her down. She didn't particularly want to take a dip in the drink and was very aware that it was right beneath her.

Christian eyed her for a moment, his gaze sliding over her face, and then he glanced to Jack, his voice grudging as he said, "Thanks for looking out for her."

"Don't thank me," Jack laughed, finally releasing her. "I enjoyed it. I'm just glad she has a friend to look out for her on land. I'd be disappointed if she fell ill and wasn't on the return journey."

Carolyn felt her face heat up and wasn't sure if it was Jack's teasing or the fact that the sides of Christian's thumbs were rubbing against the bottom of her breasts as he eased her to the dock. She stepped away from him as soon as her feet hit the wood, and then sighed as she swayed and Christian immediately took her arm.

"Hang on." Jack moved back to the helm. She wasn't surprised when he returned with another chocolate bar. Holding it out, he said, "A spare. Make sure you have one as soon as you're in the bus. And eat a big meal at the plantation."

"You're going to run out of chocolate at this rate," Carolyn said as she leaned forward to take the offering. Christian's hands were immediately at her hips to keep her from overbalancing and plunging into the water and Carolyn felt herself flush again.

Jack grinned at her embarrassed expression, and shook his head. "Nah. I'll buy another box of them while you're gone. Then I'll give you flowers, chocolate, and drinks on the way back and we'll really be going steady."

Carolyn flushed again and muttered, "Thank you," then straightened and glanced around with surprise when something like a growl came from Christian.

"The buses are waiting for us," he said grimly, urging her away, his hands still at her hips.

"Have fun, wench," Jack said cheerfully and Carolyn managed a smile and wave over her shoulder before Christian dropped his hold on her waist to take her arm instead and began to move so fast she had to watch where she was going or risk falling on her face. Not that she probably would have, he was holding her arm too tightly for that. Painfully tightly, actually, she noted with a frown. Before she could ask him to ease up, she did stumble. Christian didn't even miss a beat, but scooped her up in his arms and continued quickly to the buses.

Twelve

'I can walk,' Carolyn muttered with embarrassment as they were waved past the first and second full
minibuses to the third one.

"Not fast enough," he said shortly.

Carolyn scowled, but held her tongue as he carried her
onto the bus. She wished she'd insisted though when she
saw the curious stares they were garnering. He carried
her to the only empty bench seat in the very back on the
right and settled on it with her in his lap.

"Er . . ." Carolyn murmured, at a bit of a loss. Everyone
was staring and . . . well, she was in his lap, for heaven's
sake. It was bad enough he'd carried her on, but he could
have set her on the seat. Instead, he was holding her in
his lap as if she were an injured child . . . or a lover, she
thought as his scent enveloped her now that they weren't
moving. He smelled like the jungle on a rainy day, a
slightly musky scent that made her forget people were
staring. It also made her suddenly aware of the heat of his

chest pressing along her side and his hard lap beneath her.

Biting her lip, Carolyn raised her head, her eyes widening when she met his gaze and found herself staring into eyes more silver than black. Silver. Not gray. She'd never seen anything so beautiful . . . or impossible.

"Your eyes," she whispered with confusion as they began to move closer, almost as if his head were lowering to hers, she thought with bemusement.

Christian stilled at once, and then shifted her to sit on the bench seat beside him. Oddly enough, while it was what she'd wanted moments ago, she now felt a pang of disappointment.

"Eat your chocolate," he growled.

"But your eyes," she said, shifting on the seat to try to see them again.

"Colored contacts," he said grimly. "Eat your chocolate."

Carolyn frowned at how snappy he was being, but settled back in her seat to unwrap her chocolate bar. The damned wrapper must have been sealed with Krazy Glue. She couldn't seem to get the thing open, but gasped with surprise when Christian cursed and snatched it from her fumbling fingers. His face was grim, his jaw clenched as he impatiently opened it for her.

"There. Eat," he snarled, pushing it back at her. When she didn't take it right away, his gaze shifted to her face and he frowned. "What's wrong?"

"That's what I'm wondering," she said wearily. "You're snapping at me like I stole your favorite toy."

Christian glanced away, then sighed, peered back, and offered an apologetic half-smile. "Sorry. I'm not a morning person."

Carolyn relaxed a little and took the chocolate bar, mumbling, "Jack said that was probably the case when you were scowling at us from the dock. Or maybe I said it," she added with a frown. It was hard to recall just then. One of them had said it.

"Eat your chocolate," Christian said, every word carefully enunciated. "Your hands are shaking so bad I'm surprised you can hold it."

Carolyn shifted her attention to her hands, noting absently that they were indeed shaking. She was also all sweaty again, and her heart was racing as if she'd been running. On top of that, it was growing hard to think. When Christian suddenly caught the hand holding the chocolate bar and pulled it toward his face, she thought he was going to take a bite himself, but instead he turned her hand and pressed his nose to the inside of her wrist. Carolyn just gaped as he inhaled deeply, and then he cursed and quickly urged the hand toward her until the chocolate touched her lips.

"Eat," Christian growled.

"What's wrong with my perfume?" she asked with a frown.

"What?" he asked, the confused one now.

"You sniffed me and cursed," she explained. "What's wrong with—" Carolyn's words died as he urged the chocolate into her open mouth. It seemed she would eat or he would shove it down her throat. Scowling at him around the bar, she took a bite, relieved when he let go.

"There's nothing wrong with your perfume," Christian said grimly as she chewed. He stood up, muttering, "It's your blood that's the problem."

Carolyn stared after him with amazement as she chewed. He was walking slowly up the aisle, his gaze moving over the people on the bus as he went. She had swallowed and taken a second bite when he suddenly paused and turned to an older couple on the right. She didn't see his lips move, but suddenly the woman held up a bottle of orange liquid to him. Christian took it and immediately headed back to her, moving much more swiftly.

"Here."

She stared blankly at the bottle of orange juice when he opened it and held it out. "How did you—"

"Drink," he insisted quietly. "It will get the sugar into your system faster than the chocolate and you need it, *cara*. Your blood sugar is bottoming out."

Carolyn blinked. His anger appeared to be gone now, concern and caring in its place.

"Drink," he repeated, pressing the bottle to her lips.

She took over holding it and opened her mouth to allow the liquid to pour in. It was cool and sweet and she drank it quickly. The moment she lowered the empty bottle, Christian took it back, recapped it, and set it on the seat between them. He then gestured to the chocolate bar, and watched silently as she continued to eat it. He just sat there staring at her as if she were a child and he needed to be sure she ate the bar and didn't shove it down the side of her seat or something.

"Stop staring at me," she muttered. "You're as bad as Captain Jack."

That made his mouth twist with displeasure and annoyance creep back to replace some of the concern on his face. His voice was tart when he said, "You appear to have made a friend in Captain Jack. He was all over you on the boat."

Carolyn raised her eyebrows at his testy voice and eyed him silently as she popped the last bite of chocolate into her mouth. If she didn't know he was gay, she'd have said he was jealous of the man. But he *was* gay, so there was no reason for this reaction. Unless . . .

* * *

Uncomfortable under her narrowing gaze, Christian took
the chocolate wrapper from her, balled it up, and glanced
around, wondering if there was a garbage container at
the front of the bus. His gaze found the woman standing
beside the driver. She'd been droning on for a couple of
minutes about the highlights of Soufriere and its history.
He hadn't caught a word of it.

"You're jealous."

That accusation from Carolyn made him glance to
her sharply with surprise. It was true. Jealousy had been
eating at him like acid since he'd seen her laughing and
chatting with the boat captain. But it had positively devoured him when the man had put his arm around Carolyn as she'd placed a necklace of flowers around his neck.
He'd wanted to wring his neck, and he probably would
have had he been on the boat. She was his life mate. No
man should touch her.

Christian's reaction had been just as visceral when the
man had lifted Carolyn off the boat. He couldn't move
quickly enough to get her out of his hands, and when the
fellow had resisted his taking her and held on, he'd seen
red. Christian had been about to slip into his thoughts
when the fellow had said that bit about her blood sugar.
Christian had forced himself to relax then, but it had
been a struggle. The captain was entirely too comfortable
touching his woman.

And Carolyn hadn't protested it either, he thought
grimly. But then she had no idea yet that she was his. She
thought he was gay, which was why he was surprised that
she recognized he was jealous.

"It's okay." She patted his hand now. "I understand. He
is a hottie. All those tan, rippling muscles and the piratey
hair."

Christian ground his teeth together and considered

wringing her neck instead of Captain Jack's. How dare she think the man a hottie? And what was she doing noticing his rippling muscles? She was his, dammit, whether she knew it or not.

"Not my type," she continued. "I mean, he seems nice enough and all, and probably loads of fun, but there was just no spark for some reason."

While Carolyn was now frowning, apparently perplexed as to why that would be the case, Christian felt himself relax and even begin to grin at these words. She wasn't attracted to Captain Jack, rippling muscles and piratey hair or not. Ha!

Heaving a sigh, she said more cheerfully, "The good news is, he was only flirting with me because Genie told him to make sure I had a good time, so who knows, you may yet be in luck. He could be gay too." She looked dubious even as she said it, but then added encouragingly, "Or maybe bisexual at least."

Christian blinked as it slowly dawned on him that she thought he was jealous of her rather than of Captain Jack. Dear God!

"Oh look, we're stopping."

Christian glanced around to see that they had pulled up beside a line of outdoor stands offering island jewelry and the like. Everyone on the bus began to stand to disembark, but when Carolyn did, he frowned.

"You should wait here. Your blood sugar—"

"I'm good now, the juice and chocolate did wonders," she assured him scrambling past his legs to get out.

Christian reached to stop her, but paused as her behind was suddenly in his face.

"Damn," he breathed and nearly grabbed the two round cheeks in front of him, but then she was past and moving eagerly up the aisle behind the others.

Giving his head a shake, Christian stood to follow, knowing it was a mistake even as he did it. He'd been in such a rush to get down to the boat that morning that he hadn't thought to feed, let alone to down several extra bags to make up for the exposure to sunlight. The last thing he needed was to be out in the sun, but he couldn't leave Carolyn on her own. Her physical symptoms had been worrying enough, but when he'd sniffed her wrist the scent of her blood had been telling. Captain Jack had been right. She'd been bottoming out with low blood sugar.

Mouth tightening, Christian plunged out into the sunlight to follow Carolyn toward the first stall as everyone spread out to look at the offered wares. He followed her silently from stall to stall, his eyes moving warily from her happy face to the sun and back.

"Oh, look, Christian, this one's lovely."

Pausing behind Carolyn, Christian gazed over her shoulder to the necklace she'd picked up. It was made up of rows of small polished black stones separated by tiny silver beads.

"What do you think?" she asked.

"Nice," he murmured, imagining it against her naked skin.

"I'll take it," Carolyn said to the woman and then picked up one that had a handful of pink stones among the black and said, "This as well."

Much to his relief their guide called a halt to the shopping trip then and everyone piled back on the bus. Christian settled into his seat with a little sigh as the bus started to move again. The guide immediately began talking about the drive-in volcano where they would stop next, but his attention shifted to Carolyn as she suddenly pressed the black and silver necklace into his hand.

"Here, hold this."

Christian automatically closed his fingers around the necklace and watched her undo the clasp on the one with the pink stones and put it on. She tipped her head down, trying to see it, but then shrugged and reached for the necklace he held. He gave it up at once, eyebrows rising when she began to undo its clasp as well.

"Are you going to wear both of them?" he asked with amusement.

"Nope," Carolyn said cheerfully, then shifted to kneel on the bench seat beside him and reached up to place the black and silver necklace around his neck.

Christian froze as she leaned forward to see around his neck to do up the clasp, his entire body suddenly wide awake and alert as she inadvertently pressed against him. She'd wondered what was wrong with her perfume earlier. The answer was not a damned thing. It was spicy wildflowers and intoxicating as hell. He had to ball his fingers into fists and physically fight the urge to slip his arms around her, draw her even closer, and bury his face in her neck just to inhale it more deeply.

"There," she said, pulling back to look at his throat.

Christian stared at her as she peered at his neck. At first he thought that she was completely unaffected by the closeness that had nearly laid waste to his own self-control, but then he noted that the color was high in her cheeks. She was also avoiding his eyes and her smile seemed a bit forced. And her heart was racing again. He could hear it, but it wasn't from a drop in blood sugar this time, he was sure of it.

"It's perfect," Carolyn pronounced.

"Thank you." The words were a bare growl as he watched her settle back on her side of the seat. "I'll give it back when we return to the resort."

"You will not," she said at once, scowling. "I bought it for you. It matches your eyes. Besides, as Brent always says, you need pretty baubles to attract the male of the species. Maybe you'll catch Captain Jack's eye on the way back."

Christian grimaced.

"Although, I'm afraid that will attract a few women too," Carolyn added with amusement, casting another glance toward his neck and chest.

"Then it's good I have you to help fend them off," he said quietly.

She smiled faintly, and then turned her gaze to the passing scenery as the bus wound up the hill. It left Christian free to stare at her. Her color was good again, the juice and chocolate had done the trick, which suggested Jack had been right and she was hypoglycemic. It shouldn't be a problem once he settled everything and turned her, but he'd have to keep an eye on her until then, make sure she didn't—

"I can't wait to see the drive-in volcano." Carolyn suddenly turned to smile at him.

Christian nodded and did his best not to look like he'd been staring.

"I have this image of the road running into a cave and along the wall around the side of this huge cauldron of bubbling lava and then out through a cave on the other side." She paused and frowned, and then said, "You don't think it would be dangerous to inhale the fumes, do you?" She'd barely asked the question when she then shook her head. "I'm sure Jack would have said something."

Christian scowled at the mention of the man's name.

"And Genie wouldn't have let us come at all," she added. "Speaking of which, what did she say when you showed up this morning to get a ticket?"

"She transferred Bethany's ticket to me," he said, forcing his scowl away.

"Really?" she asked with surprise.

He nodded. "She also arranged for a car to take me to Soufriere to catch up with you."

"That was good of her," Carolyn murmured with a smile.

Christian agreed. Genie cared about Carolyn. He'd read it from her mind as he'd waited for her to finish transferring the ticket. He'd also read some of her feelings regarding him and it seemed she was wishing he was straight and interested in Carolyn, who she felt deserved some fun after the rough time she'd had. Genie thought he'd be the perfect solution if he were straight and into older blondes, like Marguerite thought.

"So," Carolyn tilted her head quizzically. "You came because you knew I'd be on my own?"

He nodded, and risked admitting, "That and I enjoy spending time with you."

She smiled and patted his hand. "I like hanging with you too. You're a good friend, Christian."

It was a start, he told himself. A good start, really, forever was a long time. A life mate had to be a friend as well as a lover.

"Why are we stopping?" Carolyn asked, glancing curiously around as they pulled into an area where several other vans and minibuses were parked. "I thought the drive-in volcano was next."

Christian looked to the front of the bus as their guide explained that they would walk from here, and commented, "I guess we don't actually drive in after all."

"Hmm." She looked disappointed and he had the urge to kiss the pout off her lips, but simply stood and turned to allow her out of the seat, then followed as she trailed the others off the bus. He was rather disappointed himself. Walking meant another round under the scorching sun, something he could well do without.

"You must be boiling in those black jeans," Carolyn said as they followed the group away from the buses. "I know you're allergic to the sun, but you could at least have worn the white T-shirt you bought the other day. And maybe pants that were made of a less heavy material to make it bearable."

"I was rushing and not thinking." Christian took her arm to steer her along. It was true, he had been rushing and not thinking or he would have had blood.

"Is it awful to admit I'm a bit disappointed?" Carolyn asked moments later as they joined the others peering over the drive-in volcano.

Christian chuckled at her expression and shook his head. "Your vision was much more exciting."

"Yeah." She sighed and peered out over the steaming field before them. "It kind of looks like an ash field . . . except for the steam. But those rocks are rather pretty."

Christian nodded as his gaze slid over the rocks streaked black, yellow, and white.

"It smells though," Carolyn muttered, wrinkling her nose.

"Sulphur," he said, his gaze sliding to the tour guide who was explaining that while tourists used to be allowed to walk to the end of the tar pits, that was no longer allowed because a local tour guide had fallen through the crust, receiving third-degree burns over most of his body. The story made Christian urge Carolyn back from the edge of the platform. The last thing he wanted was to lose her now that he'd found her.

"Are you all right?" Carolyn asked moments later as they started along the path toward Sulphur Springs.

"Yes, why?" he muttered, relieved to see that the path led into the jungle ahead.

"You're the one looking pale now," she said with concern. "Would you like my other chocolate bar?"

Christian shook his head. Chocolate wasn't going to help him. "I'm good. Keep it in case you need it later," he said and released a slow relieved sigh as the vegetation closed around them, providing shade.

"I have water too." She offered him her half-empty bottle of water.

Christian just shook his head again. It wouldn't help either. What he needed was blood, but he wasn't likely to get the opportunity to get that anytime soon.

"Are you sure?" she asked with a frown. "You really don't look good."

"I'm fine. You drink it." He urged her to the side to make room for people coming from the opposite way along the path.

Shrugging, Carolyn opened the bottle and gulped it down. She was putting the empty bottle back into her bag when they stepped out into an open area.

"Oh," Carolyn breathed as she took in the waterfalls. "Now this is impressive."

Christian nodded, but almost sighed as he followed her out of the shade. It was pretty, but difficult to enjoy. All this sunlight was beginning to affect him. His stomach was starting to cramp and his senses were all starting to zero in on the sources of blood around him. He could hear every heartbeat of every tourist they traveled with, could hear the blood pounding through their veins louder than the falls themselves, could actually smell the tinny substance rushing beneath their skin.

His fangs tried to slide out in response and Christian clenched his jaw, concentrating on keeping them in.

"Maybe we should go back to the bus."

Christian blinked. Carolyn stood in front of him, concern on her face.

"You really don't look good."

"I'm fine," he said tightly and she snorted at the claim.

"No you aren't. You look ready to pass out. Come on. You took care of me and now I'm going to take care of you." Catching his hand, she moved past him, dragging him back along the path the way they'd come.

"Really, I'm fine," he assured her, a new concern claiming him. As desperately as he needed blood, the last thing he wanted was to be closed up in a minibus with her where the scent of her blood might make him do something stupid. The temptation to bite would be unbearable. Hell, being back on the bus with a dozen pounding mortal hearts pumping all that glorious blood through their veins would be even worse. He needed to feed. His gaze slid to Carolyn, zeroing in on her neck. Her naked and now vulnerable neck he saw with dismay.

"When did you pull your hair up?" he asked with alarm.

"While we were walking through the jungle," she said without glancing around. "Didn't you see me? You were right behind me."

"No," he muttered, unable to tear his eyes from her throat. He'd been way too distracted with thoughts of his need for blood and how to get it, he supposed.

"I have another scrunchy in my bag if you want to pull your hair back too," she offered, glancing over her shoulder.

Christian forced his eyes from her throat to her face with some effort and frowned. She'd gone pale again and her eyes were a little glassy. Her blood sugar had dropped once more, he realized.

Christ, what a pair they were, he thought, catching her elbow when she stumbled. They had reached the end of the shaded path and had the long open area to cross, but Carolyn was now moving at almost a crawl. No sugar, no energy. It would take forever to get back to the minibus at this rate, and every minute of it under the glaring sun.

Grinding his teeth, Christian scooped her up into his arms.

"Christian, I can walk. I—" She snapped her mouth closed as he began to jog, jostling her in his arms.

"Your blood sugar is low again," he said grimly, moving a little faster as her scent wafted to his nose. Unfortunately, he couldn't outrun her scent when he was carrying her.

People were gaping as he ran past with Carolyn, but he didn't care. He needed to get her to the bus, sit her in it, get her to eat her chocolate bar, and then go find a blood donor. This was an emergency situation. He couldn't risk his need making him do something stupid.

Christian didn't slow until he reached the bus and found the door closed. Frowning, he glanced around, spotting their driver standing with two other men, the other drivers he supposed. But even as his eyes landed on the driver, the man was moving forward to let them in.

"Put me down," Carolyn hissed now that the risk of biting her tongue was gone.

"Your sugar's low," he said grimly as the driver opened the door.

"Yes, well if you set me down I will get out the other chocolate bar and—" She gave up the argument on an exasperated sigh as he hurried up the steps and carried her back to their seat to set her down.

"Eat your chocolate," Christian ordered, straightening and taking a step back to avoid temptation.

"Stop ordering me around," Carolyn snapped irritably, opening her bag to retrieve the chocolate bar. "I am not a child. Hell, you're the child here. I'm— Crap!" she cursed when the chocolate bar slid from her clumsy hands and dropped to the bus floor.

She started to bend to find it, but he was there first, wedging himself between their bench seat and the one in front to reach around her legs for it. Her naked legs. Damn they were soft and smooth, he thought as his cheek brushed one. They smelled of sunlight and coconut. Sunscreen, he supposed, but they smelled good enough to lick and he was hard-pressed not to turn his head for a taste before his fingers closed over the bar.

"Can't you find it?" Carolyn asked.

"Yes, I—" The words died in his throat as he glanced up and found she'd leaned forward. Her face was only inches from his, her lips soft and wet as if she'd licked or bitten them. His hand tightened on the chocolate bar as he watched her eyes dilate. He could hear that her heart rate had picked up and smell her attraction to him as her body released hormones and adrenaline in a potent cocktail.

When she licked her lips nervously and started to pull back, Christian reacted instinctively, the predator in him taking over. His hand was at the back of her head, stopping her retreat before he even realized he intended to do it, and then he was rising from his crouch, his mouth claiming hers and forcing her back against the seat as he settled on the bench beside her.

Carolyn went still, even holding her breath, and he dropped the chocolate bar on the seat to move his hand to her waist. He slid it up her side, stopping at the underside of her breast, and then ran his tongue along her lips before allowing his hand to creep up to cover her breast. When she gasped in surprise, he squeezed the soft flesh he'd claimed and thrust his tongue into her mouth.

Her resistance shattered, the sudden doubling of sensation he experienced telling him that. He was feeling her pleasure as well as his own now and the combination was a double whammy that slammed him straight in the groin, making him grow hard and heavy with blood.

Christian lost his head then and any semblance of control. He pulled her to straddle him, his mouth slanting over hers repeatedly as his hands roamed freely, sliding over her breasts and then dropping to slip under her T-shirt to find them again through the soft cloth of her bra. When he tugged the cups aside to touch her without their hindrance, Carolyn broke their kiss with a groan and let her head fall back, her bottom moving against his growing erection.

Deprived of her mouth, Christian let his lips move over her neck, licking and nibbling the warm flesh as he lightly pinched her nipples. He wanted to push her shirt up and close his mouth over the hard nubs one at a time, but couldn't seem to tear his mouth from her neck. It was so soft and smelled so good. He just wanted to sink his teeth in and—

Christian froze in horror as his fangs suddenly pushed out of his gums and scraped across her skin. Sweat broke out on his forehead as he fought the temptation to bite. He couldn't. She was in no shape to lose blood, and he couldn't make her forget if he did bite her. Carolyn wasn't ready to learn what he was. He couldn't risk losing her.

"Christian?" she mumbled uncertainly.

Cursing under his breath, he removed his hands from her breasts, tugged her bra back into place and quickly shifted her, almost dumped her really, on the seat beside him. He then launched himself out of the seat and hurried up the aisle, desperate to get away from the temptation she represented before he did something so stupid it was irreversible.

Christian stopped outside the bus, his gaze searching the area. There were public washrooms along the parking area, he noted and glanced over the few people moving around the vehicles before settling on the drivers still gathered by the first of their three buses. Christian's gaze flickered briefly over the selection before settling on a robust balding fellow. He slipped into the man's mind and sent him moving toward the washrooms even as he headed that way himself. Dinner was served.

Thirteen

Carolyn slowly let her breath out, her eyes wide as she watched Christian disappear into the men's bathroom. Then she just sat there, her mind so awash with a confusion of emotions she could hardly think. The only thing that was going through her head was one refrain. What the hell had just happened?

She wasn't really sure; she remembered leaning forward, and finding herself staring at his lips and thinking of his kisses. She didn't recall deciding to kiss him but Christian's horrified expression as he'd dumped her off his lap was fresh in her mind, and she thought she might have attacked poor, gay, too-young-for-her Christian. Attacked and nearly devoured him alive. At least that's how it had felt. She'd never been exposed to such raw need and hunger in her life as what had exploded over her as they'd kissed. She'd wanted to crawl inside his skin and merge with him completely.

Cripes, if he hadn't stopped her when he had, she might

have tugged her shorts off, pulled him out of his pants, and mounted him right there on the bus. Carolyn didn't think she'd have had the presence of mind to remember they were in public. Let alone care that he was much too young for her or even that he was gay and not the least bit interested. And those dreams she'd thought were so hot and passionate? Well, they were nothing next to the reality, or at least the small taste of reality she'd had. And she wanted more, she acknowledged. And shouldn't.

What the hell was the matter with her? She sank shakily back on the bench, and glanced down with a frown as she heard a rustle. Spotting the chocolate bar beside her hip, she stared at it blankly, then instinctively reached for it, pausing when she saw how her hand was trembling.

Right, according to Jack it was low blood sugar, she recalled slowly. She'd never had problems like this before this trip, but the chocolate bars and juice had seemed to help before. Carolyn picked up the bar, managing to open it despite her shakes and clumsiness. She began to eat it automatically, her mind still struggling with what she'd done.

By the time she'd finished the chocolate, she'd pushed her guilt and humiliation aside and had moved on to what she should do now. Several possibilities came to mind. All of them had to do with avoiding Christian. She owed him an apology, but she was just too ashamed of herself to face him right now. In fact, the idea stirred an anxiety close to panic, and she began searching her mind for ways to avoid him.

Jumping off the bus and finding a ride back to the resort was her favorite solution, but the buses were the only way out. However, she definitely couldn't handle spending the rest of the journey as Christian's seat mate. If he was even willing to, she thought on a sigh.

Crumbling the chocolate wrapper in her hand, she slid out of the seat and hurried off the bus.

Christian finished wiping the driver's mind, sent him on his way, and then moved to the sinks to turn on the taps. He splashed cold water on his face several times, and then straightened to peer at himself.

He had a little more color now, but he hadn't had enough blood. He hadn't been willing to risk weakening the driver in charge of a minibus of tourists. But he'd had enough that he was at least thinking a bit more clearly, and what Christian was thinking was that he'd made a hell of a mess of things.

Sighing, he braced his hands on the counter and briefly closed his eyes as he tried to sort out what the hell he was supposed to say to Carolyn when he went back to the bus. But his mind kept returning to how she'd rocked his world.

Christian had experienced more passion in those few minutes on the bus than he had in his entire five hundred plus years. The woman was a flame to his dynamite, or maybe she was the dynamite. He couldn't say, but she was something. He still had a damned erection. Even having to stand close to the sweaty little driver with his teeth sunk in his neck hadn't driven that off, which was pretty amazing when you considered that as low as he'd been on blood, he probably shouldn't even have been able to get an erection.

Grimacing, Christian turned off the taps and headed out of the bathroom.

Their party had returned and was boarding the mini-buses. Christian joined the back of the line of passengers at the third bus, his hand tapping nervously against his leg. He was standing in direct sunlight again, but hardly noticed, his mind taken up with worry over how Carolyn would greet him.

His cover was now blown, and she definitely wouldn't believe him gay anymore, but maybe those few kisses and caresses had been enough to tempt her into ignoring what she thought was their age difference and letting him get close to her after all.

Christian held on to that hope right up until he finally got on the bus and saw that the seat he'd shared with Carolyn was empty. Pausing abruptly, he turned toward the driver, but before he'd even spoken the man smiled and said, "Your lady friend moved to the front bus."

"I thought there weren't any seats in the other buses?" he said quietly.

"Only one on each, with the tour guide," the driver said.

"Right," he muttered, turning away to continue to his seat. It appeared the kisses hadn't been enough to tempt her. She was running.

"Caro! Finally you're back."

Carolyn laughed at Captain Jack's greeting as he took her hand to help her onboard. Riding in the front of the first bus with the guide, she'd been the first one off and so was the first onboard the boat.

"Where's band boy?" Jack asked.

"He's back there somewhere," she said vaguely as he led her toward the helm, leaving his crew to help the others aboard.

"Ah. You were so eager to see me you ran ahead," he said with a grin.

Carolyn just chuckled and shook her head as he urged her onto the seat beside his again.

"Your flowers, wench," he announced, grabbing the necklace of blooms off the wheel and placing it around her neck. He didn't step away then, but caught her face in his hands and lifted it for inspection. After a moment, he nodded with satisfaction. "Your color's good and your eyes are clear. Let me see your hands."

Carolyn wrinkled her nose and held out her hands. "Steady as a rock. I had the second chocolate bar at Sulphur Springs, but haven't had a problem since. And I had second helpings of the meal at the plantation. I'm good. No more worries," she assured him.

"Good. But do me a favor and have some blood tests when you get back home," he said seriously.

Carolyn nodded. Today's experience had scared her enough that she already intended on getting a full physical when she got home. It was only after eating at the plantation that she'd really started to feel like herself again. It was also when she'd begun to realize just how weak and disoriented she'd been before that. She was blaming that for the whole episode on the bus. She just wasn't the sort to run around attacking men.

The whole horrible scene had replayed through her head repeatedly that afternoon. The kiss, somehow winding up on his lap—she wasn't too sure how that had happened. It was all kind of a fuzzy whirl of want and need and suddenly she'd been in his lap and his hands had been on her breasts and— That part had kind of left her confused too. At least until she'd recalled that Christian hadn't been at all well either by then. He'd been pale, with sweat beading his forehead, and for all she knew had been feverish and hallucinating that she was George Michael. He'd certainly come to his senses quickly enough. The horror on his face as he'd dumped her on the seat and fled had haunted her ever since.

Carolyn had been worried that he'd approach her as soon as they arrived at the plantation and either demand an explanation or explain politely that he was gay. And what could she say, *So sorry. I've been having these wet dreams about you and for a minute there I think I just confused them with reality?*

She snorted at the very idea.

Christian had kept his distance. He'd also watched her with a wariness that made her wonder if he was afraid she'd jump him again.

Well, he was safe. She was feeling more herself and had every intention of letting him know that he was safe. Carolyn didn't have the balls to walk over and simply say, *You're safe, sonny. I won't attack you again* though, so she was going to have to show him. Somehow.

"Here you are."

Carolyn glanced to Jack as he appeared before her with a full glass.

"Firewater?" she asked, accepting it.

"Nothing less for the mascot," he said with a grin.

Smiling faintly, she took a sip, and then raised her eyebrows when he held out a chocolate bar. Swallowing, she shook her head. "I told you, I'm good."

"This is precautionary," he said, and then grinned. "Besides, I promised you flowers, drinks, and chocolate on your return."

"Hmm." Carolyn accepted the bar and teased, "I'm not sure if I'm ready to go steady yet."

"I'm willing to go slow," he assured her. This time there was no teasing in either his voice or face.

Carolyn's eyes widened. It was the first time she hadn't been sure his flirting was just for fun, and suddenly she began to wonder if he *was* interested. If so, he might be the answer to all her problems. She liked and felt comfortable with him. He could be her first fling! Which she obviously needed if only to protect those around her. Her body seemed to be crying out for sex. Giving it some might fix everything. Of course, there was the small matter of Christian liking Jack, she thought and sighed. However, if the man was straight, Christian didn't have a chance anyway, and she really needed to take care of this problem of hers before she did something even worse than today's little episode.

Carolyn stiffened as the back of her neck began to prickle. She peered over her shoulder, not terribly surprised to see Christian stepping aboard, eyes on her and expression grim. She'd felt that same prickling several times today and each time had glanced around to find Christian staring.

"Band boy's the last one. Time to set sail," Jack said, drawing her attention as he moved up to the helm and started the engine. Glancing her way, he grinned and asked, "You want to steer us out of here?"

She snorted. "You looking to get a new boat or something?"

Jack chuckled and gestured to the crew to do their thing.

They were both silent as he concentrated on steering them out of the busy bay. Carolyn took that opportunity to glance around to see where Christian had settled himself. She found him standing alone under the canvas shading the center seats, and frowned at how alone he looked. But when he met her gaze, she quickly turned away and took a gulp of her drink.

"I hope you brought your swimsuit," Jack said as they passed out of the harbor into open water. "We stop for a dip at Anse Cochon on the way back."

"Yes. Genie warned me. I'm wearing it under my T-shirt and shorts."

"Really?" he asked, waggling his eyebrows. "Feel free

to strip down then. We're always happy to allow ladies to sun themselves onboard. I even have suntan lotion if you need it. And I've been told I'm excellent at applying it."

"Excellent, huh?" she asked with amusement.

Jack nodded. "I am meticulous about ensuring that every inch of naked flesh is slathered with the slippery stuff."

Carolyn smiled and shook her head at his teasing, but she was tempted to take off her T-shirt at least. It was midafternoon and super hot. Most of the men were already bare-chested, and several of the women were even now stripping off their T-shirts to reveal bathing suits beneath.

"Come on, where's your good old Canadian courage?" Jack taunted. "Take it off. I know you want to."

Carolyn met his teasing gaze, then quickly swallowed the last of her drink and handed him the empty cup. She then removed the lei and handed him that as well. The moment he took it, she grabbed the hem of her T-shirt and quickly tugged it up and over her head.

"That a girl," he chuckled. "A couple more of these and we'll have you dancing on deck."

Carolyn turned from laying her shirt across the back of her chair to find him holding out a fresh glass of firewater.

"How did you get that so fast?" she asked with amazement, ignoring the prickling along her side that was Christian's gaze sliding over her body.

"Tristan headed over with it the moment he saw you down the first one," he said, gesturing to the big guy who had brought her drinks on the way out.

Carolyn raised her eyebrows. "Trying to get me drunk to ensure I dance on deck?"

Jack chuckled. "The boys have orders to keep the drinks topped up on the way back. It helps everyone relax enough to join in the contests, which in turn makes it more fun, and that's what they're here for."

"What exactly are these contests?" she asked suspiciously.

Grinning, he wagged a finger beneath her nose. "Uh-uh-uh. Can't spoil the surprise."

"Hmm . . . well, they can't be good if you have to get people drunk to participate."

"Not drunk, relaxed," he corrected and when she looked dubious, chuckled and admitted, "Well, one or two will get drunk, but most people are sensible enough to take it easy. Besides, there's only so much punch. Once it runs out, they're out of luck. It's not enough to get everyone drunk." His gaze drifted over her bare shoulders briefly, and then he stepped back from the helm and released one hand. "Come take the wheel."

Carolyn slid off her seat and moved to take the wheel. The moment she did, he let go and pointed past her to a compass on the dash. "Keep the needle between those two points."

She nodded. It was an instruction he'd given her on the way out, and she'd been impressed with how well she'd managed it.

Jack leaned around her to dig through his shelf of goodies beside her hip, but soon straightened to stand behind her. When his hands then settled on her shoulders and began to smooth warm lotion across them, Carolyn stiffened and glanced back at him with surprise.

"Your skin's too pale for this sun, you need lotion or you'll be a boiled lobster," he said seriously. When she hesitated, he smiled. "Relax. We're going steady. It's allowed."

Carolyn gave a nervous laugh and turned back to peer at the compass. She was damned uncomfortable though as his hands slid across her skin. He was perfectly professional about it, if you could be professional about applying lotion. His hands moved smartly over her shoulders and up and down her arms, not dallying or drifting. Still she grew tenser by the minute as they then moved to her back, and sides.

"You haven't dated since your divorce," he said suddenly.

Carolyn started to glance around, but caught herself. She didn't want to see Christian staring at her again and she could feel his eyes burning holes into the back of her head. She knew he was attracted to Jack, but it was looking more and more like the captain was straight, and she couldn't help that.

"I can tell you haven't had anyone's hands on you for a while," Jack continued conversationally. "You're as tense as a cat over water."

"Sorry," Carolyn muttered, but thought she *had* had hands on her, and very recently. Those few moments on the bus rose up in her memory, and she felt her nipples harden as her body seemed to swell with remembered passion.

When Jack's hands suddenly slowed, Carolyn forced the memories from her mind and took a deep breath. He couldn't possibly see her breasts from behind, but goose bumps had broken out on her skin and a shiver had run down her back at the flood of memories, and she suspected he'd noticed her physical response and mistaken the source. She was proven correct when he suddenly stepped closer, the heat of his body radiating along her back as his hands moved to clasp her waist.

"Well, that's encouraging," he breathed by her ear. "I was beginning to think you were completely immune to my charms."

Carolyn just bit her lip, not sure what to do or say.

"Dare I hope there's enough interest that you'd join me for dinner tomorrow night?"

Carolyn turned her head to glance back at him, and then gave a squeak of surprise as she found a wide black mass beside her. Christian's chest, she realized and raised her head to see him glowering down at her.

"If you can manage to tear yourself out of the captain's greasy hands for a moment, I'd appreciate a word with you," he said coldly.

Her mouth dropped open and she felt Jack tense behind her, and then she snapped her mouth closed and slid out from in front of Jack, muttering, "I'll be right back."

"I'll be waiting," he assured her, taking the helm again, but his narrowed eyes were locked on Christian's face and his expression wasn't friendly.

Sighing at the testosterone suddenly flying around her, Carolyn caught Christian's arm and dragged him to the rail at the back of the boat. Pausing there, she turned and scowled at him. "First off, that was rude."

Christian snorted. "Rude? He was all over you."

"Yes, but—" She paused and then shook her head. "I'm sorry. I know you're interested in him, but I wasn't coming on to him or anything, and I can't help it if he's straight."

He scowled, and she blurted out, "I'm sorry about the bus thing."

"The bus *thing*?" Christian asked grimly, each word succinct.

Carolyn winced. "My only excuse is that I wasn't feeling well and . . . well . . . you're attractive," she said helplessly. "I just got confused for a minute. I'm sorry I kissed you. But you weren't fighting me off, and I know you were probably out of it and thinking I was Elton John or someone, but it didn't help."

When he just stared at her, his jaw hanging open, she sighed and added, "Frankly, I'm starting to think that I was right and I should . . . er . . . well, you know."

His mouth snapped closed and then he said silkily, "No, I don't know. Why don't you tell me?"

Carolyn eyed him warily. "What we talked about in the restaurant."

"We talked about many things," he said grimly. "Be more specific."

Crap, he was going to make her spell it out, she thought with annoyance. "Well, I'm thinking I should start something with Jack." His eyes narrowed, his expression tightening and she rushed on, "You're right, I'm not the type to just pick up some guy at a club, but I've spent a bit of time with Jack, and he's nice. And I wouldn't rush into it. He's invited me to dinner. There's nothing wrong with my accepting and maybe letting him kiss me to see how it goes."

When he stared as if turned to stone, she found herself babbling, "I'm obviously in some serious need of attention. It was bad enough when I started having erotic dreams all over the place, but if I'm going to run around attacking my poor gay friends—" She closed her eyes and raised a hand to rub her forehead, muttering with dismay, "God, next I'll be kissing Bethany or something."

She let her hand drop and said, "Obviously, I've been too long without and need to take care of certain biological needs to keep you safe."

"*What*?" he asked incredulously. "Are you suggesting you plan to sleep with him for *me*?"

"I value your friendship, and I'll do whatever it takes to keep it safe," she said firmly, and then flushed and admitted, "God, I squirm every time I think of the horror on your face as you ran off the bus. I felt like I had raped you or something, and then there are the dreams. I feel like I'm dream-raping you every time I have them and you don't even know about them. Well, you didn't," she added with a frown, and then rushed on, "I need to get this under control. I mean I was looking it up online last night and we aren't designed to be celibate. Sex is natural, and I think I really must be hitting that menopause thing with the added hormones and horniness. I'll be humping the waiters soon if I don't do something. I—"

"*Cara*," he interrupted firmly, taking her arms. "You are overreacting here. There's no need to resort to—"

"I'm not overreacting," she insisted, her voice rising. "I never once attacked Brent like that . . . or anyone else. But I'm acting crazy, jumping on you and—It's just better if I take care of things." She heaved out a breath and then added, "Besides, unless I want to spend the rest of my life alone, I need to get back into the dating game eventually. I may as well practice with someone I'm never likely to meet again. At least that way, if I make a complete fool of myself I never have to see him again," she pointed out.

"*Cara*," he said quietly.

"No." She patted his arm and shook her head. "It's okay, I know you're upset with me, and you have every right to be after my behavior. And I know you'll probably be upset about Jack too since you like him. I mean, friends don't date guys other friends want. But there aren't a lot of options at honeymoon hell, and he's nice, and obviously interested in me. He's also straight. So, whether it upsets you or not, I'm going to go out with him." She patted his arm again. "I know you probably want some time to process everything so I'll leave you alone for a bit. But I'll still be your beard and everything. I'm sure Jack won't mind, he knows you're gay. He promised he wouldn't tell anyone," she added quickly. "And I hope eventually you come to forgive me for attacking you like that. I really can't explain this weird attraction I have for you, but I promise I won't do it again."

Turning before he could respond, she hurried back up to the front of the boat.

"Everything all right?" Jack asked, his voice oddly sober for a change.

Carolyn sighed. "Yes. He's just a little jealous. He likes you and your paying attention to me has his nose out of joint."

Jack blinked and then glanced at her with surprise. "It's me he—?"

"What? You thought your charm only worked with women?" Carolyn asked with amusement.

"*Hoped* it only worked with women, more like," Jack muttered, turning his gaze out to sea again, and then he shook his head and grunted. "And here I was thinking that for a gay guy he was acting pretty jealous over you."

Carolyn smiled faintly and shook her head, but couldn't help wishing that was so. Which just made her shake her head again. She obviously still wasn't thinking clearly.

"So, I believe I was inviting you to dinner before we were interrupted," he said his eyes never leaving the horizon.

Carolyn hesitated, her gaze sliding to Christian again. He was looking grim, a scowl on his face, but still so damned handsome she felt her heart turn over. Mouth tightening, she turned back and smiled. "And I believe I was about to say yes."

His head swiveled, revealing sparkling eyes and a grin. "Yeah?"

"Yeah," she said, and then blurted out, "But I'm kind of still on training wheels when it comes to dating. I—"

Her words died when he removed one hand from the

wheel to slide it around her waist and draw her forward. Carolyn was afraid he was going to kiss her and couldn't keep herself from tensing, but he only pulled her close to whisper in her ear, "It's okay. I meant it when I said I was willing to go slow. Some things are worth waiting for."

"Thanks," she breathed with relief, managing a smile when he pressed a quick kiss to her forehead and released her. She then glanced around with surprise when a drink appeared in front of her: Tristan with another offering of firewater.

She started to refuse, but spotted Christian over the man's shoulder, still scowling fiercely from the back of the boat, and the guilt that suffused her immediately changed her mind. She took the drink. Carolyn suspected she'd need it if she didn't want to freeze up like some ice maiden every time Jack touched or teased her, and she was determined to see this through.

She'd go out with him and let him kiss her and—well, if she had the same reaction to his kisses as she had to Christian's, things should be all right. She just needed to relax and not panic in the meantime. Unfortunately, the very idea of doing any of that had her in a tizzy.

God I'm so pathetic, Carolyn thought with disgust, raising the glass to her lips.

Fourteen

'Gosh that was fun, wasn't it?' Carolyn asked skipping along beside him as they started up the dock.

Christian grunted what could have been taken for agreement to Carolyn's cheerful words, but wasn't. It hadn't been fun at all for him. Having to stand at the back of the boat watching as Captain Jack had pushed drink after drink on Carolyn "to relax her" while taking every opportunity to touch her had been nothing but torture.

He knew what the man had been doing. Christian hadn't missed how she'd stiffened up and looked uncomfortable every time Jack had touched her. The man had obviously set out to get her used to his touching her by doing so in a nonsexual and nonthreatening way as much as possible.

It had been bad enough on the boat, but when they'd stopped at Anse Cochon to swim it had been ten times worse. Everyone had stripped down to swimsuits then, including Carolyn. She'd slid off her shorts, revealing the bottoms that went with the deep purple bikini top Christian had mistaken for a bra under her T-shirt. It had also revealed her curvy figure and shapely legs to the captain's interested eyes.

Jack had immediately insisted she needed more suntan lotion and proceeded to "help" apply it despite her embarrassment and obvious discomfort. Then the man had set out to relax her by playing with her onshore, splashing her and teasing her before grabbing her by the waist and threatening to throw her into the water as he held her almost naked back to his bare chest.

Christian had watched grimly from the boat, resisting the urge to leap overboard, swim to the man, and rip his heart out for daring to touch her. Only the flashes of discomfort on Carolyn's face, and the way she continued to tense at Jack's touch had kept him from doing so. She hadn't reacted like that to him on the bus. And she hadn't been half-tanked at the time. The guy didn't stand a chance.

"I can't believe I won the 'shake-your-booty' contest," she giggled.

Christian grunted again, his jaw now clenching and his teeth grinding together. That was a ten minutes he wouldn't soon forget. By the time the "contests" had started, the drink had begun to have its effect and Carolyn had gaily joined in when the crew had pulled out a boom box and lined up the dozen or so women on the boat tour, informing them that they had to shake their booty and that the men would pick the winner by applause. Having seen her dance the night before, Christian hadn't been at all surprised to see her close her eyes, let the music flow through her, and begin to bump and grind like a pro. The woman was pure sensuality when music played, and he hadn't been the only one to notice. She had won easily.

Many of the other women, not having drunk as much as she had, hadn't been as comfortable doing it and had bowed out quickly or been too stiff and were voted off. Three women had been removed each round, until there had only been Carolyn and two other women left. Then they had voted for first, second, and third place. Carolyn had beat out a twenty-something young bride and a woman in her thirties to take the prize; the lei she'd been wearing all day, and still had on.

"You should have joined in when the guys did it. I bet you can shake your booty too," she said with a laugh, skipping along beside him as they entered the main building.

Christian grunted again. As soon as Carolyn had been named the winner, the men had been lined up for the same contest with the women voting. Christian hadn't joined in. Neither had he bothered to watch the other men gyrating lamely on the boat. His eyes had been locked on Carolyn as the captain congratulated her, dropped the lei over her head, and gave her a quick congratulatory kiss that had made her blush and duck her head. The man had then slung his arm around her shoulder possessively to watch the men do their thing and Carolyn had stood biting her lip and looking uncomfortable but determined.

It was the determined look that bothered him the most. The woman was apparently firmly fixed on having an affair with Captain Jack, whether she really wanted to or not, since her reactions hardly indicated any eagerness on her part. And it was all to take care of what she thought was premenopausal horniness and to preserve their friendship by "saving" him from her "unwanted attentions." Good lord! He hadn't missed the irony in that.

"So, are we having dinner tonight?" she asked as they boarded a van for the ride up the hill.

Christian blinked as they settled on the front bench

seat together, realizing that with Bethany sick again Carolyn would be free to have dinner with him tonight.

"Because if not, I should run back down to the boat after I change. Jack is taking people out on a night cruise and invited me along, but I said no because I promised to play date for you—"

"Yes, we're having dinner," Christian growled at once. There was no damned way he was letting her anywhere near Jack again. He'd made up his mind. Her determination to sleep with Jack for his sake was madness . . . and he wasn't allowing it. Perhaps he couldn't risk telling her what he was and about his people yet, but he was going to tell her he wasn't really gay. He would then kiss her silly, strip her naked, seek out every inch of skin the captain had touched, and place his own hands there to wipe away the memory of the man before making love to her until she couldn't breathe.

By the time the sun rose in the morning, Carolyn would never again be foolish enough to imagine another man could stir her as he could. Hell, he should really just drag her up to the villa now and put his plans into action. And he would if it weren't for the fact that his need for blood had hit the critical point again: his emotions were all over the place and his control almost nonexistent. He didn't even dare risk holding her hand until he'd had a couple of bags of blood.

"Okay, I'll meet you down in the lounge," she said cheerfully.

"No. I'll pick you up," Christian said at once. It was going to be a proper date for a change. He was not meeting her anywhere. He would collect her, and take her down to dinner, then—

"Oh, but—," she began.

"I'm picking you up," he said firmly as the van slowed

in front of her villa, then quickly opened the door and ushered her out.

"But—" Carolyn tried again as he leaped back into the van.

"One hour," he interrupted firmly and pulled the door closed on further protest.

Carolyn stared after the van with dismay, then turned to start up the walk to the villa door. She didn't want him picking her up. Beth would give her grief, and she really didn't want another lecture on being his beard. It would completely ruin her mellow mood of the moment, and she *was* mellow.

Okay, that was an understatement, Carolyn admitted as she staggered on the path. She was pickled. In fact, she'd had a seriously hard time walking straight on the way from the dock to the van and wasn't sure she'd accomplished it at all. She may have been staggering a bit here or there, but fortunately, Christian hadn't noticed. He'd stared straight ahead, his expression grim the whole way.

Carolyn had never been much of a drinker, only ever indulging in the occasional glass of wine with dinner. In fact, she'd had more to drink on this trip so far than she'd probably had in her whole life, and most of it today. It had been deliberate, a desperate effort to force herself to relax. It hadn't worked as well as she'd hoped. She'd still stiffened a bit every time Jack had touched her, but she was beginning to think that had more to do with the fact that Christian had been glowering the entire time. Maybe if he wasn't there looking all handsome and sexy and glaring at her for stealing a guy he was interested in, she would relax more with Jack. That was what she was hoping for anyway.

Carolyn supposed she'd find out tomorrow on their dinner date, and thought perhaps she should have a couple of cocktails before he even picked her up. She pushed that worry away for now as she reached the door and struggled to get the key card into the slot. Right now she had other matters to worry about. Like getting showered, dressed, and up the hill to Christian's villa before he left to come collect her. She really didn't need the lecture Bethany would give her if she knew she was having dinner with Christian again.

Speaking of which, she thought suddenly, what if Bethany was feeling better again and wanted to have dinner with her? That worry was fizzing around inside her head as she fumbled with the door, but as it turned out, it really didn't end up being a problem. Apparently, hearing her at the door, Bethany came to open it for her, took one look at her, and just gaped for a full minute before accusing her of being drunk. She then trailed her to her room asking all sorts of questions about what she'd drunk and so on.

Carolyn muttered mostly incoherent answers as she stumbled into her bathroom and turned on the shower. She was terribly relieved when Bethany pronounced her too drunk to even make sense, and announced that she was going back to bed. She then firmly added that Carolyn too should go to bed after her shower. She could order herself some room service when she woke up if she felt like it, but was likely to upchuck if she ate now.

Bethany left her alone in the bathroom then, saying she would fetch her some water and put it on her bedside table. She should drink it before sleeping. Water helped prevent hangovers and she didn't want Carolyn hung over on the shopping tour the next day.

"Thank you," Carolyn had mumbled, relieved at the way things had turned out. She could shower and pretend to lie down, but dress and slip out of the villa via her terrace doors instead. There would be no lectures. Bethany wouldn't even know she was gone. Carolyn had stripped and gotten into the shower, grabbing for the taps to keep from falling over as she did and then squawking as the water suddenly turned cold. She'd turned the taps, she realized after a moment under icy water, and quickly adjusted it back.

Forty-five minutes later she was dry, dressed, and slipping out through her terrace doors. She felt like a teenager sneaking out when grounded. Something else she'd missed out on growing up, Carolyn thought with a giggle, and wondered if all women acted like prepubescent idiots when menopause set in. She should be able to say she was going down to dinner with Christian. And if Bethany began to lecture her, Carolyn should be able to say she was an adult and could do as she wished and didn't appreciate lectures.

However, this was easier, and actually, kind of fun, she thought with a grin as she tossed her shoes over the terrace rail and then climbed over to drop onto the grass on the other side. Picking up her shoes, she smiled to herself as she hurried around the villa and up the road on bare feet.

Carolyn didn't stop to put on her shoes until she had almost reached the stone terrace around the villa the band was using. Pausing a few feet short of it, she quickly slid her sandals on, did them up, and straightened to brush down her skirt before continuing on. But with the first step, her strap snapped, and her foot twisted sideways out of the high-heeled sandal. Carolyn staggered to the side, trying to keep herself from falling, felt the ground give beneath her, and gasped out a surprised, "Oh," as she fell.

* * *

"Do you really think that's wise, son?" Marguerite asked worriedly as she followed him to the front door.

"Were you listening to me at all?" Christian asked with disgust as he peered out to see if the van he'd sent for had arrived yet. He'd gotten back to the villa, downed blood, showered, changed, and come out of his room to find the rest of the band up and his mother and father there. He'd spent the last half hour telling them about his horrid day and what Carolyn had decided to do, but they didn't seem to be taking her plans seriously. "She is determined to have an affair 'to save me.' I am not allowing that to happen."

"I'm sure she won't carry through on it," Marguerite said at once. "He can't possibly affect her as much as you do."

"That won't make one lick of difference. She isn't even attracted to the guy. She said there was no spark, but she's determined. Where the hell is the van?" he added in a mutter and dragged the door open to walk outside.

"I'm sure she wouldn't—"

"Isn't that Carolyn?" Santo asked.

Christian glanced around to see that everyone had trailed him outside. He then followed Santo's gaze to see Carolyn on the road, bent over and fiddling with her shoes. Even as he spotted her, she straightened, brushed herself down, took a step forward, and then suddenly pitched to the side, her eyes and mouth making perfect Os in her surprised face.

Cursing, he broke into a run, but his heart nearly stopped in his chest when the edge of the hill gave way beneath her and she toppled over, hit the ground, and immediately began to roll down the side of the mountain.

Christian already knew from having traversed it himself that the slant gave way to a straight fifteen- or twenty-foot drop where the next two roads down had been carved out of the mountainside. Changing his angle, he put on a burst of speed and threw himself forward to catch her legs just as she reached the lip of that drop.

Christian overshot. He landed on his stomach on her lower legs, his head in her lap, and her shoe jammed into his groin. It was not a memory he would soon forget, he decided, a pained groan slipping from his lips.

"Oh," Carolyn gasped. "Well, that was exciting."

Christian lifted his head slowly from her lap to find that she'd sat up and was blinking as if just having fallen out of bed onto a soft carpet.

"Hi," she said and had the temerity to grin at him.

"Are you all right, dear?" Marguerite was suddenly kneeling beside them, brushing Carolyn's hair away from her face with concern. "You took quite a fall."

"Oh, I'm fine," she assured her with a smile. "I didn't really fall far, I just mostly rolled. It was kind of fun."

"She's drunk," Gia said on a laugh.

"It's probably the only reason she wasn't hurt," Santo said quietly. "Too drunk to tense up in the fall."

"I told you she was drunk," Christian said grimly, lifting himself off of her with a wince. Damn, he was lucky he wasn't singing soprano.

"Yeah, I thought maybe a little tipsy or something. But she's totally zonked," Gia said on another laugh, helping to brush him down as he straightened.

Christian glanced to Carolyn. His mother had helped her up and was now checking her for wounds. Apparently not finding any, she turned her attention to Carolyn's face and frowned, then murmured, "Oh dear."

"What is it?" Christian asked, catching Carolyn's arm to keep her from instinctively stepping backward off the mountain when she shuffled back. "Did she hit her head?"

"No." His mother sighed, and then admitted, "But in this shape, you could be right. She could do something incredibly foolish."

"I told you," Christian growled.

Marguerite turned to Gia. "Dear, take her up to the villa and find her something else to wear. Her dress is quite ruined."

Gia nodded and started to lead Carolyn away, but paused when Julius said, "Santo, carry her back to the villa. She isn't very steady on her feet."

"I'll carry her," Christian growled, but his father caught his arm.

"Let Santo do it," he said quietly. "We have to discuss this plan of yours."

Christian hesitated, but didn't protest when Santo immediately scooped Carolyn into her arms and headed up the hill. His scowl deepened though when Carolyn smiled up at Santo and said chirpily, "Wow, you're really strong. Do you lift weights?"

Christian and the others began to follow as Santo shook his head. "No. I only lift slightly tipsy, but charming young ladies."

"I'm not young." Carolyn laughed and then patted his chest and confessed, "But I did feel young tonight when I sneaked out of the villa."

"Why were you sneaking?" Gia asked.

"Oh!" Carolyn glanced around at the other woman and waved one hand wildly, the action making her roll slightly in Santo's arms and one leg kick up. "So Bethany wouldn't catch me and lecture me on playing beard again. Bethany likes to lecture," she announced with displeasure. "She was always lecturing me in university. I should do this. I should do that. I should get laid. Blah blah blah." She sighed suddenly and then admitted, "Mind you, I probably should have gotten laid. I might not have married that abusive, gold-digging piece of crap I did if I'd had more experience with men."

Christian's eyes widened incredulously at her words, they were just so not Carolyn, at least not the Carolyn he knew. Apparently they were the Carolyn who was uninhibited by overimbibing though. The alcohol had definitely loosened her tongue if she was talking so easily about her marriage. She'd refused to even allow the subject to be brought up before this.

"Never mind though," Carolyn said, her good cheer returning. "I shall get that experience now. Is over forty too old to turn into a slut, do you think?" she asked and then peered at her feet waving on the other side of Santo's arms and said, "Where's my shoe?"

Christian glanced at her feet to see that while one had on it a very sexy, high-heeled sandal in the same shade of royal blue as her dress, the other was waving around bare.

"Zanipolo?" Julius said behind him.

"Shoe. On it," the young keyboardist responded and dropped away.

"So," Gia said with amusement, drawing Christian's attention to the trio in front of him again. "You're considering slutting around, are you?"

"Well, not as in sleeping with everything that moves or anything," Carolyn assured her. "But I've begun to suspect sex might be more fun than it was with Robert, and I think I should definitely find out, don't you?"

"Your ex wasn't good in that area?" Gia asked, egging her on.

"Not!" Carolyn snorted. "And it wasn't just that he had a teeny-weeny either."

"Teeny-weeny?" Santo choked out and she turned to him, nodding.

"It was like a short pencil next to Christian's cucumber," she informed him.

Christian was gaping in horror at this announcement when she added, "At least, Christian had a cucumber in my dream. I don't know if he does in real life because he's gay and wouldn't show it to me if I asked, I mean not that I'd ask or anything," she assured him quickly and then frowned and muttered, "I don't think I was supposed to tell you he was gay. Or do you know about it too, like Zanipolo?"

"So your husband had a small *pene*?" Gia asked quickly to distract her, and Carolyn rolled slightly in Santo's arms again to look at her.

"That means penis, right?" Carolyn asked and when Gia chuckled and nodded, she nodded as well. "Oh, yeah. But I suppose that wasn't the real problem. I mean, they say it's not the size but what you do with it, right?"

"Right," Gia laughed.

"Well, he didn't do much with it," Carolyn assured her with a sad little sigh. "Or with anything else, for that matter. He didn't even like to kiss. And I've discovered I like kissing. Christian is a really good kisser," she announced. "He's hot too. It's really too bad he's gay and everything. I could kiss him till the cows come home."

Christian heard his father ask with confusion, "There are no cows here, are there?"

"It's just an expression, dear," Marguerite murmured. "It means a long time."

"Good," Julius decided. "They'll be together a long time."

"I bet Christian doesn't have a teeny-weeny in real life either," Carolyn said suddenly.

"I should say not. He got my genes," Julius muttered behind him.

"It didn't look like he did when he came from swimming the other day," Carolyn announced, and then quickly added, "Not that I was, you know, staring or anything. But his swimsuit was clinging to him and—" She grimaced and confessed, "Oh, all right, I was looking, but I don't normally look at men's packages. I only did this time because I was still kind of wound up from the dream Bethany's call interrupted. He was doing some wonderfully delicious things in that dream, and—Oh right, I'm really sorry about that, Gia, but I think I've been dream-raping your poor gay cousin. Not on purpose or anything, of course, but—Are you okay, Santo?" She turned to peer worriedly at the man carrying her into the villa as he began to make choking sounds.

When Santo didn't respond, but continued what Christian suspected was stifled laughter, Carolyn swiveled to look at Gia. "Is he all right?"

Gia was laughing so hard she couldn't answer. But Christian wasn't laughing as he trailed them inside, and he glared at his mother when she caught his arm to stop him from following them upstairs.

"Let them go," Marguerite said. "Santo will carry her to Gia's room and she will help her dress while we talk in the kitchen."

Sighing, Christian nodded, but watched the trio disappear into Gia's room before moving again.

"Cheer up," Raffaele said, slapping him on the back. "At least you know she likes your kisses . . . and other parts."

"Ha-ha," Christian muttered as he led the way into the kitchen.

"Right," Marguerite announced as he entered. "Once Gia has helped her change we'll all go down to dinner."

"All?" He scowled. "We were supposed to be alone tonight."

"Yes, but Carolyn's very drunk at the moment, dear," she pointed out.

"So?" he asked, glancing toward the door as Santo entered.

"So in your present state I don't think it's a good idea for you to be alone with her until she's sobered up a bit," Marguerite said, drawing his attention again.

Stiffening, he asked, "What the hell do you mean *in my state*?"

"I think she's referring to your cucumber . . . which is rather prominent at the moment," Santo said calmly, and then eyes twinkling, added, "Not that I normally look at men's packages."

Christian quickly sat at the table as his mother and Raffaele dropped their gazes to his crotch. Carolyn's comments about the delicious things he'd done to her in their shared dream had brought the memories roaring back to his mind. He had a semierection.

"Well, actually I hadn't noticed his cucumber, prominent or not," Marguerite said primly. "I was referring to his thoughts."

"My thoughts are fine," he insisted.

"Tell me you weren't thinking of following them upstairs, dragging Carolyn to your room, and leaping ahead with your plan right away," she challenged.

Christian grimaced. Okay, so maybe the thought had crossed his mind. Now that he'd determined to move ahead with his plan and bed her, he found himself less than patient to commence with it.

Taking his expression as an admission, Marguerite continued, "And if at dinner Carolyn continues with her most frank appraisal of your performance in the shared dreams, I don't trust that the two of you wouldn't end up passed out on the beach, or in the nearest public washroom."

Christian grunted, glad he was sitting when under the table a certain part of his body responded to that suggestion. On the beach, in a public washroom— Hell, even in the bushes at the side of the road, any of them would do, so long as they included a naked Carolyn and his finally sinking himself into her warm, welcoming body.

"Show a little class, Christian," Julius snapped. "You were raised better than to bed your life mate for the first time in the bushes, for God's sake."

Christian stiffened, and then glared at him for reading his mind, and said, "Oh, right, cause in the john of a train on the way to York is so much classier."

"We didn't do it there," Julius responded at once.

"From the memories in your head when you two came out of the bathroom, it wasn't from lack of trying," Christian said dryly.

"Boys," Marguerite said in a pained voice.

Glancing over, Christian spotted her embarrassed blush and immediately felt bad. While he'd been addressing his father, it had, of course, embarrassed her as well which he hadn't intended.

"Sorry, Mom," he muttered.

"As I was saying," she said heavily. "Aside from ensuring you don't end up passed out and vulnerable in a public location, I suspect that dinner will help sober Carolyn up. By the time you finish your set in the lounge, she should be clearheaded enough that you couldn't be accused of taking advantage of her inebriated state."

Christian stilled as he realized that he would indeed be doing that if he didn't give her time to sober up first.

"Right," he said on an expulsion of breath. He and Carolyn were having dinner with his family.

His mother nodded her approval, but added, "Christian, while I agree that it may be better for you to admit you're straight and lure her to bed so she can experience what it is to be a life mate . . . Well, it might not work," she warned. "I still don't think she'll be comfortable with someone she thinks is so much younger than she is. It might make her run."

"Then I'll chase her," he said firmly. "But she won't know about us and what we are, so no one can wipe her memories. Right?"

"Right," she agreed soothingly.

He relaxed a little, and added, "And it might work the other way. It might increase her feelings for me."

Before she could respond, Zanipolo entered, holding up Carolyn's missing shoe. "It took me a while to find it. Mostly because I was looking at the bottom of the hill and it was at the top. The strap's broken. I think it's the reason she fell."

Christian took the shoe, muttering, "One of her shoes broke the night we arrived too."

"That's odd," Marguerite said. "Carolyn has money, she isn't likely to buy cheap shoes."

"Hmm." He peered to the doorway as the clip of high heels warned that the women were approaching.

"Here we are," Gia said gaily as she led Carolyn into the room.

Christian's jaw nearly hit the floor when he got his first look at the transformed Carolyn. Gia had an entire selection of outfits she wore onstage, all of them tight, with short skirts and low-cut necklines. But he'd never really noticed how tight, short, or low-cut they were. He was noticing now. Dear God.

He wasn't sure how Gia had done it, but she'd some-how squeezed Carolyn, who was much curvier, into a black leather outfit that halted perhaps an inch below where he suspected her panties stopped. As for the neckline, it wasn't low it was nonexistent. The dress was sleeveless, strapless, and rode across her breasts to drop between them low enough to show she had no bra on. Not that he couldn't tell that by the way her breasts were practically crawling out of the petal-shaped cups covering them. Or trying to; he was sure there was a hint of rose peeking out of one cup.

"Is that a nipple?" he asked in a squawk.

Carolyn glanced down and muttered, "Oh."

She then began tugging at the top of the dress, explain-ing, "I wanted to wear my bra. My boobs are too big and I always wear a bra, but Gia said noooo."

"The straps would show," Gia pointed out, helping her tug the leather up to cover her better. She then stepped back and nodded, satisfied they'd done the trick.

"See?" Carolyn said with a shrug. "She kept saying that upstairs too."

Christian made a choked sound. Her shrug had undone all their efforts to tame her breasts back into place. Now there was a rosy crescent above both cups.

"I like it," Zanipolo said with a grin.

"Stop looking," Christian snapped, resisting the urge to rush over and cover her up. He scowled at his mother. "She is not wearing that in public. She—"

"We can tape it in place," Marguerite said soothingly, moving to help Gia readjust the dress again.

"Tape it?" Christian asked with disbelief. "To *what*?"

"Do you have dress tape, Gia?" Marguerite asked, ig-noring him. "If not I have some at my villa, I can—"

"I have some." Gia headed for the door. "I should have thought of it myself."

Christian was silent, his gaze sliding over Carolyn again. Gia had put her in black stockings and sandals. The sandals had four-inch heels and the stockings stopped a couple of inches below her skirt, leaving a tantalizing strip of pale thigh on view. Gia had called them thigh highs when he'd once teased her that her stockings didn't go all the way up. Christian didn't remember thinking the thigh highs looked particularly sexy on Gia, but damn . . . Carolyn had fine legs, he thought.

"You're right. She definitely has a fine set of gams," Zanipolo agreed.

"No one calls them gams anymore," Christian snapped. "And get out of my head."

Zanipolo just chuckled.

Christian glared and then turned back to the women. "Mother, she can't go like this."

"Why is that, dear?" Marguerite asked with interest.

"Because I'm too old to wear an outfit like this," Carolyn laughed with a shrug that suggested it should be obvious . . . and dislodged her top again.

"You are not," he snapped. Damn, the woman had a fixation with her age, he thought and moved forward, intending to cover her boobs. He hadn't taken a step before his father caught his arm.

"Your mother can handle this," Julius said with amusement as Marguerite moved back to adjust Carolyn's dress again. "And why can't she go like that?"

"Because those heels are too damned high. She'll fall over in her state." He figured that would carry more weight than admitting that he didn't want other men looking at her in the dress.

"I probably will," Carolyn admitted on a laugh. "I'm not very graceful."

Christian stared at her with amazement. He'd seen her

dance. How the hell could she think she wasn't graceful?

"Robert always called me Clumsy Car," she announced, rolling her eyes. "It was his idea of an endearment."

"Robert sounds like a very nasty man," Marguerite said.

Carolyn nodded as they both tugged at the top of her dress, and said conversationally, "You know, Marguerite, he really was . . . and he had a vile temper too. Very unpredictable. He was kind of scary, actually. I was so glad to leave him. Life's much nicer without him around insulting me all the time. He didn't think I could do anything right."

"I found my tape," Gia announced, returning to the room and moving to join Marguerite in front of Carolyn.

Christian frowned and craned his head, trying to see what they were doing.

"There," Marguerite said with satisfaction as she stepped back.

"Perfect," Gia pronounced.

"Then we should go," Zanipolo said. "The van arrived just as I found the shoe. I—" He hesitated, his gaze sliding to Carolyn before he said carefully, "I convinced him to wait for us."

Controlled his mind, Christian translated in his head, moving to take Carolyn's arm to lead her to the door.

"Oh good, I'm starved," Carolyn said cheerfully, and then glanced at Gia. "Don't let me forget and bend over or anything."

"Why can't she bend over?" Zanipolo asked, trailing them out of the kitchen.

"Because her panties would show," Christian guessed in a growl, imagining that in his mind and wondering what color they were.

"No they wouldn't," Carolyn said cheerfully. "I'm not wearing any. Gia wouldn't let me."

"*What*?" He turned to his cousin in horror.

"They were ripped," Gia said defensively. "She couldn't wear ripped panties with that getup."

"And you thought *none at all* would be better?" he asked with disbelief. They couldn't go. He should take her to his room now.

"Gee, Christian, you're hurting me," Carolyn muttered, trying to free herself of his suddenly clenched fingers.

He released her at once, shocked that he'd squeezed so hard, but peered at his father questioningly when he caught his arm and pulled him aside. "What?"

"I have to tell you something," he said. "Santo, escort Carolyn to the van."

Santo immediately took Carolyn's arm to lead her out, and she tipped her head back to peer up at him with awe. "Wow. You're really tall, huh, Santa?"

"She kept calling him Santa upstairs too. It was making him crazy," Gia said on a chuckle as she followed.

"What did you want to say?" Christian asked his father impatiently as the others trooped out.

"Flesh colored," Julius announced, and took Marguerite's arm to walk her out.

Christian stared after him blankly, slow to realize what he was talking about. But then he recalled that he'd wondered what color Carolyn's panties were before he'd known she wasn't wearing any. Flesh-colored was the answer. But he'd already known that. His father had just held him back to keep him from dragging Carolyn off to his room.

Growling, he strode forward, intending to say something rude to his father, but he got outside and slowed as he heard his mother say, "I don't know why you two seem to be at odds so much, Julius. But I wish you wouldn't needle him so."

"We're not at odds," Julius assured her as they walked. "Christian is just frustrated and scared of losing his life mate so is taking it out on me."

"And when he's not, you're deliberately drawing his fire," she suggested.

Julius shrugged. "It's safer for him to turn his anger on me than elsewhere. Definitely safer than turning it on Carolyn or doing something else to mess this up."

"You're a good father, Julius Notte," Marguerite said as they approached the van, and then added sadly, "I wish all my children had been so lucky."

Christian paused as his father halted at the van and turned her to face him. "They had you, Marguerite. I'm sure they'd agree that more than made up for the lack in their father."

Marguerite gave him a watery smile. "I love you, Julius."

"And I love you, *cara*." He pressed a kiss to her lips, and then lifted her into the van. Pausing, he glanced back to Christian then. "Well, now that you're done eavesdropping, are you going to go close the door? Or do I have to do that as well as get you your woman on my honeymoon?"

Christian looked over his shoulder. In his rage, he'd left the villa door wide open when he'd stormed out after them. That rage was gone now and a lot of his frustration and fear with it. He wasn't alone. He had backup. If there was a way to claim Carolyn, his parents would help him find it . . . on their honeymoon, no less. Turning back, he grinned and said, "Get in the van, old man. I'll do it."

Julius smiled. "Just see you don't trip over your own feet while you do, pup."

"You'd be there to catch me," Christian said with confidence.

His father nodded solemnly. "And if possible I always will."

"Thank you for that," Christian said quietly and returned to close the door.

Fifteen

'How are you feeling, dear?'

Carolyn tore her gaze from the stage where Christian was playing his heart out—well, Christian and the rest of the band, she supposed, though you couldn't tell from her. She'd hardly glanced at the rest of the band all night. Which just proved she was an utter idiot, Carolyn thought on a sigh, turning her gaze to Marguerite.

"Fine, thank you," she answered politely, though it wasn't true. It had taken a huge meal she only vaguely recalled, a dozen cups of coffee, and about five hours, but she was sobering up. Which really wasn't a good thing, Carolyn decided, shifting uncomfortably on the edge of her seat and tugging at the short skirt of the dress she wore. She was perched on the very edge of the chair because the darned skirt was so short it didn't cover her whole butt when she sat and she didn't want to place her bare ass on the seat. What had she been thinking allowing herself to be poured into the thing?

Well, that was a bit of a ridiculous question, she supposed. In truth, she hadn't been thinking at all. It was probably a good thing she had never taken to drink. She obviously didn't handle booze well, Carolyn decided and tugged at her skirt again, grateful that she was in the back corner of the deck where no one could see her bare butt cheeks hanging off the front of the seat.

At least, she hoped no one could, Carolyn thought and glanced nervously around just to be sure, only to freeze, eyes widening when she spotted Captain Jack weaving his way through the tables in their direction.

"Oh dear," she muttered, worried that he'd forget she was supposed to be Christian's beard and say something to give away the game.

"What is it, *cara*?" Marguerite asked.

Carolyn hardly noticed the endearment she was so used to them from this group. Honestly, Italians must be the most affectionate people she'd ever met. Every one of them had really been very sweet and welcoming from the start, she thought absently as she warily watched Jack draw nearer.

"Carolyn?" Marguerite said.

She glanced around with a start, and flushed. "Oh . . . er . . . uh . . . ," she stammered, her usual eloquent self when in a panic.

"Carolyn, isn't it?"

She swung her head back at Jack's voice, eyes wide when she found he'd reached the table and was smiling at her quizzically. "I . . . er . . ."

"It is Carolyn, isn't it?" he asked with feigned uncertainty. "You were on the Soufriere cruise today with your boyfriend. Christian I think his name was?"

"Oh, yes," she breathed with relief, smiling at him gratefully as she realized he was going to uphold her position as Christian's beard.

"I thought so," Jack said, beaming. "We just got in from the night cruise and I came up for a drink, spotted you and thought I'd come congratulate you on winning the shake-your-booty contest. I didn't get the chance on-board ship."

"You won a contest?" Marguerite asked with interest.

Carolyn flushed. She only vaguely recalled the contest and suspected she didn't really want to remember it any better, but nodded weakly.

"Beat out a dozen other women to take the prize," Jack told them proudly.

"What exactly is a shake-your-booty contest?" Julius growled.

Carolyn glanced nervously his way, eyes widening when she saw the cold way he was eyeing Jack.

"We're considering taking the tour to Soufriere our-selves," Marguerite explained, smoothing things over. "It would be good to find out more about it."

Acting like it was an invitation, Jack immediately pulled out the chair next to Carolyn and sat down to ex-plain.

Marguerite listened attentively, ignoring her husband's rude glares as Jack chattered away charmingly. As for Carolyn, she sat tense and nervous, her gaze sliding from Jack, to Marguerite and Julius, to Christian over and over, like an iPod on loop. And the whole time, she was si-lently wishing he'd leave. Jack was a nice guy and she still intended to have an affair with him and everything, but really this was beyond nerve-racking. Julius was glaring, Christian was scowling, and she was sitting there with her butt hanging off the chair, for heaven's sake.

"—care to dance?"

Carolyn whipped her head back from Christian to peer at Jack blankly. "Huh?"

He chuckled at her dumbstruck expression. "I said would you care to dance?"

"It's hard rock," she said with amazement.

"It's a hard-rock ballad," Jack pointed out gently. "And lots of people are dancing. I'm sure Christian would want you to dance to his music."

Carolyn followed his gesture to the small dance floor in front of the band where couples were shuffling around to the ballad.

"Oh . . . er . . . I . . . ," Carolyn muttered, but he'd caught her hand and stood, drawing her up with him as he headed for the dance floor. She had little choice but to follow, but tugged fretfully at her skirt with her free hand as she went, hoping to God she hadn't mooned anyone.

Carolyn's eyes slid to Christian as they reached the dance floor, but then she looked quickly away. If looks could kill she and Jack would be corpses on the floor, she thought on a sigh, and pulled back slightly when Jack pulled her tightly to his chest.

"Marguerite and Julius are watching," she muttered apologetically.

"I know," he sighed. "And I shouldn't have come over, but I couldn't resist when I saw you in this dress. You look incredible."

Carolyn flushed and glanced away, whispering, "Thank you. It's Gia's. I fell down the hill and ruined the dress I was wearing and she put me in this."

"Gia?" Jack asked.

"Christian's cousin. The lead singer," she murmured, nodding to the stage.

"Ah." He barely spared Gia a glance. "Well, she did you justice. You look hotter than hell and I gather hell is pretty hot," he added with a grin.

Carolyn smiled reluctantly, but glanced away again.

"And you aren't at all comfortable looking that way, are you?" he asked with gentle amusement.

Carolyn shook her head with a sigh. "It's a little sexy for me."

"Caro, nothing is too sexy for a woman who shakes her booty like you do," he said solemnly and for some reason that made her laugh. Her laugh died though when he pulled her closer again, his hands sliding to curve over the top of her behind as he added seriously, "Give me the week and a half you have left here and I'll have you realizing that and as comfortable in this dress as a second skin."

Carolyn stared at him wide-eyed and then glanced around at the loud scrape of chair legs on the wooden floor. Julius was moving their way, his expression tight. And then the fact that the sound had been audible struck her and brought her gaze around to see that the band had finished their set. The others were putting away their instruments, but Christian was clutching his violin like a bat as he stepped off the stage and strode toward them, his face like thunder.

"Time for you to go," Carolyn whispered in a panic, pulling out of his arms.

"Right," Jack said wryly, but then frowned. "Will you be all right?"

She nodded quickly.

"I'll call you tomorrow to firm up arrangements for dinner then."

Carolyn didn't respond. Jack had already slipped away, moving toward the bar. Which was a relief, except that she was now standing alone on the dance floor with two bulls charging at her. Geez, she thought. Jack had caused this, and she really should have made him stay to face the music rather than sent him on his way.

Christian was the first to reach her. He caught her hand without a word, and dragged her behind him as he walked toward Julius. The two men paused when they met and Carolyn peered around Christian trying to see what was happening. They weren't talking, just staring at each other. When Christian suddenly relaxed, Julius nodded and took his violin, and then Christian was moving forward again, pulling her behind him.

Carolyn stayed silent as he led her from the lounge and around the pool to the main building, mostly because she hadn't a clue what to say. She knew Christian had to act jealous for Julius's sake, but suspected it hadn't all been an act and he was still jealous about Jack. She didn't know what to say, so held her tongue as they got in the van and putted up the hill roads. But when the van cruised right past her villa and took the turnaround to continue on, she glanced around with alarm.

"Why didn't he stop?"

"Because I told him to take us to my villa. We have to talk," he added quietly before she could protest.

Carolyn tried to make out his expression in the darkness. She couldn't see much, but he sounded very calm, so she sank back in the seat and simply waited.

Christian got out and turned back when the van stopped, but rather than hand her down as she expected, he caught her by the waist and lifted her out, allowing her body to slide down his as he had the first night they'd met. It caused the exact same havoc in Carolyn and she sucked in a startled breath and held it until her feet were on the ground. She couldn't help thinking though that she hadn't felt that same havoc when Jack had pressed her close.

Damn, Carolyn thought as he released her to turn back and close the door. This just wasn't right. Why couldn't she react like that to Jack? He was straight and a more appropriate partner for her, she thought with self-disgust as Christian caught her hand and led her to the villa.

"Do you want a drink?" he asked as he closed the door behind them.

"Water, please," she answered, thinking she certainly didn't need any more alcohol. Besides, she had a vague recollection of Beth saying water helped prevent hangovers and a headache had started nagging at her as she'd begun to sober up. Perhaps the water would help.

"Go in the living room and I'll get it," Christian said, moving off into the kitchen.

Carolyn moved into the living room, her feet taking her to the glass wall overlooking the side of the mountain. She stared down at the sea and then reached up to massage her temples wearily.

"Headache?" Christian asked appearing at her side with an open bottle of water and a glass.

"A bit," she acknowledged, taking the bottle, but shaking her head at the glass when he offered it. He moved away to return the glass, and she tipped the bottle to her lips, quickly drinking down half of it. She paused for breath, then did the same again. She heard footsteps approach and recede as she finished off the bottle, and glanced around in time to see Christian slipping back into the kitchen again.

Carolyn turned from the windows to head for the kitchen to dispose of the bottle. Christian had the fridge door open and was pulling out another bottle of water as she entered.

"Where do I—" Carolyn paused with surprise when Christian suddenly slammed the refrigerator door closed and faced her, his expression almost guilty.

"I was getting you more water," he explained. "I saw

you'd finished the first one, so thought I'd get you another."

Carolyn felt her eyebrows rise. For Christian, this was nervous babbling, and then he moved forward and traded the empty bottle for the full one. Tossing the empty in the sink, he ushered her out of the kitchen and back into the living room, which just made her wonder what he didn't want her to see in the fridge. Probably drugs, she thought. Weren't all musicians into drugs? Christian didn't seem the sort, but who knew? One of the others in the band might use them, she thought, but let the matter go and moved back to the window.

"Is the water helping your headache?" Christian asked.

"Not yet." Carolyn glanced over her shoulder to see him moving toward the entertainment center. As she watched, he turned on the sound system and slipped a CD into the player. When soft music began to play, he adjusted the sound a bit, then straightened and moved toward her.

Carolyn turned back to the windows, and found herself sliding the door open and stepping out onto the terrace. The evening breeze was soothing, and she walked around the pool to the rail as she removed the cap from the bottle of water and raised it to her lips.

She heard Christian's footsteps behind her as she lowered it. When his hands settled on her shoulders, she glanced back in question.

"I can help," he said quietly.

Nodding, Carolyn turned back to the rail, her eyes bypassing the villas below to slide over the star-dappled sea as his hands began to massage her shoulders, moving toward her neck. She knew at once that she'd made a mistake. This was almost like her dream on the beach and her body was reacting in much the same way now as it had then, his touch sending tingles rushing through her. But it wasn't a dream. Carolyn bit her lip. "Maybe you shouldn't—"

His hands stilled. "I'm not gay."

Carolyn just stood there, blinking at the sea. That was like her dream too, she thought with confusion. "But Gia—"

"Gia could see how attracted we were to each other and how uncomfortable it made you. She wanted you to get to know me to give me a chance, so she lied and said I was gay."

"But you're not gay?" Carolyn asked uncertainly.

"No."

Eyes locked on the sea, but no longer seeing it, Carolyn said, "So my being your beard . . . ?"

"Was all just so I could spend time with you."

"Why?" she asked with bewilderment.

For answer his right hand suddenly moved from the base of her neck, to slide around her throat and up to cup her chin. When he then used his hold to turn her head to the side and back, Carolyn found herself staring up into his eyes and blinking as she noted they were molten silver again, glowing in the dark. Colored contacts, she recalled and then his head lowered.

Carolyn stood absolutely still as his lips moved over hers, almost terrified that if she moved this would all suddenly fracture and prove to be just another one of her erotic dreams. She seemed to be having a lot of them, and each one seemed real until the phone or alarm rang, then she'd wake up in a frustrated sweat.

Please God, don't let me wake up this time, she thought and then sucked in a startled breath as his left hand drifted down from the base of her neck to run along the top of her dress over the curves of her breasts. Carolyn almost could have believed the vacuum from her gasp sucked Christian's tongue right in with the air, because it was suddenly there, slipping past her lips and filling her mouth. A torrent of passion immediately rose up inside her, and she moaned around his tongue when he suddenly peeled the leather down off her left breast, his hand replacing it.

They both groaned as he kneaded the soft globe and then his right hand left her throat to peel away the leather from her other breast and do the same. Carolyn kissed him desperately and dropped the bottle of water so she could cover his hands and encourage him briefly, then let one slip back between them to find him through his jeans. She found him hard and pressing eagerly against the heavy cloth. When she squeezed gently, it sent a shiver of pleasure through her that left her gasping.

Christian immediately tore his mouth away on a curse, and released her breasts to turn her to face him. He then urged her back until her behind bumped against the railing, muttering, "God, I wanted you."

Carolyn responded by finding and squeezing him again, but stilled as the touch sent another ripple of almost unbearable pleasure through her own body. She glanced up to him in confusion, and saw something like realization cross his face, and then he urged her hand away, caught her by the waist to lift her to sit on the rail, and covered her mouth with his. In the space of time it took for Christian's hands to find her breasts again, that odd moment had left her mind, pushed out by the passion he was bringing to roaring life within her. The next time she reached for him, he caught her hands and held them both behind her back, and then broke their kiss to trail his mouth down her throat, over her collarbone, and on to one breast.

Carolyn cried out and tugged at her hands as his lips

closed over her nipple, but he had a firm grip and kept it as he drew on the hard bud. When he let the first nipple slip from his lips and turned to attend to the other, she tugged harder and gasped, "Christian, please."

He released her hands then, but slid between her legs, pressing against her as he returned to kissing her. Carolyn immediately wrapped her arms around his neck, her body arching to press her breasts against his chest as he kissed her. But then she reached for his T-shirt and began to tug it up. She sighed with a combination of disappointment and relief when he stopped kissing her to help remove it. The moment he'd tossed it aside, he returned to kissing her, however, and she arched toward him again, groaning as the coarse hairs on his chest tickled her nipples before she pressed herself firmly against him. Christian responded by pulling her forward on the rail with one hand at her hips and grinding against her, and then she felt his other hand sliding up her thigh.

Tearing his mouth from hers, Christian began to nibble his way back down toward her breast, muttering against her skin, "It's been driving me crazy all night that you had no panties on."

Carolyn's answer was to throw her head back on a cry as his hand reached what her panties would have covered. The movement almost overbalanced her and would have had Christian not quickly raised the hand at her hips to catch her.

Cursing, he pressed her hard to his chest. Her ear was against his thundering heart, but she heard him mutter, "Bedroom." Then he caught her legs, drew them up around his hips, and caught her at the waist to lift her off the rail. Carolyn immediately crossed her ankles, clinging to him as he carried her across the terrace.

The soft strains of music reached her ears as he carried her into the house and Carolyn lifted her head to glance toward the music system. When she glanced back to Christian it was to find him staring down at her rather than watching where he was going. She had barely taken note of that when he lowered his head and kissed her again, his footsteps slowing. With one hand still on her bottom, helping to hold her up, he then found her breast with the other, and groaned along with her as he gently pinched the nipple. He started to walk again then, but then he sat down a second later, rearranging her legs so that she straddled him. Carolyn broke their kiss to glance around with confusion. They were back in the living room, on the couch.

She'd barely registered that when his mouth closed over the nipple he'd been pinching and his hand slid between her legs again. The double assault sent excitement and need rushing through her in a shockingly stark one-two punch. Carolyn cried out and nearly reared up off his lap, but the hand at her hip held her in place as the fingers of his other hand slid over her slick flesh, and then pushed up into her.

"I need you. Now," Christian growled, letting her nipple slip from his mouth.

"Yes," Carolyn gasped, riding his hand. He released her hip and she felt that hand brush against her inner thigh as he undid his jeans, freeing himself, and then his hands moved to clasp her hips, urging her down and pushed into her, hot and hard.

Carolyn clutched his shoulders, and met his gaze, eyes widening as he filled her. He just seemed so much hotter, harder . . . and well, there just seemed like so much more of him than in her dreams. Or her other dreams if this was one, she thought faintly as her body expanded to close around him like a tight glove. Robert had definitely had a teeny-weeny, she thought on a gasp as Christian filled her to the hilt. She could swear she could feel him pressing against her womb. He was pressing against something anyway, she thought faintly and then blinked open eyes she hadn't realized she'd closed when he slid a hand down to touch her even as his mouth found her breast once more.

Groaning, Carolyn wrapped her arms around his head and began to move, using her thighs to raise and lower herself. The movement combined with everything else started an overwhelming chain of waves inside her and she groaned and instinctively began to move more quickly as those waves of pleasure built to unbearable levels, mounting one on top of the other and crashing through her head until she thought she would drown in the pleasure. She couldn't hear the music anymore. Her ears were full of a roaring. Her vision was blurring to pinpricks of light. And then the roaring became a thundering and the pinpricks exploded and Carolyn screamed out, barely hearing Christian's roar as what they'd been running toward found them and pulled her under.

Christian opened his eyes with a start to find Gia peering down at him from behind the couch.

"You really should have taken her to the bedroom," she said gently. "She'll be very upset if she knows the boys saw her like this."

Christian glanced sharply down at Carolyn. She still straddled his hips, her chest pressed to his, he saw with relief. At least nothing was showing. Raising his head again, he glanced around. "Where are they?"

"I sent them to the kitchen until it's clear," Gia said solemnly.

"Thanks," Christian said gratefully.

Gia shrugged. "I like her. She and I are going to be good friends."

Christian smiled faintly and simply said, "I hope so."

"Oh, we will," she assured him. "So long as you don't muck this up."

Christian frowned.

"How did you handle the shared pleasure part of it?" Gia asked, her gaze slipping to Carolyn.

He glanced down at her as well before admitting, "I forgot all about that at first."

"You didn't let her touch you?" Gia asked, worry crowding her face when he nodded.

"But I distracted her right after. I don't think she'll remember."

"Let's hope not, but don't let her touch you again. It could raise questions you can't afford to answer right now."

Christian scowled. "Well, I'm trying not to, but it's kind of hard without tying her down."

"So tie her down," Gia said at once and grinned at his expression. "Like that idea, do you?" Chuckling, she moved away toward the stairs, saying, "I have some lovely silk scarves that will be perfect. I'll get them."

Christian peered after her as she started upstairs, and then turned his gaze back to Carolyn as she murmured sleepily and shifted against him. The small sound made his heart ache for some reason and he merely stared at her for a moment, wondering how she'd slipped into his heart so easily and quickly. It wasn't the sex, which he acknowledged had been a hundred times more powerful than the dream sex they'd shared. That had been . . . well, mind blowing frankly. It had certainly fried his circuits and knocked him out better than a good bash to the back of the head. But that wasn't how she'd slipped under his skin. It had happened before the sex. It was why panic had been clawing at his throat all day. His father was right, he'd been frustrated and panic stricken. Now he was just panic stricken. He could still lose her.

Christian carefully shifted Carolyn in his arms and stood up, grateful when his pants didn't immediately drop around his ankles. Lowering her to rest against the waist of his jeans to ensure that they didn't drop at an inopportune moment, he headed for the stairs, meeting Gia at the top. She set a bevy of colorful scarves on Carolyn's chest and then moved past, murmuring, "Have fun."

Carolyn didn't stir again until he'd reached his room and set her on the bed. She stirred sleepily the moment he released her, shifting restlessly onto her side, her hand reaching out as if searching for him.

Christian smiled and moved back to close the door, then stripped off his jeans as he returned to the bed, his eyes moving hungrily over Carolyn in her rumpled leather dress. She was on her side, the leather cups still below her breasts from when he'd peeled them back, leaving the colorful array of silk scarves the only cover on her upper body. Her skirt was now up around her hips from their joining downstairs, baring her to his pleasure.

His gaze slid to the scarves, and he decided he wouldn't tie her up while she was asleep. He didn't want her to wake up and find herself staked out on the bed and freak. But he would once she was awake if she didn't protest. The idea made him smile. Christian was erect before he even crawled onto the bed and began to draw the scarves off.

Sixteen

Carolyn stirred from sleep with a deep moan, her body already arching to press her back into something warm, lifting her breasts into something else warm as passion roused her. Gasping as pleasure swept from her breast and out to every part of her body, she opened her eyes and peered down at the hand toying with her nipple.

"Christian?" she said uncertainly.

He chuckled by her ear, nipping at it gently. "Who else would it be?"

Before she could answer, he'd released her nipple to slide his hand down between her legs and Carolyn pressed herself back against him with a gasp. Feeling the hardness pressing against her bottom, she instinctively reached back to find him. But Christian gave off touching her to catch her hand before she could.

"No touching or I'll tie you to the bed," he growled.

Carolyn gave a breathless laugh that ended on a gasp when his hand then slid between her legs again.

"But I want to touch you," she moaned, reaching behind her again. The moment she did, Christian stopped caressing her to catch her hand. He turned her onto her back, and then shifted over her, his mouth smothering her complaint as he forced her hand up above her head. When she felt something soft slide around her wrist and pull tight, Carolyn broke their kiss to glance up with surprise. A silk scarf was affixed to the bedpost and now attached to her wrist.

Carolyn turned back to peer at him with amazement, but his attention was on her other hand as he raised it and wound another scarf around it as well. Lowering his head, he peered at her and asked, "All right?"

She stared at him blankly and then whispered uncertainly, "I don't know."

"Say the word and I'll stop," Christian promised and then shifted down her body, his lips trailing over her skin, skating to first one spot and then another, stopping to nibble here and suckle there as he went.

Carolyn bit her lip, her hands instinctively grabbing at the ties binding her as he made a meal of her, nibbling her collarbone, licking his way down between her breasts and then laving the undersides of each before suckling at her nipples. Carolyn gasped, torn between uncertainty and pleasure and Christian continued down, skipping over the leather dress gathered around her waist to find and follow her hip bone, making her writhe as something between tickling and pleasure trickled through her.

"Oh," she gasped as his lips trailed their way farther down. She raised her head and watched, wide-eyed, as he began to duck between her legs.

"Oh . . . er . . . Ohhhh!" Carolyn cried, tugging hard on her ties and arching on the bed as pleasure shot through her like a bullet, hitting seemingly every nerve in her body. Carolyn wasn't aware of trying to close her thighs, but felt Christian press and hold them back. She wasn't aware of much after that except for the building pressure. It was a rough sea pounding against the shore of her brain in wave after crashing wave, stirring up mud so that she couldn't think of anything but what she was experiencing. It left her panting and unable to catch her breath, and then he rose up, caught her hips in his hands to raise her off the bed, and thrust himself into her. Carolyn tugged frantically at the ties, screaming as he pushed her over the edge to where the deep dark water closed over her head.

Carolyn opened her eyes to a cool room lit only by the light coming from the bathroom through the half-closed door. She knew where she was at once and lay still for a minute, enjoying the heat of Christian's chest at her back and his arm around her until the need to relieve herself forced her to slip out from under his arm and ease off the bed. She paused then and peered down at him, marveling at his beauty. Strong, handsome, his trouble-free face looking so damned heartbreakingly young in the dim light.

Biting her lip, Carolyn turned and tiptoed to the bathroom. She slipped inside, closed the door, and then turned confronted by her own reflection in the bathroom mirror. It brought her up short, her need to pee forgotten as she stared at herself. She still wore Gia's leather dress, though it was more of a wide leather belt around her waist at the moment, revealing breasts that weren't as perky as they had been at Christian's age, and thighs she swore she could see cellulite on.

But the true horror was from the neck up. Her hair was a disheveled mess around a face that looked horrid in the stark light. Her mascara had left dark bruises below each eye, her foundation was caked in some places, and missing in others where it had been rubbed off, and her lipstick was half eaten off and half smudged onto the skin around her lips. She looked . . . like an old tramp, she judged harshly.

"What are you doing here?" Carolyn whispered to her reflection and watched as her eyes glazed with a fine sheen of tears until her vision blurred. Sucking in a shaky breath, she moved to the sink, turned on the taps, grabbed a washcloth, dampened it, and began to scrub viciously at her face until her skin burned with the effort. Then she tossed the cloth aside and turned off the taps before risking another look at herself. She hadn't miraculously washed away the years. She just looked old and blotchy now to her jaundiced eye.

Carolyn turned away and began to tug at Gia's dress, pulling the cups back up into place and the skirt back down. Once she had it covering her as decently as it would, she paused to catch her breath and glanced warily to the door, listening for sounds from the other room. When silence met her ear, she sucked in a breath and moved silently to open the door.

Christian still lay asleep where she'd left him, but Carolyn didn't count on that continuing for long. This was the first time she'd actually been awake before him. Each of the five times she'd woken up before this, she'd been stirred to consciousness by sweet words and gentle caresses as he took her again and again to such extremes of pleasure she fainted at the end. They hadn't spoken other than gasps and moans after the first time she'd woken when he'd tied her up, and they'd hardly talked then. She had no idea what he wanted from her, or what this was all about, and she was afraid to find out.

Carolyn slipped from the bathroom and crossed on tiptoes to the hall door. She listened briefly, but when she didn't hear anything, eased the door open, cast one last glance at Christian when he murmured sleepily on the bed, then slid out, and hurried along the hall and down the stairs as if all the hounds of hell were on her heels. She didn't bother about shoes or anything else, but headed straight out the front door and burst into a run that didn't slow until she'd hit the turnaround and started down the road toward her own villa. She eased back to a jog then, but continued forward, slipping around the side to the terrace and the French doors to her room.

Her eyes landed on the bathroom door as she slipped inside her room, and Carolyn crossed to it at a quick clip. She stepped inside, pushing the door closed behind her as she hurried forward. By the time she reached the toilet, she was clutching her stomach and simply dropped to her knees and began to vomit as Bethany called out and knocked at her bedroom door.

Christian rolled onto his side in bed and reached for Carolyn, then opened his eyes with a frown when he didn't immediately find her. He stared blankly at the empty space beside him, and then sat up, his eyes swinging around the room. Spotting the cracked-open bathroom door, he got up and moved to it, but when he pushed the door open, the room was empty. There was evidence she'd been there though, he noted, spotting the makeup-stained washcloth on the floor.

A bad feeling crawling up his back, he crossed the bedroom to hurry out into the hall. But he could see at a glance that the living room was empty, and the silence that settled around him the moment he stopped walking told him that no one else was stirring.

Cursing, he hurried back into his room to drag on his

jeans and a fresh T-shirt, and then rushed back out to race down the stairs and out the front door. The moment his feet hit the hot stone walk Christian realized he'd forgotten shoes, but he didn't go back for them. He had to see Carolyn, talk to her. He should have made sure to talk to her before this, he berated himself. But every time he'd woken to find her warm soft body beside his in bed, his hunger for her had roared back to life and talking had been the last thing on his mind. It was definitely at the forefront of his thoughts now, however. And it was accompanied by a clutching panic.

"She hasn't run," Christian assured himself as he cut along the terrace and made his way quickly down the mountainside. "She just went home to change or something and didn't want to wake me."

The reassurance sounded hollow to his ears, and Christian's panic clawed its way up his throat as he made the jump to the road cut into the mountainside. He shouldn't have done it, and Christian knew it. It was midday by his guess. If anyone had seen him . . . But he didn't care. He had to get to Carolyn. That was the only thing his mind could concentrate on as he hurried up the walk to her villa and rang the bell.

He heard the bell sound inside and the patter of footsteps and felt himself relax. She was here. They would talk. It would be all right, he thought before the door opened to reveal one of the resort maids, a bundle of used sheets in her arms.

"Yes?" she asked politely.

Christian almost pushed past her into the villa, but restrained himself, and said, "I need to speak to Carolyn."

"The ladies who rent this villa are out," she said politely and started to close the door, but he caught it before it closed.

"Where is she?"

The maid turned back with surprise. "I don't know. On a tour maybe."

"But she hasn't checked out?" Christian asked grimly.

"No, they are still staying here," she said, beginning to eye him warily. "They are just out right now, I think."

"Right," Christian murmured, forcing himself to relax. "Thank you."

He released the door and turned to walk back up the path. Carolyn was still at the resort. She just wasn't in at the moment. And neither was Bethany. They'd probably gone down to lunch or something. She hadn't run . . . yet. He would go shower, change his clothes, and then find her.

"Are you sure you don't want to head back to the resort?" Bethany asked with concern. "You look terribly pale."

"No, I'm good," Carolyn said at once, but it was a complete and utter lie. She felt like hell. Her headache from the night before had returned, along with the queasiness and shakes that had plagued her the day before on the boat and the night before that in bed. But then she supposed she'd done it to herself by having only coffee at breakfast before they'd boarded the bus for the shopping tour, and then merely picking disinterestedly at her lunch. What she really wanted was to return to the villa and crawl into bed. However, Christian would be able to find her there.

If he was looking for her, Carolyn thought unhappily. She wasn't sure what would be worse, his not looking for her at all, or his looking and finding her. The idea of having to face him after all they'd done last night . . . or really, what he'd done to her, she thought with a frown. He hadn't let her touch him at all after that first time on the terrace, but had either tied her up or pinned her down, holding her hands by her head as he thrust himself into her.

But he'd untied her after each round. She'd woken to find herself in his arms and untied each time. Thank God, Carolyn thought, or that last time she'd woken she wouldn't have been able to slip away. Even as she had that thought, some part of her brain was laughing at her. The part that knew that Carolyn really wished she hadn't woken up first at all, but was still there with him. She would have been happy never to wake first and leave his bed.

"Well, if you're sure," Bethany said. "Let's go look at those shops over there. That dress in the one shop window would look nice on you. You could buy it just in case you get lucky and have a date."

Bethany headed toward the shop, but her words had made Carolyn halt abruptly as horror crept over her. The innocent comment about "in case you get lucky" had whipped at her like a lash. She'd already gotten lucky, luckier than she'd ever imagined. But it was the part about getting a date that was causing her horror. It reminded her that she already had a date. Tonight. With Jack. The guy she'd intended to have an affair with.

Carolyn moaned. The very idea of that now left her feeling nauseous again.

She didn't know what was going on between her and Christian. Part of her wanted to crawl right back to his bed, but another part was standing back and gasping in horror at the very fact that she'd slept with someone so much younger than herself even the once. Well, six times, she corrected herself, and then wondered if it counted as one or six times if it was all in the same night.

Carolyn shook her head at the ridiculous worry. That didn't matter, what did was that while she didn't know what to do about Christian, she knew damned well she wasn't ready to plunge from his bed to Jack's.

"Carolyn, come on," Bethany said, sounding exasperated and then raised her eyebrows when Carolyn's phone began to ring from the depths of her purse.

"You go ahead. It's probably the office," Carolyn said, digging through her purse. "I'll catch up."

Bethany nodded and headed into the first store as Carolyn found her phone. She hit the button to answer and pressed it to her ear, sighing, "Hello?"

"Caro?"

"Jack?" Carolyn gasped with amazement, her eyes widening with a sort of horror. It was as if thinking of him had called forth his voice.

"Yeah," he grinned. "Genie gave me your cell number when I told her we had a date tonight and I couldn't reach you at the villa. She said you're out shopping with that Bethany who rushed off the boat yesterday morning?"

"I—Yes," she breathed, her eyes automatically moving to the store her friend had disappeared into.

"Well, don't miss the shuttle. I'd have to head my boat up there to fetch you back for our date."

Carolyn gave a nervous laugh and closed her eyes, trying to figure out how to handle this. It wasn't exactly something she often dealt with. Okay, so she'd never handled anything like this before. What was she supposed to say? *Gee, Jack, that's really sweet, but Christian screwed me silly last night and I'd feel kind of uncomfortable going out with you now.*

"Uh-oh, the tourists are back. I have to get off, but—"

"The tourists?" she interrupted. "You're on a cruise now?"

"Soufriere again," he answered. "It's not nearly as much fun without you by the way."

Carolyn winced. "If you're on the boat, how did you get my number from Genie?"

Jack chuckled. "A little thing called a cell phone."

"Of course," Carolyn murmured, feeling stupid, but then she probably was stupid at the moment. Low blood sugar, she recalled. She had all the other symptoms again: the disorientation, clumsiness, and, apparently, decreased intelligence.

"I really have to go, beautiful. I just wanted to make sure you knew what time to expect me. I'll pick you up at your villa at six," he announced, and then rang off with a cheery, "Have fun shopping," before she could say anything.

Carolyn pulled the phone from her ear and stared at it blankly. She then checked her recent calls, but his showed up as an unknown caller. She couldn't call him back to cancel, she realized, dismay creeping over her.

"What do you mean she was gone when you woke up?" Marguerite trailed Christian into the kitchen as he went to the fridge.

"Just what I said," he snapped, retrieving a bag of blood. "I woke up and she was gone."

"Well, did you go after her?" Marguerite asked with concern as he slapped the bag to his fangs.

"He's been down to the villa at least a dozen times that I know of and I've only been up the last two hours," Gia answered quietly, drawing Marguerite's attention. "But she's been out all day. Her things are still there though."

"Then she hasn't run," Marguerite said with relief and turned back to Christian. "What did she say when you talked to her?"

He grimaced around the bag in his mouth and it was his father who answered. Eyes narrowed on his face, Julius growled, "He didn't talk to her."

"What?" she gasped and turned piercing eyes on Christian herself. He just stood there and let her ruffle her way through his thoughts and memories, too weary to care until she cried, "You idiot!"

Startled, Christian stared at her over the bag.

"I'm sorry. I love you and you're not an idiot," she said at once, and then paced a couple of steps away before whirling back to add, "But you *are* an idiot."

Christian just blinked at her. He wasn't an idiot, but he was? Nice. Thanks, *Mom*, he thought.

"I'm sorry," she repeated, moving back to pat his shoulder. "I meant that not talking to her was idiotic. Christian, this is too important to mess up like this. You could lose her. You need to—"

"I know," he interrupted, tearing the now empty bag from his fangs. "I should have talked to her. And I meant to. It just . . ." He grimaced. "It got away from me. I wasn't expecting it to be so . . ."

"I tried to warn you," Julius said solemnly. "When life mates get together it's like an atom bomb going off in both body and brain. You become a blithering idiot."

"Yeah," Christian turned to the fridge for another bag. "I'll talk to her tonight. I'm heading back down to her villa after I finish feeding. She has to return sometime."

"When did you last check?" Marguerite asked, moving to the dining room window to peer down at the villa below.

"Four o'clock," he answered, retrieving a second bag of blood and pushing the door closed. "Then I fell asleep for a couple of hours."

"Two hours ago," Marguerite murmured. "She must have returned between then and now."

Christian stiffened. "She's there?"

"She's leaving," Marguerite said, and as he hurried to her side, added, "With that captain person."

"That lecherous bastard?" Julius barked with outrage, following on Christian's heels.

"He isn't a lech," Marguerite said quietly as Christian watched the couple getting into a resort van on the road below.

"Ha! If you think that, you weren't reading his thoughts last night every time he looked at Carolyn," Julius muttered, scowling.

"His thoughts were a lot less X-rated than our son's," Marguerite pointed out.

"Yes, but *he's* supposed to have thoughts like that," Julius argued at once, and then scowled. "Why the hell aren't you more upset? Our son's life mate is stepping out with another man."

"He's an honorable man and won't force himself on her," Marguerite said with a shrug, and then added, "And after last night with Christian . . . Carolyn won't find any of his advances . . . stirring. This may be a good thing."

"A good thing?" Julius asked doubtfully.

"Captain Jack's kisses will be like water next to the finest champagne in comparison to Christian's. It will be good for her to find that out."

Christian stiffened, his fingers tightening around the blood bag at the very thought of Captain Jack kissing Carolyn.

"Water slakes a thirst," Julius growled.

"Then we shall have to hope she isn't thirsty after last night," Marguerite said firmly and glanced around with concern when the bag in Christian's hand burst under pressure, splashing blood everywhere.

* * *

"Was it my imagination or did your friend seem . . . er . . ."

"Angry?" Carolyn suggested wryly when Jack hesitated. She wasn't surprised by the question, just that he'd waited so long to ask it. They'd chatted idly about his day cruise and her shopping trip on the drive here to the quaint little restaurant he'd chosen, and then through drinks and the first part of dinner before he'd finally asked the question about Bethany.

"Yes, angry," he admitted with a smile. "I'm not used to women hating me on sight."

"It wasn't you. She was mad at me for not telling her about you sooner," Carolyn assured him, and thought that was something of an understatement. Bethany had been furious that she hadn't told her about Jack's flirting and their date. Seeing the way Jack's eyebrows had risen, Carolyn muttered, "I was a bit tipsy when I got back from the boat."

"A bit," he agreed. "But it was my fault. I was a little pushy with the punch. In my defense," he added quickly, "I had no intention of taking advantage, I just wanted you to relax and enjoy yourself."

"You weren't forcing them on me," Carolyn said, absolving him of guilt and then continued, "Anyway, when she saw the shape I was in, she immediately insisted I lie down, so I didn't get to tell her then."

"And after you had lain down?" Jack asked.

Carolyn forced a smile. She hadn't actually lain down, but she was fine with his assuming that, so simply said, "Then I was out with Christian and his family. And you," she added wryly, recalling her discomfort when he'd shown up at the table.

"And then?" Jack asked.

Carolyn just shrugged helplessly, feeling her face flush as she recalled what she'd been doing with Christian after leaving the lounge last night. Ducking her head, she picked up her water glass to avoid meeting his gaze.

"So when did you tell her about me?" he asked after a moment.

Carolyn sighed and admitted, "About an hour before you arrived."

When he didn't respond at first, she glanced reluctantly up to see him peering at her, eyes narrowed speculatively. Still, she wasn't prepared for him to ask her, "So what happened with band boy after he dragged you out of the lounge?"

Carolyn stared at him, feeling the blood rush from her face and then flood back, and blurted out, "He told me he wasn't gay."

Jack sank back in his seat, disappointment sliding across his face. "Right. So his jealousy was over you after all."

"I don't know," she muttered, dropping her eyes again.

"Yes, you do," he said with a laugh. "If he could have keelhauled me before we left Soufriere yesterday, he would have."

When Carolyn remained silent, he asked, "You said his cousin told you he was gay?"

"Gia," she admitted uncomfortably.

"Why?"

"Does it matter?" she asked, suddenly impatient. "He's too young for me."

"And that right there tells me exactly what I didn't want to hear," he said on a sigh. When her eyes widened in surprise, he smiled wryly. "Sweetheart, you've fallen for the guy and the only thing holding you back is his age. My guess is the cousin knew it would be a problem for you and told you he was gay so you'd get to know him and not run."

"What makes you think I'd have run?" Carolyn asked with amazement. While she had, she didn't like the idea that others could see that so easily.

"Caro, I'm the guy who got you drunk just so you'd relax and get to know me," he said with a laugh. "Woman, you have runner written all over you."

When she sagged unhappily, he said, "It doesn't take much more than a moment in your company to know you're a good, kind-hearted woman who doesn't have a lot of experience and got burned gaining the little experience you do have. Now you run rather than risk getting burned again . . ."

"But I don't want to like Christian." She snapped her mouth closed when she heard how whiney she sounded. Sighing, she took a deep breath. "I'd rather like someone like you. And I do," she added quickly.

Jack's lips twitched, and then he said with amusement, "You do realize that most women wouldn't think me a much better choice than band boy, right? I mean, I dumped my life and responsibilities in Canada to grow my hair out and loaf around on a boat in the Caribbean. My life is made up of sun, fun, punch, and a never ending parade of women."

Carolyn blinked. "A parade?"

He burst out laughing at her surprise. "I don't seem the playboy type to you?"

"Well . . . It's just—I mean . . . well, you're nice," she pointed out helplessly.

"You expected playboys would be jerks?" he asked with amusement.

"My husband was," she muttered.

"Ah," Jack said and nodded. "Burned."

Carolyn grimaced and peered at him solemnly. "So why the interest in me?"

His eyebrows rose in surprise.

"I mean, you make me sound like a mouse, skittering madly away. Why would you or any man be interested in—"

"Your skittishness is part of your charm. The fact that you will likely run makes you a challenge," Jack said quietly. "Cats like the chase." When her mouth dropped open, he smiled and shrugged. "There's no sense of conquest with women who throw themselves at you."

"So Christian is just interested in me because I'm a conquest?" she asked with dismay. If so, he'd conquested last night and she'd probably left just before he gave her the boot, she thought and then realized that Jack was shaking his head.

"Oh no," he said when he had her full attention. "Band boy is no cat, cats don't look at women the way he looks at you, or drag them away with the barely contained emotion that was seething in him when he pulled you off the dance floor. He's in it to win it for the long haul. He wants you all . . . body and soul. I'd stake my life on that one," he assured her solemnly.

"But he's—"

"Too young," Jack finished dryly and then shrugged. "Good. Then I'm still in the game. Now finish your dinner and we'll order dessert."

Carolyn grimaced at her half empty plate. She wasn't hungry, but began to eat anyway. She'd nearly fallen down the stairs of the shuttle on returning to the resort this afternoon, and would have had the driver not spotted her swaying at the top of the stairs and caught her just as she started to drop. Carolyn wasn't skipping another meal ever until she had this blood sugar thing checked out.

Oddly enough, by the time they finished eating, Carolyn and Jack were chatting as if the whole Christian subject hadn't come up. She was rather impressed with how he managed that, actually.

Afterward, they walked along the harbor, discussing places they both knew in Toronto, and places she'd been to here in St. Lucia as well as places he thought she should see. They then stopped for a drink before heading back. By the time they returned to the resort it was nearly eleven thirty. She expected him to just drop her off and go, but he walked her to one of the resort vans, announcing that he'd see her to her door.

Seventeen

'Oh.' Carolyn stared after the departing van with alarm.

"I told the driver I'd walk back. It's good for me," Jack said with an easy smile. "Besides, I didn't want him sitting there watching when I try for my good-night kiss."

Carolyn flushed and turned quickly away to hurry to her door, suddenly a bundle of nerves as she tried to come up with ways to avoid that kiss. She paused halfway there though when he started to chuckle. Turning back, she peered at him uncertainly. "What's so funny?"

"You're running again," he said with amusement. "Even though you know I like the chase."

Her eyes widened. "No, I—"

Pausing in front of her, Jack slid his arms around her waist. He peered down at her silently for a moment and then said, "You're a beautiful woman, Caro. Did Christian kiss you after he told you he wasn't gay?"

Carolyn's eyes widened and she started to duck her

head, but he simply caught her chin and lifted her face back up, saying wryly, "That would be a yes."

Sighing, she nodded.

"Right. But he's too young. So," he suggested, drawing her a little closer. "How about you let me kiss you? If I'm as good or better than he is . . . " He grinned. "Then you don't need to worry about him or his age anymore and can start worrying about me."

Carolyn was silent for a minute, her mind racing. She liked Jack, not as much as Christian, but maybe with a little time . . . He was also handsome, and close to her own age. It certainly wouldn't be a bad thing if she enjoyed his kisses as much as Christian's. Maybe it would be like that with a lot of men and she was losing her head and falling in love out of sheer lack of experience.

Carolyn blinked as that thought slid through her head. Losing her head and falling in love? What the— Unwilling even to think about something as ridiculous as that, she forced herself to relax, reached her hand up around Jack's neck, and drew his head down for a kiss.

Carolyn was braced for fireworks. After all, she liked him, thought he was attractive, and he was apparently pretty experienced so no doubt knew what he was doing. She really thought this would solve all her problems. But instead of fireworks she got sparklers. Oh, a slow, lazy warmth stole through her when his lips moved over hers, and it gained heat as he urged her lips open to allow his tongue entrance. She even sighed and moved a little closer when his hands urged her to. But it wasn't rockets and fireworks like it was with Christian, and she felt a deep disappointment when he broke the kiss and raised his head to peer at her.

"Well?" he asked, his voice rough.

Carolyn smiled. "It was nice."

"*Nice*?" he asked with disbelief. "Sweetheart, that about knocked my socks off."

"It did?" Carolyn asked with surprise.

"Well, that's not a rocket in my pocket pressing on you," he said dryly. "And I don't generally respond so eagerly to a kiss."

"Sorry," she muttered, suddenly aware of the not-rocket pressing against her.

Jack frowned and looked her over slowly. "Your eyes are dilated, you're breathing heavier, and your nipples are erect. You liked it too."

Carolyn flushed at the frank assessment, but assured him quickly, "I did like it. It was—"

"Nice," he finished with a grimace when she cut herself off. Dissatisfaction crossed his face, and then he shook his head, released her, and turned to leave, only to immediately swing back. "On a scale of one to ten, what would you have rated that kiss?"

"Ten," Carolyn answered honestly, because really it had been nice. She'd been kissed by more than just Robert, although not by scads of men. But there had been the occasional flirtation at office Christmas parties or such. On that scale, Robert had been a one, but some of the others had reached maybe five or so. Jack was definitely a ten in comparison to them.

He nodded as if she'd verified something, and then asked, "And band boy's kisses rate where?"

Carolyn sighed. "I can't compare his, they're . . . " She shook her head helplessly and admitted, "When he kisses me the world slips away. I can't hear or breathe or see anything but him, and my body just explodes with a pleasure so overwhelming I—"

"Jesus, look at you," he muttered with fascination,

moving back to examine her more closely. "You're on fire just thinking about it . . . and you're trembling."

Carolyn swallowed and lowered her head, then raised it again and blurted out, "He did more than kiss me last night."

"He bedded you." Jack didn't seem at all surprised.

"Six times," Carolyn admitted shakily. "And each time I fainted at the end. It was just too overwhelming and I passed right out every single—What are you doing?" she asked with surprise when he grabbed her hand and suddenly turned to drag her up the walk.

"Doing you a favor," he said grimly. "Where's he staying?"

"Why?" she asked warily.

"It's the villa above yours, isn't it?" Jack asked tugging her up the road.

"How did you know?" she gasped with surprise.

"Because you kept looking up there before and after I kissed you," he said dryly.

Carolyn grimaced. She had looked several times, but there had been nothing to see. The villa was dark. "He's not there. And I don't understand what you're doing anyway."

"Like I said, doing you a favor."

"What favor?" she cried, stumbling along behind him.

Pausing, he turned abruptly, catching her arms to steady her when she nearly crashed into him. Staring down at her solemnly, Jack said, "Sweetheart, I've been with more women than I can count and have never come close to what you just described. In fact, your kiss was about the hottest I've ever enjoyed and it was nothing like that. *And*," he added heavily, "I have never, ever heard of sex so powerful the woman passes out or faints. If you have that with him, then you should be with him no matter who, what, or how old he is."

"He passes out too," Carolyn muttered with disgruntlement and glanced up with surprise when he cursed and growled, "Lucky son of a bitch," as he turned to continue dragging her along.

"But he's not there," she protested again as they hit the turnaround and started up Christian's road.

"Oh, he's there," Jack assured her. "I'm pretty sure it was him standing up there with a bunch of others watching from the windows as I helped you into the van when we left earlier."

"He saw us?" she asked with dismay.

"Yes. He's probably been sitting up there stewing and waiting for you to return ever since," he said. "Besides, I could feel his scowl scorching the back of my neck while I kissed you."

Carolyn bit her lip, but asked, "A kind of prickly heat up the back of your—?"

"Yeah. That's it. Felt it every time I touched you on the boat too. That's why I recognized it."

"Damn," Carolyn breathed, and then began to tug at her hand in earnest. If Christian had seen them kissing . . . "I can't go there."

"Woman, this is no time to be a coward," Jack said firmly, dragging her forward. "What you have here is a once in a lifetime thing, maybe a once in a thousand lifetimes thing. And I guarantee you will never find it again."

"But what if he doesn't want me?"

"Oh trust me, he wants you," he assured her. "A woman who makes you faint? It's enough to make a grown man weep with envy."

"But if he saw us kiss—"

"He did. And he no doubt saw me dragging you up here too. It'll be all right."

"But—"

"Shut up, Caro," Jack said grimly. "I'd rather drag you back to my place and enjoy some of that passion I tasted just a few minutes ago. Maybe for a lifetime, it was that good. But I'd always know I couldn't compete with what he could give you. I'm doing this for you, you idiot."

Her mouth snapped closed as they reached the walk to Christian's villa and he tugged her up that. Pausing, he rang the bell, pushed her in front of the door, and turned to walk away.

"You're just leaving me?" Carolyn cried, whirling to gape after him. "On the doorstep like an abandoned baby?"

Jack paused halfway up the walk and turned back. "I like you sweetheart, and I'm doing this for you. But I like me too and wouldn't mind seeing dawn, so—oh crap."

Carolyn stilled, sure without turning that the door had opened behind her and Christian was there. She could feel his heat.

"She wants you, not me," Jack said abruptly. "I can't make her feel like you do and she made that obvious. But she's got a problem with your age difference so you'll have to—" Jack paused and Carolyn gasped as her hand was suddenly grabbed and she was jerked around into Christian's arms. His mouth was on hers at once, devouring her and setting off those rockets she'd missed when Jack had kissed her.

Carolyn thought she heard Jack finish with a wry, "work it out," but Christian's hands were moving over her now, molding her to his body and then dropping to cup her behind and raise her off the ground. Carolyn moaned into his mouth even as he did when their bodies slid together.

She thought she heard Jack mutter, "It's like a fricking forest fire," as she let her purse slip to the ground and wrapped her arms around Christian's neck and her legs around his waist. She held on as he turned to carry her away from the door.

"Uh . . . I'll just get the door for you, shall I?" Jack called out. "And put her purse on the floor here?"

At least she thought he said that. It was hard to care much with one of Christian's hands cupping and squeezing her behind, pressing her more tightly against him, while the other found one of her breasts and squeezed as he mounted the stairs.

His hand left her breast as they reached the top of the stairs, and Carolyn shivered as she felt the zipper of her dress slide down her back, and then he was carrying her into and through the bedroom, straight to the bathroom. She felt cold tile under her feet when he set her down, and when he broke their kiss she glanced around, confusion rising up through her when she saw they were in the shower.

"What—?" she began uncertainly and then gasped as Christian turned the taps on and cold water shot down over them.

"I can smell him on you," he growled, tugging her dress off her shoulders as the water warmed.

"He kissed me," Carolyn muttered and then gasped when he pulled her back into his arms to kiss her again. She felt the snap of her bra give way, and as it dropped to the floor Christian pushed down her panties. The moment he got them off her hips, the damp material slithered down to pool at her ankles with her dress. He immediately lifted her out of them and caught her between his body and the wall as she wrapped her legs around his damp, jeans-clad legs. Christian then reached for the soap and began to rub it between his hands.

"Christian, I—" Her words ended on a surprised gasp and she closed her eyes as he dropped the bar and began to run his soapy hands over her face and throat. He then slid them up and down her arms and over to cover her breasts.

Clutching at his shoulders, Carolyn gasped, "Oh," and arched into his hands as he soaped them. She then sank back with a little sigh as his hands moved away to curve over the flesh around them, and down her sides. He was being as methodical as Jack had been about applying the suntan lotion.

"He only kissed me," Carolyn whispered, beginning to feel like he was trying to wash away a taint. "He didn't touch me. You're the only one who has touched me in seven years."

"He touched you on the boat every chance he got," Christian muttered, and she reached for his face, forcing him to look at her.

"But not like you do, and he didn't make me feel like you do when you touch me," she said firmly. "I don't think anyone could."

Christian stared at her silently and then his face relaxed and the tension slipped from his body. His hands began to move again, sliding slowly now to curve under her behind and lift her a bit higher against the wall. Still, meeting her gaze, he then brought one hand around and slid it between her spread legs.

Carolyn gasped and pushed her back hard against the cold tiles, her legs tightening around his hips as his soapy fingers slid over her.

"Moan for me," he whispered, his fingers dancing across her flesh. "*I vostri gemiti sono musica. Cantano per me*— Your moans are music. Sing for me."

She was panting now, straining against the pleasure, but Carolyn shook her head and managed a crooked smile as she challenged him. "Make me."

Her eyes widened incredulously when his suddenly flared bright silver. Then she tipped her head back against the cold tile wall and cried out as his fingers slid between her folds so that his thumb could strum the core of her excitement as one finger slid into her. She then moaned as that finger withdrew, and groaned as it returned.

"Beautiful," Christian panted, his voice gravel. Carolyn immediately lowered her head and kissed him, hard. When he suddenly turned them both under the spray, she simply squeezed her eyes tightly closed as the water washed the lather away, her body twisting and writhing under his touch. Carolyn was vaguely aware of the water suddenly stopping, and movement, and then Christian was lowering her to a soft surface. The bed, she saw opening her eyes. They were in the bedroom now, and then her eyes shifted back to him as he withdrew his hand from between her legs and straightened to remove his wet jeans.

"Don't ever leave while I'm sleeping," he muttered, urging her legs apart. "Promise me you won't leave this time until we talk."

"I—" Carolyn gasped as he pulled her to the edge of the bed and slid into her.

"Promise me," he insisted as he withdrew.

"I promise," she gasped as he slid back in and then repeated it with each thrust. "I promise. I promise. I promise."

Christian opened his eyes, instantly alert, panic clutching at him as he saw the wide, empty expanse of bed next to him. She'd promised, he thought with dismay and then became aware of the heat at his back and glanced over his shoulder. Carolyn. Christian relaxed. He sat up and turned to get a better look. Her back was to him and she was on her side on the very edge of the bed. If she moved the slightest bit she was likely to tumble out.

He was a bed hog, Christian realized with dismay and reached for her, intending to move her away from the edge, but then hesitated. If he touched her, he wouldn't be able to stop, and then they wouldn't talk again and . . .

Christian grimaced. He'd already pounced on her once without talking. It wasn't a good idea to do it again. He needed to convince her to have a relationship with him. He needed to make her fall in love with and trust him, because he needed her.

A sleepy murmur drew his attention and he focused on Carolyn again as she shifted onto her back with a sigh, the sheet slipping down to reveal one breast. Christian found himself staring at the pale, perfect mound with its rosy areola. He licked his lips and immediately bent toward her, but caught himself just before he would have taken it in his mouth. They needed to talk. He had to not touch her so they could talk, he reminded himself sternly and started to rise, but paused again when he saw that her nipple had budded, growing more prominent.

Had his breath done that? he wondered with fascination, and then Carolyn shifted sleepily again, dislodging the sheet from her other breast as well. Now he was faced with a two-course feast. Damn, she wasn't making this easy for him. His gaze slid from one breast to the other, noting that the one just revealed wasn't erect like the first. It looked a little unbalanced he decided. He should really balance that out for her.

Leaning over he blew on the second nipple, and then rose up a little to compare it to the first. Damn, now the second one was much more prominent than the first, the blowing apparently causing more excitement than just breathing.

Hmm, best fix that, he thought and turned his attention to the first nipple again. He intended to just blow, but really a quick lick might work just as well. He could resist after a quick lick, he assured himself and slid his tongue out to rasp the nipple, eyes squeezing closed when a quick lick of pleasure slid through him. Damn, he'd forgotten about the shared pleasure. It was all new to him, and Christian wasn't exactly sure how it worked, but apparently he had to be in physical contact to experience it, because he hadn't felt it when he'd breathed or blown on her . . . and that gave him an idea.

Sliding from the bed, he crossed the room and went out into the hall to hurry to Gia's room. The house was silent. It was still early though, well, probably one, early for their kind. The gig in the lounge had ended at eleven, and the others had gone to hit a club in town, leaving him alone to wait for Carolyn's return.

He'd spent the time until she arrived pacing along the wall of windows, staring at the villa below while cursing, and muttering to himself like a madman. In the end, it had only been half an hour before the van pulled up and disgorged Jack and Carolyn, but it had felt like hours to him. It had felt like hell . . . at least until he'd had to watch helplessly as Jack put his arms around Carolyn and kissed her, then he'd discovered what true hell was.

Christian had wanted to crash down the mountain and rip out the man's spine through his back, and still wasn't sure how he'd maintained enough control not to do that. But then Jack had seemed to be about to leave, turned back, the couple had spoken briefly, and suddenly Jack was dragging Carolyn up the mountain like a father dragging a naughty girl home after catching her doing something she shouldn't. The man had delivered her to him even though he wanted her for himself . . . because he knew Carolyn wanted him.

Amazing, Christian thought as he slipped into Gia's room. He would never give her up . . . no matter what. If his efforts to convince her to accept a relationship with him failed and she ran, he would follow her to Canada, or the ends of the earth if necessary. He'd buy or rent a house or apartment near her, make it so that she couldn't avoid him, and haunt her sleep with shared dreams until the combination wore her down.

He couldn't lose her. It was as simple as that.

Pausing at the closet, he opened the door, his eyes sliding over Gia's clothes. She had some pretty wild outfits, and some cool accessories too: scarves, gloves, chains, and feathers among other things.

It was the feathers he had come in search of. He could run those over Carolyn's body without the shared pleasure overwhelming him. But the thought of Gia's gloves suddenly made him pause. If he wore those . . . could he touch her without being overwhelmed by shared pleasure?

Of course, Gia's hands were much smaller than his. The gloves wouldn't fit him. But he could always buy gloves that would. And they would fit Carolyn. If the bit of cloth prevented her from experiencing the shared pleasure, he could let her touch him wearing them. It was a thought. She wasn't going to allow him to prevent her touching him forever. While she hadn't seemed to notice that he'd prevented her from touching him tonight, she'd been growing impatient with his refusal to allow it by the end of their first night together. He had to try something.

Right now though, he wanted feathers. Where the hell did Gia keep things like that?

* * *

Carolyn stirred sleepily and opened her eyes as she stretched in the bed. God, she felt good. Warm, happy, sated. The last thought made her smile and glance toward Christian, or where she expected him to be, but he wasn't there. Surprised, she sat up, and then slid out of bed to cross to the bathroom.

Carolyn found the room empty and started to turn away, but then paused, lowered her head and swung back. Biting her lip, she hesitated for a moment, then slowly raised her eyes to her reflection in the mirror, and let out a slow breath.

Okay, that wasn't so bad, Carolyn decided. She was naked, no leather dress crumpled around her waist. She supposed her breasts still weren't as perky as they had been in her twenties, and she wasn't exactly svelte, but she could deal with it. What really made the difference was that this time there was no streaky makeup caked on her face, or black eyes from mascara. Christian had washed her face in the shower. She looked just . . . well . . . okay, so she didn't look great. She could do with some lipstick and maybe blush, but she didn't look as bad as she had the last time she'd woken up here.

Giving herself a wry smile, Carolyn moved to go to the bathroom, grimacing when she noted her dress, a damp heap on the shower floor. She then returned to the bedroom and glanced around. Christian still hadn't returned and when she spotted the black T-shirt, discarded on a chair, she walked over to claim it. Carolyn tugged it on over her head, murmuring with pleasure as she inhaled his scent. God, he always smelled so good.

The T-shirt stopped below her bottom, which was good enough, she decided as she tugged her hair out of the neck and crossed to the door. The villa was silent as she slipped out of the bedroom and headed for the stairs. Christian wasn't in the living room. She could see it was empty as she descended the stairs, so she turned left off the last step to head into the kitchen and glanced around expectantly as she slipped inside.

He wasn't there and disappointment immediately claimed her as she wondered where he'd gone. As far as she knew the only other rooms were the bedrooms. Had he left the villa? After making her promise not to leave before they talked? She frowned over that, worrying that he wouldn't return. That was quickly followed by the worry that he would, and she began to fret over how he would greet her, how she should greet him. This was another situation she wasn't used to.

Sighing, Carolyn walked to the dining room windows. Staring out at the night, she absently plucked at the neck of the T-shirt she wore and pulled it up over her nose so that she could inhale his scent again. For some reason the smell soothed her and made her smile. Christian did smell heavenly. His kisses were also heavenly, and his touch and . . .

Feeling her body begin to tingle as she thought of just how heavenly his kisses and caresses were, Carolyn gave a little shiver and hugged herself, hardly able to believe he wanted her. Boring little Carolyn Connor. And he definitely wanted her. There was no way for him to be faking the passion he showed her.

Why not? Robert had, the heckler in her head whispered.

But she'd been pretty inexperienced then, Carolyn argued with herself. Besides, Robert had fooled her with sweet words and limp kisses that hadn't even compared to Jack's, which couldn't hold a candle to Christian's. And Robert had never made love to her six times in one night, or done all the delicious things to her that Christian had, or . . .

No, Carolyn assured herself, Christian wasn't faking his passion. He wanted her. The problem was, she didn't know what he wanted her for. Jack had said Christian was in it for the long haul and wanted her body and soul, but she was afraid to get her hopes up. Because she was scared silly she'd gone and fallen for him.

Carolyn let the T-shirt drop back into place with a sigh and tried to sort out her feelings. She'd spent a lot of time with Christian over the last few days, most of her time with him actually. They'd relaxed together, talked a lot, and had fun. She enjoyed his company a great deal. In fact, she enjoyed his company more than Bethany's. Spending time with Beth always seemed to leave her feeling depressed and hopeless for some reason. So much so that Carolyn had actually been rather disappointed when she'd returned to the villa to find that her friend was feeling better. Mostly because it meant she wouldn't be able to spend time with Christian. She enjoyed his company more, had more fun with him, laughed more with him. He made her happy.

But that wasn't all. She'd somehow come to trust him. Carolyn wasn't sure how that had happened. But she did. She wouldn't have let him tie her to the bed last night if she hadn't trusted him. She'd also trusted him to look out for her on the cruise yesterday. Carolyn didn't think she would have drunk as much as she had if she hadn't known Christian was watching from the back of the boat. Despite his anger, she'd been confident he'd be there at the end of the trip to see her safely off the boat and back to the villa. As he had.

But what did he want from her? What exactly had Jack

meant when he'd said Christian was in it for the long haul? And was he even right about that?

Carolyn shifted from one foot to the other with frustration. She wouldn't know the answers to anything until she had that talk with Christian. But the thought of it left her nervous and dry-mouthed. Grimacing, she turned and walked back across the combination kitchen/dining room, and slid around the island to the fridge. She was thirsty and knew there was bottled water here. Christian had gotten her two bottles last night.

He wouldn't mind her getting another while she waited, Carolyn thought and pulled the fridge door open and then simply stared. There was water. Several bottles of it lined up on the fridge door shelves. The main part of the fridge though was what made her pause. It was filled with what had to be more than fifty bags of red liquid, all stacked on top of each other, that looked suspiciously like blood.

The sound of voices from the other room had her quickly closing the fridge door and moving guiltily away. She had no idea what the blood was doing in it. Christian had mentioned an allergy to the sun, but he'd never mentioned hemophilia or anything like that. Although, she wasn't sure hemophiliacs carried around bags of blood with them, and even if they did, surely they wouldn't need so much?

Frowning, she started for the door and then paused. Obviously the rest of the band had returned, and while she was covered up and relatively decent, she . . . well . . . she'd rather not be seen running around in nothing but Christian's T-shirt. God, they'd all know she— That they'd— Oh dear, she thought with a sigh.

"Caro?"

Carolyn glanced to the door to see Gia there, with the

rest of the band crowded behind her and immediately felt her face grow hot. Actually, her whole body did and she suspected she was blushing all the way down to her toes.

"Hi," she said weakly, tugging at the bottom of Christian's T-shirt, which suddenly seemed extremely short under their stares.

"Where's Christian?" Gia asked

"Er . . . actually . . . I'm not sure. I came in here looking for him," she admitted and then, seeing no hope for it, drew her shoulders up and headed quickly forward, murmuring, "I think I'll go back to his room now."

Carolyn was pretty sure her blush was darkening, and she probably resembled a tomato with legs as she hurried forward, but much to her relief, Gia stepped aside and the men backed away to make room for her to leave. Muttering an embarrassed "Thank you," she moved past them, crossed to the steps, and scampered upstairs.

Eighteen

'Christian? What are you doing?'

Turning from the closet, Christian found Gia standing in the doorway and sagged with relief. "Thank God you're back. Can I borrow—" He stopped in surprise as she suddenly crossed the room to grab one of the two robes arranged on the bed and tossed it at him.

"Cover up," she said with disgust as he caught it. "I love you, *cugino,* but not enough to have you waving the family jewels in my face."

"Sorry," he muttered, pulling on the robe.

"So what did you want to borrow?" Gia asked once he was decent.

"Oh, yes. Can I borrow a feather? And maybe a pair of gloves?"

"Why would you want . . ." Her words trailed off as she concentrated on his forehead, and then she said, "Ewww. No. You can't."

Christian was just sagging with disappointment when

she added, "You can *have* a pair of gloves and a feather, but I do not want them back. Ever."

Christian grinned at her disgusted expression as she moved to the dresser. "You're just jealous because I've found my life mate and you haven't."

"Yeah," she agreed, digging out the desired items. "Let's just hope you can hold on to her."

"I will. I'm not letting Caro go," he said grimly, taking the red feather and black gloves she held out.

"Then you'd better come up with a good excuse for the blood in the fridge," Gia said quietly.

Christian stiffened. "What? Why? She doesn't know about—"

"She woke up and went in search of you. In the kitchen, she stopped for a bottle of water and found the blood."

He felt himself pale. "What did she—?"

"Don't panic," Gia said soothingly. "Carolyn really isn't sure what to make of it at the moment. Hemophilia crossed her mind, but she didn't get much chance to think about it. We returned then and she heard us and closed the fridge door. She was standing in the center of the kitchen looking guilty when we walked in, which is why I read her memory," Gia explained, and then added, "And discovered she loves you."

Christian felt his heart stutter in his chest. "She does?"

Gia nodded solemnly. "You should maybe go tell her you love her too. If nothing else, it should distract her from thinking about the blood."

Christian nodded, but hesitated and frowned. "How the hell am I going to explain the blood if she asks about it?"

"Tell her it's fake blood for the stage show."

Christian turned to glance toward the door at that rumble from Santo. The man stood leaning against the door frame, arms crossed. Raising his eyebrows, Christian asked, "Stage show?"

Santo shrugged. "Rock bands do all sorts of weird things, biting heads off bats and such nonsense. Say Zanipolo wanted to use it in the show, but the rest of us refused."

"Why Zanipolo?" Gia asked with amusement.

"Because he's just crazy enough to do something like that," Santo said dryly.

"Good. That's good, Santo," Christian said, nodding as he moved toward him.

"Thanks," Santo said with a wry twist to his lips as he turned to let him pass. "I do occasionally do more with my head than shave it."

"And I'm glad you do," Christian said wryly as he moved into the hall. "Cause nothing was coming to my mind to explain it."

He heard Santo grunt as he hurried back to his room.

Christian found Carolyn in the bathroom wearing one of his T-shirts and hanging her dress over the shower door to let it dry out. He watched silently, trying to figure out how to bring up the subject of the blood in the fridge. He wasn't supposed to know she knew about it.

"Oh." Carolyn's surprised murmur drew his attention to the fact that she'd turned and spotted him. A slow blush slid up across her skin and he smiled.

"Sorry I wasn't here when you woke up, I went to find—" He paused and suddenly whipped the hand holding the gloves and feather behind his back. It was just better he didn't even think about those items until they'd talked, otherwise they might never get to the talking. Seeing the question on Carolyn's face he finished, "A surprise."

"Oh?" Carolyn remained where she was, looking uncertain.

"Wait here." Christian turned to move to the dresser in his room and stowed away the borrowed items, then called out, "*Cara?*"

"Yes?" She came to the door of the bathroom.

"Are you thirsty or hungry?" he asked innocently.

"Thirsty," Carolyn admitted quietly.

Nodding, Christian grabbed one of the two robes that he'd tumbled to the floor earlier when he'd carried Carolyn to the bed and held it out to her. "Come on. We'll go get a drink and see if room service is still available."

"Oh . . . er . . . your cousins are back," she said uncomfortably.

"That's why I'm giving you the robe," he said with amusement.

"Yes, but . . ."

His eyebrows rose as he noted the embarrassment and discomfort on her face and he said gently, "*Cara*, there's no reason to feel shy around my family. They understand the situation."

"Do they?" she asked uncertainly. "Because I don't."

Christian turned to toss the robe on the bed. The talk would be about them before the blood then. Obviously she wasn't as concerned about his having blood in the fridge as she was about what was happening between them. He figured that had to be a good thing. It showed some trust, didn't it? She wasn't jumping to mad conclusions and suddenly concerned that he was a freak or something.

Turning back, he caught a look of yearning and fear on her face before she quickly ducked her head, and he felt his heart tighten. Gia said she loved him, and that look made him pretty sure Gia was right. But that love wasn't going to reassure her about what she thought was their age difference. He could reassure her pretty quickly simply by telling her everything, but her feelings were too new and he was afraid of what would happen if they weren't yet strong enough to withstand what he had to tell her. He had to work with what he *could* tell her.

"I love you."

Her face came up, eyes wide, and then she began to shake her head. "I know you want me. At least I'm pretty sure you haven't been faking that, but love?"

"Yes, love," Christian said firmly and then frowned. "Carolyn, I know your husband did a number on you. It's obviously left you feeling . . ."

"Old, ugly, useless, and unlovable," Carolyn said dully.

"Bastard," Christian breathed, fighting fury as he saw her eyes glaze with tears. If he ever met the man— He cut off his own thoughts. Anger wouldn't help. He needed her to talk to him, and pleaded, "Help me understand. Tell me about him."

A struggle started on her face and, for a moment, he feared she didn't trust him enough to speak about it yet, but then she just started to talk.

"I bumped into Robert in a coffee shop on a sunny Sunday afternoon. Literally bumped into him. I turned from the counter with my coffee and crashed into him spilling coffee all over both of us. I was embarrassed and upset of course, but he was so sweet and nice about it, assuring me it was all his fault . . ." Her mouth tightened. "It turns out it *had* been all his fault. He'd planned the whole thing."

Her eyes looked faraway with a combination of anger and regret, but Christian didn't speak, he was afraid to even breathe and bring an end to her revelations. She was finally talking about her marriage, and while he knew the guy hadn't treated her well, he didn't know the specifics, and suspected he needed to know those to know how to handle things.

"Anyway," Carolyn said with a sigh. "The next thing I knew he'd bought me another coffee, ushered me to a table, and was chattering away at me . . ." She grimaced and said, "Brent had been gone for almost a year, and I was lonely, it was why I'd gone to the coffee shop in the first place. There were people there and noise and . . ." She shrugged. "We ended up staying there all afternoon.

"He was charming and sweet and I just soaked it all up, basking in the attention, the admiring looks, the pretty compliments, and all from this smart, successful businessman." She snorted. "He told me he was a VP of finance for a large, international corporation with its head office in Toronto. I found out later that too was a lie. But then so was everything else," she said wearily and fell silent briefly before admitting, "In a rare moment of honesty after I left him, Robert told me just how pathetically easy it had been for him to make me love him. Bragged about it actually. He'd hardly had to work at it at all. A little charm, a few compliments, a couple of dates and kisses, some flowers and—as he put it—a bit of drivel about how our happy accident must have been fate pushing us together—and I was easily convinced to fly off to Vegas for a quickie wedding."

He'd kill him, Christian decided calmly. He would hunt the man down and—

"Then we flew back home to find my father's lawyer at my apartment door."

"You were suddenly married and rich," he said quietly.

Carolyn nodded and said bitterly, "The luckiest girl in the world: a charming new husband, and now an unexpected inheritance that neither of us had known about. I mean, I hadn't known about it, so how could he, right?" Carolyn shook her head and said grimly, "No matter how he behaved and what he said, I was safe in the knowledge that he had married me for love and not money and everything could be worked out."

She rolled her eyes as if that was about the stupidest belief in the world, and then continued, "And he was so amazing about everything. So supportive as I watched my father die, so eager to help me settle everything, so concerned that it was a lot to handle. Of course, he gave up his VP of finance position with this imaginary corporation to become VP for me."

"How kind of him," Christian said dryly.

"Yeah." She sighed. "Well, with everything going on I didn't pick up right away on the fact that my marriage was pretty much a sham. We had separate rooms within the first couple of months, but that was my fault. My snoring bothered him and he'd poke me a dozen or so times a night to wake me and tell me I was snoring."

"You don't snore," Christian said grimly.

Carolyn shrugged. "I have wondered since then, but at the time I felt horrible that my snoring was disturbing his sleep and moved to my own room so he could get his rest. Sex then became practically nonexistent. Not that I minded," she added wryly. "It wasn't all that wonderful anyway. I mean, it was definitely nothing like . . . er . . ." She flushed and glanced away.

"Like our lovemaking?" he said gently.

Carolyn bobbed her head, and rushed on, "Not that I think it could possibly be this good with anyone else anyway, but he . . ."

"Didn't trouble himself to please you," Christian guessed quietly when she hesitated.

She sighed and then said bluntly, "If he knew I had breasts or anything else besides a hole between my legs, you couldn't tell from him. He didn't even like to kiss once we were married. Sex with him was cold and sometimes even painful despite the fact that he . . . er . . . wasn't as well . . . er . . . set up in certain areas," she muttered, her eyes skating to his groin and away.

Christian's lips twitched with gentle amusement at her obvious embarrassment, but his hands also clenched at his sides as he imagined the marriage bed she'd been conned into.

"Anyway, the sex stopped altogether after the first couple of years. I'm not sure now why he even bothered with it that long, but as much as I didn't care for it, I felt horrible when it stopped. I was failing him in that area as well, and was sure the sex thing was my problem. I was too hung up and frigid."

"You are not frigid," he said firmly.

Now her lips twitched into a brief smile. "Yeah, I've kind of figured that out thanks to you." Her smile faded almost before it was fully formed and she added, "But I believed him when he said I was. And I believed everything else too when his nicey-nice act died and he started in with the criticisms. I was stupid, ugly, clumsy, useless . . . Basically, there was nothing good or worthwhile about me, and really I was very lucky that he put up with me . . . as he spent my money." She shrugged. "You get the idea."

Oh, he got the idea all right. The man had systematically set out to con her into marriage for her money and then to keep her as his cash cow by making sure she didn't think anyone else would want her. It was really rather amazing that she'd been able to pull herself out of that, Christian thought now. She'd had no family or friends, no support system at all. No one to counter Robert's insults and abuse.

"How did he know about the money before you did?" he asked abruptly.

"He worked for the private detective agency my father

hired that last time to find me. He was an office grunt who was handy with a computer and had aspirations to be Magnum PI," she said with a dry laugh. "He was the one they put on the task of finding me through my social insurance number. And he found it, and then with a little more computer wizardry, he found out I was single. I gather this information made him consider a career change. Millionaire was so much more attractive than PI," she said grimly. "So he held back the information he'd found and told them there was no SIN number for a Christiana Carolyn Carver."

Christian blinked, still not used to the idea that her real first name was the feminine version of his.

"Robert then took a two-month leave of absence, claiming his father had cancer, and flew to Toronto to find out more," Carolyn continued. "He figured out pretty quickly that I was alone in the world and lonely and arranged to 'bump into' me. Then once the I dos were done, he e-mailed his boss a resignation and a bashful admission that, in his worry over his father, he may not have been thorough in the SIN search for me and they might want to have someone else do it again."

"Nice," Christian said dryly. "And how did you find all this out?"

"A *true* happy accident," she said with a slow smile. "The investigative agency that found me, hired our advertising agency for some work. Jason Conroy, the owner, wanted a new Web site with more punch, some magazine and radio ads, and possibly a television commercial though he wasn't sure on that one. He was very concerned about the right tone, however, and flew to Toronto to meet with me and the head of the creative department to discuss suggestions. Robert was leaving my office when Conroy arrived. Robert stopped dead outside my door and went pale. I'd never seen him like that. Conroy seemed surprised to see him too, and asked how he was, but Robert was in such a panic he just muttered and hurried out of the office. Both Conroy and I stared after him with surprise, and then my head of creative showed up and we moved to the meeting room to discuss his campaign.

"Everything went well, but I could tell Conroy was distracted during the meeting." She smiled grimly. "He was adding things up. I was Robert's last job for the company. He was my VP. My name was now Connors—"

"But it was Connors when his company found you," Christian said with a frown. "Robert didn't send him the e-mail until after the I dos in Vegas."

"But it took place in Vegas. It had to be registered in Canada, and I had to apply for new identification. I hadn't done any of that when we flew back. In fact, between my father's dying and everything else, it was months before it was done and then Robert took care of it. I was still legally Christiana Carolyn Carver when they found me."

Christian nodded, and she continued. "As we were shaking hands after the meeting, Conroy said, 'Your last name is Connors now. You've married?' I said yes, that in fact Robert was my husband, and I noticed they seemed to know each other. He just stood there, holding my hand, his expression still for a minute and then he asked to have a word with me. I took him to my office and he started asking what I thought were very strange questions. How and when had I met Robert? What had he told me about himself and so on . . . and then he was silent for a long time. But finally he began to speak."

"He told you Robert had worked for him, and had been on your case," Christian said quietly and thought that meeting truly had been a happy accident. Without it, Carolyn might still be married to the bastard. She might never have come here, his mother might not have met her, and he wouldn't have found her.

"He told me more than that," she said grimly. "It seems Robert had lied about his age too. He was ten years younger than me, but had claimed to be the same age. His face is weathered, he looks old for his age, but he also dyed his hair gray at the temples to add to the lie. When he stopped dying it and let it go natural, I thought he'd actually started to dye it to look younger," she admitted tightly. "Something else he laughed about when I confronted him. How he'd expected questions about it when I saw his birth date on the wedding license as I signed it, but I hadn't even looked, I'd just quickly signed and stepped back. But then I was incredibly trusting and gullible, he informed me. How else could I have imagined someone as handsome and virile as he was would be interested in a boring old broad like me?"

"Virile?" Christian muttered, but he was thinking that not only had Robert been an abusive gold digger, he'd been ten years younger and had used that against her at the end . . . which he supposed explained a lot of Carolyn's attitudes.

"He thinks he's virile," Carolyn said and sounded more amused than angry now. "And I believed that too at the time, but then other women seemed to agree," she added and explained, "He chases women like a dog chasing cars. I can't even count the number of affairs I caught him in while we were married. Of course, each time he apologized, even as he explained that he only had them because I was so frigid, but he loved me and didn't want to leave me, and this was the best solution. I stopped caring a long time ago," she added. "But since meeting you I—"

"You what?" Christian asked quietly.

Carolyn flushed, but then lifted her chin defiantly and

admitted, "I've imagined telling him he doesn't even know what virile is. That he has chicken legs, a potbelly, the chest of a twelve-year-old, and no family jewels to speak of, let alone any skill in using them. And if it weren't for a pretty face and a way with words, I doubt he'd ever get laid. I'd tell him that was probably why he had so many affairs, because the women were more experienced than me and moved on quickly . . . And then I'd show him a picture of you and say *this* is virile."

Christian's lips twitched with amusement. "Then that's what we'll do."

Carolyn blinked and then flushed at the thought and shook her head quickly. "Oh no, I would never do that."

"Why not?" he asked curiously.

"It would be mean," she said simply.

Christian raised his eyebrows. "You're worried about being mean to a piece of crap like that?"

Carolyn eyed him solemnly. "It isn't about him. It's about me. Perhaps he deserves it, but I'm not going to be the one to do it. I won't lower myself to it. And why expend any more energy on him than he's already claimed? Life's too short to waste it on petty revenge and nastiness."

She shrugged. "Divorce is no fault in Canada. It's going to cost me half of everything the advertising agency and my investments have made these last ten years to be rid of him. It's not as much as he'd hoped for, because he can't touch the original inheritance, but it's still a fortune and my lawyer wanted to fight it, but I said no. It's worth it to be free of him.

"Of course," she added wryly, "that doesn't mean I'm stupid. He's tried to grab for more, claiming I was frigid and so on, which is why the divorce has taken so long. He kept throwing up excuses for why he should get more and threatening to force it into court if I didn't agree, which he knew I would want to avoid." Her mouth tightened. "It's humiliating enough knowing he married me for my money, but having it come out in court? And having everyone know just what I put up with for so long?" She shook her head. "So my lawyer kept responding with refusals and efforts to settle. But finally, a month ago, I just couldn't take it anymore. I wanted out. So I said, 'Fine. We'll go to court . . . and I'll bring in Conroy.' All of a sudden he backed off, and now it's just a matter of the paperwork making its way through court and then I'll truly be free of him."

Carolyn paused and shrugged wearily. "Now you know it all. You know just how stupid and pathetic I really am."

"Pathetic?" Christian asked with disbelief and crossed the room to take her face in his hands, forcing her to look at him. He then said solemnly, "*Cara,* a weaker woman would have turned to alcohol or drugs. She might even have killed herself faced with a decade of such systematic abuse. He did everything he could to make you feel completely valueless. And you were alone, without any sort of emotional support.

"You aren't pathetic," he said firmly. "You are smart, and beautiful and you obviously have a core of inner strength that most people could only wish for, because despite everything, he didn't crush you. Your spirit is in there, it peeks out at times when you aren't on your guard and I love that about you. I love your kindness and your wit and your sense of fun and your strength. You are more valuable than gold to me."

Uncertainty crossed her face and she tried to duck her head again, but he wouldn't let her and said solemnly, "I do love you. And I have no need or desire for your money. I will even transfer all my assets into your name, and insist on a prenup to prove—"

"Prenup?" she squawked with alarm, trying to break free of his hold. "I'm not marrying you, Christian. I've only just met you. I'm not going to be rushed into another marriage and—Hell, I'm not even divorced yet!"

"I know, I know," Christian said quickly, pressing her to his chest as he added soothingly, "I didn't mean right away. I am just saying that my attentions are not fleeting and that when the time comes I will do whatever it takes to prove it is you I want and not your money." Much to his relief she stopped struggling then. "I don't need your money. There is no reason for me to lie or con you. I have never lied to you. And I never will."

She pulled her head back to snap, "You already have. The gay thing, remember?"

"That was Gia. She told you I was gay," Christian said at once, pressing her head back to his chest as he admitted, "and I was rather distressed at the time and wanted to tell you the truth, but my mother convinced me to let the lie stand so that you would get used to me."

"*Your mother*?" Carolyn was out of his arms so fast he didn't get a chance to stop her, and then he just stood, staring with surprise, as she backed away, squawking, "Your *mother* knows about us?"

Christian blinked, realizing what he'd said, but then his gaze shifted to her again as she began to pace and wring her hands muttering, "Oh my God, your mother knows. She probably isn't much older than me. She'll think I'm a cradle robber. A man-eating cougar out to devour her baby boy." Whirling suddenly, she cried with distress, "How could you tell your mother about us?"

Christian raised his hands, palms out as if soothing a wild horse. "*Cara,* it's all right. She is fine with us, happy for me."

"How could she be fine with us?" Carolyn demanded

with disbelief. "Does she know I'm at least twenty years older than you?"

"You aren't twenty years older than me," he said firmly. "And she does know your age, and is fine with it."

"How could she possibly be fine with it?" she asked with patent disbelief.

"She—"

"How old is your mother?" Carolyn interrupted, and then paced away, muttering, "She's probably fifty or something. Closer to my age than you are. Dear God, I—" She whirled back. "How old is she?"

Christian stared at her blankly. He'd just promised not to lie to her. He'd been trying not to before this anyway, saying things like "Zanipolo knows my sexual preference" when she'd asked if Zani knew he was gay, but there was just no way not to lie in answer to this question.

"Well?" she demanded. "How old—"

"She's much older than you," he finally said and then added, "I'm thirsty. Are you thirsty? Let's get a drink."

Grabbing her hand, he headed for the door, dragging her behind him. It was a way to distract her of course, but it suddenly occurred to him that he couldn't now lie to her about the blood in the refrigerator. But then again, he couldn't tell her the truth either. It was better if he had backup for this conversation; Gia and the others would help out and distract her when necessary.

Nineteen

Carolyn tugged at her hand, trying to get free as Christian dragged her out of the bedroom, but she couldn't break his hold.

"Christian," she finally muttered. "I don't want to go downstairs. We have to talk about—"

"We'll keep talking," he promised. "I just want to grab some water first."

Carolyn opened her mouth to protest again, but paused as she recalled the bags of blood in the fridge. She'd quite forgotten about that what with one thing and another. She supposed though she really should find out about that now too, so held her tongue, curious to see if he'd allow her to see the blood or would try to hide it. That would tell her a lot about how much she could really trust him, she supposed and stopped trying to tug free.

When Christian glanced over his shoulder, she just shrugged and said, "I'm thirsty too."

He immediately relaxed and slowed down, his hold on her hand loosening as they started downstairs. Halfway down, he offered, "I can order food up too if you're hungry?"

"No, thank you," Carolyn murmured. She was kind of hungry, but if she was going to be naked around Christian, it seemed a good idea to try to rid herself of some of those curves of hers, she thought with a sigh.

They were silent the rest of the way down. Carolyn had no idea what he was thinking, but her mind was spinning a bit, bouncing between the fact that his mother knew about them—how mortifying—and that he had a fridge full of blood which just seemed kind of strange to say the least. Although, she was sure there was a good explanation. She just couldn't imagine what that might be.

Her gaze slid to Christian and she noted that he seemed deep in thought, his expression troubled. She wondered what he was thinking about, and then they were approaching the kitchen and she glanced ahead to spot Gia, Santo, Raffaele, and Zanipolo gathered around the kitchen counter.

Carolyn immediately recalled that she was in nothing but a T-shirt and was again about to try to tug her hand free of Christian's, but then noted that the foursome each had what appeared to be bags of blood pressed to their mouths. Gia's and Santo's were full, but Zanipolo and Raffaele's bags were both empty or nearly, and even as she noticed that, Zanipolo ripped his empty bag from his mouth and she caught a flash of fangs before he turned to toss the bag in the garbage.

Carolyn promptly stopped dead.

Drawn from his thoughts, Christian glanced to her in question. "*Cara?* What—?" He paused abruptly and released her hand to move in front of her to raise her face with concern. "You've gone deathly pale, *cara*. Do you feel unwell again?"

Carolyn just stared up at him with a sort of horror and began to shuffle backward.

"*Cara?*" he repeated, his concern deepening. "What—?"

Carolyn didn't wait for more; her horror had suddenly given way to panic, and she whirled on her feet, before heading for the nearest exit, the front door. She knew he was following, but her fear gave her wings and she swore her feet barely touched the floor as she raced toward escape. She was just passing the stairs when the door ahead suddenly opened and Marguerite and Julius started into the villa. Carolyn immediately changed direction, charging up the stairs instead.

"Christian? What's going on?" she heard Julius ask.

"I don't know," he barked, and she could actually feel his breath on the back of her neck.

Carolyn was sure he would grab her at any minute, but he merely tailed her along the hall, staying close but not stopping her, and Carolyn began to realize he had no idea what she'd seen. He hadn't seen it. He'd been lost in thought. If she could just keep her head, she could get out of this, she told herself as she hurried through the bedroom door.

"*Cara,* what is it?" Christian repeated as he closed the door behind them. "Don't you feel well?"

"No," she muttered, grasping at the excuse, and turned toward the bathroom.

"What did you have for dinner?" he asked, following.

"I—" She stopped abruptly at the door and turned to raise a hand to stop him. "I think I'm going to throw up."

His concern deepened. "Then I'll get you a cold, damp cloth and hold your head while you do."

Carolyn blinked at the offer. Her mother used to do that when she was a child, but no one since. Robert's idea of nurturing had been to say, "You look like hell. Go lie down so I don't have to look at you."

Her thoughts were distracted when Christian suddenly took her upraised hand. "You're trembling, and cold as ice. Is your blood sugar low again?"

When she stared at him blankly, he cursed and scooped her into his arms to carry her to the bed. He set her down gently, and pulled the blankets up to cover her, then brushed the hair from her face, frowning when he saw the tears pooling in her eyes.

"Don't cry. I'll run down to the main building and get you some juice. You'll feel better soon," he reassured her, caressing her cheek. "But don't get out of bed until I get back. I don't want you to fall and hurt yourself. I love you too much to lose you now. Okay?"

When she just stared, he bent to press a tender kiss to her lips, then straightened and hurried away, promising, "I'll be as quick as I can."

For one moment, Carolyn didn't move. Her mind was filled with the concern and caring on his face, the tenderness he'd shown and his vow of love. She was sure he cared for her. Perhaps there was an explanation.

For blood in the fridge and fangs? her friendly heckler asked dryly. *Sure there is. You've stumbled into a den of vampires and are on the menu. Surely it isn't coincidence that you suddenly developed a blood problem after meeting him? Is it low blood sugar or just low blood?*

Carolyn sat up abruptly. Surely he hadn't been feeding on her? She immediately began to check her arms and legs for bite marks, then felt her neck, but there was nothing that she could find. She was just relaxing when her heckler suggested, *"Maybe he bit you where you can't see. The back of the neck, or between the legs, he seemed to like it down there when he tied you up and that would explain why you kept passing out at the end.*

Carolyn leaped out of the bed, but then just turned in a circle as it occurred to her that she'd had the low blood sugar thing on the boat, before they'd ever had sex. It couldn't be because he'd bitten her.

Or maybe those erotic dreams weren't dreams at all, her heckler suggested. *Maybe he's been coming to you in your sleep, like Dracula did to Lucy. Creeping in your window and doing things to you as he sucked you dry.* The heckler let that sink in and then added, *Jack did say he thought Christian wanted you, body and soul. He just probably didn't know how right he was.*

Carolyn was at the curtains, ripping them aside and slipping out through the French doors before that last thought was finished. She hurried down the stairs leading to the pool, sure with every step that someone would catch and stop her.

"Christian? Where are you going?"

He paused impatiently at the front door to glance back as his mother led Julius out of the kitchen. "Down to the main building. Carolyn's blood sugar is low again. I need to get her some juice."

"Well, you're not going like that," Julius said dryly. "Get your ass upstairs and put on some pants. And you'll need your wallet if you plan to buy anything."

Christian glanced down, amazed to find he wore only the robe. Muttering under his breath, he hurried back to the stairs.

"Gia and the others were feeding when we got here," Marguerite announced, suddenly in front of him.

"That's nice," Christian said with disinterest and made to go around her.

"Did Carolyn see them feeding?"

The question made him glance at her with surprise. "No, of course not."

"So they weren't feeding when you saw them in the kitchen as you approached?"

He blinked. "No. I mean, I don't think—I never really saw them, I was preoccupied with my thoughts, and Carolyn stopped suddenly and I looked at her and—" He frowned as he recalled her expression. He'd been distracted by her pallor, but her expression had been—

Cursing, Christian turned and hurried upstairs, aware that his parents were following. At the bedroom door he hissed, "Go away," and then pushed inside and glanced to the bed. When he found it empty, he crossed quickly to the bathroom and peered inside. It too was empty. Her dress was still there though, hanging from the shower door, and he grabbed it before he turned out of the room.

"She ran," Marguerite said sadly, drawing his attention to the fact that his parents had followed him into the room.

"She must have slipped out this way." Julius pulled the curtains aside to reveal that the French doors weren't completely closed.

Christian merely grunted and walked over to push past him. Julius didn't move, however, and said patiently, "Pants. You can't run around like that. You'll draw too much attention."

Cursing, he swung back to the room and accepted the pants his mother was already holding out. Still clutching the dress, he tugged them on and quickly shrugged out of the robe. But he didn't bother with a T-shirt or shoes, and simply headed for the French doors again.

"We'll come with you," Marguerite announced.

He paused abruptly and turned to shake his head. "No, I'll handle this."

"You can't control her," Julius pointed out.

"I don't need to control her. I'm just going to explain things and—She'll accept it. She loves me. Gia said so," he added and didn't like the desperate edge to his voice.

"And if she doesn't accept it?" Marguerite asked.

"Mother," he began grimly, and then forced himself to calm down and said, "Mom, I love you. And I know you two are trying to help. But you can't. This is my life, my life mate. I have to do this on my own."

"But I can help you," Marguerite said, and moved forward, pleading, "Let me help you, son. I missed so much. I wasn't there for you for so long. Let me help you."

Christian smiled crookedly, and reached out to hug her tightly, saying, "You have nothing to make up for, you know. It's not your fault you weren't there for me these last five hundred years. I don't blame you for it, and you need to stop feeling guilty about it." Pulling back he added, "And you already have helped me. You brought me to her and you made sure we got to spend time together. Now, it's up to me. I can do this," he added firmly. "I have to."

She hesitated, and then stepped back, but said, "If you need help we are here. And there is no shame in asking us. I helped your brothers and sister with their life mates. I will be more than happy to help with yours. We both will," she added as Julius moved to slide his arm around her.

"Thank you," Christian said quietly, and slipped through the French doors.

"Caro? What on earth?" Bethany gasped, clutching her robe closed and gaping at Carolyn when she opened the door to find her on the doorstep in just the T-shirt.

"I'm sorry I woke you," Carolyn said as she slipped past her into the villa. "I didn't have my key."

"That's not all you don't have," Beth snapped, slamming the door. "Where are your clothes? And your purse? Did you have sex with that captain?"

"I'll explain later," Carolyn muttered, heading for her room.

"I don't think so, girl." Bethany caught her arm as she reached the door to her room. "You can't just come in from a date looking . . ." She paused and then simply waved at her bare feet and legs and said, "Looking like this and not explain yourself. What the hell happened?"

"I— It's—" She gave up her efforts and cast a hunted look to the door as the bell rang. She knew at once it was Christian, and when Beth moved to the door, cried, "Don't answer it!"

Too late, Bethany was already pulling the door open. Christian was on the stoop, her ruined dress in hand. He barely spared Beth a glance before spotting Carolyn. When he started toward her, she turned with a squeak and hurried into her room. He was there before she could close the door though and she backed away, eyes searching frantically for an escape as he advanced into the room.

"Carolyn? Should I call security?" Bethany asked, appearing at the door, the villa's cordless phone in hand.

Christian turned and peered at her silently. After a moment, Bethany's face went blank. Then she set the phone on the bedside table and retreated, pulling the door closed behind her.

Carolyn gaped at the closed door, but then scrambled back as Christian started forward again. "What did you do to her?"

"I took control of her mind, made her relax, and sent

her to her bed thinking everything was all right. She'll stay there until morning no matter what she hears."

His words brought her up short and she breathed, "Oh, God, you really are a vampire."

"No, I am not a vampire," he said solemnly.

"You're lying," she said at once.

"I love you. I promised you I wouldn't lie to you, *cara*. And I'm not. I am not a vampire," Christian said firmly as his hands closed on her arms. It was only then that Carolyn realized she'd stopped backing up.

Forcing down the panic that tried to claim her, she remained perfectly still and said grimly, "I saw the blood in the fridge and Zanipolo's fangs. I—"

"There is an explanation if you will only listen," he said quietly. "Please, *cara*. Let me explain."

Carolyn was tempted, but said, "Show me your teeth."

Christian hesitated, and then opened his mouth to reveal perfectly normal teeth. No long incisors that could pierce bags and skin.

"You don't have fangs." She sagged against him with relief and his arms closed around her as she babbled, "Oh, my God. I thought—I was—When I saw them all in the kitchen and the blood and—I was ready to catch the first plane back to Canada," she admitted with horror, and then glanced at his face. "Was it some kind of joke? Or . . ."

Carolyn paused because while she really, really wanted to believe it was a joke, it had suddenly occurred to her that she'd never noticed Zanipolo or the others having fangs before tonight either. Not that she'd seen fangs on the others, but they'd had bags to their mouths as well . . . And Christian had controlled Beth, she recalled. How could she have forgotten that he'd controlled Beth?

"Please let me explain," Christian said, apparently seeing the dawning realization on her face.

"Show me your fangs," she said grimly.

Much to her surprise, though he didn't look happy, he did open his mouth again. Only this time his incisors suddenly slid smoothly down out of his gums to make two fine points.

Carolyn stared at them and cried, "You said you weren't a vampire."

His teeth slid back and he said quickly, "I'm not. I'm an immortal."

Carolyn frowned, not having a clue what that was about other than it sounded much nicer than a vampire, but then her mind returned to her worries in the villa and she asked abruptly, "Have you been feeding on me?"

"No, I have never once bitten you," Christian assured her, but added apologetically, "although, it was very close that time on the bus . . . and then again each time I've made love to you it has been a struggle not to bite you as well."

He sounded pained to admit it, but the very fact that he had made her believe him, and she asked, "Why? I mean, you have all that bagged blood, why bite anyone?"

"We don't," he assured her. "Except in cases of emergency or . . . er . . . mutual agreement. The situation on the bus would have fit under the emergency heading. I was low on blood, the sun was affecting me, and I almost bit you. But I didn't," he added quickly, and explained, "That's why I dumped you and ran off the bus. The horror on my face wasn't because I felt like you were raping me, as you imagined. *I* kissed *you*, not the other way around. I couldn't resist you. You smelled so sweet and looked so beautiful, and then once I gave in and kissed you, I couldn't resist touching you, but that just made it worse. I wanted to rip your clothes off, push you down on the bench seat and sink my teeth into you as I claimed you with my body and I just . . ."

Carolyn felt her body responding to his words and the memory of that day. That and the recollection of the sudden explosion of passion that had rolled over her then, combined now with the picture he painted of what he had wanted to do and made an echo of that passion roll up through her again. She wasn't even put off by the thought of his biting her as he made love to her, Carolyn realized with dismay, and forced the memories away to ask, "And were you low on blood last night and again tonight when we—"

"No," Christian assured her, and then cleared his throat and admitted, "I was just overexcited."

"Overexcited?" she asked uncertainly, not sure what that had to do with biting.

His expression pained, he admitted, "When I'm with you, *cara,* I just lose it. I want to touch and lick and kiss you everywhere, and I want to make love to you in every position in every place in that villa—Hell, every place in the world. But the life mate passion rolls over me and I lose control and our bodies are merged, and our senses are merged, and it's a real struggle not to sink my teeth into you and merge with you in blood too."

"Oh dear," Carolyn breathed. His words were just making the desire that had been slithering through her stronger. Or perhaps it was his arms around her, and his scent enveloping her, or the erection growing against her belly, Carolyn thought, and then noticed that his eyes were more silver than black as she'd seen on several occasions. "You aren't wearing colored contacts, are you?"

Christian shook his head. "My eyes flare silver when I need blood."

"So you need blood now?" she asked uncertainly.

"No, I had several bags while waiting for you to return from your date last night," he assured her, and then cleared his throat and admitted, "They also go silver when I want you."

Carolyn blinked, and asked with disbelief, "So it's like an ocular boner?"

He gave a startled laugh, but nodded. "Basically, yes, I suppose it is."

"Huh," she muttered staring into his eyes, and shifting against him, which only seemed to increase the excitement shimmering through her.

"*Cara?*"

"Hmm?" she asked, shifting again.

"You have to stop doing that, or we won't get to finish our talk," Christian said in a pained voice.

"Stop what?" she asked with surprise, shifting again to lean back a bit.

"That," he said grimly, reaching for her hips to hold her in place so she'd stop unintentionally rubbing against him.

"Oh." Carolyn felt herself flush. But every shift had sent shivers of pleasure through her and she was terribly aware that she was in his arms in nothing but a T-shirt, and that he had both an ocular and a penile boner and . . . Geez, she'd just discovered how good sex could be. "Ummm . . . Christian?"

"Yes?"

Carolyn raised her head again, her blush deepening.

"Maybe we could talk on the bed?" she suggested, and then breathed, "Wow," as the silver completely overtook his eyes and turned molten. It was accompanied by a definite growth spurt against her belly too. Christian growled, his arms tightening around her and his head lowering toward hers, and then suddenly jumped away as if he'd been burned.

"No," he growled, and then softened the rejection by saying, "Believe me, I want to, but we have to talk first. I don't want to be overwhelmed by passion and then wake up only to find you have panicked and fled. I need to explain everything so you understand and feel safe."

"I feel safe," Carolyn assured him, feeling bereft now that his arms were no longer around her. "You're an immortal, not a vampire. You drink bagged blood, have never bitten me, and you really, really want me," Carolyn said, smiling as a sense of power she'd never experienced before swept through her. She felt desirable, beautiful even. Wanted. This gorgeous man's eyes were glowing for her, his body hardening. She had no idea how or why she affected him so, but just the fact that she did was one hell of a turn-on. It made her want to test her new powers.

"Caro," Christian growled in warning.

"What?" she asked innocently.

His eyes narrowed. "You have a very naughty look on your face. Whatever you're thinking of doing, don't. We need to have this talk."

"Naughty?" she asked with a throaty chuckle.

"Yes," he said firmly. "Naughty."

"And if I did do anything naughty, would you spank me?" she asked with interest.

"Caro—"

"And what is considered naughty? Would borrowing your T-shirt without permission be naughty?" she asked. "It probably is. I should give it back."

Carolyn saw his eyes widen with realization, but she was already pulling his shirt off over her head and walking toward him.

Christian immediately began to back away. When the back of his legs hit the bed, he dropped with dismay to sit on it. His voice was tortured when he said, "*Cara*, we need to talk. I can't risk losing you. I love and need you too much. You're my life mate."

"You won't lose me." She stepped between his legs and glided her fingers into his hair. When he raised his head to meet her gaze, she said, "Immortal or even vampire, I don't care what you are. I need you too much too. You make me laugh and smile and happy. And you make me feel beautiful and desirable and I've never felt that way in my life. I've never enjoyed such passion or pleasure. My life was a wasteland before you, and now it's an orgy of pleasure. I'm not giving that up easily," she assured him. "I love you for all of that and much more. You're stuck with me. You'll have to kick me out of your life when you tire of me, and then I'll probably stalk you like a crazy lady. But I'm done running."

"You are my life mate, *cara*, I will never tire of you," he vowed, his hands rising to clasp her by the waist and turn her onto the bed.

"What's a life mate?"

Christian blinked his eyes open to find Carolyn leaning over him, her hair framing his face. Smiling wryly, he said, "Good morning to you too."

"It's only three thirty, not morning yet," she assured him. "What's a life mate? You've called me that two or three times now."

"A life mate is the one person we cannot read or control who can be a proper mate to us. With them we can enjoy shared dreams, shared pleasure, and passion beyond measure, but we can also relax and not guard our thoughts with them," he answered solemnly.

"And I'm that for you?" Carolyn asked with surprise.

He nodded.

She considered that and then frowned. "How do you know? I mean, what if you've got the wrong girl?"

Christian grinned at her worry. "Do you remember

on the beach when I smoothed cream into your back and started to make love to you on the lounger before Beth called to interrupt us?"

Her eyes and mouth went round, and then she gasped, "But that was a dream."

"A shared dream," he corrected.

"You mean you and I—?"

He nodded. "As were the other dreams. It is a sign of a life mate, as is eating again, not being able to read their mind or control them. As well as the shared pleasure."

"Shared pleasure?" she asked.

"When I make love to you I experience your pleasure as my own," he said quietly. "And so will you feel mine."

"I don't recall feeling—"

"When you touched me on the terrace," he prompted, and slow realization dawned on her face. "I distracted you then and have tried to keep you from touching me since because I couldn't explain it without telling you everything and I worried you weren't ready for it." He hadn't given her the chance to touch him tonight yet either. Her admission of love had quite overset him earlier and it had been a very short, passionate session before they'd both been screaming and passing out. His thoughts scattered as he felt her fingers slide down his chest toward his groin.

Christian's gaze shot to hers, but knowing she was testing out the shared pleasure, he simply watched her face as her fingers found and closed around his suddenly awakening member. Her eyes widened at the first touch, but then drifted shut as she closed her hand around him and drew it along his growing length. His own eyes drifted closed, so Christian was taken completely by surprise when she suddenly climbed to straddle his hips.

* * *

Blinking his eyes open, he found himself staring with amazement. She was smiling. Carolyn knew exactly how she was affecting him and was reveling in it. Enjoying the power she wielded, she grinned wickedly and lowered herself, taking him into herself in a slow, torturous manner that had him clenching his fists to keep from grabbing her hips and taking control. A relieved groan slid from his lips when he was finally buried inside her to the hilt, but her torture wasn't over yet. Grin widening, Carolyn leaned forward to press a kiss to his lips, then slowly began to move, apparently determined to drive him wild with her slow torment. It was sexy as hell.

"Why do we faint each time?"

Christian opened his eyes, expecting Carolyn to be leaning over him again, but this time she lay on her side beside him, head on her upraised hand as she waited for him to explain why they fainted at the end of each lovemaking session.

He hesitated, his brain slow to wake fully, and then answered, "That happens with life mates for the first year or so."

"All life mates experience this?" she asked, running her fingers lightly along his arm.

Christian raised his arm, and drew her against his chest before lowering it again. Running his own hands down her back, he admitted, "I have only heard of one couple who it didn't happen for right away."

When she tilted her head up in question, he kissed her forehead, and murmured, "My cousin Vincent and his life mate, Jackie."

She raised her eyebrows. "Weren't they life mates then?"

"Yes, but Jackie had a bad experience with an immortal as a teenager," he explained, his hand finding her breast. Pleasure slid through him at once and his voice became a little rough as he continued, "My mother believes the experience caused an ingrained wariness that made her erect a natural wall that wouldn't allow their minds to merge fully until she learned to trust him completely. After a couple of weeks they apparently started fainting as well."

"Oh." Carolyn breathed, arching into his caress, and then mumbled, "You have a lot of cousins."

"More than you can imagine, *cara*. And they will be yours too," he assured her, pulling her to straddle his thighs as he sat up.

Twenty

Christian stirred lazily and opened his eyes. A smile tugged at his lips when his gaze landed on Carolyn, sleeping beside him. He'd woken up before her this time, he thought and started to reach for her, but then retrieved his hand and rolled out of bed instead when his bladder complained of a need for relief. He quickly crossed the room, and slipped into the bathroom to tend to the matter.

Carolyn wasn't in bed when he returned and he paused, but relaxed when he spotted her by the closet. She must have heard the door open, because she turned then and smiled.

"Have I mentioned how incredibly handsome and sexy you look first thing in the morning with your hair all tousled like that?" she asked as her gaze slid over him, and then her eyes drifted back to his face and she added dryly, "And young."

"I've told you, I'm not as young as I look," he said, starting toward her.

She tilted her head. "How old are you?"

"I was born in 1491, I'm five—" He broke off to rush forward as Carolyn's knees buckled and she started to slide toward the floor.

Catching her before she hit the carpet, Christian carried her to the bed, and sat her on the end of it. He then straightened and said wryly, "Well, you didn't take that quite as well as the rest of it."

She just stared at him and he shifted uncomfortably.

"I told you I wasn't younger than you are," he pointed out and then cleared his throat and said worriedly, "I know you have a problem with having a younger lover, but how do you feel about an older one?"

Carolyn just stared at him.

Christian ran a hand wearily around the back of his neck. It had seemed to be going well before this, but now . . . well his age had apparently knocked her for a loop and he didn't know what to say to make it all right again. It was also incredibly difficult to think with her sitting there naked on the foot of the bed.

"What's the difference between a vampire and an immortal?"

Christian breathed out. At least she appeared to be over the worst of her shock. Well, she was talking anyway.

"Vampires are mythical creatures, fabled to be cursed and soulless," he answered quickly. "Immortals are a result of scientific advancement. We have nanos in us that kill off illnesses and cancers, and so on, and repair damage done to the body by the sun or aging."

Carolyn absorbed that and then said, "Which is why you're alive and strapping at . . . My God, you're more than five centuries old," she breathed.

"Yes." He grimaced. "And some days I feel every one of those centuries." Like now, he decided and thought wouldn't it be ironic if, after refusing to get involved with him because he was too young, she now refused because he was too old?

"And the blood?" Carolyn asked suddenly, drawing him from his thoughts. "Why do you—?"

"The nanos use blood to propel and replicate themselves," Christian explained. "They also utilize it in repairs. But it takes a lot of blood, more than a human body can produce. Immortals need an outside source of blood aside from what they can produce." He paused, and then added, "We didn't start out with fangs. The nanos altered my ancestors to aid them in getting what they needed."

"The nanos gave you fangs?" she asked with surprise.

Christian nodded. "And other benefits. We're faster than other humans, stronger, and see better at night . . . among other things."

"Other things like controlling Bethany and making her do what you want?"

Christian nodded unapologetically.

"So while you feed on bagged blood now . . . ?"

"We didn't always have that option," he said quietly.

She seemed to accept that, and then asked, "So are you an alien?"

He smiled faintly. "No. We're human just like you . . . and you'll be immortal just like me when I turn you."

Carolyn stilled. "What?"

"If you want," Christian added quickly. "I would never turn you without your permission. It's not allowed, but even if it were I wouldn't. I—" Christian paused and sighed, then moved to sit next to her on the bed.

"Carolyn," he said, taking her hands. "You're my life mate, and that's a very precious thing. I also love you, which is inevitable between life mates. The nanos pick the perfect mate, and—" He paused, realizing that sounded about as romantic as dog food. He tried again. "The point is, you are my life mate. I will never cheat on you, never stop loving you, and would sooner cut out my own heart than hurt you . . . And I want to spend the rest of my life with you. I would like to turn you and claim you as my mate for so long as we both live."

Carolyn frowned and hesitated, and then asked, "So I wouldn't age anymore? I'd always look forty-two to your twenty-five?" Before he could answer, she added wryly, "Which I suppose is better than looking sixty-two to your twenty-five if we had met later. Still, it seems unfair that for the rest of . . . well . . . however long we live, everyone will think I'm the older woman with the boy toy when you're really ages older than me." She shook her head and leaned it against his shoulder, moaning, "Why couldn't we have met twenty years ago? I'd look the same age as you then."

"You wouldn't look forty-two," he said quietly, relief already washing through him. She was willing to turn. "You'll look somewhere between twenty-five and thirty years old."

Carolyn stiffened and slowly lifted her head. "What?"

"I told you, the nanos repair damage," he said gently.

"Yeah, like from the sun and illness and—"

"And aging," he put in. "They are programmed to keep their host in peak condition. They will repair everything, including any damage aging has done."

She blinked and then squawked, "That's not repairing, that's reversing."

"Yes, I suppose," Christian acknowledged.

"Well . . ." Carolyn frowned. "I don't know if I want to look twenty-five forever. For heaven's sake, nobody gives twenty-five-year-olds respect. Not even me. I've been thinking of you all as a bunch of young punks since meeting you. Well, until I got to know you at least, and—" She stopped talking and frowned when Christian suddenly started to laugh. "What's so funny?"

"You," he said gently. "What you're talking about is ageism. And it happens no matter the age. Twenty-year-olds think teenagers don't know a thing, thirty-year-olds feel the same about twenty-year-olds and teenagers, and so on." He quirked an eyebrow and asked, "Do you really think fifty- and sixty-year-olds don't look at you and feel the same way?"

Carolyn scowled at the thought.

"And it gets no better among immortals. My brother Lucern is over six hundred and treats anyone under four hundred like they're young punks." He paused briefly and then said, "And I hate to point this out, but most women would be pleased at the thought of being their peak age and physical condition for the rest of their lives . . . Always young, always healthy and vibrant."

Carolyn sighed. "I've always been weird."

He grinned. "It's part of your charm."

"Hmm," she said, and then suddenly stiffened. "Will I have to drink blood?"

"Not drink it, no. You needn't even taste it," he assured her quickly, suspecting that would be a problem. "If you puncture the bag with your fangs, they draw the blood directly into your system without it ever crossing your tongue. But you will have to feed to allow the nanos to do their work and keep you at peak condition."

She thought for a moment, and then asked, "Peak condition?"

"Yes." Christian peered at her curiously.

"Does that mean perky breasts and no cellulite?"

Christian's eyebrows rose. "I haven't noticed any cellulite, and I like your breasts."

"Yes, yes, I love you too," Carolyn muttered, obviously thinking he was only saying that out of love. "But would the nanos—?"

"Yes," he assured her patiently.

"Oh." She sighed and said, "Well, there's that then at least."

She made it sound like a booby prize. Frowning, he said, "*Cara,* I—"

"How am I supposed to explain it to my employees?" she asked suddenly.

"Ah." Christian frowned. "Well, that's—"

"I suppose I could let them think I had face-lifts and stuff."

"Er . . ."

"But I'd probably have to sell the advertising agency and do something else after a couple of years," she continued with a frown. "I mean, eventually they'd pick up on my not aging."

"Yes," he said with relief, glad she'd concluded that on her own and he hadn't had to tell her that would have to happen.

"Actually, it would probably be better if I did that before turning anyway," she muttered. "I mean, you live in Italy . . . I don't think I could bear to be without your arms around me for weeks and months on end, and—" She paused on a gasp when he suddenly scooped her into his lap.

"You will never spend weeks or months without my arms around you," he assured her.

Carolyn smiled and slid her arms around his neck. "That will make it all worthwhile then."

Christian just stared at her for a moment, then shook his head and said softly, "God, you are the strangest creature . . . and I love you more than life itself."

He caught the sheen of tears in her eyes, and then she drew his head down and they were kissing when the door opened.

"Carolyn, if we want to make breakfast— Oh, my God!"

Christian lifted his head, and turned toward the door where Bethany now stood gaping at them, but glanced back with surprise as Carolyn nearly toppled off his lap in her panic to get up. He steadied her quickly, and then glanced back to Bethany as she began to squawk.

"What the hell are you doing? Last night you come back half naked from a date with that captain guy and then today you're screwing gay boy? What the hell? You're supposed to be frigid and suicidal, not slutting around like some Mata Hari!"

Christian started to narrow his eyes on the woman, but Carolyn stepped in front of him.

When Christian glanced her way, Carolyn gave him a warning scowl. She'd recognized his concentrated look from last night. He'd been about to control Bethany and send her away again as he had then, but it wasn't necessary. She'd handle this. She wouldn't allow her friends to be controlled.

Carolyn waited for Christian to nod and relax, and then moved to pick up his discarded T-shirt.

"Christian's not gay. Obviously," she said pointedly as she tugged the T-shirt on. "And I am not slutting around. I didn't sleep with Jack." Propping her hands on her hips, she added, "And you're the one who keeps saying I should have a fling, so—" She paused suddenly and then barked, "Frigid? Who the hell said I was frigid?"

"Nobody," Bethany muttered, scowling at her.

Carolyn eyed her silently. She'd never told Beth about

her marriage, and she knew Genie wouldn't have. That left— "It was Robert, wasn't it?"

When Bethany avoided her gaze, Carolyn frowned and added in a rising voice, "And what do you mean, I'm supposed to be suicidal?"

"She's been trying to drive you to suicide," Christian said quietly.

"What?" Carolyn glanced his way with amazement. His gaze was focused on Beth. He was reading her, she realized, but surely he had that wrong?

"That's not true," Bethany said at once, but Christian just continued.

"She brought you here hoping that being surrounded by honeymooners while in the midst of a divorce would just add to the depression that has been plaguing you since your marriage fell apart. And then she feigned illness to ensure that you were alone to add to your sense of being a failure and a loser."

"Th-that's ridiculous," Bethany stammered.

"She's been feeding you her diabetes medication in the bottled water to make you feel sickly and add to your troubles. Though she wouldn't have minded had you had an accident while feeling poorly and disoriented. She even messed with several of your shoes to aid in the endeavor."

"How do you know that?" Beth asked, pale and shaking with horror.

Carolyn felt a slow burn starting in her gut. "Seriously, Beth?"

"I—" Beth shook her head, confusion and horror on her face, and then anger plowed everything else under and she shrieked, "Well, what did you expect? You've made Robert's life a living hell for ten years and now you're trying to take him for everything he's worth? You're just a frigid little gold digger and he—"

"*I'm* the gold digger?" Carolyn asked with disbelief. "How can I be the gold digger when the money is mine?"

"Oh, don't give me that crap," Beth snarled. "You were poor as a church mouse in university. Besides, Robert told me everything. How you refused him sex and kicked him out of your bed. How you spent his inheritance like it was water, and are trying to clean him out. We're going to marry as soon as the divorce is over, but you keep dragging it out, trying to squeeze more out of him with that fancy lawyer of yours."

Carolyn was trembling from head to toe by the time Bethany finished, but calmed when she felt Christian's hand on her leg. She leaned against his legs and asked quietly, "How long?"

"How long what?" Bethany asked resentfully.

"How long have you been sleeping with Robert?"

Bethany's teeth ground together and then she said, "We fell in love when you hired me to sell the first house. But we aren't lovers. He refuses to be unfaithful."

"Except for the dozen or so women I've caught him with and the ones I haven't," Carolyn said dryly.

"That's a lie. He's always been faithful to you, despite the fact that you didn't deserve it since you wouldn't sleep with him."

"Right," Carolyn said wearily. "And whose idea was it to off me in St. Lucia?"

"He—I—" Bethany flushed and paled by turn and it was Christian who answered for her.

"His. He suggested the vacation here and wanted her to kill you, but she couldn't bring herself to do it. The best she could do was try to make you as miserable as possible and hope you killed yourself. The diabetes drugs were the most she was willing to do, because she thought they would just make you feel poorly and more suicidal. Her conscience could deal with that."

Carolyn nodded solemnly. She stared at Beth for a moment, and then said slowly, "So he's got you so in love with him that you were willing to kill for him."

"No. I would never kill anyone," Beth protested at once, horror on her face.

"Don't fool yourself, Beth, driving me to suicide is killing as much as if you had fed me an overdose or sliced my wrists open," Carolyn said coldly, and then picked up Christian's jeans and handed them to him before turning to grab the phone.

"What are you doing?" Beth asked with alarm.

"Doing you a favor, the last and best favor I'll ever do for you," Carolyn said as she punched in numbers. The phone rang twice and then Genie's voice sounded, pleasant and professional. "Genie, it's Carolyn."

"Oh, hey, hon," Genie said cheerfully. "How went the date?"

"I'll tell you about that later, I promise. But right now I need a favor."

"Okay, no problem. What is it?" Genie asked at once.

"I'm going to hand the phone to Beth and I'd like you to tell her everything you know about my marriage to Robert," she said quietly.

"Everything?" Genie asked with surprise.

"The affairs, the inheritance, Conroy . . . *everything*," Carolyn said firmly. "She thinks she's in love with him."

"What?" Genie squawked. "Oh, my God, put that idiot on the phone."

Carolyn handed the phone to Beth, and turned to Christian. Seeing that he'd put on his pants, she held out her hand. When he took it, she led him from the room.

"If you had died," Christian began as they stepped into the hall.

"I haven't made a will. As my husband, Robert would have gotten everything," she said and then grimaced. "I guess I shall have to do it now to discourage him from trying again, but at least this gave me a heads-up."

"You're not going to call the police about this, are you?" While it was couched as a question, it really wasn't one. Still, Carolyn shook her head, and he frowned. "You're just going to let them get away with it?"

Carolyn shrugged with indifference. "Get away with what? Nothing happened except that I didn't feel good for a couple of days. Besides, Bethany's basically in the same spot as I was ten years ago. She's as much Robert's dupe as I was. Well, except for the willingness to see me dead," she added dryly. Shaking her head, Carolyn grimaced. "I'm guessing if Bethany had succeeded at making me kill myself, she would have been his next victim. She's good at what she does and makes a heck of a lot of money." She smiled wryly and added, "Besides, I kind of owe her in a way."

"Owe her?" he asked with disbelief. "For what?"

"If she hadn't fallen halfheartedly in with his suggestion, he might have tried to kill me another way, one that might have been more successful. At least I now know I need to watch my back," she pointed out.

"Your back will be watched by many," he assured her solemnly. "You have a whole family now, *cara*."

"And that's the real reason I owe her," Carolyn responded. "Because if she hadn't brought me here, I never would have met you."

When he stopped walking, she smiled faintly. "Hadn't thought of that, had you?"

Christian shook his head, a slightly stunned look on his face.

She peered curiously at his expression. "What are you thinking?"

"I've just realized you think very like my mother," he said with wonder.

"Er . . ." Carolyn frowned, not sure that was a good thing. Finally, she asked, "How is that?"

"She can see past the pain and suffering to the good too," he said solemnly.

Carolyn smiled. "The silver lining. I learned it from my mother. She always found the silver lining. It's how she survived the worst of times. How I did too."

"You'll have to teach me that." He scooped her up and carried her to the door.

"Are we going to your villa?" Carolyn said, automatically opening the door for him to carry her out. Neither of them worried about closing it. When he nodded, she pointed out, "I'll have to come back for clothes at some point."

"Gia and Mother would probably be happy to tend to that if you wish to avoid Beth in future," he offered.

Carolyn stiffened. "Your mother is here in St. Lucia?"

"Ah." Christian grimaced. "Actually, yes, and you've met her."

Her eyes widened. "I have?" She paused and stared, taking in his hair color and the shape of his eyes with a sinking feeling. "Not Marguerite?"

He nodded apologetically.

"But I— She—"

"She volunteered the band to replace the one that canceled because she recognized that you were my life mate," he explained gently.

She stared at him blankly. "Then Julius is your . . ."

"Father," he finished.

"Oh, dear God," she breathed. "He doesn't look any older than you."

"We all look around the same age," he reminded her quietly.

"Yes, of course," she murmured, and couldn't resist asking, "How old are your parents?"

"My mother is a couple hundred years older than me."

"Is that all?" Carolyn asked faintly.

"And my father was born in 534 BC."

"B-BC?" she stammered. "But that's— That's more than 2,500 years old," she said incredulously.

"Considerably more than 2,500," he agreed easily.

"But . . . Who created these nanos? I mean, there can't have been that kind of technology back . . . Well, not even five hundred years ago, let alone 2,500. It's just not possible."

Christian hesitated, but then decided he'd best explain now, because once he got her back to the villa they wouldn't be talking much for a while. One of his arms was under her bare legs, the other around her back, his hand was resting against the curve of her breast through the T-shirt, and her scent was teasing his nose as he walked. Not unexpectedly his body was responding. It would be a while before they could be in each other's company without wanting to get naked. Best to get all the explanations out of the way that he could, he decided and asked, "Have you heard of Atlantis?"

If you enjoyed

UNDER A VAMPIRE MOON,

turn the page for a sneak peek at the
next book in Lynsay Sands' Argeneau series,

THE LADY IS A VAMP

Coming August 2012
from Avon Books

'Last day, Fred,' Jeanne Louise commented, offering a smile to the guard as she approached the security station. The mortal man had worked the exit of the science division of Argeneau Enterprises for nearly five years now and was being rotated out to another area to prevent him from noticing that many members of the staff didn't age. She would miss Fred. He'd been a smiling face wishing her a good night and asking about her family for a long time.

"Yes, Miss Jeanie. Last day here. Off to one of the blood banks next week."

Jeanne Louise nodded, her smile fading slightly and expression sincere as she said, "They'll be lucky to have you there. You'll be missed."

"I'll miss all of you too," he assured her solemnly, walking around the counter to the door to unlock it for her. He pushed it open then and held it, turning sideways to let her slip past as he said, "Night, Miss Jeanie. You enjoy the long weekend now."

"I will. You too," she said, smiling faintly at his calling

her Miss Jeanie. He always made her feel like a child . . . which was impressive when he was only in his late fifties and she was more than forty years older than him. Not that he would believe that. She didn't look over twenty-five. It was one of the benefits to being a vampire, or immortal, as the old-timers preferred to be called. There were many such benefits and she was grateful for every one. But it didn't stop her from feeling bad for mortals who didn't enjoy those perks.

Great, a guilt-ridden vampire, she thought wryly, and gave a chuckle at the cliché. Next she'd be angst-ridden, mopey, and whining about her long life.

"Yeah, not gonna happen," Jeanne Louise muttered with amusement, and then glanced around at the sound of a stone skittering on pavement. Spotting one of the guys from the Blood Division entering the parking garage behind her, she offered a nod and then turned forward to make her way to her car. Slipping into her convertible, she started the engine and quickly backed out to exit the garage, her mind distracted with considering whether she should stay up and take care of some chores today or just go home to bed.

That was one problem with being a vampire, Jeanne Louise acknowledged as she turned out of the garage and started up the street. The hours were off-kilter with the rest of the world. Her shift generally ended at 7 a.m., but she'd stayed behind to finish up when the others had left. It was now 7:30, which meant that to perform some of those chores she was thinking of, she'd have to stay awake for another two hours and then head out to those places that weren't yet open. Under a hot, beating sun.

Frankly, at that moment, staying up another two hours was an exhausting thought.

Home to bed, Jeanne Louise decided, taking one hand

off the steering wheel to stifle a yawn as she slowed to a stop at a red light.

She'd just come to a halt when movement in her rear-view mirror caught her attention. Glancing toward it sharply, Jeanne Louise caught a glimpse of a dark shape popping up in the back seat, and then a hissing sound was accompanied by a sudden sharp pain in her neck.

"What the—?" She grabbed her neck and started to turn at the sound of the back door opening and closing. But then her own door *was* opening and the dark figure was reaching past her to shift the car into park.

"What?" Jeanne Louise muttered, frowning at the garbled word and how slow her thought processes suddenly seemed. And then the man was scooping her up to transfer her into the passenger seat and slide himself into the driver's seat. Vision beginning to blur, Jeanne Louise watched him shift the car back into drive, and then she lost consciousness.

Jeanne Louise stirred sleepily and tried to turn onto her side, but frowned as she found she couldn't. Opening her eyes, she stared at the ceiling overhead, noting that it was a plain white, not the pale rose of her bedroom at home. She tried to sit up and recall what had woken her and found that she couldn't move. Jeanne Louise saw that she was restrained, gaping down at the chains crisscrossing her body from her shoulders to her feet. Good Lord.

"It's steel. You won't be able to break it."

Jeanne Louise glanced sharply in the direction from which the voice had come, sliding over what was a very small room, all white with nothing but the bed she lay on. The only interesting thing in there with her was the man addressing her from the doorway. Although he wasn't overly tall, perhaps four or five inches taller than her own five feet, six inches, the man was built, with wide shoulders and a narrow waist. He was also rather attractive in a boy-next-door sort of way, with brown hair, a square jaw, and eyes a brighter green than she'd ever seen . . . and she'd seen a lot of mortal eyes in her one hundred and two, almost one hundred and three, years of life. These easily beat out every other set she'd ever seen.

"How do you feel?" he asked with what appeared to be real concern.

"I've been better," Jeanne Louise said dryly, glancing down to the chains again. Steel, he'd said. Cripes, he had her bound up like a crazed elephant or something.

"The tranquilizer I used on you can cause headaches and a fuzzy feeling as it wears off," he announced apologetically. "Are you experiencing anything of that nature? Do you need an ibuprofen or something?"

"No," Jeanne Louise said grimly, knowing it would go away quickly on its own, thanks to the nanos. She then narrowed her eyes on the man's face as she instinctively tried to penetrate his thoughts and take control of him. She intended to make him get her out of these ridiculous chains, explain himself, and then call her Uncle Lucian and have him send someone to deal with him. That was the plan anyway. It didn't go that way, however—because she couldn't penetrate his mind or take control of him.

Must be the drug he gave me, Jeanne Louise thought with a frown, and gave her head a shake to try to clear it a little more before trying again.

"Nothing," she muttered with bewilderment. The drug definitely had to still be affecting her, she surmised, and then scowled at him. "What did you give me?"

"The latest tranquilizer we've been working on in R and D," he said mildly, and then disappeared out the door and briefly out of sight.

Jeanne Louise frowned at the empty space, his words running through her head. R and D was research and development. But R and D for where? It couldn't be a normal tranquilizer for mortals; that would have hardly slowed her down, let alone knocked her out. But—

Her thoughts scattered as he returned and approached the bed.

"Do you work for Argeneau Enterprises?" Jeanne Louise asked, eyeing what he held in one hand with interest. He was clutching a tall glass of what appeared to be ice water, and she was suddenly terribly aware that her mouth and throat were parched.

"I do. I'm in R and D like you, only I help develop new drugs while you have been working on genetic anomalies, I believe," he said easily as he paused beside the bed.

Jeanne Louise frowned. Bastien Argeneau, her cousin and the head of Argeneau Enterprises, had hired her directly after she'd graduated from college seventy-five years ago. She'd worked for Argeneau Enterprises ever since. At first, she'd actually been in the department this man claimed to be in, but twenty-five years ago, Bastien had asked Jeanne Louise to choose who she wanted from R and D and form a team. She would be heading up a new branch of the department, one dedicated solely to the task of finding a way to allow her cousin Vincent and her uncle Victor to feed without the need to bite mortals. They desperately wanted to be able to feed off bagged blood like everyone else did. It made life much simpler. However, both men suffered from a genetic anomaly that made bagged blood as useful to them as water. They would starve on a diet of bagged blood. She was supposed to figure out why and if they could be given some sort of supplement to prevent that. She'd been heading up the team working on the problem ever since and they still hadn't figured out what the exact anomaly was that caused it, let alone how to fix it.

Sighing at what she considered her failure, Jeanne Louise glanced to her captor again, noting that he was standing beside the bed looking from her to the water and back, his expression troubled. Catching her questioning glance, he asked, "Can you drink water? I mean, I know you people can eat and drink, but will it help or do you need blood only? I have some laid in for you."

Jeanne Louise stared at him silently. I know you people can eat and drink? You people? Like she was another species altogether. An alien or something. The man knew she wasn't mortal. But what exactly did he know? She eyed him solemnly, once again trying to penetrate his thoughts, and once again failing. Then her gaze slid back to the water. It looked so damn good. The glass was sweating, rivulets running down the outside, and Jeanne Louise would have paid a lot just to lick up those drops. But she had no idea what was in the glass besides ice and water. He could have drugged it. She couldn't take the chance. If he worked in R and D at Argeneau Enterprises, he had access to drugs that could affect her.

"It's not drugged," the man said as if reading her thoughts, which she considered rather ironic. He was mortal, one glance at his eyes proved that, and mortals couldn't read minds. Immortals could, yet she couldn't read his, while he seemed to be able to read hers. Or her expression, she supposed.

"There's no need to keep you drugged," he added as if to convince her. "You'll never escape those chains. Besides I need you clearheaded to consider the proposition I'm going to put to you."

"The proposition," Jeanne Louise muttered with irritation, giving a tentative tug on her chains. With a little time and effort she might have broken the chain . . . if he hadn't gone crazy with it, wrapping it around her and the bed as if it was linen around a mummy.

"Water or blood?"

The question drew her gaze to the glass again. There was no guarantee the blood wouldn't be drugged too. She debated the issue briefly and then gave in with a grim nod.

He immediately bent, sliding one hand beneath her head and lifting it, then placed the glass to her lips and tipped it. Jeanne Louise tried to just sip at the water, but the moment the liquid touched her tongue, so cold and soothing, she found herself gulping at the icy drink. Half of it was gone before she stopped and closed her lips. He immediately eased the glass away and laid her head gently back on the bed.

"Are you hungry?" he asked then.

Jeanne Louise considered the question. Her last meal of food for the day was usually breakfast in the Argeneau cafeteria about an hour and a half before heading home. She wasn't hungry . . . But he'd have to unchain her to feed her, and that thought was appealing enough to bring a smile to her lips.

"Yes," Jeanne Louise said, quickly hiding her smile when she noted the way his eyes narrowed.

He hesitated, and then nodded and turned away to leave the room once more, presumably in search of food for her.

Jeanne Louise watched him go, but the moment the door closed behind him, she turned her attention to the chains, trying to sort out if they were one long chain wrapped around her and the bed over and over again or several of them. She supposed it wouldn't make much difference. Bound up as she was, she couldn't move enough to get the leverage to try breaking one, let alone several, lengths of chain.

Her best bet was for him to unchain her so that she could sit up and eat. She could overpower him easily then. Of course, it would be easier all the way around if her mind wasn't still affected by the drug he'd given her and she could just take control of him. She'd just make him unchain her and save herself a lot of bother. Jeanne Louise had no idea what this proposition of his was, but mortals who knew about them were few and far between. They were either trusted retainers, higher-ups in Argeneau Enterprises, or exceptionally brilliant scientists who had to know what they were dealing with to do their jobs. He was obviously one of the latter—a brilliant scientist working on drugs in R and D. But no matter what group they belonged to, mortals in the know had tabs kept on them. They were given sporadic mind checks to see that they were okay mentally and not planning anything stupid, like going to the press about them. Or kidnapping immortals, chaining them to a bed, and propositioning them.

Somebody had obviously fallen down on the job here, Jeanne Louise thought grimly. The knowledge didn't worry her much. She wasn't scared, just annoyed that her routine was being disrupted this way and that she'd probably be up most of the day as this mess was being cleaned up. They'd have to find out what the man's plans had been and who else, if anyone, he'd told about them. Then the man's mind and memories would have to be wiped, and the situation set to rights. Jeanne Louise wouldn't have to take care of all that. The Enforcers were in charge of things like that, but she'd probably be kept up for hours answering questions and explaining things. It was a huge inconvenience. Jeanne Louise disliked having her routine disrupted.

Her thoughts scattered and she glanced expectantly

toward the door as it opened, satisfaction curving her lips when she saw the plate of food her captor held. He would definitely have to unchain her to eat. However, she soon figured out that the guy wasn't just smart at his job when he shifted the plate to one hand and bent to do something beside the bed that made the top end rise with a quiet hum.

"Hospital bed," he said straightening, a grin claiming his lips at her vexed expression. "They're handy."

"Yes," she said dryly as he paused and glanced around with a frown.

"Be right back," he announced, and set the plate on the floor beside the bed before heading out of the room again. He wasn't gone long. Not even a minute passed before he reappeared with a wooden chair in hand. He set it down beside the bed, then scooped up the plate again and settled into the chair. The fellow immediately scooped up some food on a fork, but when he held it toward her, she turned her head away with irritation.

"I'm not hungry."

"You said you were," he pointed out with surprise.

"I lied," she said succinctly.

"Come now, I warmed it up and everything. At least try it," he coaxed as if speaking to a difficult child. When she merely cast a scowl his way, he smiled charmingly and held up the forkful of food. "It's your favorite."

That drew her attention to the plate, and her eyebrows rose slightly when she saw that it was indeed her favorite, a cheese omelet and sausages. It was what she had for breakfast in the cafeteria at work each morning. When her gaze shifted to his face in question, he shrugged.

"I thought you should be comfortable while you're here. I have no desire to make you uncomfortable or unhappy."

Jeanne Louise's eyes widened incredulously and then dropped meaningfully to the chains. All she said, however, was a sarcastic, "Helloooo?"

"I'll remove those after you've heard my proposition," he assured her solemnly. "I just needed them to keep you in place until I do."

"You can stick your proposition," she growled, and then narrowed her eyes on his face again and tried to slip into his thoughts, but again came up against a blank wall. The drugs were still affecting her. She fell back on the bed with annoyance and scowled at him.

"Fine. Tell me about this proposition of yours," she said finally. Anything to get out of there.

He hesitated, but then shook his head. "I don't think you're in a state of mind to listen. You seem rather annoyed."

"I wonder why," she said dryly.

"Probably because you're hungry," he said mildly and held out the forkful of food again.

"I told you I'm not hun—" Jeanne Louise paused, scowling as her stomach gave a loud rumble. Apparently she was hungry, after all. It was probably the smell of food causing it, and the fact that she'd been so wrapped up in work she'd only eaten half her breakfast that morning. At least that's what she'd told herself when she'd pushed her half-eaten meal away. Forget the fact that she'd recently been skipping meals a lot and only eating half meals when she did bother with food. It just didn't seem to be quite as flavorful or tempting as it used to. Even chocolate didn't seem as yummy as it once did.

In truth, Jeanne Louise suspected she was reaching that stage where food lost its appeal and became more a bother than anything else. Mind you, while her breakfast had seemed bland and boring that morning, the same thing smelled damned good now, and she actually was feeling a bit hungry, she acknowledged, eyeing the fork-ful of food. When he began to move the fork from side to side as if trying to tempt or amuse a child, she turned narrowed eyes his way. "If you start making airplane sounds, I'm not eating for sure."

A startled chuckle slipped from his lips and he grinned. But the fork steadied. "Sorry."

"Hmm," she muttered and accepted the food. It was as good as it smelled, and after chewing and swallowing, she asked reluctantly, "How did you know it was my favorite?"

"I've had breakfast the same time as you in the mornings for years. Well, I did until a month ago," he added and then shrugged. "It's what you always get."

Jeanne Louise peered more closely at him now, noting the buzz cut hair, dark brown eyebrows, baby blue eyes, and pleasant smile. He was a good-looking man. It was hard to imagine she hadn't noticed him in the cafeteria at some point over these supposed years they'd had breaks together. But then she did tend to get into her work and walk around a little oblivious a lot of the time, she supposed. Jeanne Louise wanted so desperately to find a cure for her uncle and cousin, she even took her notes with her when she went for her breaks so that she could glance over them while she ate. As distracted as she got with her obsession, Jeanne Louise supposed Uncle Lucian himself could have been in the seat next to her, and unless he said or did something to catch her attention, she probably wouldn't notice.

Her eyes shot back to the man as something he'd said caught her attention. She asked, "Until a month ago? Don't you work for Argeneau Enterprises anymore?"

"Yes, I do," he said quietly. "I took a couple months off."

Jeanne Louise stared at him silently, processing this information. If this plan, whatever it was, hadn't been in his mind before he'd taken the break . . . Well, it may be that no one had messed up. There wouldn't have been anything for one of the team who kept tabs on mortals to find.

"Eat?" he asked quietly, urging the forkful of food closer to her lips.

Jeanne Louise's eyes dropped to the fork and she almost shook her head in refusal on principle alone, but it seemed like cutting off her nose to spite her face when her stomach was rumbling eagerly and her mouth filling with saliva at just the prospect of what he offered. Sighing, she opened her mouth somewhat resentfully, closed it around the fork when he slid it carefully inside, and then drew the food off with compressed lips as he removed it. They were silent, eyeing each other as she chewed and swallowed, and he scooped up another forkful for her.

"It would be easier if I could just feed myself," she pointed out dryly when he raised the next forkful.

"Yes, it would," he agreed mildly, and when she opened her mouth to snap a bit impatiently about her preference, he slid the fork in, silencing her before the first word could leave her lips. As she chewed, he added, "But I know your kind are very strong and I don't want to risk you trying to escape. I'm sure once you understand the situation, there won't need to be such caution. But until then . . . This is just the better way to handle things."

"My kind," Jeanne Louise muttered the moment she'd swallowed. "We *are* human you know."

"But not mortal," he said quietly.

"The heck we aren't. We can die just like you can. We're just harder to kill. And live longer," she added reluctantly.

"And stay young, and resist disease, and can self-heal," he said quietly, slipping more food into her mouth.

Jeanne Louise eyed him as she chewed and swallowed, and then said, "So let me guess, you want that. To be young, to live longer, be stronger, be—"

He shook his head and silenced her by slipping food past her lips, even as he assured her, "I don't."

"Then what do you want?" Jeanne Louise asked with frustration when she could speak again. "What is this proposition?"

He hesitated, and she could see the debate going on behind his eyes, but in the end he shook his head again. "Not yet."

This time, when he raised the fork to her lips, she turned her head away and muttered, "I'm not hungry," and meant it. She was too frustrated and angry to care about food anymore. Besides what she'd eaten had taken the edge off her hunger.

He was silent for a minute, but then sighed, set the fork on the still half-full plate, and stood. "I'll let you rest for a bit. The drugs should be out of your system by the time you wake up again. We can talk then."

Jeanne Louise didn't even acknowledge his words with a glance, but stared grimly at the wall as he bent and did something to make the bed slide back into a flat position. She didn't move until she heard his footsteps cross the floor and the door open and close. Then Jeanne Louise slowly allowed herself to relax and let her eyes slip shut.

She wanted out of there and back to her own life. But she was also tired, and there was little she could do until the last of the drug wore off. The moment that happened, she would take control of the situation and make the man release her, Jeanne Louise promised herself. He wouldn't be expecting that. While there were mortals who knew about them and knew some of their skills and strengths, the immortals' ability to read and control minds was not usually one of the skills revealed. Mortals didn't take the knowledge of those attributes well. It tended to freak them out to know their thoughts could be heard, and "her kind" had learned over the years to just keep that bit of knowledge to themselves. Of course, if his job had depended on that knowledge, he might have been given it. But Jeanne Louise doubted that was the case or he would keep her drugged rather than wait for her head to completely clear to make this proposition he had.

Whoever *he* was, she thought with a frown, as it occurred to her that she had no idea what his name was or much of anything else really. All she knew was that he worked in R and D at Argeneau Enterprises and took the same breakfast break she did.

Which meant he probably worked the night shift too. That was interesting. Mortals usually didn't like the night shift. It was usually full of immortals, while the mortals stuck to the day shifts. She wondered briefly why he would work the night shift, and then let the matter go. She needed to rest. Jeanne Louise wanted to be awake and alert when he returned.

Paul pulled the door closed behind him with a little sigh and moved up the hall to the stairs, his mind running over everything he'd done so far, looking for any problems that might arise, but he didn't see any. He'd waited until she was off Argeneau property and away from the cameras on the grounds before making his move, and it had all gone as smoothly as he'd hoped.

Hers had been the only car at the traffic light when Paul had hit her with the tranquilizer. That, of course, had been pure luck. God or the fates had been smiling down on him this morning.

The tranq had worked as quickly as it did in testing and it had only taken seconds for him to get out of the back seat, shift her to the passenger seat, and slide behind the wheel. The whole thing had been over within a minute.

The only place where he could see a problem was when he'd crawled out of Lester's trunk and got into the back-seat of her car at Argeneau Enterprises in full view of at least three security cameras. But he'd worn dark clothes and a balaclava to cover his face. There wouldn't have been much for the cameras to catch. Paul had snuck onto the property in the trunk of Lester's car, but there wasn't anything the other man could tell them. Paul had broken into Lester's garage, jimmied his trunk open, got in, and hitched a ride into Argeneau Enterprises. It meant he'd had to hold it not quite closed until the end of the long night shift.

Moments before Lester had returned to the car, Paul had slid out of the trunk and made his way to Jeanne Louise Argeneau's car. His main concern had been that it might be locked, but few bothered in the patrolled parking garage. It was so well guarded and had so many damn cameras, no one would try anything there as a rule. Much to his relief, Jeanne Louise hadn't locked her car and she hadn't worked past her usual half hour after end of shift, but had arrived just moments after he'd got in. If Paul was spotted moving from one car to the other on the cameras and security had been on their way, they'd been too late. His only worry now was that Lester might be thought of as a co-conspirator in the whole business and get in trouble. That would make him feel bad. Lester was a good guy.

Aware that he couldn't do a damn thing for the man right now, Paul pushed that worry away as he mounted the steps out of the basement. He came out in the kitchen and he headed for the sink, intending to dump the food Jeanne Louise had left unfinished and rinse the plate. But halfway there he changed direction and instead walked out of the room and up the hall to the stairs to the second floor. Paul mounted those quickly, slipping one hand under the plate as he went to check that the food was still warm. It was and still looked fresh and tasty enough that it made him hungry. He only hoped Livy would think so too but feared she wouldn't. Nothing seemed to tempt her appetite anymore.

"Daddy?"

Paul forced a smile at that soft query as he crossed the pretty pink bedroom to the canopied bed to peer down at the little blonde slip of a girl who almost disappeared in all the soft fluffy pillows and comforter. "Yes, baby. I'm here."

"Mrs. Stuart said you went to work last night," she said with a hurt expression.

"Yes, baby. Just for a bit. I'm back though," he said quietly, not surprised that she knew. Paul had driven Jeanne Louise's car to the parking lot where his own car waited, relieved to find it empty. He'd quickly switched her to his car, then had driven straight home and into his garage. He'd carried her down into the basement through the garage door to chain her up before heading into the house and finding the babysitter.

Mrs. Stuart had reported that Livy had suffered a rough night. He'd been disappointed but not surprised by the news. They all seemed to be bad lately. But not for long, Paul reassured himself, and then tipped the plate of food slightly for her to see. "Are you hungry?"

"No," she said dully, turning her head away from the food he presented.

Paul hesitated, but then said gently, "Sweetie, you have

to eat to keep your strength up so you can get healthy again."

"Mrs. Stuart said I wasn't going to get healthy again. That God was . . ." Livy frowned, as if trying to recall the exact wording, and then said, "calling me home to be with him. She said if I was very good and He liked me, maybe I'd get to see Mommy. But she doubted He would 'cause I was naughty and crying. Do you think God will like me even though I was crying?"

Paul simply stood frozen. All the blood seemed to have slid from his head and down his body to pool in his feet, leaving him empty and weak. His brain was having trouble processing what she had said. And then the blood came pounding back, rushing up through his body and slamming into his brain, bringing a burning rage with it.

He didn't say a word; he didn't dare. The expletives roaring through his head were not for a child's ears. After a moment of struggle, Paul managed to bark one word, "Yes." Then he turned stiffly and simply walked out of the room, straight downstairs and back into the kitchen. His movements were jerky and automatic as he scraped the food off the plate into the garbage pail. He then walked to the sink, but rather than rinse it under the tap as he intended, Paul suddenly found himself smashing the empty plate across the top of it. He didn't even realize he was going to do it, and hardly noticed let alone cared that bits of shattered china flew up to spike his face and neck.

The stupid, vicious, nasty, old cow. He never should have had Mrs. Stuart watch Livy. He'd known she wouldn't be able to keep her Bible-thumping to herself, but he'd had no choice. Mrs. Stuart used to be a nurse before retiring, and there was no one else he'd trusted to know what to do if there had been a problem. But he'd never let the old bitch near her again. If she was good

God might like her? But he probably wouldn't because she'd cried? The child was dying of cancer, being eaten alive, wasting away and suffering a pain that he couldn't even comprehend and couldn't prevent. They had given him a prescription for the strongest dosage of pain meds they could for Livy, but they did little for the girl. The only other option was to keep her sedated in the hospital until she died, and he refused to do that. He wouldn't simply watch her die. He wanted her cured, but until then, nothing seemed to ease the pain she was suffering, and for Mrs. Stuart to suggest that her crying because of that excruciating pain might make God not like her so she wouldn't see her mother—

"Daddy?"

Stiffening, Paul sucked in a breath to calm himself, and then turned to peer blankly at the five-year-old girl standing in the kitchen doorway. In the next moment, he was rushing forward to scoop her up. "What are you doing out of bed, baby. You shouldn't be up."

"I'm tired of staying in bed," Livy said unhappily, and then reached up to touch his chin. "You're bleeding. Did you cut yourself?"

"No. Yes. Daddy's fine," Paul assured her grimly, carrying her back up the stairs. She was all bones and pale skin, and his heart ached as he held her. The child was precious, the most precious thing in his life. Paul lived for her, and he'd die for her too, if he had to. But for now, he'd put her back to bed and then catch a couple hours of sleep himself. He'd stayed awake all night and needed to be alert and on the ball when he talked to Jeanne Louise Argeneau. He needed to be clear and persuasive. He needed to convince her to make his child one of her kind. He'd give her anything she wanted to get her to do that, including his own life, just so long as she turned her and taught her to survive as a vampire. He'd give anything and everything to know she lived on. He'd failed her mother, his wife, Jerri. But he wouldn't fail Livy. He had to convince Jeanne Louise to save her life. She was his only hope.

SINK YOUR TEETH INTO
DELECTABLE VAMPIRE ROMANCE FROM
USA TODAY BESTSELLING AUTHOR

LYNSAY
SANDS

BORN TO BITE
978-0-06-147432-3

Legend has it that Armand Argeneau is a killer in the bed-room. But with all three of his late wives meeting unfortunate ends, it's up to Eshe d'Aureus to find out if this sexy immortal is a lover or a murderer. As an enforcer, it's her job to bring rogue vampires to justice, even if the rogue in question makes her blood race red hot.

HUNGRY FOR YOU
978-0-06-189457-2

As one of the most ancient in the Argeneau clan, Cale Valens has given up on finding a life mate. His friends and family, however, have not. In fact, they believe they've finally found his perfect match. Getting them together, however, requires one little white lie . . .

THE RELUCTANT VAMPIRE
978-0-06-189459-6

Rogue hunter Drina Argenis has been many things in her years as an immortal, but bodyguard/babysitter to a teenage vampire is something new. There's an incentive, however: the other vampsitter, Harper Stoyan, may be Drina's life mate.